I0668361

Guile

By Geoffrey Neil

Copyright Information

This book is a work of fiction. Any references to historical events, real people, or real locales are used fictitiously. Other names, characters, places, and incidents are the product of the author's imagination, and any resemblance to actual events or locales or persons, living or dead, is entirely coincidental.

Priorities Intact Publishing
8306 Wilshire Blvd., #7076, Beverly Hills, CA 90211

No part of this book may be reproduced or transmitted in any form or any manner, electronic or mechanical, including photocopying, recording or by any information storage and retrieval system, without permission in writing from the publisher.

Written by Geoffrey Neil, copyright © 2020
Cover art by Geoffrey Neil, copyright © 2020

Printed in the United States of America

10 9 8 7 6 5 4 3 2 1

ISBN-978-0-9850223-7-2

Table of Contents

"Nothing is more common on earth than
to deceive and be deceived."

— *Johann G. Seume*

For Mickey

Love you, love you, love you.

One

IF HE HAD known what was in store for him, Ian Shaw would have used the gun. A simple trigger-pull would have spared so much pain. The small bullet would have done the world a huge favor. His loved ones would forgive him. As awful as it sounds, they'd secretly be grateful.

Everybody's rock bottom looks different. At 28 years old, Ian's was a portrait of abject misery painted by a cascade of horrible decisions. This afternoon, his mobile home grew hot enough to bake him after a decision to max out his last credit card on beer instead of fixing his air conditioner. He stretched out in his underwear on a tattered recliner with a bottle of Pabst Blue Ribbon warming between his legs. The torn pieces of his overdrawn bank statement lay strewn over unopened bills and demand letters on the floor beside him. His eyes glazed over while he looked at the stack, each envelope a complete waste of postage.

Unemployed, broke, heartbroken, and lonely, Ian was due for some good luck—at least that's what the kinder people told him. "Hang in there, and life will get better," some said. "Good things are right around the corner," others promised. A few tried to cheer him up with tired expressions. *It's always darkest just before the dawn.* He hated that one most because he knew it was bullshit. After countless nights spent camping, he knew the pre-dawn sky was as dark as midnight, and his life felt blacker than both right now. Sure, his encouragers meant well, but he had no faith in their prophecies.

The closest thing to optimism Ian felt was that his life couldn't get any worse. That's where he was wrong. Like most people, he didn't know that a deeper, insidious level of misery lurks beneath rock bottom. The poor souls who find it become trapped in the utmost agony and despair. Here, only death offers mercy, obscuring other exits, which is why visitors rarely survive. It's difficult to reach without a perfect combination of foolish decisions and terrible luck. Ian would unwittingly begin drilling down to this abysmal level in the following days, thanks to his penchant for unwise decisions. As for the awful luck, he was dripping with it.

His life's downward spiral became a plummet two months ago when Kate, the love of his life, dumped him after a five-year relationship. Her non-negotiable breakup devastated him. He withdrew from friends and family. He stopped shaving, stopped eating, stopped caring, and started drinking.

He and Kate had run a small sandwich shop for two years. Kate handled the books and operations while Ian managed inventory and fulfilled his dream of becoming the closest thing he'd ever been to a chef.

Poor management and an inability to sustain enough operating capital caused the business's financial health to decline in lockstep with the health of their relationship.

Ian still kicked himself for letting Kate blindside him. Missing all the clues, slathered a thick layer of embarrassment on top of his heartbreak.

The first hint of trouble came six months ago when she announced that she'd purchased a flight for a weekend trip to a self-improvement seminar. Early in their relationship, she and Ian regularly took out-of-town excursions together, so it was reasonable for Ian to assume he'd go with her.

"Where are we staying?" he asked.

"I'm sorry, I should have told you," Kate said, wincing to soften the blow. "It's a women's retreat."

"Good for you!" Ian said, forcing enthusiasm.

"I thought you'd be upset."

"Nah! Why would I be?" he said, feeling upset. "Going with girlfriends?"

"No. Solo."

"Fantastic!" The enthusiasm took more effort.

Kate kept the additional details of her trip under wraps. While out of town, she contacted Ian only once with an obligatory call to tell him she'd arrived safely. When she returned three days later, she found Ian in the back of their sandwich shop, stocking new deliveries. After a tepid hug and a few clichéd exchanges about her flights and the weather, Kate said, "I think we should try abstinence."

Ian laughed.

Kate didn't.

"Am I that horrible in bed?" Ian said.

"It has nothing to do with quality."

"Whew!" Ian wiped his brow. He went to her, put his hands on her waist, and pulled her close. "If we're starting a diet, shouldn't we enjoy a little bite to eat first?"

She gently pushed him back. "Stop, Ian. This is important."

"You're serious?" he said, still searching her face for any hint of a joke. "Abstinence, just like that?"

Kate nodded.

"Why?" He stepped away and picked up a case of sodas from the floor.

"For some couples, abstinence improves the relationship," Kate said. "It strengthens the emotional connection by detaching the physical. It's counterintuitive, but studies have supported it."

Ian went to a shelf and slid the case onto it. "Is this something they pushed on you at that seminar?"

"It was one topic, but that doesn't matter. What's important is that abstinence is a powerful investment that could pay off for our relationship, and I want us to try it."

He came back to her, this time giving her space. "Don't couples who choose abstinence agree to it from the get-go?"

"Not always."

"Who begins abstinence after the fact? If this is some moral thing, it's too late to save ourselves for marriage." He picked up another case and heaved it onto the first.

"It's not about morality," Kate said. "It's called PCA, Post-Consummation Abstinence. Many couples have dramatically enhanced their emotional connection by abstaining from intercourse."

"Sounds backward to me," Ian said. He picked up a mesh bag of cucumbers and plopped it beside the sink. His sex life with Kate was great by her own admission. Something had happened to her on that trip. She'd normally be nervous while talking to him about such a sensitive topic. But now she exuded an unsettling calmness while making an announcement she had to know would rattle him. "This doesn't seem like you," he said. He turned on the faucet and began scrubbing cucumbers.

She came to stand beside him. "If abstinence can reveal a deeper commitment to the relationship, we need that."

"How long?"

"The suggested first round is sixty days."

"First round?" Ian scrubbed harder, lips tight, teeth clenched.

Kate watched him, waiting.

Ian stopped. "So, is this a test for me?"

"It's a test for us," Kate said. "If it's any consolation, it will be difficult for me, too, but I want you to agree to try."

If Ian knew one thing about Kate, it was that if she got some bizarre new idea like this in her head, her mind would not change until it played out. Veganism, yoga, multiple detox diets, and two new-age religions were among Kate's personal fads that had popped and fizzled. He knew abstinence was doomed, too, but having to tug out his sexual release for whatever number of days while Kate came to her senses was an annoying price he'd have to pay. He pulled a shriveled cucumber from the bag and slammed it into the trash bin. "Looks like I have no choice."

Kate flashed a frown. "Of course you do."

"Then my answer is no."

"Okay," Kate said. She shrugged.

"Just like that, you're willing to skip this abstinence thing?"

"I respect your decision. Abstinence is a difficult investment that not all couples can make." She paused, sliding her thumbnail back and forth against her fingertip, a nervous tick Ian instantly recognized.

"Are you disappointed?" he asked.

Kate sighed. "Yes."

"Fine. We'll do the abstinence thing."

"No, we won't."

Ian slapped the faucet handle down to turn the water off. "Making love when I know you don't want to is a buzz-kill, babe."

"When we make love, it will be because I want to," she said.

Ian looked at her skeptically.

Kate raised her right hand.

• • •

The next evening, Ian cleaned the back of the sandwich shop after another day of paltry business. Kate had gone home early after announcing that she didn't feel well.

Ian's phone buzzed with her number. "Hey, babe."

"Are you still at the shop?" Kate asked.

"Yep."

"Can you stay there for a bit longer?"

"Sure. Why?"

Then came the words Ian had recently grown to despise.

"We need to talk," she said.

He briefly pulled the phone from his ear and rolled his eyes. "Sure, what about?"

"In person will be better." Her strange calmness was back.

"If it's about abstinence, I'm still willing to try it—for a while," Ian said.

Kate hesitated. "I'll see you soon."

When she entered the back of the shop wearing a taut expression, Ian got up from his chair. "Hey, what's wrong?" he said, going to her with open arms.

She held up her hand, snubbing his hug, then pointed her finger back and forth between them. "We aren't working out, and we both know it."

The words impaled Ian. He opened his mouth but couldn't speak for a noticeable moment. "If it's about the abstinence—"

"It's so much more than that," Kate said. "You know we have some big issues."

"Issues worth ending us? C'mon, Kate! You didn't want to get married. I went along with that. You didn't want to move in together. I went along with that, even though sharing a place would save money and give us more time together. What issues are you talking about?"

"Let's not argue. This was a tough decision, and I'm sorry."

Her sympathetic expression showed the sensitivity he loved about her but also carried a chilly resolve he didn't recognize.

He tried joking to loosen her up. "Am I too horny for you?"

Kate fought the slightest smile that would typically have swelled into a laugh. "No."

"Then what is it?" he asked.

"Ian, you are probably the most resourceful person I know. And I know you'll desperately want to fix our situation. It'll be easiest if we agree that nothing's broken. The parts just no longer fit."

"What parts? We fit fine! And we're business partners. What about the shop?"

Kate gave him a pitiful look. Ian hated that look because it gave him the sensation of shrinking.

"The business is dying on the vine," she said. "It's time to cut losses." She looked around their cramped back office. "We can decide which of us gets what from the shop. I won't fight you for anything important to you."

"You are important to me," Ian said.

Kate looked away.

Ian's heart skipped when he thought she might be hiding tears, but she turned back to him, eyes dry, voice steady, and said, "I'm sorry, Ian. I realize this is painful."

Ian covered his face and slid his fingers up through his hair. "If you're still frustrated with our sales, that's all about to change. I told you I'm on the verge of signing our first catering contracts—big ones. I've got verbal commitments. They're basically done deals. I swear."

"A couple of contracts can't fix us." Then Kate surprised him by taking his hand.

Normally, Ian would have loved her touch, but the sympathy coming through her fingers shrank him more. He pulled away. "Kate, don't make this rash decision. Let's sleep on it and decide tomorrow."

"Sleep hasn't changed my mind for many nights. I'm sorry to have to hurt you this way. But I know we'll look back someday and agree that we made the best possible decision."

"We aren't making this decision, *you* are!" Ian said, anger rushing in to replace his shock.

"Please don't raise your voice to me. Let's not make this harder than it is."

Ian slowly shook his head, staring at her in disbelief. "What do you want me to say—that I'm fine with it?"

Kate looked down at her hand, working her thumbnail against her fingertip again. "I have a request I'm hoping you'll accommodate."

"Now what?" Ian crossed his arms.

Kate took a deep breath and said, "I think it would be easiest for both of us if we didn't see each other or communicate for a while."

Ian felt the urge to quickly agree in order to appear more decisive than he felt. But accepting these terms ruined any chance of negotiation.

Kate didn't wait for his agreement. She turned and headed through the door to the front of the shop.

Ian hurried after her, saying, "Why don't we just take a break? We'll give each other some space. Let's start with... maybe a week. I'll cover the shop."

"I'm not willing to prolong the inevitable," Kate said, navigating between dining tables.

"Inevitable? Why is this inevitable?" Ian tried to get in front of her to block her exit, but couldn't before she pushed through the front door. Outside in the parking lot, he sidestepped beside her. "You've met someone new. You've cheated on me, haven't you?"

"Ian, don't even go there," she said, reaching for her car door handle.

Ian threw his hands up. "What am I supposed to think?"

"If I could control what you think, this breakup would have been easier," Kate said. "I knew it would get complicated." She got into the driver's seat.

Ian stepped closer, blocking her door. "What's gotten into you?"

Kate closed her eyes and held up her hand. "Enough."

Ian stepped back.

She pulled the door closed.

Ian's eyes welled up while he watched her drive from the parking lot. He took a few steps as if he might chase her on foot. His throat tightened when her car disappeared around the corner. "Goddammit, Kate." His voice cracked.

The next morning, when he opened his front door to leave, he found a cardboard box. It contained some clothes, two pairs of shoes, a toaster, and an unopened bottle of wine from months ago, his miniature Valentine's card still taped to the side. A roughly folded note stuffed under the box flap read:

Ian,

Your stuff from my place.

If I missed anything, I'll reimburse you.

All the best,

Kate

Ian squeezed the note into his fist. He mumbled, "All the best," as he threw the box inside and slammed the door.

Two

IAN RESPECTED KATE'S request for radio silence for three days before succumbing to curiosity about her true motivation for breaking up. The pleasure of their relationship's peaks had far outnumbered the challenges of their valleys, at least from his perspective. He assumed that the financial sacrifice and sweat-equity they invested in running a business would create a mutual dependency that would help them weather any rough patch in their personal relationship. Kate had ruined that theory.

If she had found someone new, she should have just said so. When Ian accused her of meeting someone new, she said, "Don't go there." And saying this wasn't a denial. It was a warning. She must have known the truth would hurt him. He deserved the truth, so she owed him the truth. But he didn't believe Kate would confess it. And if she wouldn't, he had no choice but to take it. After a quick search on his phone, he drove into town to browse the delightful offerings of a spy shop.

That night, on his way to drive by Kate's apartment to see what he could see, his resolve to learn the truth strengthened. He never imagined he'd have an urge to spy on Kate, but here he was. He reassured himself that this act didn't make him a stalker. This was just a quick solution that would give him the information he deserved so he could move on.

He pulled his Kawasaki Z1000 to the side of the road across the street from her apartment. The motorcycle had been another source of friction between him and Kate. After taking a minor spill on it that resulted in only a few scrapes a few months ago, Kate had argued with him, insisting that he stop driving it. Ian won the argument.

He pulled off his helmet for a better view. Kate's car was gone, and her windows were dark. Perfect. Unless Kate had announced her breakup to her neighbors, it wouldn't be suspicious for him to walk to her door after only a few days of absence. Her apartment building stretched parallel to the road like a motor lodge. Her unit was almost perfectly positioned at the building's halfway point. He relaxed while strolling toward her door, holding his key in his pocket. He softly knocked and waited for Mrs. Jenson, the cat lady next door, to part her window shades to see who was there. Ian felt relieved when that didn't happen.

He smoothly slid the key into the knob, but the lock cylinder wouldn't turn. He jiggled the key, then took it out and flipped it. Inverted, it wouldn't even insert into the keyhole. He cursed his nervousness, trying the other way again. It slid in but still wouldn't turn. He pulled out his phone and illuminated the keyhole. The doorknob had a shiny new key cylinder that didn't match the worn brass knob. He froze, realizing the implication and trying to resist feeling insulted. Had Kate changed the lock because of him? Never once had he lifted a finger to her. He'd never stolen from her. She knew he wasn't vindictive. Why did she feel the need to change the locks so quickly? He considered it a personal insult until a more acceptable explanation came to mind. Maybe Kate had moved away, and the apartment manager followed protocol by promptly re-keying. He stepped back from the front door to see Kate's bedroom window. Her houseplants and beloved Georgetown banner were still there. She would never have abandoned them.

Ian reached into his other pocket and felt the magnetic bug and radio transmitter he planned to hide in her bedroom ceiling fan. He'd mentally rehearsed the installation probably fifty times. But now, the hardware he had been counting on to give him answers was useless without having a few minutes of private access to her place. He looked again at the window, considering whether he should try to slip in that way, but quickly dismissed the idea. Breaking and entering would draw too much attention. He returned to his bike and sped away. The following day, he returned the eavesdropping hardware to the spy shop and promptly spent the refund on a pair of binoculars.

· · ·

Fifty-seven days did nothing to dull the pain of losing Kate. Her absence became unbearable. He missed her uncanny ability to dissolve the lowest of his moods with her smile. He missed seeing her gorgeous face framed in that ginger hair. From how her chin slid in to rest perfectly on his shoulder when they hugged to their innate understanding of each other's emotional nuances, they were perfect for each other—or so he thought.

The two-month hiatus allowed him to perform over sixty ego-battering drives past Kate's place. He still had no idea where she had gone after dumping him. Bringing her up several times in conversation among some of their common friends yielded nothing. Either no one knew anything about her whereabouts, or they were helping her hide.

On today's lunchtime drive-by, Ian saw her car for the first time since he had watched it disappear from the sandwich shop parking lot. After nearly two months, Kate's white Toyota Camry was parked in its space a few paces from her apartment door. The sight sent a surge of adrenaline through Ian that got his heart thumping. He fought the urge to stop and watch her windows for a glimpse of her. Doing so at midday would be foolish. Kate would not only recognize his motorcycle on sight, but she often knew when he had arrived in her driveway long before he got to the door because its sound was familiar. With no traffic behind him, Ian slowed but didn't stop, making sure not to rev the engine. He rolled past her driveway and gently sped up, hoping to keep the engine sound below Kate's ability to hear it. He couldn't wait for sunset.

When he returned to his place, he grabbed a beer from the fridge and fanned the front of his shirt on his way to the recliner. He turned on the TV, feeling excitement he hadn't felt for a long time. Finally, he'd soon have the answers he deserved.

After Kate's new door lock ruined his ability to get an electronic bug into her place, a stakeout was the only way to covertly get the truth about Kate. The more he considered the idea, the more sense it made. After a few more beers, Ian was convinced of his plan's perfect logic.

When dusk fell, he grabbed half a turkey sandwich and a beer to prepare for his mission. By the door, he held the sandwich with his teeth while he slid a Beretta into the concealed holster under his belt. He carried the gun with him everywhere. His older brother, Tim, had loaned him the pistol last year. Tim was a hunting fanatic and regularly encouraged Ian to join him, letting Ian try various firearms. He did his best to infect Ian with a love for his hobby, but Ian had little interest in guns. Instead, Ian's preference for cooking perplexed and often frustrated Tim. This changed when Ian and Kate were robbed at gunpoint at the sandwich shop. The loss included about $233 from the register and the thorough destruction of their sense of safety and security. This was when Tim loaned Ian the gun, commenting that Ian could hold it indefinitely.

When the police arrived, Kate had been too flustered to give her account. While Ian provided a report to officers in the front of the store, Kate sat hunched over in the storeroom, trembling and hyperventilating.

The armed robbery revealed a vulnerability and helplessness that Ian hated. He began carrying a concealed pistol everywhere despite Kate's adamant disapproval. Ian obtained a legal concealed carry permit, but this didn't matter to Kate. She hated guns—the sight of them, their sound, their purpose, and everything about them. She even resented Ian's hunting trips with his brother and their dad.

The ability to protect himself and Kate transformed the pistol into Ian's security blanket. He refused to appease Kate by giving it up, but out of respect, he never took it to her place and tried to keep it hidden from her anywhere else they went together.

Ian went outside, walked past his bike, and climbed into his old Nissan Sentra. He felt the steel of the gun's muzzle tucked snugly under his belt. Besides protection, possessing the gun gave him a satisfying sense of rebellion against Kate. The ability to protect himself provided a sense of control when he felt none. Bringing a gun to her apartment while they were together would have been a top-tier offense, punishable by a scathing rebuke from Kate and three to five days of cold-shoulder treatment. As he got into his car, he imagined pulling out the gun right in her living room while she watched. Her shocked expression might be like the one he had worn while she dumped him.

As he drove onto the highway, he felt a fleeting twinge of trepidation about his plans. He knew the information he sought could be painful, but didn't care. Not getting it would be a worse punishment.

It was dark when the lights from Kate's apartment building came into view in the distance. He strained to see if her car was still parked in front. His pulse raced when he saw it was. Then her kitchen window came into view, its drawn yellow curtain illuminated. She was there. He pulled to the side of the road, parking across the street in a place he knew was difficult to see from Kate's windows.

The lights on the edge of the building were strong enough to illuminate an unfamiliar lime-green Camaro parked beside Kate's car. The sight of it clenched Ian's jaw. He squinted at the out-of-state license plate, searching his memory for recognition. Her apartment building had only ten units, and after spending more of their five-year relationship at her place than his own, Ian knew every make and model of every neighbor's vehicle and their guests. This green car definitely didn't belong. He wiped his sweaty hands on his shirt. *Who paints a muscle car such a stupid shade of green?* Ian thought. *Somebody who's starved for attention.* If it belonged to someone dating Kate, Ian would love to give him some attention.

He rolled down the window and turned off the engine. Kate's door and windows were too far away for eavesdropping. He reached behind his seat and shook the binoculars free from a crumpled plastic bag. This was the first opportunity for them to be helpful. He pressed them to his eyes and adjusted the focus, the price tag still dangling.

He watched the kitchen window for an hour, waiting for a shadow, or worse, two shadows to darken the curtain. He saw nothing. He waited for a half-hour, beginning to feel perplexed at seeing no movement at the window. Kate's kitchen was tiny. Any movement to a cabinet or the refrigerator should be visible through the curtain. Another half an hour passed. If Kate was with someone, and all the windows were dark except the kitchen, maybe she had gone somewhere with that person. But Kate never left her lights on while she was out because she was too conscientious of her electric bill.

A horrible thought clobbered Ian as he panned his binoculars to Kate's dark bedroom window. Despite his constant gushing over her beauty, Kate had always preferred to make love with the lights off, typically insisting on it. Her bedroom window had been dark for at least an hour. His heart thumped harder.

He rolled down the window. After a car passed, he leaned out, held his breath, and listened for the worst sound he could imagine. All was quiet except for some faint classical music that seeped through a neighbor's open window.

Viewed from the street at night, Kate's bedroom window was shadowed by an overhang, making it difficult to see. He panned back toward the lit kitchen curtain. "Dammit!" He pounded the steering wheel and took a deep breath, suppressing his urge to run to the apartment and confirm the worst.

He hunkered down, put his head on the headrest, and prepared to wait as long as necessary for the truth. After another hour, he wiped his eye with his knuckle, and the soreness he felt on his eye socket from pressing the binoculars triggered another rush of shame that he tried to shake off. *What the hell am I doing here?* Several satisfying scenarios came to mind. The most wonderful was Kate inside, having returned home only to be triggered by memories of her life with him, her hands over her face, miserable and sobbing about her mistake. Another fantasy was watching Kate make a call on her phone before his phone buzzed in his pocket with her caller ID. He felt gutted when he realized how impossible either scenario was.

He had just placed the binoculars on the seat beside him when he thought he saw movement in the kitchen window. He grabbed the binoculars, homed in, and held his breath. Nothing. "Now I'm hallucinating," he mumbled.

He eventually dozed off a few times, occasionally waking for passing cars and once when the beers required him to relieve himself behind the trees that flanked his side of the road. At about 4:15 a.m., the headlights of an approaching car woke him. He watched it, squinting as it closed in on him. This vehicle moved slower than previous cars, which was strange on a wide-open road at this hour. He wondered if it was someone scoping out vehicles or the apartment building for mischief. The car continued to slow at a rate that seemed it might come to a stop beside him.

He slipped his hand under his belt, gripping his pistol, then scooted deeper into the seat.

Ian wondered if someone had spotted him and called the police. Who else would be driving around at this hour? When the vehicle pulled beside him, he saw it wasn't a police cruiser. It was a pickup truck. It slowly passed by, nearly coming to a stop. Ian tried to see the driver, but it was too dark. The truck abruptly sped away.

After his adrenaline subsided, Ian dozed off, startling awake when his phone alarm vibrated at 6 a.m. He looked out the window, bleary-eyed, as the sun added detail to his view. He knew that the next few minutes would be the best to discover who, if anyone, was with Kate. She had a strict exercise regimen that should have her leaving for the gym at any minute. His mind went to another dark place. The only exception to Kate's gym trip would be if she had gotten enough exercise the night before—a private joke they shared. The thought flooded his stomach with acid.

A strange combination of relief and fear struck Ian when he saw her apartment door open a few minutes after 6 o'clock. True to form, Kate was dressed in her workout clothes. Ian felt for the binoculars on the passenger seat. He focused on her door. A rush of prickles spread up his back when he saw what he hoped he wouldn't but expected. A man followed Kate outside. Together, they strolled to her car, not holding hands, just walking. Ian held the binoculars steady, watching every step, scanning for details. The guy looked to be in his early twenties—younger than Ian. He was about Ian's height and had blond hair, which surprised Ian. It wasn't that Kate had an aversion to blond hair. She simply had always dated guys with dark hair. This guy wore khaki pants and a polo shirt and looked skinny. The guy didn't look like he'd be comfortable in the gym, so bonding over fitness wasn't likely to have brought them together. *God, what does she see in him?*

It hurt that Kate looked happy. While they moved down the sidewalk, she pointed toward the trash enclosure and then to the mailboxes at the end of the building. *Oh yeah, she's giving him the full-on tour,* Ian thought.

They stopped beside her car. She opened the driver's door, then tapped her watch, saying something that made them laugh. They hugged, and the guy headed back toward her apartment.

Only a hug? Ian thought, then he remembered Kate's modesty about public affection. That she let this man hang out in her place alone disturbed Ian. She had changed the locks to keep Ian out, but was now allowing this new guy free, unsupervised reign? Kate was extremely private. She must've fallen hard for him.

When the guy entered Kate's apartment and closed the door, Ian seethed. Getting a look at his replacement had silenced his imagination, but spawned a dark urge he had never had. Seeing Kate with someone new hurt much more than he thought it would.

He heard her car engine start. She didn't immediately back it out. She was on the phone. Had she forgotten to tell her new lover something?

Ian threw the binoculars to the passenger seat and picked up the Beretta. If she was rebounding with this guy, her fling wouldn't last. But if not, she must have been cheating with this guy long before dumping Ian, which was worse. Ian pulled out the Beretta and checked it. It had a full magazine and a bullet chambered. He could knock on the door and push his way in without showing the gun. Once inside, he could end Kate's new relationship as promptly as she had ended her relationship with Ian. He considered kicking up the retaliation more. What if he then laid beside the body and shot himself? He imagined Kate stumbling onto the scene when she got home. It might've been the darkest thought he had ever conjured, and that he entertained the thought chilled him. He quickly dismissed it. He didn't want to physically harm anyone. But his all-consuming need to relieve the pain made desperate measures feel more rational than they should.

His phone buzzed. He set the pistol on the passenger seat beside the binoculars. His phone displayed his brother's name. He and Tim were close and spoke at least two or three times a week by phone, if not in person, under normal circumstances. They had spoken only once since Ian had lost Kate. Tim never approved of Ian's relationship with Kate, and it created fiction even in the best of times. After the breakup, which Tim wanted, the brothers' relationship had cooled. Ian sent the call to voicemail, and as he was trying to slide the phone back into his pocket, it slipped and fell between the driver's seat and the center console. "Dammit!" He squeezed his hand down into the crack, trying to pinch the phone with his fingertips, but only pushed it deeper. He opened the car door and kneeled on the asphalt for a better angle to sweep his hand underneath the seat. He found the phone, and his finger hooked something else that felt like a chain. He pulled a necklace out with his phone. The silver chain was threaded through two chrome puzzle pieces. Memories flooded him. The necklace was a gift to Kate last year. He remembered her jumping up and down, clapping and leaping into his arms the day he gave it to her. He could still feel her warm arms hugging his neck. One puzzle piece was engraved with his name, the other with hers. On the back of both were the words:

LOVING EACH OTHER TO PIECES.

Ian climbed back into the driver's seat and closed the door. He checked across the street. Kate was still on the phone in her car. He caressed the necklace with his thumb, feeling the grooves of the lettering. He also remembered the day she lost it. They had gone to the lake, and she didn't want to risk losing it while swimming. She must've set it precariously on the car's dashboard. For weeks, she lamented having lost it.

The finding and holding the necklace brought on a fresh wave of emotion. Ian's throat clenched, and before he could stop the tears, they flowed as he sobbed. His anger toward Kate for hurting him so badly had been dislodged, at least for the moment, by a poignant memory that cut through him. He still loved her.

He looked at the loaded gun on the passenger seat and then tucked it back into his holster. He covered his face and, through his fingers, said, "My God, I've gone insane." In a moment of clarity, he realized that everything—the spying attempt, the eavesdropping, the stalking, the gun fantasies would never bring him relief. Each would lead only to more pain. His reconnaissance had delivered the information he had sought. Hurting Kate would hurt him more, putting his own well-being in jeopardy. Being free without Kate edged out rotting in prison without her.

As Kate backed out of her parking space, Ian started his engine. If he waited too long, Kate was sure to see and recognize his car. He was hungry, thirsty, and exhausted. By the time Kate exited her driveway, Ian was gone.

• • •

Ian stopped his car at the edge of his long driveway to get his mail from the mailbox. His home sat tucked far from the street. Ian liked it that way because the distance muted the passing traffic, providing more privacy. He pulled into the driveway and rolled to the side of his mobile home, parking under a canvas awning supported by four tent poles he'd set up as a makeshift carport. He got out next to the motorcycle he preferred for ninety-nine percent of his travel.

Walking toward the front door, he flipped through the mail. Knee-high weeds slapped his legs along the beaten path. As usual, most of the envelopes were past-due notices.

Inside, he tossed the entire stack into the trash bin and went straight to his bedroom. He flopped onto the bed and plunged into a much more comfortable sleep than in his car. He slept until the afternoon. The extended nap took the edge off the sleep deprivation caused by his successful but unsatisfying stakeout. The catharsis of seeing the truth about Kate had loosened his obsession with her enough to take his first shower in days. After he finished, he went to the refrigerator. While they had their sandwich shop, his refrigerator had always been well-stocked with skimmed inventory, but things had changed. He pushed aside some expired milk and threw away some questionable produce and meats. He grabbed a beer bottle and started to walk away. Before the fridge closed, he caught the door and grabbed a second bottle.

The midday sun beat down on the roof of his mobile home, quickly making Ian's living space too hot for comfort. He went to a window-mounted air conditioner and smacked its side, bringing it to life with a loud grinding. He adjusted the vents to aim at his recliner before plopping down. He turned on the television and enjoyed the breeze as he guzzled half of the first beer.

He stared at the screen glassy-eyed as he flipped through the channels, eventually landing on an online dating ad. After watching a few moments of images featuring happy couples and an audio message with the promise of finding lasting love, Ian clicked off the TV and threw down the remote. He took another big swig of beer. Until a few months ago, he had never been much of a beer drinker, but recently, it had become his self-prescribed heart-numbing medication.

He tilted his head back and relaxed his arm on the armrest, holding the bottle's rim with his fingertips. Soon, he dozed off again, and the beer dropped to the floor.

He woke to the phone ringing across the room and climbed to his feet. He staggered to it, kicking the beer bottle and spinning it across the floor. He answered the old wired phone connected to a short wall cord.

"Hello?"

"Oh, sweetheart, thank God!" His mom could sound both tense and relieved at the same time. "Where have you been?"

"Around," Ian said.

"We've been trying to reach you and couldn't even leave a voice message."

Ian looked at his ancient phone. "I don't have voicemail on my landline anymore," he said.

"Why not?"

"Just use my mobile phone," he said, failing to stifle the agitation in his voice.

"There's no need to get angry."

"What do you want?" Ian strained the phone cord so he could reach the refrigerator door handle.

"Since you mentioned Kate, and just out of curiosity, have you talked to her?"

"No." He briefly moved the phone from his ear, stretching to grab a beer in the fridge.

"I'm so sorry. I believe she'll come back to you."

"Whatever," Ian said. The fallout from his breakup extended to his parents, who were crazy about Kate. Even when things were wonderful, Ian grew tired of hearing them frequently proclaim that she was the best thing that ever happened to him. When he shared news of the breakup with his mom, she broke down, weeping on the phone. He ended the call as gracefully as possible, but his mom's reaction fanned his feelings of failure. His dad could not conceal his anger and blamed Ian, saying, "I don't know why you couldn't make it work out. She would've been great.

If I were you, I'd do whatever it takes to get her back." After the initial shock of the news wore off, his parents made the awkward offer to finance therapy for him and Kate together with the hope of reconciliation. Ian later found out that they had contacted Kate directly with the offer. She refused.

"Have you reached out to her?" his mom asked.

"Mom, if there is any change in our status, I'll let you know."

"How are you—emotionally?"

"Mom, please!"

"When we don't see or hear from you, I worry. The only reason we haven't called the police is that your father drives by your place and notices your car and motorcycle changing positions. It's unkind to let your loved ones worry about you that way." After an awkward silence, she added, "Your voice sounds weak. You haven't been eating."

"I really need to go."

"Why don't you come over for dinner? I just finished making an antipasto salad, and there's lasagna in the oven. I could even bake your favorite rhubarb cobbler for dessert."

God, that sounds good, Ian thought. Although he hadn't stepped on the scale, his bathroom mirror showed weight loss in his face, dramatic enough for him to notice. Depression had robbed him of almost all appetite for food. It also made shopping and preparing his own meals too much work.

The idea of listening to his mom's reconciliation options while his dad bathed him in long looks of disappointment was the last thing Ian wanted. Enduring their questions about what he'd been doing these last weeks was certain.

On the other hand, his mom's cooking had always inspired him to cook. He had spent hours in the kitchen with her. He considered each of her delectable dishes a work of art. If she had calculated what she knew to be his favorite dish, she nailed it, and the timing was right. At this moment, the idea of simply stepping into his parents' home for a fully prepared hot meal was worth the price of the discomfort of their interrogation.

Ian relented. "I suppose I could stop by."

"Wonderful! I could use some help with a half-finished cobbler."

"What help do you need?" Ian asked.

"You made one a few months ago and told me you tweaked my recipe somehow. Your father absolutely loved whatever you did. I think I'm missing something. The last two were delicious but didn't turn out like yours. Are you hiding a recipe item?"

"It's probably the brandy," Ian said. "A shot or two of peach brandy makes all the difference."

"I knew it!" his mom said, "You rascal!"

"Mom, are you telling me you've never hoarded a recipe secret?"

"Who, me? I wouldn't think of it!"

They laughed.

"I'll be over in a few minutes," Ian said.

"Wait," his mom replied. "Don't come right away. Why don't you come by at about 5 o'clock?"

"Why?" he asked. The request was odd. He was always welcome at his parents' house and never remembered his mother or father preferring a particular time.

"Because…" His mom hesitated. "Because I need to run to the store—for the brandy."

"Don't bother, I have some brandy. I'll bring it," he said.

"I, uh, need to pick up some other things, too. I'll be back before 5 o'clock. Show up any time after then."

"Mom, what's the problem? I can just let myself in if you're gone when I get there."

"No, Ian—I want to watch you add the brandy to the cobbler."

Ian frowned. "Alright. See you after five." He hung up and rubbed his neck as he walked to the bathroom. A delicious hot meal prepared by his mom created a welcome sense of anticipation he hadn't felt for weeks.

He splashed some cold water on his face, and while he patted it dry, he wondered about his mom's strange request to wait until 5:00 p.m. It wasn't simply her request. She was a horrible liar. Her face and voice showed every emotion she felt. Ian brushed it off for the time being.

At 5:05 p.m., he slipped on a leather jacket and went to his motorcycle for the quick six-minute drive to his parents' home.

Three

IAN GREW UP in Pinedale Park, where his parents, Mitch and Carol Shaw, had lived for 30 years. The town was proud of its title as one of America's top-ten safest places, having never experienced a homicide. Neighbors left their doors unlocked and garages open.

When he turned onto their street, he saw a familiar car approaching from the opposite direction. As it came closer, he recognized Mrs. Wiggert, the local reverend's wife. As they passed by one another, Ian waved, but Mrs. Wiggert turned her head away to look out the passenger window at the perfect moment to miss him. Ian wondered why she was there. It was most likely that she had visited his parents because no other neighbors on the street attended church or had a relationship with the reverend.

The Shaw family's two-story brick house was set far from the street, the last property at the end of a cul-de-sac. He turned into the driveway and drove up the curved, gentle incline flanked by evenly spaced saw palmetto trees. A few mature silver maple trees provided shade along the front of the house, and a hammock was strung between the two closest to the porch.

His mom's Mercedes and his dad's Range Rover parked side-by-side, a few paces from the front door. They rarely went through the effort of moving them to the detached garage at the back of the house. Typically, his dad didn't get home until later in the evening, so seeing his car there at this time of day surprised him.

He parked his motorcycle where he always did, on the side of the house where the driveway had been extended for the RV they used to own. As he got off and removed his helmet, he was relieved to feel none of the angst he had expected. Maybe dinner would go well this evening. Perhaps the time together might ease some of his dad's anger and his mom's sadness about losing the woman they dreamed would become their daughter-in-law.

When he came to the front door, he heard a commotion inside and listened, but the house went quiet. The silence was broken by the sudden chatter of nearby birds behind him.

Ian grabbed the doorknob and tried to turn it, but it was locked. *What the hell is going on?* He hesitated to use his key because of his mom's strange request that he wait until after five. It wasn't his birthday, so he couldn't be stumbling into a surprise party. He rang the bell and knocked.

While waiting for an answer, he cupped his hand over his eyes to look into the small window mounted high on the door. The foyer was dark, but the kitchen light was on at the end of the hallway. As he fished his keys from his pocket, he heard footsteps approaching. He looked inside again and saw his mom hurrying to the door.

She pulled it open and wiped her hands on an apron. "Hi, honey," she said.

"Why isn't Dad at work?"

"Oh, that… your father was so excited that you were coming for dinner that he took off early from work."

Ian's expression turned suspicious. "Dad did that—because of me?"

"Of course! We haven't seen you in so long, I think he's making dinner a bit of a celebration."

This explanation fell flat for Ian. Tensions were high between him and his dad. And Mr. Shaw's regular rants of disappointment that Ian couldn't hold on to Kate had only made things worse.

"He isn't still pissed off at me?"

She frowned. "Why do you use that term?"

"Sorry. He isn't still angry at me?"

"You know your father only wants the best for you. He sometimes has a difficult time expressing it."

"And why was your door locked?" Ian asked.

"That was all my fault," Mrs. Shaw crossed her hands over her chest to emphasize her apology. "I must have accidentally locked it while elbowing my way back into the house with my hands full of groceries. I'm sorry, Sweetheart."

Ian squinted at her, wanting the explanation to make sense.

She tugged his arm for him to enter, then closed the door behind him. He followed her down the hallway, raising his chin to inhale deeply through his nose, enjoying the delicious aroma of spices and melted cheese of lasagna and garlic bread. The scent brought Ian a flood of happy memories. As they neared the kitchen door, he briefly caught a whiff of something different. It was subtle and unfamiliar. "Are you wearing a new perfume?" he said.

"No, why?" His mom opened the swinging door to the kitchen and held it for him, motioning for him to go in.

This gesture, too, struck Ian as odd. The flimsy, slatted door swung easily on spring hinges. There was no need for her to hold the door for him.

"I smell something different. It's sweet."

"It's probably the cobbler prep."

"No, it's floral-sweet."

His mom shrugged and went to a large silver bowl, taking the handle of a wooden spoon that protruded from it. She stirred the cobbler filling.

She seemed nervous, watching him while she stirred.

"That won't work," Ian said, pointing to a large bottle of cheap peach brandy on the counter beside the bowl.

His mom paused, and her shoulders drooped. "I thought you told me I needed peach brandy."

"I did, but I also told you I'd bring some for you. Here you go…" He pulled a fancy miniature bottle of Kuchan Indian blood peach brandy from the inside pocket of his jacket and slid it across the counter to her. "This brand will add honey overtones and the slightly spicy finish Dad probably liked. Let it marinate a bit before cooking. It'll make all the difference."

"Ian, you could have told me what to buy, and I would've gladly purchased it."

"It's difficult to find, Ian said. This one's on me."

She picked up the bottle and looked down her nose at it to examine the label. "I can't believe you held out on your mother on such a delicious tweak to the recipe." She wagged the bottle at him. "We chefs have to stick together. We shouldn't have such secrets between us!"

"Wasn't holding out on you, Mom. And when have you ever written down a recipe?"

She laughed and pulled a large pan from the oven, already lined with the cobbler crust. "How much brandy should I use?"

"God, that's huge!" Ian said. He quickly made room on the counter, opened a drawer, and tossed hot pads onto it.

"It never goes to waste, right?" His mom said, setting it down.

"With a pan that large, you should freeze some," Ian said. "I should have brought you two bottles of brandy, but we can probably come close to the flavor you want with one."

Mrs. Shaw poured the brandy over the filling. Before she resumed stirring, Ian saw her take the briefest glance toward the swinging doors and then returned her focus to pouring the bottle.

"What's the matter with you? You're tense," he said.

"Oh, nothing at all!" She said.

Ian didn't buy it. She answered too quickly. He knew his mother.

Mrs. Shaw went to the trash and tossed the empty brandy bottle but missed, and it fell to the floor. She retrieved it, and her second try succeeded.

Ian stared at her until she noticed.

"What? Everything's fine."

"Why do I feel you're hiding something?" Ian went to the sink to wash his hands.

"Before you do that, come help me a minute." She pointed to a glass casserole dish on a cabinet shelf that was a little high, but well within her reach.

"Before I wash my hands?" Ian approached her suspiciously and took the dish down for her.

"Thank you." She set it beside the sink and then faced him, blocking the sink and the window above it.

Ian said, "Mom, what's going on? From the moment I drove onto the property, everything has been weird here."

She said, "Why don't you relax? Everything will be fine."

"*Will be* fine? What isn't fine right now?" he asked, resisting panic.

"I just mean with your breakup and everything. Soon, you'll recover and feel healthy again in no time."

"Recover? My health is fine, Mom."

Mrs. Shaw reached for the bowl of cobbler filling and stirred it while holding it to keep her position in front of the sink.

Ian tried to walk past her, but she planted her feet while stirring hard. He looked over her shoulder. He saw the garage door was sliding down from about knee height. Ian glimpsed two sets of vehicle tires and someone's feet walking between them before the door closed, obscuring his view.

"Who's in the garage?"

"Uh," his mom stammered, "that would be your father."

"Why is he closing it? Did I see cars in there?"

"I didn't see any cars," Mrs. Shaw replied.

Ian headed for the back door.

Mrs. Shaw blurted, "Wait! Where are you going?"

"I'm going out to find out from Dad why everything here is weird."

"I wish you wouldn't!"

Ian stopped. "Why not?"

"Because I want you to stay here and keep me company. He'll be in soon enough." She beamed at him with a smile too broad to be authentic.

"Mom, you're freaking me out. You're acting crazy."

Mrs. Shaw moved to the cobbler crust dish and began pouring the rhubarb filling, ignoring his accusation. "Now, to make sure you aren't hoarding any more recipe secrets, how long do you bake it?"

"Twenty minutes at 400 preheated. Mom, something's not right here. I need to look around." Ian went to the swinging doors to the hall.

"No, wait!" his mom said.

Ian stopped, looking back at her.

"Before you do that, I need your help again." She paused, then went to the cabinets on the farther side of the kitchen, wringing her hands.

"With what?"

She opened a cabinet and pointed up to the top shelf. "Up there. Can you get me that large salad bowl? I can't reach it."

Ian slowly approached her, looking back and forth between the swinging doors and her. He studied her expression closely. He reached up and retrieved the bowl. As he brought it down to her, he leaned close and whispered, "If someone is holding you against your will, say, 'I want you to taste my rhubarb.'" He pulled his gun from his holster and held it behind his back.

She looked up into his face with a smile that contradicted the anxiety in her eyes. "Put that away, and don't be silly," she said.

"Then tell me what's going on," Ian said louder.

A cough came from the hallway.

Ian spun, raising his pistol.

"Honey, no, it's okay." She took his wrist and tried to take the gun, but Ian resisted. "Ian Shaw, give me the gun," his mother said firmly. "You have nothing to worry about here."

"Then who coughed?"

His mother motioned with her finger for him to come closer and whispered, "I'm hoping you'll be pleasantly surprised."

"You know I don't like surprises."

"I do know that, but this is an exception." Her consolation and persistence paid off when Ian relinquished the gun to her. She opened a drawer and tucked it under some towels.

"Give back my gun. I won't use it."

His mom pressed her finger to her lips and said, "Shh, just wait."

"I've had enough of this." Ian pushed through the swinging doors to the hallway. The door to the den was closed. Just as the front door was never locked, the Shaws never closed the garage or the den's sliding door. "You guys have everything closed up like you're expecting bad weather," Ian yelled back to her. He reached for the den door handle.

"No!" his mom said. "Ian, just wait a minute for your father. He can help me explain."

The back door from the garage to the kitchen opened, and after a few footsteps, Ian's dad entered the hallway.

"Hey, Son."

Ian flashed a brief smile and raised his chin in acknowledgment. "Mom's acting weird," he said, trying to open the den door, but it was locked. "Somebody needs to tell me what the hell is going on in this house!" he shouted.

"Son, first, you need to relax," Mr. Shaw said, approaching him.

The den door startled Ian when it slid open from the inside. Ian looked inside and froze. He felt a warm hand gently nudge him from behind, urging him to enter the room. His mom whispered, "Go inside, sweetheart. It's okay."

Ian stepped to catch his balance after Mrs. Shaw's gentle push. He gazed through the doorway.

Mr. Shaw moved around him, blocking the hallway to the front door. "We need you to go inside, son," his dad said, pointing.

Ian's brother, Tim, had warned Ian of their parents' recent concern for Ian's well-being. Tim had broken their trust by revealing to Ian that they had been planning to send him off for treatment—forcibly, if necessary. His parents knew Ian would never go willingly, so the meaning of the strange secrecy became clear, panicking him.

He turned and lunged, slamming into his father. Mr. Shaw grabbed him. They crashed against the wall, dislodging a picture that fell to the floor.

Mrs. Shaw screamed, "Ian, stop!"

Ian regained his footing and fled.

Mr. Shaw grabbed the back of Ian's shirt. It tore as Ian broke free, racing away.

Shouts from the den joined in with his mother, calling for Ian to stop.

He sped up to a full sprint, closing in on the front door. When he came to the living room opening, a large figure came from the side, tackling him to the floor just outside the foyer. The muscular man pinned him. "We're gonna do this with you rested, or we will do this while you are tired. It's your choice," the man said. Ian recognized the voice of his Uncle Thomas, a muscular ex-Marine.

"Get off me!" Ian said, twisting and kicking.

Uncle Thomas gained control of Ian with little effort, putting him in a headlock.

"Do not resist," his father said. He kneeled and swung his leg over Ian's legs to keep them from kicking.

Uncle Thomas said, "I will loosen my grip, and you will cooperate. Do you understand?"

Ian nodded, wheezing through his nose.

Uncle Thomas slowly released the headlock.

Mr. Shaw cautiously took his weight off Ian's legs. "Now, let's go back into the den and get this over with." He reached down to help Ian up.

Ian shoved his father's hand away and climbed to his feet alone.

Mr. Shaw and Uncle Thomas followed him, exchanging satisfied nods as Ian took several steps toward the den. Before the men could fall in behind him, Ian bolted for the door again. This time he reached it, but when he grabbed for the knob, it was encased in a metal cuff that spun loosely, preventing the knob from turning from the inside. Ian slammed his shoulder into the door but couldn't break through it.

Uncle Thomas and his father had positioned themselves behind him in a way that blocked him from escaping past them in the hallway.

His dad said, "You're not leaving until we do this. You'll avoid a lot of pain if you don't fight it."

When Uncle Thomas tried to grab Ian's arm, Ian shoved him in the chest and tried to run between the men. His dad shoulder-blocked him, sending Ian crashing into the wall. The impact slowed him enough for Uncle Thomas to make another tackle from behind, slamming Ian to the floor.

Ian's dad again subdued his kicking legs while Uncle Thomas secured Ian's arms behind him. He pressed his knee into the back of Ian's neck.

"Can't… breathe," Ian gasped.

"Easy, Thom," Mr. Shaw said, climbing to his feet now that Ian was again under control.

Uncle Thomas got up and pulled Ian to his feet. "We should bind him."

Mr. Shaw moved to face Ian and said, "Do you hear your uncle right now? Do we need to fully restrain you to force you to do the right thing, son?"

"No," Ian grunted.

They marched him down the hallway. This time, Uncle Thomas kept a tight grip on one of Ian's arms while his dad held the other.

Ian heard chairs sliding and footsteps in the den. When they came to the open doorway, he saw six people. They sat in a row, using the wooden fold-up chairs the Shaws only brought out when they had company.

Mr. Shaw pointed and said, "Take a seat."

They let go of Ian's arms. Uncle Thomas shoved him toward an empty chair that faced the others.

Ian stumbled in and stood beside the chair. Until a few minutes ago, the den represented Ian's fondest childhood memories. He and his family had spent thousands of hours watching television on the familiar striped sofa now pushed off to the side. Shelves on the wood-panel wall still contained high school baseball and soccer trophies he and his brother, Tim, had earned.

He scanned the people in the room. When he sat down, their expressions relaxed—a little.

Mrs. Shaw came in and took a seat on the end chair. She clutched a wad of tissue while looking sympathetically at Ian. She forced a brief smile that Ian didn't return.

Next to her sat Reverend Wiggert, his hands comfortably folded on a Bible that rested on his lap. He had known Ian since Ian was a baby.

Beside him sat Ian's older brother, Tim. He wore his typical attire: cargo pants, hiking boots, a camouflage hunting shirt, and a backward baseball cap. He chewed a plastic straw. His exasperated expression made him the only person in the room who looked as uncomfortable as Ian.

The person next to Tim was a surprise. Brandon was Ian's best friend from high school. They occasionally kept in touch by phone but hadn't hung out in person in nearly a year. Brandon's face was the calmest of the group, looking at Ian with a small smile tinged with concern.

Sidney Fletcher, his former boss, sat in the next chair. The gathering felt like a lame attempt at a *This-Is-Your-Life* show.

The last chair was occupied by a slightly heavyset woman in a long black skirt. She had shoulder-length red hair and wore too much makeup, including overdone rouge that extended to her temples. She held a small box on her lap, its woodgrain finish polished to a mirror shine.

Uncle Thomas slid the door closed behind him, then assumed an intimidating guard-like stance. He flexed his chest several times and raised his chin to dominate Ian with a look.

Standing beside Uncle Thomas, Mr. Shaw wore his own I-dare-you expression. The men had obviously forfeited their reserved seats on the sofa to ensure Ian couldn't flee.

The unfamiliar woman said, "Can we begin, Mr. Shaw?"

Ian looked over his shoulder at his dad.

Mr. Shaw nodded.

The woman picked up a handbag, slung its strap over her shoulder, and carried the box to the corner of the room, placing it on a lamp table. She blocked everyone's view with her body while she removed something from the bag, placing it inside the box. After clicking the lid closed, she brought the box to her seat and slid it under her chair. She smiled at Ian, cleared her throat, and said, "Hello, Ian. I regret we got off to such a rough start. It typically doesn't happen this way."

Ian crossed his arms and slouched in his chair. "Who the fuck are you?"

"Ian! Language!" his mom snapped.

The woman's smile broadened, revealing a straight row of undersized teeth. Ian looked closer at her and saw that her overdone makeup failed to mask some rather deep-set wrinkles, including pronounced crow's feet at the corners of her eyes, and that her smile failed to deepen.

"My name is Dagny. As you've probably guessed, we are here to conduct an intervention."

"For...?" Ian said, examining his fingernails.

"For you!"

The group laughed, seizing on the humor to release the tension.

"So, this is funny to you people?" Ian said, scanning the faces.

His reprimand snuffed the laughter, and the residual smiles quickly dissolved.

"I apologize," Dagny said. "My comment was inappropriate. Ian, the people in this room have each expressed having a closeness with you. They have taken time out of their busy schedules to be here because they care about you. They are worried about your well-being."

"Be specific. What's going on?" Ian said, glaring at Dagny.

"Everyone here shares a genuine concern about your use of alcohol and what seems to be your increasing dependence on it."

"How would anybody here know that?" Ian pointed to the other people.

"Their conclusions are based on their observations. Everyone in this room agrees that the road you are on will prevent your future happiness and that your habit has had a detrimental effect on your relationships with each of them."

Ian sat forward in his chair. "That's bullshit!"

"Ian Shaw, watch your language!" Mrs. Shaw said, raising her voice. She patted her hair and adjusted herself in her seat.

"I'm not an alcoholic," Ian said. He swept his finger across his spectators. "These people know nothing about my life."

"Well, if they are all mistaken, this is the perfect opportunity to clear that up."

Ian sat back and crossed his arms.

Dagny continued. "We are here to support you. My job is facilitating the experience, making it as comfortable as possible."

Ian rolled his eyes. If these people represented the best emotional pressure points his parents could devise for an intervention, he'd give them a D+. If they genuinely wanted to influence him, Kate would be sitting here. Ian wondered if they even tried to contact her.

He tried to remember when and where anyone might have seen him drinking. Maybe they had hired a private investigator to spy on him. He wondered how long ago they had planned to trap him this way. He was familiar enough with interventions to know that the choice to take part would ultimately be his—at least it should be. He couldn't wait to reject the offer.

Dagny said, "The people in this room have some important, heartfelt messages for you. Are you willing to listen?"

Knowing he had no choice, the question irritated him. His drinking wasn't out of control. And if he occasionally got excessive, he stayed home, bothering no one. If it was a problem, it was only his problem. He stared at Dagny, saying nothing.

"Answer the woman," Mr. Shaw snapped from behind him.

"Mitch, please," Mrs. Shaw said.

"Carol, I don't care how old he is. The boy needs to mind his manners."

"Please!" Dagny interrupted. "I know emotions are raw, but we need to stay positive. So, I'm going to ask, for Ian's sake, that we limit any communication to our prepared messages. I don't want Ian to experience any more stress than he's already feeling. Makes sense?" She returned her attention to Ian. "Let's begin. Ian, each person will share a prepared message with you. When they finish, they will ask you a simple question. Your only job is to listen carefully and answer. Makes sense?"

Ian poked his tongue into his cheek and barely shrugged.

Dagny clasped her hands together. "Good, then. Reverend Wiggert, why don't you begin?"

The reverend stood and rubbed his hands together as if boasting that he didn't need to read his words from a piece of paper.

"No, no, no," Dagny said. "We don't stand during the personal messages. The posture is dominant and confrontational. We reviewed this, Reverend. Please address Ian from in your seat."

The reverend reluctantly sat, cleared his throat, and said, "Before we go any further, I think it would be wise for us to invoke God's blessing on this important gathering."

Ian rubbed his temples and hissed through his clenched teeth.

"Does that make you uncomfortable?" Dagny asked Ian. Since Ian stopped attending church a few years ago, his encounters with the reverend have been creepy. The reverend had given off a stalker-ish vibe whenever he said, "We know we'll get you back soon." Ian looked at him and said, "If your prayers worked, we wouldn't be here, right?"

"Oh, Brother Shaw, prayer always works!"

"I'm not your brother and don't need your prayer. I need to get this over with so I can leave."

"If any situation needed God's blessing, it's this one," the reverend replied, undaunted.

Dagny said, "We aren't here to argue with Ian. We are here to support him. He doesn't want to pray, so there will be no prayer."

The reverend glanced over to Mr. Shaw and then Mrs. Shaw.

Mr. Shaw felt the pressure and said, "What's the harm in a brief prayer?"

Dagny stood. "Let me ask you something, Mr. Shaw. Do you want to help your son today?"

"Of course."

"I'm going to ask you to trust my experience. Here, keeping Ian comfortable is the key to success. If the reverend or any of you have a problem with that, you may leave now."

Ian watched Dagny advocate for him. He smiled with half his mouth. As a therapist, or whatever, she wasn't horrible.

"It's okay, Reverend Wiggert," Mrs. Shaw said. "All of us will pray in our heads." She smiled at Ian, claiming victory.

"Let's just get this shit over with," Ian said.

"Lord, forgive him—language!" Mrs. Shaw said, scowling at him.

"What's the matter, Mom? Worried my language will reflect poorly on you?"

Ian's dad came toward him.

Dagny jumped up, stepping between them. "Mr. Shaw, please let it go!"

Ian bowed his head and smiled, enjoying the interference Dagny was running for him.

Mr. Shaw reached around Dagny and put his finger close to Ian's face. "You show your mother respect. And watch your mouth. We are in mixed company."

Dagny gently took Mr. Shaw's arm and moved the finger away from Ian's face, saying, "Please, Mr. Shaw, let's refocus."

Mr. Shaw yanked his wrist away and backed to his place at the door beside Uncle Thomas.

Dagny leaned down to Ian, enveloping him in the sweet floral scent of the perfume Ian had detected in the hallway.

He wrinkled his nose and leaned away.

"I need to tell you something." She motioned for him to come closer.

Ian sat up only slightly.

Dagny cupped her mouth to his ear and whispered, "If you work with me, you just watch the respect I squeeze out of these people for you. Trust me, and let me amaze you."

Everyone watched, wondering what Dagny's secret message had been.

Ian wasn't sure how to feel about the offer. It wasn't bad. The unfamiliar interloper had so far been the strongest advocate for him in this room. The irony of it sent a disgusted puff through his nose.

"Reverend, please try again to give Ian your statement," Dagny said, returning to her seat.

The reverend gave Ian an extended look of pity before he smiled and said, "We haven't seen you at church for quite some time…" He paused to see if the statement triggered any hint of shame in Ian.

Ian rolled his eyes.

The reverend continued. "I'm here representing your flock. Your church family has always lovingly supported you. I want you to know that God has a plan for you, but you must listen and obey. The crafty devil has made headway in the battle for your soul. It's not too late for God to peel back the devil's fingers and free you. He has sent this wonderful woman," the reverend pointed to Dagny, "and God will use her talents to make you whole again. Oh, how the church has prayed for you. We pray you will return to the fold and renounce the temptations that have led you astray. We understand this task is too big for any man to handle alone. But by God's grace, you can do it with the support of these wonderful people." He looked around at the other guests. "If, on the other hand, you reject God's loving gift of rehabilitation, I will have no choice but to bring your name before the church committee for discussion and disfellowship. Brother Shaw, let's avoid this unnecessary and shameful step by agreeing to get help. Will you accept treatment today?" the reverend grinned.

Ian checked his watch and said, "Next?"

The reverend's grin dissolved.

"Don't be an ass," his brother said. "Why can't you just answer the goddamn question?"

"Timothy! Language!" Mrs. Shaw said.

"That was an answer," Ian said. "By 'next,' I meant hell no!"

Mrs. Shaw blew her nose and said, "Ian, we need you to trust us."

"Unbelievable!" he gaped at his mother. "You are asking me for trust? After you tricked me?"

"Why would you say that?" Mrs. Shaw said, visibly embarrassed.

"You lured me here with my favorite meal. Then Dad and Uncle Thomas assaulted me and held me against my will, and now you dare to ask for my trust?"

Mrs. Shaw opened her mouth to respond but struggled to get any words out.

Ian thumbed over his shoulder. "At least Dad's clumsy, persistent anger is straightforward. After today, how can I ever trust you again?"

"Don't say that!" Mrs. Shaw blurted, covering her face. She cried.

Mr. Shaw watched the exchange. His temples flared with each clench of his teeth. He glared at Ian, looking like he might lunge at any moment. "Boy, you have really sunk to a new low, talking to your mother like that."

"Please leave!" Dagny said to Mr. Shaw.

"Excuse me?" he said.

"Mr. Shaw, I am asking you to leave," she said, pointing at the door.

At first, Mr. Shaw smiled with disbelief. "You're not going to kick me out of my own—"

"I mean it," Dagny insisted. "Respectfully, if this intervention is to succeed, I need you to leave—please."

Uncle Thomas kept his eye on Ian while he opened the door with the care and paranoia of a corrections officer.

Mr. Shaw's cursing echoed in the hallway until Uncle Thomas closed the door.

Mrs. Shaw sat, visibly stunned. Her husband's expulsion had jarred her from her weeping.

Dagny said, "If anyone else raises their voice, shames, or speaks rudely to Ian, they'll be invited to leave as well. My organization boasts a perfect record, achieved through respect and nurturing, not degradation. Can we lift Ian up, respecting him, embracing his uniqueness, and expressing only love, or should I pack up and leave now?"

"Please, let's continue," Mrs. Shaw said.

"Good, then it's your brother's turn." She motioned to Tim.

Ian said, "Yes, let's hear from the favored son."

"Don't be an ass," Tim said.

Mrs. Shaw squeezed her eyes shut and grimaced.

"Careful, Tim," Dagny warned. "No name-calling."

Tim had relished being a protective older brother for most of their younger years. They and their dad often took camping and hunting trips together. Ian's closeness to Tim grew through their teen years. Tim often stuck up for Ian in high school when kids would pick on him. Tim went to college, then dropped out, returning as an avid environmentalist and outdoorsman. Fishing, hiking, camping, and hunting consumed Tim, and he could live happily on a minuscule budget. Over time, their diverging interests had cooled their relationship. One topic, in particular, was a powder keg. Tim never approved of Ian's relationship with Kate. His comments about Kate frequently angered Ian, further eroding the brothers' closeness.

"Listen, these people are trying to help you," Tim said. "You can at least give them the courtesy of cooperating for a few minutes. I mean, deal with it, Bro."

"I'm dealing with this better than you would," Ian laughed. "In fact, you drink more than I do."

"But I'm not in your situation, am I?" Tim said. "That makes all the difference."

"What the fuck do you know about my situation?"

Mrs. Shaw bowed and rubbed her temples, saying, "Jesus—please."

"Just read your note." Ian waved him off.

Tim pulled an index card from his pocket and unfolded it. He took a deep breath and said, "I know life has been hard for you lately. Life gets tough. Even though you are my little brother, I always saw you as a badass. I still think that, but whatever you've been going through lately has really fucked you up." He paused to look at Mrs. Shaw.

She squeezed her lips tighter.

Tim continued. "And I agree with everyone that we can't ignore what we see. Late last night, I drove by your place. You weren't home. I called your mobile, and, as usual, you didn't answer."

"I was gone, and my mobile phone's been deactivated," Ian interrupted.

"Sorry to hear that," Tim said. "Anyway, no one has heard your voice for almost two weeks. On a hunch, I drove by your ex's place." Tim pulled an iPad out from under his chair and flipped open the cover. He tapped the screen, then turned it for Ian to see a photo. The image, taken through a vehicle window, showed Ian sitting in the driver's seat of his car, looking directly at the camera, a worried expression captured in explicit detail.

Ian instantly linked Tim to the truck that had slowed by his car last night.

"You spied on me?" Ian said.

"Listen to me. You gotta let Kate go. She's wrecking you."

"Of course, you'd say that. You never liked her. You never gave her a chance."

"I told you she was no good for you from day one." Tim closed the iPad. "You can do so much better, Bro."

"So you get a divorce, and suddenly you're an expert on recognizing terrible relationships?"

"That has nothing to do with it, and you know it. The lock she had on you was insane!"

"I see what this is about. You were jealous of Kate because I wanted to spend time with her instead of hunting with you."

"That's not it at all," Tim said.

Ian leaned on the edge of his chair. "We shared a love I wouldn't expect you to recognize." He felt his throat clench along with the pre-cry prickling behind his nose. He paused.

Tim said, "Listen, if you two were still together, I might not have shown up today because I know it would've been futile. But knowing that you broke up made me feel like this was a genuine opportunity to help you aim in a better direction without her distracting it." Tim flipped over the index card and read the last line. "If you refuse treatment today, I will have to cut off all communication, including telephone, text messaging, and in-person. Will you accept treatment today?"

Ian looked at Tim in disbelief. "You seriously think that's pressure?"

"Maybe it's not, but it's all I've got," Tim said.

Dagny said softly, "Ian, please, we need you to answer the question."

Ian thought momentarily, then said, "I don't even know what the treatment looks like. I do not agree to anything unless I know exactly what I'm agreeing to."

Dagny said, "The agreement is for a few short days of treatment conducted at a wellness retreat known as A Taste of Heaven."

"Where is that?"

"Just outside Jamesburg, a tad over an hour away."

"Never heard of it."

"That doesn't surprise me," Dagny said. "I can assure you it's a magnificent, luxurious resort where you'll be safe, comfortable, and respected. Our success rate is virtually 100%. In fact, I wouldn't be surprised if we had to force you to leave."

Ian said, "I'm sure it is lovely, but you're trying to fix a problem I don't have. No deal." He crossed his arms.

"Alright, then," Dagny said, "We'll continue. Next, we have a person I think you know quite well." She motioned toward Sydney Fletcher, Ian's former boss. Ian did not know why anyone thought this man's presence would help. A couple of years ago, Mr. Fletcher laid Ian off from the Braybar Grille, a local restaurant where Ian had hoped to become the executive chef. Mr. Fletcher claimed the layoff was financially necessary. But Ian found out from another employee that Mr. Fletcher had immediately hired his underqualified son-in-law at higher pay, eventually making him the chef.

"I bet you're surprised to see me here," Mr. Fletcher said tentatively.

Ian said, "I'll only be surprised if you don't spin this meeting into profit."

Mr. Fletcher wrung his hands. "I understand you may still harbor some bitterness about my having to let you go."

"You mean firing me?"

Dagny said, "Ian, I will gently request that you hear him out. You will have the opportunity to respond at the end."

Ian motioned for Mr. Fletcher to hurry.

"When I found out you were going through such a difficult time, I didn't hesitate to offer my support at this intervention. We had our differences, but you were a good worker. You were responsible, prompt, and competent. From what I hear, your wonderful traits have been affected by the bottle."

Ian put his head back and covered his eyes with his arm. "That's not true! I'm not an alcoholic. How many times do I have to tell you people?"

"Shh, take it easy," Dagny said.

"Ian, I'm going to make you an offer," Mr. Fletcher continued. "If you will accept the help that you need in treatment, I would consider rehiring you. Not only that, but I'd also be willing to put you on a fast track to become our chef."

Ian smirked at him. "Your son-in-law not working out?"

"We are here to discuss you, not José," Mr. Fletcher replied.

"I happen to know José got arrested for DUI after an accident." Ian looked at Brandon. "And didn't you tell me José got injured in that accident and can't work anymore?"

Brandon's face flushed red. He winced when Mr. Fletcher looked at him. "It was just something I heard."

"That's right," Ian said. "Brandon doesn't call much anymore, but this was juicy enough news for him to pick up the phone. Are you taking notes on this intervention to plan for José's?"

Mr. Fletcher laughed nervously. "That's not your concern. Today, we are here for you, and after making you such a generous job offer, your lack of gratitude is stunning."

"Let me tell you what's stunning," Ian said.

"No, we need to stay on track," Dagny said.

"Dammit, lady, shut up."

"Ian Mitchell Shaw!" his mother yelled.

Ian pointed at Dagny. "She keeps telling me I will have a chance to speak, then I never get one!"

"Go ahead, Ian," Dagny said. She folded her hands and sat back.

"Let me tell you something," Ian said, scowling at Mr. Fletcher. "You expect gratitude from me after lying to me about your reasons for firing me? Then you hired your alcoholic nephew, who brought you exactly what you deserved. Do you want me to express gratitude? I'll be grateful to the first person in this room who can help to muscle me out of this goddamn hellhole. My answer to everyone is no. Are we done here?" He looked at Dagny.

"Almost. It's your mother's turn."

While she took her time to unfold a note, Mrs. Shaw said, "First of all, I apologize to everyone for my son's language."

Several in the group glanced toward the window at the sound of an approaching vehicle. The drawn shades allowed light while blocking any detail. Had they been open, it would have made no difference, anyway. Most of the driveway wasn't visible through the den window. The vehicle's engine was deep, growling like a truck stopping beside the house. At this point, Ian wouldn't be surprised if they had transported him in an armored truck to prevent his escape.

Mrs. Shaw's hand trembled as she began reading. "My son, I love you so much…" Tears flowed again. She held up a finger and stopped. For almost 30 seconds, she fought to gain her composure.

A door slammed closed from the vehicle outside.

When Mrs. Shaw tried to speak calmly, emotion flooded back, overwhelming her. She blurted, "Please agree to get help, or we can't have you back…" She dissolved into sobs. When Tim leaned toward her and placed his hand on her back, she got up and rushed to the door while crumpling the paper in her fist.

Uncle Thomas opened his arms to comfort her, but she pushed past him and disappeared into the hallway where Mr. Shaw waited.

"Do you see how much love there is in this room for you?" Dagny asked Ian.

Ian studied his thumbnail, not responding.

"Allow me to ask on behalf of your mother," Dagny said. "Will you accept the treatment we are offering today?"

"Not a chance in hell," Ian replied.

"Then we move on," Dagny said. "Brandon, your turn."

Brandon pulled a card from his pocket. Before he could speak, Ian said, "Who brought you into this?"

Brandon flicked the card on his leg several times, searching for a non-incendiary response. "It's not important, buddy."

"You know it is. Tell me, dammit."

A firm knock at the den door rescued Brandon from Ian's interrogation.

Ian expected to see his mom return after having composed herself.

Uncle Thomas answered the knock and leaned out into the hallway. When he returned, he signaled Dagny a thumbs-up before closing the door.

"Ian, we've yet to hear messages from Brandon, your father, and your uncle. Based on your responses so far, I have no confidence that the heartfelt testimonials from these three men will make any difference."

"Finally," Ian said. "I wholeheartedly agree with you. I don't need to hear another word from any of you people."

"In that case, I'll simply ask you one final time. Ian Shaw, will you accept the treatment we offer you today?"

"You people are insane," Ian said, standing up.

Dagny reached down and slid the wooden box out from under her chair, placing it on her lap.

Ian continued. "If you had accused me of being depressed and a little more reclusive than usual lately, I'd grant you that, but I'm not an alcoholic. Frankly, what I do on my time in my house is none of your business. I don't understand why you people are so determined to solve a problem that doesn't exist."

"I'd say you've thoroughly convinced us," Dagny said.

"I have?" Ian said, surprised.

"Yes, we are all convinced *you* believe that," Dagny said.

"So, now I'm delusional and unable to recognize my own problem. Is that what you're saying?"

"Think of it this way," Dagny said. "If you are correct and don't need rehabilitation, then attending our treatment shouldn't concern you. We can't fix what isn't broken. We assume all the risk by spending money and resources to give you the experience of a five-star resort unnecessarily. You win, we lose. The joke's on us. What's the harm in some free pampering while you suffer none of the withdrawal symptoms of addiction that our other patients experience?"

"How much clearer can I make it for you?" Ian said, sounding angrier. "I don't want or need your pampering. The only thing I need is to get the hell out of here before I press charges for holding me against my will, you bunch of fucking hostage-takers."

Dagny leaned forward in her chair and looked at the others. "Goodness gracious, I'd say he's made his position quite clear. It looks like our only option is to respect his wishes." She sat back and signaled Uncle Thomas with a slight nod.

He opened the door, stepped aside, and extended his arm, inviting Ian to exit.

Ian hesitated, looking at Uncle Thomas suspiciously and then at the other people in the room. Something wasn't right. They wore content expressions, no longer seeming upset by his rejection of treatment. "So, you are saying I can walk out—just like that?" he asked.

"You're an adult, and this is America," Dagny said. She smiled and motioned with her chin toward the door that opened to his freedom.

Ian eased past his uncle, expecting him to grab him, but Uncle Thomas stepped back more, giving him even more room.

In the hallway, he found his dad hugging his mom, trying to comfort her.

"Sorry for being such a disappointment," Ian said as he paused beside his parents.

"If you've refused our help, then just go," Mr. Shaw said, refusing to look at him while gently rocking Mrs. Shaw.

Ian continued toward the front door, frequently checking over his shoulder as if a surprise hand from somewhere might reach out and grab him. He reached the front door. The metal cuff had been removed. No one in the group had followed him. His parents remained embraced a few paces away. He reached for the knob and turned it. The door opened. Behind him, the house was quiet. He stepped outside and saw something that took his breath away. Kate stood just off the porch. She looked up at him and smiled.

Four

IAN THOUGHT HIS knees might buckle as he gazed at Kate. At some point, after he had seen Kate leave her house this morning, she had changed into a white sleeveless summer dress that highlighted the beautiful skin of her shoulders and arms. She wore white leather cross-strap sandals, and her ponytail had been freed, her hair falling behind her shoulders. She looked perfect. Absolutely perfect. He couldn't speak.

Kate raised her hand and twiddled her fingers in a wave. "I was pretty sure you'd be surprised," she said.

Ian used brute force to stammer, "Wow."

"I've been worried about you," she said softly.

The words sent a warm rush through him, instantly dissolving any resentment he felt toward her. The rush deepened when she tilted her head and smiled at him.

"Sorry I'm late," she said.

"Late for what?" Ian instantly recognized the silliness of his question but didn't care. He wanted Kate to say more, and he'd do anything to prolong their interaction—to hear her voice.

"The intervention."

"Oh, right. You were in on that, too?" He took a tentative step closer, as if worried it might scare her away.

"Yesterday, your parents called me," Kate said. "They told me about your situation."

"I hope you didn't believe them. I'm doing fine. Great, actually."

"I figured you would say that, so I told them not to worry. I told them how strong I knew you were."

"You said that? Really?"

"Of course."

Ian used brute force to resist rushing to throw his arms around her.

Kate said, "They told me about the intervention. They were nervous and worried it might fail. In their desperation, they contacted me, asking my opinion about whether you would cooperate."

"And you said…"

"I told them it depends. I reminded them you are a problem-solver and recounted the many times I saw you rescue yourself from impossible situations."

"Except with us." Ian looked away.

Kate closed her eyes and sighed. "Ian, no rehash. Please."

GUILE
 45

"Sorry."

Kate shook off Ian's misstep. "So, I offered to attend the intervention today. They initially worried that I would be too much of a distraction. I finally convinced them to let me participate, but I'm late, so it looks like I missed the most exciting part."

Ian rolled his eyes. His parents hadn't needed to go through the trouble of coordinating the sneaky visit by the reverend, a friend, Tim, and a former boss Ian had no respect for. They could've lured Ian anywhere on earth by simply saying, "Kate will be there, and she hopes to see you." She was the only participant the intervention needed. Despite their breakup, she still had more influence on him than everyone at the intervention combined.

Kate raised onto her toes to look over Ian's shoulder at the front door. "Have I missed the whole meeting?"

"You can thank me later," Ian said.

Kate smiled with a small laugh. "How did it go?"

"Ended well for me, not so well for them."

"I assume you didn't agree to treatment." Worry spread on her face.

Ian's heart sank when he realized that despite her confidence in him, Kate might have bought into the intervention after all. She *had* to know he wasn't an alcoholic. He could count on one hand the times Kate had seen him drink while they were together. And she wouldn't know anything about his life after the breakup.

Ian heard a click behind him. He looked over his shoulder. His dad had quietly appeared and unlatched the screen door, staying behind it.

Ian stepped closer to Kate and whispered, "You know I'm not an alcoholic, don't you?"

When Kate seemed to search for an answer, Ian's eyes grew enormous. "You've got to be kidding me!" he said.

"Honestly, I never saw you struggle with alcohol."

"My God—thank you!" Ian said, clasping his hands in a prayer sign as if she were a jury delivering a not-guilty verdict.

"Not while we were together, at least," she added.

The caveat hit Ian hard. "And I haven't since then! What do you even know about me anymore?"

"Would you let me hug you?" Kate said, opening her arms.

"Let you?" Ian practically lunged. Her warm embrace instantly vaporized his irritation with her.

"Come with me," she said, leading him away from the front door. Her hand felt warm and familiar. An exuberance flooded him he could hardly contain. He felt a flash of panic that he'd wake up at any moment to realize this dreamy encounter with Kate was really just a dream.

She looked closer at him as they walked to the corner of the house. "You haven't been eating," she said.

"I'm okay," Ian said. If he confessed the reason for his weight loss, Kate would accuse him of more forbidden rehashing.

When they rounded the corner to the side of the house, Ian saw the vehicle they had heard while in the den. It wasn't an armored truck. It was the damned green Camaro. And Kate's new man leaned against it.

Ian let go of her hand. "Why would you do this?"

"Do what?" Kate said, confused.

"Flaunt him," Ian said, pointing to the guy.

Kate tilted her head, squinting at him for a moment. Understanding quickly replaced her confusion. She said, "Ian, I'm sorry. I thought that bringing my nephew, Preston, would be okay."

"Nephew?"

"Yes, he's staying with me for a week before he goes back to college."

Preston heard the exchange and offered a weak, almost fearful wave.

Ian turned away. Embarrassment sent blood rushing to his face.

"It's okay," Kate said. "Preston is my sister Tracy's son. On my fridge, I had photos of him taken a few years ago, but it was unfair of me to assume you'd still recognize him—he's grown so much."

"I'm sorry," Ian said.

"Forgiven already," Kate said, shrugging. Then she delivered another smile. That damned smile always wrecked him. Missing this part of her beauty had been torture. Why couldn't she be a bitch? It would make losing her so much more bearable. Instead, her beauty, compassion, and concern for his well-being fed what he knew would be torture when it was time for them to leave separately.

"Tell me why you refused treatment," she asked.

"Because I don't need it." He thumbed over his shoulder. "I won't let them haul me away for unnecessary treatment. My folks still adore you and will probably agree to anything you suggest. Please tell them this isn't necessary."

Kate said, "That's the hard way. The easiest way at this point is to go along. If the treatment isn't necessary, so what? Take a vacation. I hear it's lavish."

Ian looked at her suspiciously. "How did you know that?"

"A woman named Dagny called me last night. She wanted to ask me some questions. I thought it would be quick, but we ended up talking for almost an hour."

"About what?"

"She said she was doing prep interviews to ensure the program would be effective for you. She asked me about your likes and dislikes, fears, and aspirations. She even wanted to know your favorite foods and foods they should avoid. If they took my input to heart, you will be well cared for!" Kate laughed and gently poked him. She took both of Ian's hands. "The reviews on this place are stellar. If you don't think you have a problem, just enjoy it. It'll release the pressure from your family. I don't see a downside."

They heard another vehicle approaching the front of the house.

"Why are you doing this?" Ian asked.

"Breaking up took away none of my concern for your well-being. After I finished the call with an update from your parents, I became more worried about you. This might surprise you, but I'm willing to do whatever it takes to help you."

"You requested that we not communicate for a while. If that's the case—"

Kate put her finger to his lips to stop him. "Wait. I had hoped that you would accept treatment without me being a distraction from the process."

Ian looked confused.

"I've had plenty of time to think things over while we've been apart. The silence and distance between us revealed a lot. Most of all, it made me realize what a great guy you are and how much I've missed you."

This time, Ian interrupted her when his resistance gave way. He pulled her to him, and they hugged. He felt himself welling up and held her close so she wouldn't see.

"Are you okay?" Kate asked.

He could only nod, knowing she felt his head moving against hers.

She said, "This might surprise you, but I want to ask if you'd be willing to give us another chance."

Ian couldn't hold it anymore and sobbed.

Kate rubbed his back. "I'm sorry things have become so difficult for you. I don't know what I was thinking. If I'm honest, my life was better with you."

Ian felt faint. Kate's confession fulfilled his ultimate fantasy. "I swear this better not be a dream," he said.

Kate laughed. "I'll take that as a yes!" She reached around and pinched his butt. "See? You didn't wake up!"

"Hey, no more pinching, too risky!"

They laughed.

Ian sniffled and hugged her again. He pressed his lips against her hair and slurred the words, "God, I've missed you."

"Listen, babe," she said, gently pushing back to see his eyes. She wiped a tear from his cheek. "I want you to do the treatment. When you get back, maybe we'll go to a vacation resort together instead of the treatment resort. Will you do it for me? For us?"

"Totally unfair."

Kate gave him an inquisitive look.

"Because I would do anything for you, and you know it." Ian wiped his face on his sleeve.

Kate led him around the corner of the house to the front. The group had left the den and waited outside. A brown Ford Crown Victoria with an open rear door was parked at an odd angle outside the front door. Dagny got out of the driver's side and met Mr. Shaw at the front of the car to exchange words. When Dagny saw Ian and Kate, she motioned for them to approach.

"It's okay," Kate said, squeezing his hand.

Mr. Shaw went to stand by the open car door.

Ian and Kate came to Dagny. "This one sure loves you," Dagny said, pointing to Kate. "Did she read her statement for you?"

"It wasn't necessary," Kate answered. "He's decided to accept treatment."

Dagny clasped her fingers under her chin, beaming. "This is fantastic news!" She seemed so excited Ian thought she might start dancing. "Thank you for allowing us to help you!" She glanced at her watch. "My goodness, we need to get going. I want you to have plenty of time to settle in and begin your royal treatment."

"Let's get at it, son." Mr. Shaw loudly patted the car's roof.

Kate tried to lead Ian to the open door, but he pulled back on her hand.

"Wait, I haven't packed anything."

"No need," Dagny said, looking at Kate.

"Oh my God, I almost forgot!" Kate said. She disappeared around the corner of the house to where her nephew's Camaro was parked.

While they waited, Dagny said, "You have a veritable guardian angel in her!"

Moments later, Kate hurried back, toting some stuffed plastic shopping bags. She came to Ian and opened one for him to look in. "Last night, I picked up a few clothes in your size, but they might be a little loose because of your weight loss." She caressed his stomach with the back of her hand. "There's also a soft-bristle toothbrush, your favorite Gillette razors, hypoallergenic soap, and some sweets I know you like."

"Load it up, darling," Dagny said. She raised her keys and pressed a button on her FOB. The car's trunk popped open.

As Kate took the bags to the trunk, Mrs. Shaw emerged from the house wearing oven mitts and carrying a couple of large casserole dishes. She stepped carefully, joining Kate at the car's open trunk.

Dagny said, "Although we have wonderful chefs who I'm sure will amaze you, moms will be moms!" She put her hands on her hips, feigning frustration with Mrs. Shaw. "Your mother is packing up some of her delicious lasagna and rhubarb cobbler so you can enjoy her home cooking during your stay."

Mrs. Shaw came to Ian as she pulled off her oven mitts. "Sweetheart, that special peach brandy made all the difference!" She kissed her fingertips and then hugged him.

"Let's get 'er done, son," Mr. Shaw said, standing at the open rear door.

"What about my bike?"

Mr. Shaw said, "I'll store it in the garage for you. Now quit stalling!"

"It's okay, it's okay," Dagny said, not wanting Ian's dad to intimidate him.

Kate guided Ian to the open car door. Dagny followed closely.

Large, faded, oxidized paint patches covered the car's hood and roof.

Mr. Shaw stepped aside, and Ian climbed in. The car's interior was dated but mostly clean, with noticeable wear on the carpet and seats. The leather seat-tops were cracked and sun-faded closest to the windows. Ian saw Dagny's polished wooden box on the floor behind the driver's seat. He wondered what it contained and why she had stored it there instead of the trunk. He wanted to take a quick peek inside, but Dagny came to the open door and said, "Excuse me, doll," easing past Kate. She took hold of the seatbelt and leaned over Ian to fasten it for him.

"I can fasten it myself," he said, trying to take it from her.

"Trust me, this one is tricky." She pulled the buckle wide, stretched it over Ian, and inserted the buckle after a few tries. Her perfume engulfed him.

Ian held his breath.

Dagny tugged the latched seat belt several times to ensure it was secure. "There we go," she said, stepping back with a satisfied smile.

Mr. Shaw closed the door.

Dagny hurried around the car to the driver's door and said, "And off we go!"

"Hold on," Kate said. She knocked on Ian's window, and he rolled it down.

"Will you call to let me know how things are going?" she asked.

Ian hesitated. "I would if I could."

"What's that supposed to mean?"

Confessing that he had tried to call her number during their agreed radio silence was awkward, but he had no choice if he wanted to talk to her while in treatment. It was time to own up to it. "I called a while ago and got a number-not-in-service recording."

"Oh, that," Kate said, looking around at the others, intrigued by their exchange.

Dagny started the car.

"I'll explain that later. Give me your phone. I'll put in my new number for you." She held out her hand.

Ian pulled his phone from his pocket and handed it to her.

She swiped the screen, but it was locked. "What's the code?" she asked.

"I haven't changed it. Use the date we met." Ian watched her, enjoying having forced her to remember it.

Kate's second attempt succeeded. She stepped away to update her number.

Mrs. Shaw came to lean on the window. "I'm so proud of you for doing the right thing, sweetheart. This will be a life-changing experience for you."

"It'll suck," Ian said. "But at least your food will take the edge off, so thanks, Mom."

Mrs. Shaw leaned in and kissed Ian's cheek.

"We better get going," Dagny said.

Mr. Shaw came to the open window and said, "Son, I know we've had our differences, but I respect your decision here. Accepting help isn't a weakness. It's a strength. " He rapped his knuckles on the window and stepped back.

Uncle Thomas called out without approaching the car, "I wish you luck, too. Based on your behavior today, as someone who's gone through rehab, I can tell you that this is the best thing for you."

Ian looked at him and said, "What do *you* know? You're still an alcoholic. Fuck you."

"Ian, please!" Mrs. Shaw said.

Uncle Thomas lunged forward. "Maybe they'll treat you for that nasty case of arrogance you've got, too."

"You don't know me!" Ian yelled. "You have no idea what I've been through. Don't you dare judge me."

"You could use some hard discipline, you cocky prick."

"Do not harass him!" Dagny shouted. She put the car in drive and hit the accelerator.

As they pulled away, Ian leaned out the window to see his uncle and shouted, "To hell with you!"

Uncle Thomas slowly shrank behind them, still strutting and spitting in a show of dominance. The others waved to Ian. His mom blew a kiss. His father nodded with his hands on his hips. Dust swirled up behind them, leaving the figures in a thin haze. He saw Kate jump up and down, waving both hands before running toward the car. She cupped her hands around her mouth and yelled something before continuing to wave. Her support meant the world to Ian. He wouldn't have agreed to treatment without her nudge.

Dagny turned onto the main road and accelerated hard. "We're a little late, but I think we can make up the time," she said.

The wind blowing across Ian's face felt good as they sped away.

After about a half-mile, Dagny rolled up Ian's window from the driver's console.

Ian detected the slightest scent of bleach. He looked around the rear seat compartment for the source, but nothing was obvious. He turned his head left and right. The scent of bleach remained faint but was more prominent when his head was turned to the right. He pulled the shoulder strap of the seatbelt away from him and discovered it was severely frayed at about chin level. Its tight threading had been unraveled, making it look like a fuzzy hamster clung to it. He brought it closer to his nose and realized the seat belt and the door's rim both exuded the scent of bleach.

It seems they could have afforded a better car for a rehab facility that touted itself as a resort. Dagny and his family better not have lied to him. If the program didn't live up to the expectations they had set, he'd Uber the hell out of there within minutes of arrival. That's when, out of habit, he reached for his phone and felt his empty pocket. "Stop! We have to go back! I left my phone!"

"Negative. We're late," Dagny said. Her cheery demeanor was gone.

"I don't give a shit. I need my phone. Go back!"

"That isn't possible," Dagny said, wringing the steering wheel. "Besides, you've experienced enough criticism for today." She sped up.

"Take me back, or I'm canceling the treatment."

Dagny laughed. It was a different laugh than the cheery chuckles coming from her at the intervention. This laughter was deeper, and he saw how it deepened her wrinkles, making the crow's feet more pronounced at the corner of her eyes. "Ian, where you're going, a phone is useless."

Five

DAGNY IGNORED IAN'S shouts to turn back. She accelerated, looking ahead, wringing the steering wheel. She wore a slight smile, but it was broad enough to show her tiny teeth that seemed smaller than before in her roundish head.

Ian reached down to unbuckle his seatbelt, then changed his mind when he realized how fast they were going.

"Goddammit, lady, I'm not kidding," Ian said. "Turn this fucking car around now!"

"Temper, temper, temper," she finally replied, raising her eyebrows. "You've just highlighted another important task for your treatment. Your outburst has shown a need to resolve your impulse control. But everything will work out just fine for you once we take care of that demanding tone. Makes sense?"

Ian stared at her in disbelief. "My phone has all my contacts, addresses, passwords, everything I need."

"Which will make your reunion with it spectacular when you finish your program," Dagny said, checking her watch. "I want to get you processed as quickly as possible." She checked her phone. "According to the navigation app, we could still get there just in time."

"What happened to me being in control and adjusting to my needs? What happened to respect for me?"

Dagny laughed again. "Oh, we respect you, that's for sure. And soon, you'll see how much." She slowed the car as they approached a red traffic light.

Ian scanned their surroundings. They were still at least a ten-minute drive from town. There were no other cars in sight. Even with Dagny's heavy foot, they couldn't have yet traveled more than a mile. Thick woods lined both sides of the street. Ian knew he could disappear into them in less than 10 strides if he jumped out of the car. From there, it would be an easy jog to his parent's house, where he could get his phone before Kate left, and then he'd abandon the whole treatment.

He sensed Dagny watching him in the mirror and confirmed it when he looked up. She gazed at him with a detached smile, frozen like a photograph.

As they neared the intersection, Ian kept his shoulders still while reaching for the seatbelt release button. 100 feet, 75 feet, 50 feet… The car had slowed to a speed that would probably result in a tumble and roll, but it was survivable. *Slow down just a tad bit more,* he thought. When he reached up for the door handle, Dagny punched the accelerator. The car screeched through the red light.

Ian gripped the armrest. "What the hell are you doing?"

"I'm getting you to where you need to be." She tapped her watch. "I have a job to do, and I won't fail. You will be given treatment, Ian. The sooner you accept it, the less discomfort you'll need to experience. I can promise that." Her detached smile had vanished.

Ian couldn't believe what he was hearing. Dagny's sudden change in demeanor chilled him. He vowed to jump out of the car the next time it slowed to a safe speed.

He looked down at the wooden box behind Dagny's seat. She would likely notice if he leaned forward to reach it because her eyes immediately went to the rearview mirror each time he so much as turned his head. He leaned forward slightly and then some more, extending his hand toward the box while looking out the window in the opposite direction. He didn't feel it and leaned a bit more.

"Everything okay?" Dagny said, craning her neck to see him in the rearview mirror.

"Everything's wonderful," Ian said, infusing as much sarcasm as possible. He made a final push forward and swiped for the box, but it was just out of reach with his seatbelt on. He positioned his thumb on the seatbelt release button, then reconsidered. He didn't want to press it yet in case this car was equipped with sensors that chimed when a seatbelt was unbuckled while the car was in motion.

They rode for about ten more minutes before entering the small town of Portsford. He leaned toward the center to see through the windshield. The town was small, featuring a main road with only two traffic signals. Ian cursed under his breath when both lights remained green as Dagny passed through each intersection, traveling far too fast for him to bail out.

"Praise God, the traffic lights are merciful today," she said as they drove out of town. She slipped her fingers through the back of her red hair. "I'm getting hot," she said. She squeezed a big wad of hair and pulled off a wig, exposing a tangle of stubby jet-black hair. She tussled it with her fingertips, teasing it into short spikes that jutted out in all directions like a punk rocker. "That's much better," she said, taking a hard turn onto a highway on-ramp. They quickly sped up to 80 mph. Ian knew they had to be at least fifteen miles from his parents' house. Kate had no-doubt left by now. He could not know if she had taken his phone with her or left it with his parents. Either way, he couldn't Uber back without it.

Dagny continued weaving between cars as they sped through moderate traffic. A few cars blew their horns when she cut them off.

Ian's resolve to jump out of the car at the first opportunity strengthened. Better yet, maybe a cop would pull her over for driving like a maniac. He wondered if some conversation would ease her foot on the pedal. "So, how long have you worked at A Taste of Heaven?" he asked.

Dagny seemed not to hear until Ian noticed her shoulders shaking. Her laughter grew until she threw her head back.

"Was that funny?" Ian asked.

Dagny fanned her face while catching her breath. "Whew, you are a piece of work."

"Why not bring me in on the joke?" Ian said.

Dagny reached under her seat and handed a brochure to him over her shoulder. It featured an opulent lodge with a lush green lawn and a glass entrance with an ornate fountain in the lobby. A uniformed bellhop stood at the entry door, smiling with his hands tucked comfortably behind him. Well-manicured flowerbeds extended to the building's end from either side of the entrance.

"You poor thing. You must've misunderstood," Dagny said. "During your intervention, I said it's *known* as a taste of heaven. And we often informally refer to it as such. But the actual name is Biding Wellness Center."

The information jarred Ian. "What?"

"That's right," Dagny said, wiping her eyes. "Many of our patients have remarked that their treatment felt like preparation for heaven."

Ian stared at the brochure. He recognized the name Biding Wellness Center from an investigation a couple of years ago that was heavily featured on the news. The facility was run by a religious sect called the Sadens, who had gained a brief period of national notoriety for some extreme rituals that were purported to include human rights violations. The allegations could not be proven. The Sadens deftly managed the PR crisis by heavily investing in advertising campaigns that highlighted their positive contributions to the community in the form of services by funding local shelters for the homeless and financing a safe house for battered women. They abandoned evangelistic efforts, cloaked their religious beliefs behind a robust veil of secrecy, and moved their practices underground.

Some families of patients who had been treated by Biding Wellness Center filed missing person reports after loved ones simply disappeared from the facility. The Sadens claimed that each patient had completed treatment and signed out of the facility on their own. They even provided camera footage, showing each patient exiting the facility and walking toward the parking lot. When that footage was later found to have featured a fraudulent time stamp, Biding Wellness Center became the focus of a full-fledged criminal investigation. Ian didn't remember all the details but did remember a follow-up report months later of an undisclosed monetary settlement that included the facility's loss of license.

Ian regretted not having his gun. His mom confiscating it had removed an essential option for breaking free of this dire situation. He said, "Do my parents know I'm going to Biding Wellness Center?"

"Are you kidding? They selected it. Your mom stumbled upon our website and was good enough to invite me to their home for a presentation. I shared every aspect of our program with her and your dad. I must tell you they were impressed most by the fact that we virtually guarantee results."

"So, they had no problem with it?"

"Why would they? What, specifically, is your concern, Ian?" She glanced at him in the mirror.

"It's just that I specifically asked where the treatment would be. Why didn't you give me the name?"

Dagny's expression grew serious. "You seem concerned about something." She raised her chin and gave him a long stare in the rearview mirror. "Tell me what's bothering you," she said.

"Look out!" Ian shouted, pointing.

Dagny swerved back into her lane, narrowly missing an oncoming truck.

After a few moments of stunned silence, Ian unclamped his fingers from the seat and armrest.

Dagny said, "Whew! I'll take that as another sign from God that you are precisely where you are supposed to be." Without skipping a beat, she said, "So, you were going to tell me what bothers you—about our wellness center."

Ian sensed a sudden risk in answering honestly.

"The name sounds familiar, that's all."

"Hmm. Something about your concerned expression tells me you have bigger concerns than you admit."

"No, this is my expression after narrowly avoiding a head-on collision."

"That's funny," Dagny said without smiling.

"Why don't you tell *me* about Biding Wellness Center?" Ian said.

"You have the brochure in hand. If I tell you more than that, it ruins the surprise. I hate to dip a patient's toe in the experience before our arrival. It's better that we drop you in with both feet for a full splash."

He decided to mention something more innocuous than the truth to see if it would satisfy her suspicion. "I do vaguely remember something about a licensing issue," he said.

"I see it's coming back to you. Anything else?" This time, she was more careful to divide her attention between Ian and driving.

"Wasn't there some sort of problem with patient discharge?"

"Ahhhhh, there's the truth. I had a feeling you were trying to deceive me."

"I wasn't being deceptive. It's just that I couldn't possibly remember the details," Ian lied.

Dagny said, "Normally, I wouldn't discuss this with you, but I'm hyper-sensitive to my patient's anxiety, and you're oozing with it, so let's just get this out of the way. There were reports of people going missing from our facility."

"Really?" Ian tried to sound surprised. "Should I be concerned?"

"Not yet—we're not even there yet!" She locked her gaze onto him in the rearview mirror again, grinning.

"Please," Ian said, pointing ahead.

"Of course," Dagny returned her eyes to the road. "Would you describe yourself as a resentful person?"

"At the moment? Yes."

Dagny's fake detached smile returned. She wrung the steering wheel and then shifted her entire torso to look back over the seat at him. "We cure resentment, too, you know."

Ian quickly nodded to release her attention back to driving.

"Our patients are very sick, and lots, and lots, and lots, and lots of them arrive feeling resentment. None of them leave with it, though." She laughed. "This puts us in quite a quandary. You need to understand that most people we treat are chock full of resentment. They resent themselves for acquiring the habits that made their visit necessary. They resent the loved ones who did the right thing by confronting and sending them to us. And, as unfathomable as it is, they have the unmitigated gall to resent Biding Wellness Center for rescuing them and making them whole again."

"I don't really feel resentful. I was kidding," Ian said.

"Well, then you're an odd bird," Dagny said. "Think of it… After harboring enormous resentment for weeks in our facility, why would anyone assume that such a patient would want their family to pick them up at discharge time? The resentment toward family members can linger for years. Patients are free to leave, and they do. If they had family issues before intake, they aren't magically resolved. So it's perfectly understandable that patients would choose to disappear, creating a new life somewhere new, never wanting to be found again." Dagny's voice had grown louder.

"I see what you mean," Ian said as consolingly as possible.

"Can anyone blame them for never wanting to be seen again?" Dagny shouted.

"No, I can't blame them," Ian said, trying to appease her as his concern about her stability spiked.

They drove for another twenty minutes, never slowing enough to ditch the car safely. Based on the position of the late afternoon sun, Ian calculated that their direction was roughly northwest. Mile after mile of forest sped past his window, broken only by occasional fields and farmhouses. He could only remember traveling out in this area when he visited the county fair held at a campground they had passed a few minutes ago. He never had a reason to travel further into this backcountry.

He saw a *Highway Ends* sign ahead as the road narrowed and lost its paint stripes. The woods became thicker, or maybe the trees were closer to the road. Ian strained to see as far ahead as possible, looking for anything that might bring them to a stop, but there was nothing. Then, for no apparent reason, Dagny slowed the car. He sensed her watching him and looked up to see her eyes focused on him in the rearview mirror. She let the car coast to a stop on the road's dirt shoulder. They had driven far from town. There had been no homes or businesses for many miles. Ian was torn between jumping out of the car now and testing his survival skills in these woods or riding a little further, hoping to find a better opportunity to make a break in a populated area. He decided to wait. "Why are we stopping?" he asked, unable to hide the tension in his voice.

"I need you to do me a favor," Dagny said.

"What is it?" Ian said, hedging on commitment.

"We'll be making a turn just ahead. Our facility is in a rather covert location, and we must keep it that way. So, I want to ask you to close your eyes for just a few moments. The staff at our wellness center was supposed to cover the street sign with a blanket whenever a new patient is transported for intake, but they don't always remember. Would you oblige me?"

Ian looked ahead. In the distance, he saw an intersection. "That's all? You want me to close my eyes?" he asked, looking at her suspiciously.

"Or I could blindfold you—if you feel the temptation to peek would be too great. In fact, that might be easiest." She fumbled under her seat.

"No, I'll do it." Ian closed his eyes tightly.

"Thank you for respecting our privacy," Dagny said as she put the car in gear and drove ahead. "Thank you so, so, so, so much."

Ian rested the corner of his forehead against the window. He turned his head to the right enough to make sure Dagny could see that his left eye was tightly shut, but he opened his right eye to see outside. At first, he saw nothing but more passing trees. Then he felt the car slow and round a corner. He knew Dagny was watching him, and with his right eye, he saw the pole of a street sign. He strained, desperately trying to get his eye to focus. A large burlap sack draped over the top of the sign came into view. It covered the street name.

After driving only a hundred meters past it, Dagny pulled to the side of the road again. She turned off the engine and sighed.

Ian heard her hands flop onto her lap.

"There we go. All clear," Dagny said.

Ian closed his open eye before turning his head toward her to ensure she saw him open both eyes. He squinted to show the discomfort of adjusting to the sudden brightness.

Dagny pivoted in her seat and raised a phone to within inches of Ian's face. It flashed, temporarily blinding him, before she lowered it to her lap, smiling.

"Why did you take my picture?"

Dagny continued to look down, not answering.

"Can you hear me? What's the photo for?" Ian said.

She turned to look over the seat at him with a broad smile that had no warmth.

"Is there a problem?" Ian asked. "Why are you looking at me that way?"

"Until a few moments ago, I hadn't noticed that you have the most beautiful hazel eyes," Dagney said.

Ian looked confused.

"And your performance was impressive," she added.

Ian frowned. "Pardon?"

Dagny raised her phone, holding it so he could see the screen, but not close enough for him to reach it. "In fact, your gorgeous irises perfectly contrast the dilated pupil of your obedient eye."

"Obedient?"

"Yes, look!" Dagny spread her fingers on the screen to zoom in. "See? When I took this photograph, your obedient, dilated left pupil was shrinking down lickety-split to match the size of your naughty peekaboo pupil, but it couldn't shrink quickly enough to beat my camera." She shook her head at the screen. "It was such a simple instruction." Her voice grew louder. "I don't know why it was so difficult for you to obey it." She shouted, "It was one itty-bitty request, but you couldn't handle it!"

"I'm sorry," Ian said, feeling sweat coming through his palms.

"What exactly are you sorry for?" Dagny asked. Her expression dared him to answer incorrectly.

Ian's mind raced for an answer that would appease her. "I'm, uh, sorry for disappointing you."

"Wrong! I'm not disappointed," she said. "It's more accurate to say I'm appalled by your weakness. Disappointment only happens with expectations that aren't met. Frankly, I expected you to disobey. Disobedience is another symptom of your pathetic condition. You suffer from a lack of impulse control. Expecting you to obey with such a limitation is like expecting a man with bound ankles to run. Biding Wellness Center will cure you with a special treatment program that will address your alcoholism, resentment, *and* obedience issues." She tossed the phone onto the passenger seat.

She faced forward again. "Interesting," she said, slowly nodding in thought. She pulled her bag close and began fumbling through it. She took the keys from the ignition and got out with her bag.

She closed the door. Ian felt his pulse pounding in his neck. What was she doing? Her bizarre outburst triggered by the photo of his eyes made the survival-in-the-woods option more appealing. In fact, waiting for an opportunity to ditch her in a more populated area seemed foolish. A better idea came to him. Dagny looked strong and healthy, but Ian wondered if he could overpower her. Having the car would be the ultimate option. He couldn't believe he was considering assaulting someone, but since he had arguably been kidnapped, justifying it as self-defense was easy. The absolute seclusion of their location gave him lots of options. If he could tackle her and drag her far enough from the car, he could take the keys, rush back, and lock her out before she reached him. From there, he could drive to safety. But if she had a phone, she could call the police to report the car stolen. He'd have to get her phone for sure. It was just after 6:30 p.m. and would be dark within a couple of hours. They had passed probably less than ten oncoming cars on this road. With some luck, even fewer vehicles might travel at night. If he succeeded, his odds of reaching help before Dagny could flag someone down were good.

Ian took a deep breath, then made his move. Keeping his eye on Dagny, he rested his hand on the door handle while pressing the seatbelt button with his other hand, but the latch didn't release. He pushed the button again harder, but the seatbelt remained fastened. He pulled it with both hands, desperately trying to free the buckle, but the seatbelt was solidly locked and wouldn't release.

He watched Dagny stroll toward the front of the car. She pulled her bag's strap higher on her shoulder, then fumbled through it, searching for something.

Using brute force, Ian used both hands to pull the seatbelt. He tried to create enough slack to slip his legs out from under it, but it held tight. He grabbed the door handle. It flopped loosely when he pulled it and wouldn't open the door.

Dagny finished fumbling in her bag and rounded the front of the car, keeping one hand still concealed in her bag.

Ian sat up straighter. His heart pounded harder.

She stopped outside his door and took a moment to smile through the window at him with her tiny teeth. She opened the door and stepped closer.

Ian considered grabbing her, but restraining her with the disadvantage of being locked in the seatbelt wasn't realistic. And making such an attempt without knowing what she held in her bag was probably foolish, but what other options did he have?

Dagny said, "Allow me to give you some advice," she said. "Break my rules, and the consequences will break you. Any sneakiness during your treatment will backfire. Disobedience will not profit you." She leaned closer, within striking distance. "Have I made myself perfectly clear?"

"I'm so sorry for my weakness," Ian said, covering his face with his hands. He shook his shoulders, feigning an emotional breakdown, hoping Dagny would come closer to console him.

It worked. Dagny leaned closer.

Ian swiped, grabbing her bag's strap with one hand and, with the other hand, swung his fist, landing a blow to her jaw.

Dagny fell back, yanking her bag from his grip as she fell onto her back on the road's shoulder.

Ian launched into a new frantic effort to break free of the seatbelt. He pounded the latch button with his thumb and tried again, using both hands to push and pull the seatbelt, but he couldn't.

Dagny's bag spilled some of its contents onto the dirt, including a long, serrated knife. She sat up and dabbed some blood from her lip. She stared at the blood while rubbing it between her fingers and said, "Have mercy. Mercy me."

Ian could only watch, terrified, still flailing under the seatbelt, trying to escape the consequences he knew were coming.

Dagny returned her attention to Ian as she slowly climbed to her feet. She stepped back into the open door and waited for him to finish his struggle like a spider patiently waiting for a fly to tire.

Ian finally stopped and looked up at her. "Please," Ian said.

She clucked her tongue a few times and said, "I told you back at your mommy and daddy's house that the seatbelt was tricky." She grinned bloodied teeth at him before slamming the door closed. She kept her eyes locked on Ian while she repacked her bag, then strolled around the front of the car to the driver's side. A waft of bleach hit Ian's nose. His struggle with the seatbelt had left the frayed shoulder strap against his neck. He pulled it away to look at it again. At both edges of the frayed shoulder strap section, he saw faint patterns he realized were teeth marks.

Dagny climbed into the driver's seat, closed the door, and sighed.

Ian leaned forward as far as he could and tried to swing at her from behind. Her head was just out of reach, and his fist slammed into the headrest.

Dagny reached up to the center of the dashboard and pressed a switch.

A motor hummed from somewhere inside his seat-back. The seatbelt slowly retracted, pulling his waist tightly onto the seat.

"Stop! That's enough, stop!" He yelled. "It's too tight!"

Dagny let go of the button. The motor stopped, but the pressure remained. She reached into the glove box and pulled out a bottle of water. She cracked the top and sipped it on the uninjured side of her mouth.

Ian strained under the seatbelt pressure to say, "Please loosen it!"

Dagny took her time to set the bottle down and dabbed her mouth with a tissue.

"It hurts," Ian grunted.

Dagny slowly reached for the switch and pressed it to the opposite side. A brief hiss in the seat behind his back released some of the seatbelt's pressure. It had definitely loosened but remained snugger than it had been before his escape attempt.

Ian's whole body sagged with relief. "Can you loosen it a little more?"

She shifted in her seat to reach back to him and held out her hand. "I need your watch, please."

"Why?"

She withdrew her hand and returned a finger to the button.

"No! Here!" Ian said, tugging at his watchband. "Have it." He pulled it off and threw it over the seat.

Dagny picked it up and said, "A focus on time creates unnecessary anxiety."

As does being kidnapped and tortured with a seatbelt, Ian thought.

"Let's begin your resentment therapy, shall we?"

"The seatbelt is still too tight. Can you please loosen it more?"

Dagny said, "Since you obeyed me halfway with your little peekaboo trick, it's only fair that I grant half your request by releasing half the pressure. Makes sense?"

"I'm sorry for not fully obeying. This is still too tight," Ian said, hooking his thumbs under the seatbelt.

"It took me a few minutes to recover from your betrayal, so I think a couple more minutes would be fair. Agree?"

Ian glared at her.

"Keep in mind, I'm monitoring your ability to manage your resentment."

Ian clenched his teeth but maintained a neutral expression to avoid punishment.

"That's much better. Now, we must prepare you for your daily affirmations that will be part of your treatment program." Dagny handed Ian a sheet of paper. "I want you to read these aloud for me. I want you to say them with conviction."

Ian took the paper and silently read four bulleted phrases.

DAILY AFFIRMATIONS

1. I'm thankful for the help I'm getting.

2. I promise to overcome my vices.

3. I'll do whatever is necessary to return home completely healed.

4. I'm in the capable hands of professionals.

5. There's nothing to worry about.

"Begin when you are ready," Dagny prodded.

Ian said, "I'm thankful for the help I'm getting."

"Louder. Much louder," Dagny said. Part of the affirmation is to make sure you say it with as much feeling as possible.

Ian cleared his throat and, with a louder voice, said, "I'm thankful for the help I'm getting... I promise to overcome my vices and do whatever is necessary to return home completely healed... I'm in the capable hands of professionals... There's nothing to worry about."

"Excellent," Dagny said. "You will need to repeat that for me every day. You'll be surprised how much vocalizing it makes it come true." Her phone rang, seeming to startle her. "I always forget about that. Another reason I stop at this location with patients is because this is one of the few places on our journey with a signal, thanks to that cute little fixture right over there." She pointed across a small field to a radio tower. She put the phone to her ear. "Hello?" She opened the driver's door and swung her legs out. "Yes, this is she... Oh, of course, I remember. How are you?" She plugged one ear, listening.

Ian thought of yelling for help, but there was no way the person on the phone with Dagny could know where to send help. And further antagonizing her would only make things worse. He could only listen.

"No, that won't be necessary, but I thank you for that generous offer, Kate."

Ian sat up straight. "Kate! Is that Kate?" he said. "Please let me talk to her."

Dagny glanced at him.

He made a prayer sign toward her.

She held up a finger for him to wait while she exited the car. "It'll only be a few days, so Ian insists that he won't need his phone, so you'll hold it, won't you?" She slammed the door closed.

"Wait! Kate! Help! You've got to help me!" Ian shouted, pounding on the window.

Dagny walked a few paces ahead of the car to mute Ian's hollering. She rested her free hand on her hip, facing away, occasionally gesturing a few times during the conversation. When she returned to the driver's door, Ian tried to read her lips as she finished the call, but couldn't. She slid the phone into her pocket and climbed back into the car.

Ian seethed. "Please call her back. I need to talk to her," he said. His voice had grown hoarse.

Dagny fastened her seatbelt and started the car. "Your ex-girlfriend was willing to make a trip to deliver your phone in person to you, but we discourage visitors except on discharge day. Too much of a distraction."

"She's not my ex. We're still together." Despite his current misery, making that statement out loud felt terrific, and for a moment, the anxiety of his circumstances vanished.

Dagny glanced over the seat and smiled. "Is that what you believe?"

"I believe it because it's true," Ian said, flaunting defiance.

Dagny laughed and shrugged. "In any case, she promises to keep your precious phone safe and sound, and she's so looking forward to seeing you when you are cured. Shall we get going?"

"Listen, the way you are restraining me—I don't feel safe. It's hurting. I'm sorry I offended you. Can you please release it?" Ian said, wiping his forehead.

Dagny exhaled deeply after another guzzle of water and pressed the button. A hiss released more seatbelt pressure, but not nearly enough for him to escape without unlatching it.

"I wish I could trust you to ride completely unbuckled, but there's a good reason for what we call the perma-latch." She air quoted. "As you can imagine, transporting new patients to our facility can be dangerous. Patients are under tremendous stress that often causes them to behave irrationally. The perma-latch not only keeps you snug as a bug but also protects me. I mean, look around us." Dagny pointed out the windows on either side of the car. "You've already made a poor decision to harm me out here. Had you succeeded, it might have taken hours, if not days, for someone to find me." Dagny shuddered. "How awful."

"You're gonna be facing a kidnapping charge. You realize that, don't you?"

Dagny threw her head back and laughed, then raised her chin to see him in the rearview mirror. She thumbed behind them. "What you tried to do to me back there was absolutely illegal. If investigators got involved, keep in mind that only my body shows evidence of physical assault—so far. Given my injuries and the fact that you are on your way to addiction treatment, a charge of attempted murder wouldn't be out of the question."

"What!" Ian gawked at her. "I wasn't trying to kill you!"

"Not for me to conclude," Dagny said.

After riding in stunned silence for a few minutes, Ian said, "I'm sorry for hitting you."

"Oh, I have no doubt you're sorry that you failed. But I'll give you some good news..." She shifted in her seat to face him. "I won't be pressing any charges. Sound good?"

Ian looked at her incredulously. "You aren't going to charge me?"

"That's right. My ability to treat successfully, you will give me all the recompense I need. For the life of me, I can't see how charging you with a crime would help me reach my goals. Now, can I get a thank you?"

"You want me to thank you?"

"That seatbelt must've squeezed the hearing out of you! Yes, I want you to thank me." She gave him a tiny-toothed grin.

When Ian didn't answer soon enough, she opened a small compartment next to the radio console on the dash. She drew her fingers across more switches inside and said, "You've already experienced the seatbelt-snuggy switch. Here, I have more."

"Thank you," Ian said.

"There's my thank you!" she closed the compartment and started the car.

As Dagny accelerated back onto the road, she said, "If it's any consolation, you aren't unusual. 90% of our patients are one-eyed peekers on the way to Biding Wellness Center. Honesty and self-control are key goals of treatment. That punch you landed *was* a surprise." She caressed her lip with her tongue. "The bad news is that's going to be detrimental to your assault-propensity score."

Ian said, "How much further?"

"I know you're excited!" Dagny said. "It won't be long now."

"I need to use the restroom."

"Oh my," Dagny said, "You'll need to hold it."

"I can't."

"Well, I'm going to ask you to try."

"I'm not kidding. Pull over. I won't run away. I promise."

Dagny smiled, shaking her head as she returned her focus to the road. "Just like clockwork."

"What are you talking about? I *need* to go."

"A request for a potty break on this trip is almost as predictable as the peekaboo game each of our previous patients has wanted to play."

Ian said, "I don't think I can hold it."

"Then go ahead and relieve yourself. When we get to the facility, we'll get you and the vehicle cleaned up spick and span."

The truth was that Ian didn't initially need to use the restroom, but talk of it, combined with his growing anxiety, brought the feeling on strong.

"Then can you loosen the seatbelt a little more? Please."

Dagny reached for the switch and pressed it briefly twice, producing two quick hisses from within Ian's seat. The belt loosened, relieving Ian, but his urgency to go was quickly growing. He crossed his legs and swayed his torso forward and back in his seat, trying to focus on things that would distract him from his filling bladder.

Dagny saw this and laughed.

Ian was tempted to unzip and aim his stream over the seat right at her head, but was deterred by the console switches Dagny threatened.

The car slowed as they approached another town that appeared to be a little larger, with a few shops and eateries lining the Main Street. Ian saw plenty of people out and about on the streets at dinnertime.

He looked at the window button on the door. Knowing his door didn't open from the inside, he wondered if the window button had been disabled, too. If there was any chance that this window button worked, and Dagny slowed enough, he might lower the window long enough to yell for help—if he timed it correctly. In a perfect scenario, he'd spot a police officer he could call out to. He wanted to test it but knew that Dagny would hear it and possibly disable it if it wasn't already.

He straightened his back to raise up as high as he could. He could see the speedometer. They slowed from 30 mph to 20 mph. A small group was gathered at some tables outside of a coffee shop. He checked Dagny. She appeared to be focused on the road.

A few doors down from the coffee shop, Ian spotted a man sitting outside at a patio table with two young children enjoying ice cream cones. If anyone would be sympathetic to a kidnapping victim, it was a father. They closed in. Ian felt that this might be his best opportunity. 50 feet... 30 feet... 20 feet... He put his finger on the window button, ready to pull it away if Dagny looked back. When they reached their closest point to the father and his children, the car stopped. In a stroke of luck, Ian realized they were stopped at a traffic light. He pressed the window button hard. A piercing buzzer sounded inside the car. The window didn't move.

Dagny looked back at him.

Ian frantically pressed the button again and again, harder.

"Need some air?" she asked.

"Uh, yes. I do."

"I'll turn up the vent," she said.

"Could you just roll down my window for a few minutes—if you don't mind? I'd really like some outside air." Ian figured if Dagny complied with his request, he could call out to the father before Dagny could roll the window back up.

"Oh, no worries," Dagny said. "The vent isn't recirculating. I have it set to bring in air from the outside. So sorry things got stuffy. You should've said something sooner."

Ian reached into his pocket and pulled out his keys. He threaded them between his fingers, squeezing them in his fist.

The traffic light turned green, and they pulled away from the man and his children, now laughing at some whipped cream dabbed onto the young boy's nose.

Ahead, Ian saw a long stretch of desolate road as they neared the edge of town. He knew this might be his last chance, so he pounded the window with his keys, trying to break it while screaming, "Help!" at the top of his lungs.

The man and his children paused momentarily, looking in Ian's direction, but clearly couldn't understand where the screams were coming from.

Without saying a word, Dagny calmly opened the compartment beside the radio. She drew her finger across the four switches, pausing on each as if deciding which to press.

Ian screamed louder. "Please! Somebody help me! Help!"

Dagny pressed a switch. A pane with limousine tint slid upward inside the glass of both rear windows. The blacked-out windows eliminated any possibility that someone outside the car could see him waving for help.

"Ian, I hate to sound like a broken record, but you are meeting all my expectations. It's intriguing how each patient suddenly wants fresh air when we slow down in town. You'd want to have the window down while we were moving. Don't you agree?"

Ian pushed the shoulder strap aside and leaned forward, burying his head in his arms.

Dagny said, "Have we urinated yet?"

Ian ignored her.

"Looks like you might need the encouragement of a different switch."

"No!" Ian said, sitting up. "I've been holding it. Please, I'm not trying to anger you. I just really want to get out of the car. Is there anything I can say or do that will convince you?"

"Absolutely. Heed the advice I gave you before. Be a good patient.

Rebellious patients are never comfortable. Cooperative patients are always comfortable. The choice is yours. Makes sense?"

"Yes," Ian said softly. They made a turn onto a narrower road. Ian's attention returned to the wooden box. He couldn't reach it with his hand, so he subtly moved his left foot, resting his boot beside it. The box had a lid without a latch. He pressed the rubber edge of his boot sole to the lid and pressed. The box moved away. He put his boot on top of the box and slid it closer. He pinned the box between his boot and the transmission hump on the floor between the seats. He carefully pressed against the lid and lifted it until it flopped open. Terror spread over him when he saw what was inside. Large syringes filled with yellowish liquid were lined in four velvet molds. He tried to keep his foot steady while trying to close the lid. When it was almost closed, it slipped and clapped shut. He held his breath, watching to see if Dagny had noticed.

"You know," she said, "having someone to talk to makes each visit to Biding Wellness Center so much easier for me, even if my passengers often feel resentful during the journey."

"Is that so?" Ian said, sliding his leg back from behind her.

"Yes, it's preferable to transporting a patient that sleeps the whole way. What I mean is that I could have encouraged you to sleep. Actually, I could have insisted on it, but then you would awaken feeling groggy, and the side effects of a forced nap are always uncomfortable. Makes sense?"

Ian nodded, recognizing her explanation for the syringes. God, he wished he had his gun.

She met his eye in the mirror and held it until the car bumped on the rough gravel of the road's shoulder.

"Watch out!" Ian said.

Dagny jerked the wheel, pulling them back onto the road.

After they had traveled approximately ten more miles through more lush woodlands, they came to a curve. When the road straightened, they slowed, approaching a structure on the left that looked like an abandoned motel. Dagny stopped the car in the middle of the road directly in front of it. A curved, disintegrating driveway threaded a carport overgrown with ivy.

Dagny carefully checked the road ahead of and behind her.

Ian examined the front of the property. Something about it seemed familiar. He wondered if it might be the motel his parents had taken him as a young child prior to hunting. Then it hit him. He picked up the brochure from the seat beside him. A quick comparison showed that it was the same building, only now it was severely dilapidated. The flowers in front shown on the brochure were no longer visible, replaced by a thick tangle of overgrown weeds. Grass and dandelions had bored through the asphalt, sprouting from a series of cracks veining across the driveway. The windowed front that appeared sparkling clean with crisp signage in the brochure was now filthy, caked up with dust and droppings splattered by the swallows that nested above them in the rafters.

The building barely resembled the brochure, from the plant debris spread across the roof to the weather-beaten wooden columns that supported the carport.

Six

DAGNY KEPT THE car stopped in the middle of the street for almost 30 seconds before she sped up, turning hard into the driveway. Instead of following the curve to the left, which would've taken them to the entrance under the carport, she forked to the right, following a narrower dirt drive that rounded to the back of the building.

She came to a stop beside a brown van. The old van's paint was heavily oxidized, and its sides dinged and scratched. It sported mismatched tires. Dagny turned off the car, got out of the driver's seat, and came around to Ian's door. Before opening it, she pulled her phone out and placed it to her ear. After speaking a few words, she ended the call and opened Ian's door. "Welcome to your new home!" she said.

The comment irritated Ian so much that he refused to look at her to hide his disgust.

"Out you go," Dagny said, opening the door.

He didn't move.

"Oops, silly me," Dagny said. She opened the front passenger door, leaned in, and pressed one switch on the console. "There we go."

Ian reached down to his side and unfastened his seatbelt with a simple click.

She held out her hand for him.

Ian refused it.

"Now, now, now," Dagny said. "One of the first things you must learn is how to accept help."

Ian climbed out on his own.

She closed the door and led Ian toward the back door.

He heard a rumbling of some type of motor from behind propped wooden planks about 20 meters away at the edge of the rear yard. A short distance from that, he saw a shed and heard multiple dogs barking inside. The dogs sounded big. Their deep barks were accompanied by claws scratching as they jumped against the walls. He followed Dagny, looking toward the sounds as they walked.

"It's a diesel generator," Dagny said. "You see? We've taken every measure to ensure that your stay is comfortable. Almost there," she pointed ahead to the facility's rear entrance.

Ian heard a familiar sound that excited him. It grew as they neared the door. Dagny stopped walking and said, "Oh great, he's here."

A man riding a motorcycle appeared around the corner, following a wide arc across the lawn.

Dagny watched him, smiling.

The biker stopped a few paces from them and pulled off his helmet. He wore cargo pants, boots, and a black windbreaker. He dropped the kickstand and climbed off.

Ian recognized the motorcycle as a Suzuki GSX-R performance bike. His cousin had owned one a couple of years ago and had let him try it. Ian wished he could just run to it, jump on, and feel the breeze of freedom on his face. He imagined Dagny in a futile foot pursuit, her face reddening as she shrank in the distance behind him. He'd love to see that.

"This is our new patient," Dagny said to the biker.

The man approached, pulling off black gloves finger by finger. When one hand was free, he waved. "Great. Has he seen his room yet?"

"No, we just arrived. You're just in time to see the surprise."

The biker came to stand beside them. He saluted Ian and said, "Name's Garland."

"Ian Shaw," Ian mumbled.

Garland said, "You couldn't be in better hands. This is the best treatment program east of the Mississippi."

Ian offered a halfhearted smile to satisfy Dagny's warning look. He looked beyond Garland and noticed the keys still in the ignition.

Dagny said, "Ian's mother was kind enough to send some homemade cooking for him. Please retrieve it from the trunk and take it to the kitchen."

Garland said, "Sure!" He opened his arms wide and, with a big smile, said, "What other facilities on earth would accommodate such comforts from home?" He returned to the Crown Victoria to retrieve Mrs. Shaw's lasagna and rhubarb cobbler.

Dagny led Ian to the back door while she pulled out a large key ring.

Ian stared at the motorcycle while he walked. He knew the bike's capabilities very well. It could take curves at least three times as fast as the Crown Victoria could handle.

Dagny fumbled through keys, searching for the right one.

It was the first time since leaving his parents' house that Ian wasn't virtually handcuffed by the car's seatbelt. He wondered if it was actually possible that he could be lucky enough to be looking at a perfect set of circumstances.

He looked over his other shoulder to where Garland leaned into the open trunk, arranging the food trays, momentarily concealed from view.

Dagny found her key and opened the rear door. An alarm sounded, echoing down a long hallway.

Ian wondered why an alarm was necessary for such a rundown

building in such a rural location.

She turned back to Ian and said, "Oh darn it, we'll get that annoying screamer turned off in a jiffy." She pocketed her keys as she hurried into the building, rushing to a blinking alarm console on the wall a few paces from the door.

Ian stood just outside the open door. After Dagny reached the alarm console, Ian slammed the door closed. He ran to the motorcycle and jumped onto it.

From behind the door, Dagny hollered, "Garland, get him! Get him! Ian, stop!"

Ian shoved the bike forward off its kickstand and hit the ignition, bringing the engine to life.

Garland leaned out from behind the open trunk. He instantly charged toward Ian, shouting, "No, no! Stop!"

Ian put the bike in gear and accelerated in a loop, rounding back behind the vehicles, quickly distancing himself from Garland, who had cupped his hands around his mouth as he continued shouting during his futile chase on foot. As Ian sped along the dirt road on the side of the building toward the front, he glanced at the back door. It flew open, and he saw Dagny run out, waving her hands while running toward him.

Garland changed directions in a full sprint, attempting to cut Ian off, but the bike was too fast, and Garland soon realized he had no chance of catching Ian. The Suzuki carried Ian to the front of the facility in no time. He made a sharp turn onto the driveway and raced through the carport and over the crumbling pavement toward the main road, where he turned right to go in the direction from which they had arrived. Within seconds, he sped up to 80 miles per hour on the straightaway before slowing for the first curve. He screamed, "Yes! Yes! Yes!" The cool wind in his face couldn't have felt more refreshing. He inhaled deeply. The bike was beautiful. Smooth, powerful acceleration brought the invincible feeling that had made him fall in love with riding years ago.

As he neared the next curve in the road, he started planning the next leg of his escape. If Garland called the police to report his bike stolen, Ian knew he could expect to be intercepted. Although intersections were few in this rural area, he remembered seeing a few of them on their way to the facility. He took every turn and detour he found to elude his capture until he reached a town—any town large enough for him to safely ditch the bike and get help.

As he rounded the next curve, he saw a beautiful straightaway where he could let the engine fly. He hit the throttle, but the bike's engine sputtered, and after only a few moments, it died. Ian clicked it into neutral, repeatedly pressing the starter as he coasted, quickly losing momentum.

"No, no!" he said, frantically trying to restart the bike. No matter what he tried, the starter only clicked.

As he coasted to a stop, he saw something that sent a chill up his spine. In the distance ahead, two men dressed in all black emerged from the woods, one on either side of the street. They approached one another. When they met in the center of the road, they turned to face Ian and began walking toward him. Each had a shotgun and raised it, aiming at Ian as they speed-walked toward him. One of them shouted, "Off the bike!"

Ian considered dropping the bike to run into the woods, but the dark holes of the shotgun barrels dissuaded him. As the men closed in on him, he saw their earnest expressions. The other man said, "Move to the side of the road."

Ian laid the bike down and slowly raised his hands as he stepped to the side. He wondered if any people who had gone missing from Biding Wellness Center had experienced what he was experiencing now.

One of the men kept the gun aimed at Ian while the other went to the toppled motorcycle and raised it, moving it to the road's shoulder.

The man with the gun said, "You stay put. No one will ever know if you make us put you down right here."

"I understand," Ian said.

Less than a minute later, a car approached. The familiar brown crown Victoria soon rounded the corner and skidded to a stop on the shoulder near them. Garland sat in the driver's seat. Dagny got out on the passenger side. She marched directly to Ian, putting her face close to his, and said, "Once again, you've met our expectations. We're taking you back home, where we'll fix everything wrong with you."

"Listen, I'm sorry," Ian said, stepping back from her.

Garland got out of the car and came around to open the rear passenger door.

Dagny closed her eyes and nodded, saying, "I know. Get in." She pointed to the open rear door.

When they returned to the car, Ian said, "I've changed my mind about the intervention. Why can't you respect my wishes?"

"Being ruled by your own wishes got you into this predicament. Look at what your wishes have done. Your behavior shows that we have work to do."

"Thank you," Ian said, accidentally putting more sarcasm into the reply than he meant to.

Garland started the car, but before pulling away, one of the men dressed in black got on the motorcycle. The other got in the seat behind him. The bike's engine roared to life, and they sped away.

Garland drove back toward the facility.

Dagny said, "You see, Ian, the seemingly benign disobedience you exercised in the car when you peeked is one thing. Grand theft auto is a much more serious impulse you failed to control. But don't worry, we don't plan to press charges."

Ian didn't respond. He sat slouched in his seat, looking out the window, seething.

Back at the facility, Dagny and Garland flanked Ian as they walked to the rear entrance of the facility again. This time, Garland stayed close to Ian. They entered the same door Ian slammed shut right before his escape attempt.

Inside, a long hallway with stained carpet was lined with doors. Some lights lined along the ceiling's center were yellow, and some burned out, leaving a shadow of darkness that concealed the far end of the hallway. It wasn't the luxurious resort he'd been promised. Not even close.

They led Ian about a third of the way down the hall to a door with a stenciled 151 on it. Dagny pulled the ring of keys from her pocket and, after sorting through a few of them, separated one and slid it into a doorknob. The door opened, and Dagny said, "In you go."

The room was mostly bare and poorly lit. A cot was placed against the wall. A rush of musty air wafted out when the door opened.

Ian wrinkled his nose. "You've got to be kidding me," he said, looking inside. "I'm not staying in this shithole."

"Your treatment has begun," Garland said. "We need you to enter the room, please."

"I want to use a phone," Ian said. He heard a door open from the dark end of the hallway, followed by footsteps shuffling to a stop. He couldn't see into the shadows. He wondered if it was the gunmen.

"Patients are forbidden to make telephone calls during treatment," Dagny said. "Let's focus on getting you settled in." She pointed into the room, motioning for him to enter it.

Ian said, "Listen, I'm sure my parents will pay you whatever fee they agreed to, but this place is not what I need. It won't help my life. I'm not an addict. I'm just asking you to please let me make just one quick call."

Garland reached under his jacket, pulled a coiled bullwhip from behind him, and released a finger on it, allowing it to unravel to the floor.

Ian backed into the open doorway.

"Good choice," Garland said. "Your obedience problem might get the quickest cure. One lick from this snake and your obedience problem will be cured quicker than the others. Now, don't make me decorate your backside."

"There's no problem," Ian said, backing into the room with his hands up.

"See to it." Garland pulled the door closed until it latched.

Ian put his mouth to the door's crack and said, "Can you make a call for me? Please!" He knocked on the door, but there was no response. He heard the faint sound of Dagny and Garland's footsteps fading away.

Seven

IN LESS THAN two minutes, Ian became familiar with every significant object in the room. The dim lightbulb provided only vague details. The space looked like a gutted motel room. One wall had the faint outline of a credenza. On the opposite wall, wallpaper brightened in a rectangular shape with a queen-sized headboard covering it. A padded cot sat in the corner, a blanket folded at its foot. The recessed opening that used to be a window had been covered with a perfectly sized painting of ducks swimming in a pond. It prevented any view of the outside. There was no television or radio.

Just inside the door, another door led into a small bathroom. The light seemed brighter than the light coming from the bulb in the center of the ceiling in the main room. A half roll of toilet paper rested at an angle on a broken toilet paper holder. The dirty sink had no soap, and one of the under cabinets was missing a door. It produced water, but without cups, he'd need to drink directly from the faucet. The Taste of Heaven was a shithole.

He had just examined the water stains high on the wall near the ceiling when the lights flickered and went out, leaving him in complete darkness. The diesel generator outside had gone silent. He heard footsteps passing by in the hallway. He ran to the door and pounded on it. "Hello? … Hey, can you open the door?"

The footsteps didn't stop, but faded toward the rear exit. Ian heard the door to the outside open. He felt his way back to the cot and sat. After waiting in the darkness for what he guessed was about a half-hour, the generator sputtered to life outside. Moments later, the lights flickered on. Several giant roaches scattered, fleeing the light. They disappeared into the cracks along the base of the walls.

He felt a metal bar crossing the center of his cot. As he suspected, he laid down, and the bar of the cot's frame crossed the middle of his back. He triple-folded the blankets and placed them across the bar, which provided only slight improvement.

His position on the cot made him notice several faint sets of tally lines on the wall above his head. Some were in pencil, and others in blue marker. The first set totaled 29, the second set 17, and the third set 36. Each set of tally marks was of different sizes and different styles.

A small paperback book was propped against the wall on the floor. Entitled *Our Beloved,* the cover featured a man climbing a rugged hill on his hands and knees. The man gazed upward, his eyes excited for whatever he saw. It was the only book in the room, which made it feel force-fed. His first guess, based on the title, was that the book would contain a metaphorical journey, including passages of encouragement from family members to those struggling with addiction. He opened it and saw that the author was a minister. He skimmed through several sections to get its gist. The story followed a tired and weary traveler who overcame all odds to travel to a hidden city and was rewarded with the undying love and affection of the city's inhabitants after proving himself to be worthy.

Ian closed the book and tossed it to the floor. He laid back on his cot, his hands behind his head, listening. Aside from the hum of the generator and the occasional barking of the dogs, the absence of any other sound in the stillness of his room was already creating a maddening monotony.

He thought of his family and imagined how they would react to seeing his living conditions. His dad might approve of the tough love, but even he would consider this extreme. His mom would be up in arms if she knew the truth about where they had sent him.

Ian shook his head as he considered how many of his rights had been violated. Dagny had misrepresented entirely the experience he'd have, luring him into her car with the full approval of his loved ones, who had obviously been tricked. And then holding him hostage was another egregious offense. There was no way to do anything about it unless he could escape or somehow contact law enforcement from this hellhole. The facility was so remote that Ian couldn't remember passing its closest neighbor while they approached it. With electrical power produced by a generator, there was likely no utility record of its current use.

Visually, there was no reason for any passerby to stop in and investigate it. Some windows had been boarded up as though someone had prepared the structure for a storm. The dilapidated façade showed that the former motel, or resort, or whatever it was, had been permanently abandoned. There was no telling how long it could be before someone had a reason to pull in and check the interior. Ian wondered who owned it.

He remembered how Dagny had checked for possible traffic in either direction before she sped into the driveway and raced around to park in a place in the back, completely obscured from the street. Were they secretly squatting at this place? Any remaining notion that this treatment facility had any legitimacy had evaporated. He had fallen into the hands of bad actors. What did they want with him?

As his eyes adjusted to the dim light, he noticed something above him he hadn't seen before. Something was scrawled on the ceiling directly above his cot. Although the lettering was bold, the dimness still made it difficult to see. Ian stood on the cot for a closer look, straining to read it.

DAILY AFFIRMATIONS

1. I'm thankful for the help I'm getting.

2. I promise to overcome my vices.

3. I'll do whatever is necessary to return home completely healed.

4. I'm in the capable hands of professionals.

5. There's nothing to worry about.

"There's everything to worry about," Ian mumbled.

He remained locked in the room for hours, unable to sleep. He felt increasingly anxious, a symptom he could quickly treat with a beer if he was back at home. He couldn't fathom Dagny bringing him a cold brew.

Since Dagny had confiscated his watch, he had no way of knowing how long he had been here. And with the room's window completely sealed with the painting, he couldn't even reference the rough time of day from the sun. The lack of stimuli and total boredom made him feel like he had been trapped in the room for days already.

The discomfort of lying on the cot kept him trying to sleep while sitting and leaning against the wall, but he could get no sleep. He made several visits to the bathroom for water.

A few times, his anxiety spiked, and he pounded on the door, desperate to get out. Even seeing the hallway would be mentally refreshing. The hours in isolation gave him plenty of time to consider options for escape, none of which played out successfully in his mind.

He discovered that the framed painting covering the window was secured to the wall by steel bolts around the perimeter. He had no tool which he could carve through the drywall. Even if he did, he couldn't break out quietly, as they would undoubtedly investigate the commotion.

If Dagny and Garland returned and he could get past them, he knew the exit door at the end of the hallway was locked. And even if it wasn't, a successful break for the outside meant fleeing on foot. They could easily track him, especially if Garland had a motorcycle, unless Ian went for a trek into unfamiliar woods. Getting lost in the wilderness was better than the torture he was enduring in this dungeon.

The hum of the diesel generator was frequently interrupted when it lost power. In each instance, the roaches rushed in while the room was dark. He could almost hear them. The restored light always sent at least a dozen of them, with their freakishly long antennae, fleeing to the cracks at the edge of the room for cover. The darkness was so deep that the restored dim light initially appeared bright. The longer the blackout, the more roaches. During the most prolonged outages, they covered the floor. Ian envied their freedom to leave the room.

Each blackout also brought footsteps in the hallway, sending Ian running to the door to beg for release. More than once, he crushed unlucky roaches on the way. The footsteps came and went, always ignoring his pleas.

Eventually, the door opened. Ian jumped up from the cot.

Garland leaned in with his bullwhip and said, "Do not approach."

Ian complied, keeping his distance and his hands up. "Thank God," he said. "Please, I'm begging you to let me out, just for a few minutes."

Garland and Dagny stepped inside, closing the door behind them. "Good morning, Ian!" Dagny said. She held a food tray.

Ian habitually looked at his wrist where his watch had been. Dagny's greeting confirmed the completion of his first overnight stay in this hell. "When does treatment start? I need to get out of this room," he asked.

"Soon," she replied, setting the tray on the floor beside the door. The tray contained food, a napkin, and a box of apple juice. "I need to hear your affirmations."

Ian looked confused. "The ones you had me read in the car?"

"Very good. Let's hear them."

"I, uh, don't have them memorized."

"They are above your bed."

Ian looked back at the cot and realized they were referring to the scrawl on the ceiling.

Ian went back to stand beside the cot and looked up.

"Read them aloud and be sure you memorize them," Dagny said.

Ian read the affirmations.

DAILY AFFIRMATIONS

1. I'm thankful for the help I'm getting.

2. I promise to overcome my vices.

3. I'll do whatever is necessary to return home completely healed.

4. I'm in the capable hands of professionals.

5. There's nothing to worry about.

"Excellent. Take those words to heart," Dagny said.

"Is that the food my mom sent?" Ian pointed to the tray.

"No, this is breakfast. You'll enjoy your mom's food for dinner—on good behavior." She winked. "But before you enjoy your delicious breakfast, we must dispense with a few intake questions. This will be short and sweet." She flipped a page over on a notepad and clicked a pen. "If something difficult is placed in your path, will you try to conquer it? Or would you simply choose another path?"

"I would conquer it."

"Excellent. Would you consider yourself a resourceful person?"

Ian remembered Kate's opinion of him and how she often praised him for his resourcefulness and ability to solve almost any situation.

"Yes."

"Great. Have you ever had thoughts of death?"

"You mean suicide?" Ian asked. He didn't want to add any other problems to Dagny's growing list of treatments for him.

"No," Dagny said. "Have you ever wondered how you might die?"

"No." He frowned.

Dagny raised her finger. "Don't look so surprised. Many people do. Let's move on. Have you ever studied martial arts or had military training?"

"No."

"Do you have any physical disabilities?"

"Besides being trapped here? No."

"Very good." Dagny continued scribbling at the bottom of the tablet. "If given a choice between having one woman or a harem, which would you choose?"

Confusion filled Ian's face again. He paused, wondering which answer was better for Dagny.

She looked up from her notepad. "Here's a hint. Be honest. Which would you prefer? A woman or multiple women?"

Ian pretended to think, even though he didn't need to. The only woman he wanted was Kate. And given that they'd soon be together again, a crappy relationship with her would be better than any harem. "I'm happily monogamous," he said.

"Is that your preference, or are you trying to be good?" Dagny asked.

"I gave you my answer," Ian said.

Dagny made a final scribble and slapped the pad closed.

Garland nodded.

Ian wondered if he had given the wrong answer.

"Ten minutes to eat," Dagny said, exiting the room.

"Wait," Ian said, getting up.

Garland snapped the whip, creating a deafening crack that jolted Ian. Garland then backed out of the room after Dagny. Before closing the door, he bent down and picked up a folded dark green shirt, pants, and black shoes from the floor outside the door. He dropped them beside the food tray. "You will put these clothes on."

"I'm okay. I'd like to keep on what I'm wearing."

"A word to the wise is sufficient," he said. "Put them on." The door clicked shut.

Ian went to the tray and brought it to his cot. It contained six rubbery slivers of carrot, a tiny bowl of cold baked beans, and a cheese sandwich on white bread. The pathetic presentation was ornamented with a wilted piece of parsley that hung off the plate. It was as though they had mistaken him for someone with a food addiction. He picked up half of the cheese sandwich. The underside was soggy, and the top stale. He took a bite of carrot, then wrinkled his nose, forcing himself to swallow it.

Eight

ONE DAY AFTER sending Ian off for treatment, Mitch Shaw came into the kitchen and sat across from Carol at the table for dinner.

"Any news?" he asked, picking up a fork and knife for a steak.

"Not a word," Carol replied. "And Dagny promised we'd get a check-in call from him after they arrived at the facility."

"Maybe you should try calling them again."

"I already have, twice today, once this morning and again right after lunch. I let the phone ring over twenty times, but no voicemail picked up."

"I wouldn't worry," Mitch said, chewing steak.

Carol sighed. "I know, but I'm a mother... and there's something else."

Mitch stopped chewing, waiting for her to continue.

"Did you find the behavior of that Dagny woman strange when they were leaving?"

Mitch swallowed and said, "Not in particular, but what exactly did you see?"

"After Ian left the meeting, I tried to speak to Dagny in the hallway, but she brushed right past me, so focused on Ian that I couldn't get her attention. Then she pushed Thom away from the door to get outside before him."

"The woman loves her job. Ian *was* the focus of the intervention."

"I realize that, but something about her wasn't right."

"So, what are you suggesting that means?"

"I don't know. It's just a gut feeling. Dagny was encouraging and reassuring during the meeting, and she completely transformed into a different personality when outside. Why was it so urgent for her to leave quickly? Did you see how she urged Ian into the car and insisted on connecting his seatbelt for him? At the time, it was only weird, but now, being unable to reach Ian, it's becoming creepy. That woman's aggression didn't fit the nurturing environment she promised Ian only a few minutes earlier."

Mitch nodded, sawing another piece of steak while he considered Carol's concern.

"So, you don't find any of her behavior odd?" she asked.

"There was one thing," Mitch said, swallowing, "Ian is practically biologically attached to his phone. For the life of me, I can't believe he didn't ask Dagny to come back for it."

"True," Carol said. She leaned onto the table and pressed her fingers to her temples. "Something isn't right."

"Have you talked to Kate?" Mitch asked.

"She didn't pick up my call this morning. When I got out of the shower, she had left a message saying she wanted to drop off Ian's phone to us today. I called back, but she didn't pick up."

"Maybe she's heard from him. Try her," Mitch suggested, motioning to the phone with his fork.

Carol went to it and dialed Kate's number, nibbling her lip while she watched Mitch eat. Her face relaxed when Kate's voicemail picked up after four rings.

"Hi Kate, this is Carol Shaw. I'm wondering if you could return my call. Dagny indicated Ian would call us after settling in. I know it's only been a day, but I haven't heard anything, and the treatment center isn't picking up. Have you heard from Ian? Please let me know. Thank you. Bye-bye." Carol hung up the phone and returned to the table.

Mitch reached out and took her hand. "He's fine, Carol. Ian hadn't called us for weeks before you finally reached him yesterday. And after his reaction to the intervention, do you really think he's eager to chit-chat with us?"

"You're probably right," Carol said.

"Of course I am!" With his mouth already full, Mitch took another bite of steak and mumbled, "Give the boy some time to cool off and get adjusted."

Carol nodded in agreement, then added, "I don't need to speak to him directly if I could reach a receptionist to confirm that he arrived safely. I'm telling you, I have a strange feeling something isn't right."

"Honey, let's not get ahead of ourselves," Mitch said. "Ian will exit the program in full control of his demons—isn't that what Dagny promised?" Mitch picked up a wineglass and raised it to her.

Carol raised hers.

They toasted and sipped.

"Ah, that's delicious," Mitch said. "What's the address of that treatment center again?"

"I'll get you the card." Carol crossed the kitchen to pick up a business card on the countertop beside the phone. "This is the only information Dagny gave me." She sat and slid it across the table to him.

Mitch picked it up and read the bright rainbow lettering of the heading:

Taste of Heaven Re-Creation Center.

He looked at the address. "Corbaline Road," he said. "That's right off

Highway 79. I know exactly where that is. If we don't hear from him tonight, I'll drive there in the morning."

Carol nibbled her fingernail. "I think we should go check now."

"Hold on, let's not panic," Mitch said. "This address is over an hour away. The facility isn't going anywhere. Tomorrow will be fine."

Carol reluctantly agreed, losing none of the tension in her expression.

Mitch flipped the card and examined some fine print on the back. "Hmph. It says here that they do spiritual counseling as part of their program."

"Fantastic," Carol said. "I wonder why Dagny didn't mention that."

"Definitely wouldn't kill him to get back on track with God." Mitch stood. "Some spiritual counseling might be precisely what he needs."

"I've been praying as hard as I can," Carol said, raising crossed fingers.

Later that evening, while the Shaws lounged in the den, taking in some TV, the phone rang.

"See? I'll bet that's him," Mitch said.

Carol jumped up and rushed to answer it. "Hello?"

"Hi, Mrs. Shaw, this is Kate."

"Oh, Kate, thank you for returning my call. Have you heard from Ian?"

"No, is there a problem?"

"It's just that we haven't heard from him yet and wondered if he reached out to you."

"I haven't heard from him, but that's unsurprising. If I know him, he's feeling resentful, and that will take a while to wear off, so I wouldn't expect a call for another day or two."

"Yes, that's what Mr. Shaw said, too. Thank you. That makes me feel a little better. But what about the facility's phone number? I simply wanted to confirm that he arrived safely, but no one picked up."

Kate said, "When Dagny interviewed me a couple of days ago, I asked her if I could surprise Ian with a phone call during his treatment. She mentioned they're strict on inbound calls to prevent patients from being distracted from their focus on treatment."

"I don't see how a call to a receptionist or other staffer would be a distraction, but I guess we'll have to live with that," Carol said. "I'm sorry to be so uptight, but when you are a mom, you'll understand."

"I understand. Why don't I call as well? Maybe between us, we can at least get some confirmation that he arrived safely."

"Would you do that?"

"Of course."

• • •

Ian didn't need ten minutes for the pathetic meal Dagny and Garland had given him. He put the tray on the floor and shoved it with his foot, sliding it back to the door. He returned to the cot, wondering how many days he'd have to live on the disgusting food and how long he could stretch out his mom's food when he finally got it. He closed his eyes and envisioned it. Nothing would taste better than a big slice of lasagna and a big helping of rhubarb cobbler. He then imagined being back in his sandwich shop where he regularly put together overstuffed sandwiches, dripping with dressing and garnished with all his favorite ingredients.

He got up and went to the door. He picked up the clothes they had left for him. He didn't want to put them on, but more than that, he didn't want to antagonize Dagny and Garland further. He removed his boots and stripped out of his clothes. He put on the camouflage pants and the black shoes that appeared to be some sort of flexible water shoe that felt more like a moccasin. Before he could put on the shirt, a sharp knock on the door startled him.

Garland opened it and stepped inside, holding his bullwhip. "Back away from the door," he said.

Ian complied.

Garland looked down at Ian's crumpled clothes and the folded camouflage shirt beside them. He smiled at Ian and said, "You failed to dress. You've earned a demerit."

"You gave me ten minutes."

"Over ten minutes have passed."

"What's a demerit?" Ian said.

"You'll see. It's time for your group session." Garland pointed his whip down the hall.

"What's my group session?" Ian asked.

"All of your questions will be answered. Go." Garland stepped back.

Ian passed by him. His relief to be out of the room was tempered by concern about where he was headed.

"Faster," Garland said, following close behind Ian. He uncoiled the whip and pulled it back over his shoulder to lash him.

Ian lurched forward and raised his hands in defense. "Okay, just take it easy." He continued walking toward the dark end of the hallway. Garland pulled out a flashlight and aimed it at the door. "Open it," he said.

Ian turned the knob and pushed the door open. They stepped into an equally dim space that used to be the motel lobby. The relatively large space contained a long wooden check-in counter, dated tile flooring, and an empty brochure stand. Centered in the open space was an out-of-use fountain drained of its water.

"Into that room," Garland said, pointing a few paces ahead to a door on the right. A sign above it read: *Management Only.*

Ian stepped inside the office. Dagny sat in an oversized padded chair that completed a circle of seven other chairs. She wore a navy blue military uniform. The jacket had lapel pins and insignia sewn into the chest pocket and shoulder.

Six people sat around her: three men and three women. They appeared to range in age from early 20s to a gentleman who looked to be in his 60s. There was one empty chair Ian assumed was for him. All the other attendees wore the dark green shirt and pants Garland had brought to Ian's room. Although Ian stood out for being shirtless, none of the people in the room looked at him when he entered. They all kept their eyes straight ahead.

To Dagny's right, a white man in his forties sat with his hands folded in his lap. Without moving his head, he glanced at Ian as if afraid of being caught. His green pants looked too short for his lanky legs. With salt-and-pepper hair and a somewhat dignified presence, he seemed like he'd be more comfortable in a business suit than in the camouflage scrubs provided.

Next to him, a brunette woman with a crew cut sat with her muscular arms crossed. Tattoos ran from both wrists to where they disappeared under her shirt sleeves.

Next to her sat a sickly looking man. Ian would have assumed he was too frail to be at the facility, as ill-equipped with comforts as this one. He coughed and cleared his throat.

"Are you okay?" Dagny asked.

With a raspy voice, he replied, "Yes, Ms. Conger. Thank you, Ms. Conger."

A black gentleman with a scruffy beard sat with his legs crossed, his hands resting on his knee, and his fingers interlocked. He seemed perfectly at ease, even wearing a slight smile despite keeping his eyes fixed straight ahead.

Beside him was the least attentive person in the group. She was in her early twenties, her jet-black hair pulled back tightly to accommodate a nub of a ponytail. Her nose and bottom lip were pierced with silver hoops, and tracks dotted her forearms. She sat on her hands and kept her head down, eyes closed as though she had gone elsewhere.

Garland pointed the bullwhip to the empty chair.

Ian went to the seat and slowly sat, now fully self-conscious of his missing shirt, although the other group members ignored him.

"Don't tell me," Dagny said. "We didn't give you enough time to change?"

Ian shook his head.

"We answer with our voice," Dagny said.

"No."

Dagny raised her eyebrows and leaned toward him.

"At this facility, you will refer to me as Ms. Conger."

"No, Ms. Conger," Ian said.

"Excellent. You'll find that respectfully vocalizing your answers avoids additional demerits."

"What is a demerit?"

Some of the other people turned their heads away from Ian. A couple of them closed their eyes and shook their heads.

Dagny shouted, "Silence until you are acknowledged!" Her face turned red. She calmed down and then said, "It turns out we have a demerit cancellation for you to observe as part of your orientation."

All the people in the circle tensed in their chairs, sitting up straighter but keeping their eyes down. Ian saw the unmistakable tension on their faces.

"Before we get to that, however, let's open the floor for progress reports. Who would like to go first?"

Every person quickly raised their hand as high as they could and turned to Dagny for recognition. Some hopped in their seats like school children, eager to answer correctly. The enthusiasm surprised Ian, and he slowly looked at each of them. The tension in their faces evaporated, replaced by a pleading hope that they would be called first.

"Annabel, why don't you begin?" Dagny said.

Annabel, the young woman with the piercing, burst from her introspective shell and clasped her hands as though she had just won a prize. She adjusted herself in her chair before saying, "I want to thank Biding Wellness Center for all they've done for me."

"Amen," the group said in unison.

Dagny glared at Ian. "Refusal to take part is a demerit you won't want to earn."

"Amen?" Ian said sheepishly. It seemed to satisfy Dagny because she cleared through and said, "Let's continue."

Annabel said, "I've been sober for 23 days now…"

Ian joined in when the other participants clapped.

Annabel continued, "Without the loving help of Ms. Dagny Conger, I would still be a slave to my selfish desires. Without the guidance of Biding Wellness Center, I would regularly yield to the temptations that imprisoned me, keeping me handcuffed by my urges and dragging me deeper and deeper into the mire of misery. So, for all these reasons, I want to thank Ms. Conger for giving me the gift of freedom."

"Well stated, Annabel," Dagny said.

Everyone clapped again.

Annabel's words didn't seem precisely scripted, but they lacked sincerity. Ian had studied Annabel's expression while she spoke. Her fervent words didn't seem like a factual recounting of genuine experience but a preemptive way to avoid something horrible.

The other participants raised their hands again, every eye locked onto Dagny, urging her to call on them.

"Clarence, you may go next."

Clarence was the bearded black man, maybe 35 years old. Of the participants in the group, he was the only person who actually smiled at Ian, exuding a warmth that was in stark contrast to the bland expressions of the others. When Dagny called on him, he answered while looking at Ian. "I want to thank Biding Wellness Center for my outstanding progress. Everything's gonna be okay for me, thanks to Ms. Conger." He nodded hard to confirm his own statement.

Clarence continued, "Without the loving help of Ms. Dagny Conger, I would still be a slave to my selfish desires." Clarence repeated what Annabel had said verbatim. When he finished, he smiled and bowed his head.

One by one, each of the remaining group participants took a turn reciting the same accolades for Biding Wellness Center and their gratitude for its positive effect on them.

Dagny studied each speaker, her face mostly expressionless except for occasionally smiling when her name was mentioned. When all participants had finished speaking, she said, "Ian, this is normally the time partners share their growth experiences directly with one another after having been isolated in their rooms. This social time allows them to heal one another with that special empathy only available from a fellow addict. It's beautiful to see the weak-minded supported by others like them."

The words shocked Ian. He looked around at the participants. None showed any reaction.

Dagny said, "Instead of our social time today, we have a demerit that requires cancellation."

Again, the participants stiffened in their chairs and all looked down at their folded hands. As Dagny looked around at them, one at a time, the room went so silent that the tick of the clock's second hand became audible.

Dagny said, "I'd like everyone to raise their hand to show how many demerits they have earned."

All the participants raised one finger in the air.

"As you can see, each person has earned only one demerit. Unfortunately, one of these raised hands has an incorrect number." Dagny looked from one person to the next. Some raised hands and trembled when she came to them.

"One hand should raise two fingers because of an incident that happened yesterday."

Garland and a new man Ian had never seen entered the room and strolled toward the group. Two members closed their eyes tightly, lips moving in prayer.

"Ian, I will warn you that this might be difficult to watch, but keep in mind demerits are incredibly easy to avoid. Canceling them is uncomfortable, but it's also a beautiful process if you consider the cleansing it signifies."

Garland and the man walked in opposite directions outside the circle. Everyone leaned forward in their chairs further when the men approached them. The men made one full circle around the group before they stopped behind Clarence. He tried to jump up and run, but they grabbed him and threw him to the floor.

"No! Please!" Clarence cried out, kicking and flailing. "What did I do? Please tell me what I did?"

The men pulled Clarence up, forcing him to his feet. They dragged him from the room through a door one man kicked open with his foot. The inside looked like a converted supply closet. Chains and cuffs hung from the ceiling. When they came to the door, Clarence got a foot on the doorframe, preventing them from getting him through it. Garland delivered a blow to Clarence's gut, and they dropped him to the floor. He curled up into the fetal position. The men dragged him into the room and slammed the door closed.

Some participants in the group covered their ears. When Dagny saw this, she said, "Hands down!"

They forced their hands to their laps. Most of them turned their heads away from the closet door and closed their eyes, as if trying to distance themselves from what was about to happen.

"Demerits are so unnecessary. And why is it important that we listen?" Dagny asked.

"So we may learn from the mistakes of others," the group said in unison.

Through Clarence's begging, a metallic clanking came from behind the door. Within moments, Ian heard heavy blows landing on flesh, followed by the most gut-wrenching, bloodcurdling screams he'd ever heard come from a man.

Dagny said, "During our socialization session yesterday, Clarence was overheard remarking about the gluttony of his vice he would enjoy after being discharged. We can't allow inconsiderate, weak-minded addicts to sabotage one another's progress."

Clarence's screams continued while the other participants listened. A tear ran down Annabel's face. Clarence's cries came in waves for two minutes before the room became quiet. Moments later, Garland and the other man came out.

Ian saw Clarence lying on the floor. Blood had soaked through the back of his shirt, and the back of his pants were torn to shreds. The men closed the door and returned to their posts at the door to the hallway.

Dagny went to the door and motioned for everyone to stand up. As the participants filed out, each praised her for running such a great session, while Dagny smiled and nodded.

Garland and Dagny escorted Ian back to his room. They stopped in the hallway outside his door. Garland flipped through the key ring.

"Can I please get a different room, Ms. Conger?" Ian asked.

Garland chuckled, opening the door. He directed Ian to enter.

"Over there," Garland said, pointing toward the cot for Ian to stand.

When Ian moved there, Dagny said, "The answer is no, but I adore how this experience has already enhanced your appreciation of freedom and life's comforts. If you continue to desire change, your circumstances will improve."

Garland pulled the door closed. The latch clicked.

Ian returned to the door, noticing a thin piece of plastic protruding from the top of the door's pneumatic closer at the top. He rose onto his toes, reaching for it. He pinched it between his fingertips and slid it from its slot. He took it into the bathroom for better light and examined it. It looked like a broken part from a piece of plastic ware, but its function wasn't obvious. It was too large to insert into the door's keyhole and not strong enough to slide into the door crack to open the latch. He returned to the door and slid it back into the slot. The small piece of plastic was the only small loose object in the room besides the *Our Beloved* book and the toilet paper roll. He returned to the cot, wondering how he might use it.

• • •

After another stint of seemingly endless hours, Ian lay stretched out on his cot, staring at the stains on the ceiling. He coped with a throbbing headache, along with his insomnia. The misery only made him angrier that Biding Wellness Center claimed to be treating an addiction he didn't have.

The group session he had observed the previous day had jarred him. He could still hear Clarence's gut-wrenching cries piercing the air with unfathomable agony that Ian had never heard before. Ian's stomach clamped down. He closed his eyes and breathed deeply to calm himself. His muscles relaxed. The generator's hum had become so familiar he could filter out its white noise to hear other sounds. This morning, he heard an unfamiliar sound. A faint pinging came from a small wall vent near the floor and about an arm's length from his cot. He wondered if a distant fan blade somewhere inside it was loose. But the sound was not only rhythmic but had a distinct pattern.

He got off the cot and kneeled to hear it more clearly. The pinging grew louder, then stopped. After a few moments, he heard something that startled and excited him. It sounded like a sniff. The pinging resumed, this time with a distinct pattern. Ian moved his mouth to the vent's grate and said, "Pssst."

The pinging stopped.

"Hello?" Ian said.

"Shh," a faint voice replied.

The unexpected response jerked Ian's head. He waited a moment and whispered, "Can you hear me?"

"Wait," the voice said.

Ian pressed his ear against the vent's grate, straining to hear more. For the first time since his arrival, he wished the generator would fail. Through the vent, Ian heard a door open and then another voice. He recognized it as Dagny, but she wasn't talking through the vent. Her words weren't even intelligible, but there was no mistaking her tone. She was talking to someone. Ian strained to listen, but the conversation was too distant and faint to understand.

After an exchange of about a minute, the talking stopped. The vent went quiet.

Ian waited. He flicked the back of his fingernail on one of the vent's metal fins, sending his ping into it.

A ping returned, followed by, "Are you there?" The voice was barely audible.

"Yes… Who is this?" Ian asked.

"Can't say."

"Why not?"

"You're the newbie. You haven't learned yet that Dagny favors people who report misbehavior. Nothing personal, but I don't know you, so it would be stupid to trust you."

"Then why are we talking?" Ian said.

"Shh, whisper! Didn't you just see what happened in the group session yesterday? If that bitch catches us communicating, we'll be in for torture you can't imagine."

"Okay," Ian whispered. He tried to put a face to the voice, but because the person only whispered, he couldn't discern whether they were male or female.

The voice said, "So, did your so-called loved ones send you here, or did Dagny capture you in town?"

"Capture?"

"That answers my question, newbie. So, your family took the bait."

"Wait a minute, what bait?"

"Dagny. She convinced them she'd rehabilitate you, right?"

"Something like that," Ian said.

"What's your vice?"

"They claimed it was alcohol."

"Don't tell me you don't think you are an alcoholic, and Dagny told them this place would be full of luxuries."

"Yes, both true."

"Of course."

"So, what's your story?"

After a pause, the voice said, "My family sent me, too, for a heroin habit. I stole from them. At my sister's wedding, I made out like a bandit. Unfortunately, the venue had camera footage. I embarrassed her so much she pressed charges against me. My parents convinced her to drop charges on the condition that I commit to a treatment program. So, here I am at the five-star Biding Wellness Center."

"Tell me something," Ian said. "Are these people the same Sadens that were in the news a few years ago?"

"You know about them?"

"Of course. The suspicion about them in the disappearances dominated all the media back then."

"All I can tell you is they've gone completely underground. Everything they do is covert. They've tried to detach themselves from the bad press they used to get. If you haven't caught on, you're not here for rehab. This place definitely transforms people, but not in a good way."

"So, what do they want with us?" Ian braced for the answer.

"That's the worst part about it. None of us know. During my first days here, I thought they were simply sadistic monsters. Now I know there's more to it than that. I started thinking that we were being prepped for organ harvesting. But they don't feed us well enough for that. Whatever they do, we are a product that requires a regular supply. It doesn't take a genius to figure out why. The rehab they advertise is a scam that gets them a regular supply. It's brilliant because people in so-called treatment are completely isolated from their families. This gives these sadists a guaranteed time period of privacy with them. At the end of the rehab, Biding Wellness Center claims that the rehabilitated individuals are adults free to disappear into the world. They explain the disappearances by blaming it on resentment held by patients against the families who sent them here."

"My God," Ian said, feeling light-headed. "I hate that everything you said makes sense."

"We've had plenty of time to figure this out. The only missing puzzle piece is what happens to each of us when we disappear."

"When you say 'we,' what do you mean? How do you talk to other people?"

"Very carefully. Communicating is a sin they'll punish harshly. I could sneak a hushed exchange with several other victims when Dagny briefly stepped out of group meetings. The second time I tried this, I got caught. I was terrified that my demerit would happen last night. I feel sorry for Clarence, but to be completely honest, I'm so thankful it wasn't me."

"So, you're due to get what Clarence got last night?"

"Eventually. Demerit cancelations happen on Dagny's whim."

"So, family members never come here to investigate?"

"Are you kidding? This address isn't the one they give your family. Did you see the front of this place? Who's gonna stop in to check on a dump like this? That's by design. I've got news for you. I don't know where your family thinks you are, but I guarantee it isn't here. If they found the correct address, they'd drive right on by, certain they had made a mistake. Dagny and her people are not only secretly squatting on this property. Whatever they're doing is criminal."

"I can't believe no one has reported this to the authorities," Ian said.

"Any phone inquiries to Biding Wellness Center are easy to handle. They can hide the truth behind protecting their patients' confidentiality and privacy. Now that your family has shipped you off, by the time an unreasonable amount of time has passed without contact from you, it'll be too late."

"This isn't sustainable," Ian said. "They can't get away with this for long."

"They don't need to get away with it for long. It's lucrative. They demand up-front payment for treatment. I wouldn't know how much except that, to shame me, my family admitted to forking over twenty grand for my treatment. If you are in here for addiction, your family paid at least as much."

Ian knew this could be true. Dagny had obviously sold his folks on treatment. He knew they would have doled out even more money if they thought treatment might include therapy that might bring him back to God. "Maybe we can break out," Ian said.

"That's original. You think every one of us hasn't thought of that? Before you get your hopes up, remember that you're in a locked room connected to a locked hallway watched by attentive guards at a facility with dogs on watch outside—which reminds me, have you heard the dogs?"

"How could I not?"

"They're killers, and they're well trained. Dagny forced us to watch a video of what the dogs do. Your mandatory outfit is washed with a detergent that triggers them."

Ian pulled his shirt sleeve to his nose. He detected only the faint scent of soap.

The voice continued, "The dogs' vicious behavior in the video could only be caused by starvation or hatred. One of the people watching it threw up. There are at least six dogs kenneled out back with a door that has a remote release. The only thing these animals live for is to tear anything that smells like you into pieces."

"Lovely." Ian sighed.

"If the pooches aren't cut loose to catch you, you'll have at least a one-mile sprint to the nearest neighbor. Dagny says she pays them handsomely to hold and return escapees. Good luck."

"So, you just give up?" Ian said.

"I didn't suggest giving up. I have important information to share with you."

"What is it?"

The voice didn't reply.

"Hello?" Ian said.

The voice quickly said, "Heads up—your door!"

A key slid into Ian's doorknob. The door opened. Dagny stepped in, carrying a food tray. Even with the millisecond of a warning from the voice, Ian still jumped. He quickly sat up from the vent.

"Good morning," Dagny said, looking at him suspiciously.

Ian wondered if she had noticed him jerk his head away from the vent.

"Did I hear you talking?" she asked as she reached back to push the door closed behind her.

"Probably. I talk to myself all the time," Ian said, climbing to his feet.

Dagny stood watching him momentarily, allowing Ian to feel her examination before she set the tray on the floor by the door.

She brushed off her hands and said, "Remember that your first days here may be among your toughest as your withdrawal symptoms set in. You will probably feel shaky and sweaty and experience an elevated sense of anxiety. These symptoms are to be expected and are no cause for alarm. They will fade as we heal you. Makes sense?"

Ian nodded.

"Let's verbalize," Dagny said. "How do we respond?"

"Yes, Ms. Conger."

"Excellent. Addressing me properly helps us steer clear of demerits. Now, I might have something special for you later. You should look forward to it."

She exited.

When the door latched, Ian rushed back to the vent and whispered, "Hello… Are you there?"

There was no reply.

He went to the tray and found an apple juice box, a tiny portion of cold scrambled eggs, a rubbery half slice of white toast, and four cubes of crunchy, under-ripe cantaloupe. Hunger had overcome his distaste for the food. He downed the small meal, grimacing through most of it, then washed it down with the apple juice. He went into the bathroom to supplement it with a deep drink of water from the sink.

When he came out, he heard the tapping from the vent again. He went to it and kneeled. "I hear you," he whispered.

"Enjoying the chow?" the voice asked.

"What were you going to tell me? You said it was important."

"You might be the luckiest prisoner at Biding Wellness Center."

"I don't understand," Ian said.

"You're in room 151, right?"

Ian remembered the stenciled number. "Yes."

"Then you are the only one of us with a way of escape."

Nine

CAROL PARKED IN the driveway of the Shaw home beside the front door, returning from a shopping trip. When she exited the car, she heard their landline phone ringing inside the house. She rushed in and ran to the closest phone in the den.

"Hello…"

"Hi, Mrs. Shaw," Kate's voice brought a flood of hope.

Carol clutched her chest and said, "Kate, oh thank God! Have you heard anything?"

"I haven't, and that's why I'm calling." Her voice sounded tenser than usual. "I called the number on the website and, like you, got no answer. I called information, and they had no listings. It's strange. I can't figure it out."

"That's concerning, Kate. Based on your stellar review, we chose this treatment facility and assumed you were in direct contact with them."

"Actually, I didn't have any direct experience with them. I heard about A Taste of Heaven from a girlfriend who had a very successful rehabilitation with them and remains close with the staff. I've left word with her, and she always gets back to me. I'm sure she'll be able to help."

"I certainly hope so. I was looking forward to experiencing the excellent follow-up shown in the reviews on their website. Their lack of response makes me wonder how they got any positive reviews at all."

"Mrs. Shaw, I can't tell you how sorry I am about the anxiety this is causing. If it helps, deep down, I know Ian is fine. I just…"

"Kate? … Are you there?"

Kate sniffled and then, with a shaky voice, said, "If only I had remembered to give his phone back to him, we'd know exactly where he is because he has at least two phone locating apps installed on it. That was so stupid of me."

"Blaming yourself isn't productive, Kate. Do what you can and please let us know what you find. Call my mobile phone rather than the house phone in case we are out."

"I will do everything possible to get in touch with him and call you back the instant I do."

"Thank you. We appreciate it."

When Mitch got home a short while later, Carol updated him on her conversation with Kate. They immediately got in their car for the drive to A Taste of Heaven at the address displayed on the business card.

As they sped onto the highway, Carol said, "Kate is typically cool as a cucumber, but I've never heard her behave this way. Her voice wobbled, and I thought she might break down in tears. She seemed really worried."

"I'm sure she feels like she's let us down," Mitch said.

"Poor thing," Carol replied. "I tried to tell her not to take it so hard."

Mitch nodded. "The good news is that we can forget about all this the moment we hear from him."

. . .

Ian's vent conversation had abruptly ended when the voice on the other end went silent. Moments later, he heard footsteps come to a stop outside his door. Ian sat back on his cot to hide the attention he had been giving the vent.

His door opened, and Dagny entered, followed by Garland, the bullwhip coiled in one hand. "Good afternoon, Ian," Dagny said.

"Hello, Ms. Conger," Ian said, looking at the whip.

"It's a wonderful day," she said.

"Yes, and may I please make a request?"

"Certainly," Dagny replied.

"I'm hungry and cold. I'd like to request some more food if possible. And if I could get a second blanket, it would help me tremendously."

Dagny and Garland exchanged a brief glance. "Anything else?" she said.

"Those two small things are all I ask now—ma'am."

"Good, then. The answers are no and no."

Garland let the whip unravel to the floor.

Dagny said, "You are experiencing withdrawal from your addiction. You've gone well over a day without alcohol. I wouldn't be surprised if your heightened appetite was a withdrawal symptom that could also cause the chills."

"With all due respect, I disagree," Ian said, working to suppress his rage.

"Easy," Dagny said. "I see your temper working to break free."

Garland flicked his wrist, sending a wave through the whip.

Dagny said, "The desire you've expressed is timely because I'm here to introduce you to the next phase of your treatment. Today, we are working on your resentment issues. I need you to follow us."

Ian got up from the cot and went to the door.

Garland backed into the hallway, keeping a safe distance and a close eye on Ian.

Dagny pointed toward the lobby.

Ian obeyed, walking toward the darkness that concealed the door at the end of the hall.

"I want you to keep in mind that you won't be leaving this facility unless and until we find that all your treatments have been deemed successful." She stepped around him and unlocked the door, holding it for him to enter the front of the facility.

Excitement flooded Ian when the aroma of his mom's lasagna and garlic bread filled the air. He inhaled deeply, his nostrils drawing in the delicious comfort of home.

Off to his right, he saw the closed door to the manager's office, where Clarence had been tortured in the group session the day before.

Dagny led Ian past the check-in counter in the lobby. The windows were boarded up with plywood, except for the large double glass doors, now covered with blinds. Several foldable tables were set up, and the other patients sat at them. They all wore paper bibs stained with tomato sauce. Their plates had been scraped clean. Three other muscular male staffers roamed the room like prison guards, some of them chewing.

The only patient not taking part in the meal was Clarence, who lay on a cot off to the side with his swollen eyes closed. He had an IV in his arm.

Another patient, the forty-something gentleman, picked up a bowl and put his face down into it, licking it clean.

Next to the man, Annabel's cheeks puffed out like a chipmunk. She didn't acknowledge Ian, staring at her empty plate as she chewed.

On a separate table, his mom's casserole dishes that had been filled with lasagna and rhubarb cobbler were empty.

Ian could barely suppress his rage. "My mom sent that food for me, not the group," Ian said, glaring at them. He turned to Dagny. "It was for *me*!"

"Were you unwilling to share?"

"Of course, I'd share, but look…" Ian pointed to the empty dishes. "It's gone!"

"What a compliment to your mother. It was absolutely delicious. You must get me her recipe," Dagny said.

Ian squeezed his fists behind him.

She said, "Not to worry, though." She leaned closer to Ian and whispered. "We saved you some."

The words barely took the edge off Ian's anger, but prevented him from taking a swing at her. "Where?" he said.

"Can we say 'thank you, Ms. Conger'?"

Through clenched teeth, Ian said, "Thank you, Ms. Conger."

Dagny nodded to Garland. He coiled the whip and tucked it under his arm before going behind the check-in counter. He returned with two small paper plates. In the center of one plate was a tablespoon-sized dollop of rhubarb cobbler that looked like it had been portioned with a melon scoop. The other plate had an equal amount of lasagna positioned at its center. Garland held out the plates to Ian.

Ian looked down at the insulting portions, using brute force to keep from losing control. "This is all you saved me?"

Dagny crossed her arms and said, "You're welcome."

Garland shook the plates closer, urging Ian to take them. When Ian didn't, he set them on the countertop, reached behind it, and pulled the whip from under his arm.

"You had no right to give it all away. I would have shared it. My mother intended this food for me. She didn't send it as charity to feed your other patients."

"And she didn't intend for you to become an alcoholic, did she?"

Ian's temples flared while his eyes bored into her.

Garland gently slapped the whip against his leg while he watched with a slight smile.

"To be perfectly honest," Dagny said, "after getting a taste of your mom's delectable cooking, I'm surprised we salvaged any of it for you. The other low-life addicts here are bona fide savages. You'd think they had become rabid animals if offered something special to eat. Getting them to limit themselves to a single portion was an absolute battle. You really should have seen it."

In Ian's peripheral vision, he focused on the front doors. Although the blinds obscured the glass, it had a push bar, and he knew it opened to the outside. He had a clear path. He took it, racing to the door.

"Stop!" Dagny yelled.

Garland raced after him. The crack of the whip pierced the air behind him.

The other patients hollered. One table toppled when several patients jumped up from it.

Ian slammed into the door's push bar, which was locked, and he stumbled back. Behind him, Garland wound up to lash him with the whip.

Ian sidestepped and darted around a fountain in the center of the floor. He turned to the hallway door that led to his room just as the whip cracked inches behind him. He slammed into the door, discovering that this one, too, was locked. When he turned around, all the patients at the tables were standing, watching. Garland had him blocked in.

Ian dropped to his knees and covered his head, bracing for the first searing stripe from the leather slashing his back.

"Hold on, Gar," Dagny said, strolling to them. The lash didn't come. Dagny squatted beside him and said, "Look at me."

Ian looked up.

"One thing you need to learn quickly about us, Ian, is that we follow protocol. It would be appropriate for me to let Garland decorate you with stripes—and he'd enjoy that. But your fellow addicts in treatment just enjoyed a spectacular meal lovingly prepared by your mom. I'd hate to make them lose their food while watching your backside get bloodied. We will take care of your burgeoning list of demerits at our next group session. You can thank me later for my mercy."

"Whatever," Ian said, wiping his eyes.

"We're going to take you to your room where you can think about how you will realign your attitude on a more beneficial trajectory. Simply do what we want you to do, and you can't imagine how wonderful your world will become."

"Get up," Garland said, flicking the whip in front of Ian's face.

Ian climbed to his feet.

Dagny unlocked the hallway door, and they escorted Ian to his room.

• • •

Mitch and Carol Shaw spent most of the drive speculating about reasons they couldn't reach A Taste of Heaven. Their conversation ended when they rounded the last corner before reaching the listed address on Corbaline Road.

"Here we go," Mitch said. "It should be right up ahead."

Carol clasped her hands, craning her neck to make out any sign or other indication of the building's identity. As they drove closer, the sign in front came into view. "Oh, no, don't tell me…" Carol said.

"Hold on, let's get some information before we panic," Mitch replied. "Keep in mind that a lodge has the ideal infrastructure for a treatment facility." He turned into the driveway and parked outside the office under a sign for Redchester Lodge.

Carol flicked the business card against her hand. "No Taste of Heaven anywhere, Mitch."

"Time to find out what's going on," he replied, unbuckling his seatbelt.

They strolled toward the office door, looking around for any sign that this could be a treatment facility. Inside, an older woman with half-rimmed glasses and overalls looked up from behind a tall counter she could barely see over.

"Hello there, weary travelers. Need a room?"

The Shaws exchanged an uncomfortable glance.

"No, we're looking for A Taste—"

"—of Heaven Treatment Center," the woman finished the name for her, then stood, putting her hands on her hips. "I hate to disappoint you, but your search isn't over. You're the third couple in as many months to ask."

"So, this is not a treatment facility?" Mitch said, taking the business card from Carol to recheck the address.

"I'm afraid I can only provide a comfy place to sleep." She came around the counter to them. "I swear those people are going to be the death of me. I've repeatedly asked them to update their business cards and website, but they haven't."

"Is there any way you can direct us to the correct address?" Carol asked.

"If I could do that, I would've put a sign outside to save you the trouble of stopping."

Mitch said, "You mentioned asking them to update their address information. Were you able to speak to someone at their company?"

"No, I asked them in a voicemail. Every time I call the number, I have to let it ring about 30 times before the voicemail will pick up. And that's only if it doesn't announce a full mailbox."

"We've never been able to reach voicemail," Carol said.

The woman fingered for Mitch to give her the card. She took it and said, "Yep, that's the number. I sure wish I could be more helpful."

The Shaws returned to their car. Carol recognized Mitch's tense expression. It was a sure sign that he was more worried than he would admit.

When they turned onto their street, he said, "Based on everything, we should probably get the police involved."

"So, I'm not crazy," Carol said.

Mitch shook his head. "I considered calling the police earlier, but I didn't want to get law enforcement involved prematurely. We've done all we can do to contact him. Even if we successfully reach someone from A Taste of Heaven, Ian is a grown man and a medical treatment facility isn't likely to share information about patients without a warrant."

"What can we expect the police to do?" Carol asked.

"They can help us get to the bottom of this fraudulent address."

"Mitch? All things considered, I don't mind admitting that this situation scares me. The woman sped Ian out of our driveway like a bat out of hell! We both know Ian would have insisted that she come back for his phone. She was so pushy with their program and its openness that suddenly, being unable to reach them, was a major red flag. Not to mention that look in her eyes just before she got into the car. I'm rarely wrong about the type of suspicion I'm feeling."

Mitch didn't argue. He nodded as his reluctance to admit the seriousness of the situation drained. "Fine. When we get home, we'll check messages and see what the police can do for us."

"First, let me reach out to Kate again," Carol said. She dialed and put the phone to her ear. After several rings, she hung up and said, "No answer. I'm going to blow her mind by sending a text message. She knows I never use my phone for that."

Carol typed:

Kate, it's Carol Shaw. Address on card is fake. Calling the police.

She sent the message. Within moments, Carol's phone buzzed. "Hello?"

"Hi, Mrs. Shaw. It's Kate. You just called while I was on the other line getting some good news for you."

"You have good news?"

"Yes, I was able to reach my girlfriend. She found the mobile number of one staffer at A Taste of Heaven. I called right away, and the kindest gentleman named Garland answered. I asked for Ian. Garland said Ian was in a private counseling session but had arrived safely. Garland said you could call back after an hour, and they would gladly put Ian on the line with you."

"That is fantastic news, Kate! Thank you so much!" She pulled the phone away, turned to Mitch, and whispered, "Kate got us a contact. Ian will be available to talk in an hour." Carol opened the glove box and pulled out a pen but couldn't find any paper. "Okay, Kate, I'm ready."

Kate read her the number.

Carol wrote it on her hand. "Thank you so much! You are so wonderful!"

"You're welcome. Can you do me a favor?"

"Certainly."

"If you don't mind, call me back and tell me how Ian is doing after you speak to him. I don't want to be a distraction. I really want him to succeed."

"Of course. That's the least I can do for you after putting us in touch with him. You're a lifesaver. I'll call you later."

Ten

IAN WALKED THE perimeter of his room, dragging his fingers along the wall while waiting for some response from the voice in the vent. After telling Ian that there was something special about his room, the voice had gone silent. Ian had whispered into and tapped the vent probably 50 times during the last couple of hours, but there had been no reply. Finally, he heard three distant pings from the vent. He ran to it and kneeled. "Are you there?"

"Yes," the familiar whisper said. "How are you doing?"

"Aside from incarceration, starvation, physical, and psychological abuse? Just great. "

"I'm sorry about the lasagna incident."

"You are one of the people in the room?"

"Yes, and I felt bad watching her do that to you."

"Not your fault."

"She made us eat it. She said any food left on a plate earned a demerit."

"She's fucking sadistic. My mom would be so pissed off. I swear to God she'll pay for that."

"Maybe you'll have a chance."

Ian hunched down closer to the vent. "Before we were interrupted, you said something about me being the only one with a way of escape."

"That's right. I was going to tell you about a person no longer with us. He used to be in your room."

Ian swallowed. "What do you mean by 'no longer with us?'"

"His name was Riddick Selmer. We communicated through this vent just like we are now. He was an unbelievable man."

"He escaped?"

"We assume so if they didn't catch him. But either way, he's free." The voice trailed off.

"Fill me in," Ian said.

"Riddick had been in the program for almost three weeks. Five nights ago, we all heard the generator sputter and quit. He made his move. The back door alarm didn't sound. Generator silence always wakes Dagny even though her suite is furthest from the generator. But this night, it was silent for well over an hour. We expected to hear the dogs immediately, but they were quiet, too. The wind must have been right. The guy who tried to escape before Riddick set off the back door alarm. I heard it and knew what was happening, so I timed it. In less than three minutes, Garland ran down the hallway, yelling to cut the dogs loose. We heard their excited barks fade into the woods. We found out later that Dagny wasn't at the facility that night. When she returned the next morning, we heard her yelling at Garland outside, saying he should have checked with her before releasing the dogs. She sent him and her other henchmen hiking into the woods. About three hours later, they returned, dragging what was left of a body on a makeshift stretcher with a rope."

"How do you know that?"

"She brought all the patients out of our cells and forced us to look. One of Dagny's men held the dogs on a leash nearby. We had to stand in line while they dragged the mangled corpse past us. She told us to look carefully at the firsthand results of the ultimate demerit. Nobody moved because the dogs were still jumping against the leash and snapping at us with their bloodstained muzzles. She said that the dogs would still have no trouble tracking us if we stripped out of our uniforms, showered, and ran 20 miles into the woods through wildflowers. She said we better know how to climb a tree if we wanted to keep our bodies intact for our families to bury. Then she took us, one by one, into the Cancellation Closet where Clarence took his beating and interrogated us until she was satisfied that no one had no prior warning of the escape attempt."

Ian said, "And Riddick still tried to escape?"

The voice said, "Let me ask you something… How badly do you want to get out?"

"I want to get out, but I'm not suicidal."

"The first guy that the dogs killed attempted his escape after only three days. He should've waited for a better plan. Riddick was much smarter. He planned out every detail of his escape. He was also lucky because Dagny didn't call for a room check like she usually does after a generator outage. Because of that, they didn't even know Riddick was missing until morning. When they brought his breakfast tray, they saw he was gone. We heard the expected running in the hallway and out the back door, triggering the alarm. They just let it ring while they cut the dogs loose. We could barely hear them, and their barks faded again."

"So Riddick is probably dead," Ian said, sighing.

"No, I don't think so. It's been five days, and if the dogs got to him, you can be sure that Dagny would have forced us to look at what was left of him. There might be more reasons to be hopeful. Riddick was lean and muscular. He had lived in this county all his life. He claimed to know every square foot of these woods for miles. He worked for the Bureau of Land Management and told me that one of his recent projects was a topographical survey to reestablish the boundaries and subdivisions of

5,000 square acres of public land. Some of that land buttresses this motel's property line. He knew that trying to escape via the main road by simply jogging or hitchhiking wasn't an option, given Garland, his motorcycle, and the armed men who seemed to appear out of nowhere whenever Dagny called them. He said that from Biding Wellness Center, it would require hiking at least a half-day through the woods to reach the closest location that had a telephone."

"If he made it, do you really think he'll bring help?"

"Without a doubt, which is why I worry a little, because I would've expected it by now. I still have a lot of faith in him, and if he lived, there's no way he would leave us here to die."

"Dagny must've been furious."

"That's an understatement. She immediately cut the dogs loose, even though she knew a lot of time had passed. She and Garland scoured Riddick's room. Through the vent, I heard them talking. 'Check here, look there, scrape that. Is something sticking out here?' And then, after over an hour, I heard one man say, 'Bingo.' That had to be when they found a map Riddick had drawn on a tattered piece of napkin."

"Crap."

"No, it's good. Riddick left it as a decoy. He told me he tore a seam in his cot and slipped it there for them to find. He left some threads loose to make sure it was conspicuous. That map sent them in a direction opposite of his true escape route."

"How would you know his escape route?"

"I'm getting to that. Riddick included an address on his fake hand-drawn map. He drew an arrow toward McAndrews Berry Farm, about seven miles away, just north of the main road. Frankly, I can't believe they were stupid enough to think Riddick left a map that would show his intentions, but in less than a minute, I heard Dagny's car start, and they sped away. I can't imagine the interrogation they gave whoever lives in that house. I can only hope Dagny believed them when they claimed to know nothing of Riddick."

"Dagny couldn't have hurt them. That would attract too much attention."

"I pray she didn't, but don't be so sure. That evening in the group session, Dagny said, 'I don't know how many of you might have knowledge of or are involved with the incident we had last night. If you are, let me simply say that the berry farm down the road is permanently closed'. This brings me to the most important thing I need to tell you...'"

"Hold on," Ian said, freezing for a moment. He thought he heard something outside his door. He adjusted himself so that if someone walked in, he'd be sitting beside the vent rather than kneeling to face it.

"Do you want it or not?" the voice asked.

"Yes, go ahead. I'm listening."

"The last time Riddick talked with me through the vent, he said he was leaving two hidden treasures behind. The first was some type of key to get out of the room, but he wouldn't tell me specifically what it was."

"Why not?" Ian said, skeptical.

"For the same reason that I haven't told you my name. He was afraid I might report it to Dagny. Frankly, I couldn't blame him for the caution, but the fact remains that there's something in your room that can get you out."

"And the other thing?" Ian asked as he looked up and around the walls, scouring every inch for a possible hiding place for anything.

"This second thing is most important."

"What is it? Tell me!" Ian said, his heart pounding.

There was a loud click, and the lights went out. The generator went silent. "Hurry! Tell me," Ian whispered.

The voice didn't answer.

"Please," Ian said again, his voice squeezed through the whisper.

Still no answer.

Ian listened carefully, wondering if someone had entered the voice's room, but he heard no conversation.

He felt for the cot and pulled himself up onto it. Then he heard footsteps in the hallway. No wonder the voice had gone silent. When the footsteps faded, he heard the now-familiar tapping through the vent.

"I'm here. Are you?" Ian asked.

"Yes."

"Tell me. Please hurry—tell me the other treasure that can help me get out."

"I'm surprised you haven't found it."

"Listen, whoever you are, I'm asking you to clue me in. If you have some information, please share it."

"There's an escape map in your room."

Ian thought for a moment, then said, "Where?" He looked around at the walls. "The room is bare, and I've scoured every inch of the bathroom, behind and inside the toilet, under the sink, and rubbed my hands over every square inch of the walls. There can't be a map. You told me Dagny and her people searched this room and were highly motivated to cover every inch."

"You're wrong. The book. Have you read the book?"

Ian patted his hands around him on the floor, searching for the *Our*

Beloved book. He found it a short distance away, propped against the wall where he had last placed it. He remembered skimming the pages before tossing it aside. "No, I haven't read it thoroughly," he said.

"Well, you sure as hell will want to now," the voice said. "This was another example of Riddick's genius. He knew these Sadens loved the book, and every one of them had it memorized. He hid a map where the staff would never need to look. He didn't tell me where in the book, but he asked me to tell the next person trapped in your room that they'd find the hidden map if they searched hard enough."

Ian fanned its pages, willing the lights to come back on. The voice's tip about the map was exhilarating, but utterly useless until the map was visible, and he found the tool that would allow him to escape the room. He clutched *Our Beloved* with both hands like it was a verified winning lottery ticket.

"Does me no good if I can't see," Ian said.

"Hang tight. Lights will be back on soon. Listen, now you have the map in hand, but Riddick wouldn't tell me the location of the special tool he fashioned to get out of the room. I'm afraid you're on your own for that. If you want to brainstorm, tap, and if it's safe, we'll talk."

Ian waited in the darkness with the precious *Our Beloved* book on his lap, willing the lights to come back on. "I have a question," he said.

"Go ahead," the voice said.

"Why are you sharing this with me? What's in it for you?"

"Are you serious? Whoever lands in room 151 is the only hope any of us have to escape from this place. I want you to get out and send the police as soon as possible if Riddick didn't make it. I can't believe you would ask that."

"Of course. I wasn't trying to offend you."

"Look, I've passed on to you everything Riddick told me. You have no way to pass that book to anyone else. Even if you did, the person wouldn't have Riddick's tool to get out of their room, so it's up to you now. If you are caught with the map, they'll presume that you drew it, and I think you can imagine the punishment Dagny will put you through. If you are willing to go for it, please do it soon. Otherwise, just go lay on your damn cot and wait to die like the rest of us!" Emotion welled up in the person's voice and rose above a whisper for the first time. It was still too difficult to determine whether the voice was that of a man or a woman. Ian tried to remember each person in the group session, but couldn't link the voice to a face.

"Footsteps. I have to go," the voice said.

"Okay, you don't have to worry about my willingness to break out. I want to be free more than anything."

A moment later, the lights blinked on. Ian jumped, and prickles of terror shot up his back when he saw Dagny standing inside his room with him. Her hand rested on the doorknob, and she had a leather bag over her shoulder.

Ian stood and said, "You scared me! I didn't hear you come in."

"You should expect that I'm always in here with you. That'll keep your behavior on track. Now, what do you want to be free of more than anything? I missed the first part."

Ian froze, wondering if that was true and how much of his conversation she had heard. "I—I want to be free of my addiction—more than anything."

Dagny let the door go. It clicked shut, which surprised Ian, since Garland wasn't with her. She strolled toward him with her thumb hooked under the bag's strap and tongue poked into her cheek. She pointed to the book in his hand. "Have you begun to read it?"

Ian said, "As a matter of fact, I had just cracked it open when the power went out."

Dagny held out her hand for the book.

Her taking the book from him now was the worst thing he could imagine. His arm felt like a powerful magnet was attached, preventing it from raising the book to Dagny's open hand. According to the voice, Dagny had just asked Ian to hand over his only chance to escape this nightmare.

When she took it from him, he kept his eyes locked on it. She went to his cot and sat. To Ian's horror, she bent the book and fanned the pages close to her face, inhaling its aroma and showing a pleased expression. "I encourage you to learn the story well," she said, tapping the book's cover. "Patients who read *Our Beloved* from cover to cover invariably have successful stays."

"I plan to read every word."

"Would you like me to show you some of my favorite passages?"

The question took Ian's breath away, and he stammered, "You know, I wouldn't want you to spoil the plot. I'm more of a binge-reader. Once I start a book, I like to plow straight through without stopping." He rubbed his hands together.

Dagny slapped the book shut with one hand and stood. "I can see that you're eager to continue the story." She handed the book back to him.

Ian placed it on his pillow and made the motion of brushing some dust from it before exchanging a forced smile with Dagny.

She slipped the leather bag from her shoulder. "I have something special to share as part of your treatment." She pulled three envelopes from the bag and handed them to Ian.

Ian shuffled the envelopes, immediately recognizing the writing on each. One was from his mom, another from his dad, and then he noticed the unmistakably rounded, oversized lettering of Kate's handwriting. He saw that the top edge of each envelope had been sliced open.

Dagny said, "Go ahead. Read them now, and they'll be included in your exit bag at discharge time."

Every envelope had been sliced. Ian's mouth tightened as he tried to mask his anger. He cleared his throat and said, "They've been opened."

"This is a secure facility. I'm sure you understand we must screen the mail. I assumed you'd prefer letters that have been opened rather than no letters. Makes sense?"

Ian slipped his dad's note from its envelope first.

Son,

Keep your chin up. Embrace your new

beginning. See you when you are better.

Dad

Ian assumed that a red checkmark on the top right side of the page indicated Dagny's approval of the message.

He pulled his mom's note from its envelope. Her note filled two sheets of paper instead of one. She had written a virtual treatise on her love for him and her desire to help him overcome the virtual demons that were battling for his soul. He skimmed it and then moved on to Kate's.

He saved Kate's message for last because he knew it would be emotional for him to read. He desperately wanted Dagny to leave so he could be alone with Kate's words. Reading them with an audience was better than not at all, so he pulled the folded note from the already-opened envelope. Immediately, his teeth clenched. A thick black marker redacted multiple words and phrases in Kate's handwritten message. In the first paragraph, Kate wished him success in the recovery program. She apologized for any contribution she may have made to his illness. The second paragraph began with Kate saying.

When I think of you, I feel...

The following six words were redacted. The hair on the back of Ian's neck stiffened as he tried to hold back the rage welling up in him. "What is this?" he said, turning the letter for Dagny to see. He pressed his fingertip against the black redaction. The note trembled in Ian's hand.

"Some parts of Kate's message were deemed emotional triggers that could interfere with your recovery. Luckily, we caught it in time to obscure her distracting sentiments to protect you. However, don't you worry. We photocopied her unabridged version and will happily give you a copy if you complete treatment."

Ian spoke through gritted teeth. "You opened and read my private message from her."

"The signature on your paperwork grants us permission to screen all your correspondence."

"I signed nothing like that."

"Your family admitted you. Their signatures sufficed. Reading all inbound mail is a strict policy. We have a responsibility to manage any communication that could inappropriately influence you. Makes sense?"

When Ian didn't look satisfied, Dagny reached for the letters, saying, "Of course we can end this special treat if your enjoyment is ruined by a feeling of having been violated."

Ian held the letters away.

"I expected you to be happier. That last one must be from your ex, correct?" She pointed to Ian's hand.

"She's not my ex. We're together."

"That's the second time you've mentioned that to me."

"Because it's a fact," Ian said defiantly.

"Does she know you are back together, or is it just in your head?" Dagny asked.

"Look, this is none of your business."

Dagny smiled. "All your business is my business while you are here."

Ian said, "Look, we're together, and that's that."

"I can save you some pain," Dagny said.

Ian didn't reply, only stared at her.

Dagny put her hands on her hips and said, "Ian, I wouldn't mistake Kate's desire for you to undergo treatment with a desire to get back together with you."

"I'm not making a mistake. We discussed it. And what would you know about that, anyway?"

"You should know I spoke to her for hours before your intervention. We discussed everything about you, and I mean everything. She shared the details of your desperate and losing fight to keep her. Of the three letters in your hand, Kate's was the most difficult to get. She was so worried about sending you mixed signals about her interest in you."

Ian bristled. "Kate is the most honest person I know. She would never lie to me. She sugarcoated nothing when she broke up, knowing how much it would hurt me. There's no reason for her to lie about getting back together."

"Suit yourself, but I can tell you Kate deserves your skepticism more than I do. At first, she wanted no part in this intervention. But when she agreed with me that your life was in danger, I asked which would torment her conscience more: your death from addiction because she wouldn't help us intervene or the shame of telling you a tiny little lie to save your life. When I put it like that, she magically became willing to say whatever was necessary to get you here with me. All's well that ends well. Makes sense?"

Ian could only look at Dagny, his jaw clenching.

Dagny said, "Now, whether your relationship rekindles after your treatment is between you, her, and her new boyfriend."

"That wasn't her boyfriend. It's her nephew."

"Ohhhh, she's good!" Dagny said, grinning. "Is that what she told you? Brilliant. She must want to limit your stress during treatment."

Ian stepped away to help restrain himself. He wanted to attack her. It would be a foolish move, with Garland standing outside the door. He already had a demerit cancellation coming, and if they beat him like they had beaten Clarence, Ian would be too physically depleted to make a run for freedom, whether he had a map or not. Through his teeth, he said, "What you're doing to me is wrong."

Dagny laughed and said, "I'll accept that criticism. You'll change your mind when we release you completely rehabilitated and free of your vices."

Ian felt tears coming.

Dagny noticed and said, "I can see we've touched a nerve. I assumed that the pleasure of hearing from your folks and Kate would offset the disappointment of limiting the messages."

Ian briefly raised the envelopes to look at them again, then dropped his hand. He wiped a tear.

Dagny said, "I'll tell you what... I'm going to make an exception by leaving these letters with you. But I must warn you that if I don't see appropriate progress in your recovery, I will confiscate them until we dispatch—I mean discharge you. Sound fair?"

"Certainly. Thank you, Ms. Conger." Ian squeezed the words out, infusing them with as much courtesy as possible.

"Excellent." Dagny took her bag and left the room. Garland leaned in and pulled the door closed behind her.

Ian set the letters beside the cot and picked up the *Our Beloved* book. He put the book on his lap and began flipping through the pages. He sped up, scanning page after page of text for anything resembling a map or drawing.

As he neared the end of the book, his heart sank as the odds of finding anything unusual dwindled. When he reached the final chapter, he turned each page slower. At the bottom of the last page, he saw the words:

The Beginning

Ian rolled his eyes at the cute twist on the traditional *The End*. The following page was blank, but he saw something that made his heart skip. The indentations of a ballpoint pen were visible. He drew his finger across the page, feeling them before he flipped to the next page. There it was. Riddick had used one of the blank pages at the end of the book for a hand-drawn map in black ink that filled the page, edge to edge. A skull and crossbones marked the location of the facility. Hundreds of stick-figure trees showed the forest behind the facility. The center of the map had a blank horizontal strip with arrows beside text that read: **A few miles**, which made the map's scale challenging to estimate. From the size of the hand-drawn facility, road in front, and other geographical markers, the map could encompass many miles. On the left side, an arrow pointed toward McAndrews Berry Farm, showing that it was 7 miles away. He had drawn a smiley face beside it.

On the opposite side of Biding Wellness Center, Riddick had drawn a narrow road that intersected the main road about a mile away. An arrow pointing to it read:

Dirt road hidden from view by trees.

A dotted line representing the road snaked deep into the woods for what looked like many miles. At the end, Riddick had drawn several small rectangles beside the words:

Occupied Outpost. Help is here.

At the bottom of the map, Riddick had drawn a right-pointing arrow. Ian turned the page and found an odd message.

Let the door close gently.

The cryptic message puzzled Ian. Was it a riddle? He looked at the door. So far, he was given no control over when the door opened or closed. He reread the strange message, trying to make sense of it. Whenever Dagny or Garland entered the room, they kept him away from the door. It was impossible for Ian to approach it to slow it down. The other problem was that the door latched with an audible click. There was no doubt Dagny and her staff listened for this sound, even if their backs were turned as they made their way along the hallway.

Ian got up and began pacing around the room, thinking. He examined the bathroom door, but nothing about it made sense of the cryptic message.

He went to the vent and said, "Hey, are you there?" in a loud whisper. The voice didn't respond.

He climbed onto his cot and picked up the *Our Beloved* book. He tried to commit to memory as many of the details of Riddick's map as possible in case Dagny took or traded the book or, worse, moved him to another room. He noted several creeks Riddick had added and a few blank areas of the page that he assumed to be open spaces or fields next to the dotted line that led to the encampment. About a third of the way to the outpost, the dotted line crossed a river. At the intersection, Riddick had showed an orange trestle bridge.

Of course, the map was useless until Ian had discovered how Riddick had escaped the room. He set the book aside and stared at the door. He heard voices in the hallway. Someone in an adjacent room had a staff visitor. After trying to eavesdrop on a muffled, unintelligible conversation, Ian heard the door close in the room next to his. Footsteps faded, and then the recognizable sound of the door to the building's rear exit opening and closing.

Ian's eyes focused on the top of his door. He got up from his cot and walked to it. He reached up to the door closer and pulled out the small piece of plastic he had found shortly after arriving in his room. He looked at it more closely and noticed that one edge appeared to have been scraped to shape it. He turned it over several times, examining it before he reached up to put it back. His finger brushed a tightly folded piece of paper on top of the door closer. It was attached with something sticky to keep it from falling off. He gently peeled the paper free of what felt like a glob of chewing gum. He unfolded the paper and discovered a message that said:

You found it. Use the tool to adjust the closers screw to slow the door. Then, you can catch it before it latches without rushing. Snap the latch with your thumb to simulate the sound of the door locking. Reset the closer to normal speed and place this note and the tool where it was for the next victim. I wish you luck. Run like hell.

Godspeed.

Ian took the small piece of plastic and felt along the top of the closer until it slipped into the groove of the closer's screw. He turned it and felt a change in the tension. He returned it to its original position. He tried to keep his hands from shaking as he gently placed the paper note and the plastic piece back on the closer. He was awed by Riddick's genius and attention to detail.

He went back to his cot and sat. His mind raced. Escape had suddenly become a real possibility.

• • •

Carol could hardly dial the phone number quickly enough. She pressed the phone to her ear and nibbled her lip while waiting for an answer.

Dagny sat in the manager's office, picked up the phone, and answered after the first ring. "Hello."

"Hi, is this Ms. Conger?"

"Who's asking?" Dagny said skeptically.

"This is Carol Shaw. I'm the mother of Ian Shaw."

"Oh, yes, of course. Hello, Mrs. Shaw. How are you?" Dagny's voice quickly thawed.

"We've been better. I'm so glad we could finally reach you. When we met at our home, you indicated we would get a follow-up call to confirm Ian's safe arrival. However, we haven't heard back, and I must tell you it's disappointing."

"I do apologize for that. Things have been so busy with a frenetic intake, and I frequently become so engrossed in my work that our confirmation call completely slipped my mind. I do hope you'll forgive me."

"Of course. Is everything okay with Ian?"

"Couldn't be better. You've raised him well. He is a joy and off to a fantastic start."

Dagny's consolation brought Carol enough relief to give Mitch a thumbs-up sign.

He smiled.

"We'd really like a brief word with him. Is that possible?" Carol asked.

Dagny said, "You know, under normal circumstances, that would be fine, but I can see from Ian's behavior that the fewer distractions he has, the better. Can we book a call when he's further into the program?"

"Interesting," Carol said. "I'd prefer a quick hello with him now. It'll take only a moment. I'm sure you can understand a mother's concern. I'd like to just briefly hear his voice and for him to hear mine. I'm sure you understand. I promise I won't need further communication until he completes treatment."

"You are obviously a fantastic and caring mother," Dagny said. "I would love nothing more than to put Ian on the phone with you, but he's currently taking part in a group meeting, and I'm reluctant to interrupt it. Can we book a call for another time?"

"Just a moment, please," Carol said. She pressed the phone to her shoulder and whispered to Mitch, "She apologized for not calling yesterday. She doesn't want us to talk to him now because she said it's distracting, and he's in a group meeting."

Mitch pressed his lips together and held out his hand. Carol gave him the phone.

"Dagny, this is Mitch Shaw," he said.

"Oh, hello, Mr. Shaw."

"Listen, my wife, Carol explained that you don't want to interrupt Ian for a quick word with us. If you don't allow it, you might do irreparable harm to my marriage. I hope you can understand my predicament."

Dagny laughed.

Carol smacked Mitch with the back of her hand, pretending to be offended, then smiling.

Mitch continued, "I realize you are focused on his treatment underway, but I have a difficult time understanding how a quick hello would cause a problem. Maybe you could make a small exception to make up for not having contacted us yesterday."

After a pause, Dagny said, "I understand completely. Although we typically wouldn't allow it, give me a moment to see if I can interrupt his counselor to get Ian on the line for you."

"Much appreciated," Mitch said. He handed the phone back to Carol. She put it on speakerphone so they could both hear their son.

Dagny put the call on hold, got up from her desk, and went to the opposite side of the office, where she removed a laptop from the top drawer of a file cabinet. She strolled back to her desk and sat. After waiting for it to boot up, she opened a music player with five audio clips queued up. She took a deep breath, took the call off hold, and said, "I see Ian walking down the hall. One moment while I call him over."

Mitch said, "Thank you." He and Carol leaned closer to the phone, anticipating Ian's voice.

Dagny said, "I have Ian here with me now." She gently placed her phone beside the laptop's speaker, briefly covering her phone with her hand to dampen her voice. "Ian, your parents are on the line, and they seem to be worried about you. Can you speak to them? They seem concerned about your well-being." Dagny pressed play for the first clip. Ian's voice said, "There's nothing to worry about." Dagny pressed pause.

"Oh, thank God," Carol said. "Sweetheart, it's so good to hear your voice. Is everything okay?"

Dagny clicked another clip. Ian's voice said, "I'm in the capable hands of true professionals." She pressed pause.

"We know, Son," Mitch Shaw chimed in. "We're glad you got there safe. We're rooting for you."

Ian's voice said, "I promise to overcome my vices, and I'll do whatever is necessary to return home completely healed."

"I've always loved your determination. You are wonderful," his mom said. "When you get home, we'll celebrate. Are you feeling good about things?"

Dagny clicked the next clip. Ian's voice said, "I'm thankful for the help I'm getting."

Dagny broke into the conversation. "There you go, Mr. and Mrs. Shaw. We need to get Ian to his next appointment, which is a spa treatment before dinner."

"My, oh, my!" Carol said.

Dagny laughed. "It's some extra pampering that we include exclusively for new arrivals to take the edge off homesickness and withdrawal."

"Dagny, we can't thank you enough," Mitch said. "We promise not to further interfere in Ian's treatment, but the phone number on the card you gave us only rings with no answer."

Dagny said, "I apologize for that. I don't want you using that number, anyway. Ian is such a special patient that I want you to have direct access to me. The number we are speaking on is my mobile number. I'm giving you permission to use it whenever you have a concern, no matter how small."

"What a relief!" Carol said.

"And your relief makes me happy. You two take care, won't you?"

Mitch said, "And thank you for saving my marriage!"

Everyone laughed.

After hanging up, Dagny sat back in her chair and smiled.

Eleven

THE KNOT IN the pit of Ian's stomach grew tighter every time he remembered that the time for his demerit cancellation at the group session was growing closer. Hours went by, then more hours. He couldn't fall asleep, and his withdrawal symptoms had him on edge. Even the sudden generator failures startled him.

He tapped on the vent and called out in whispers, trying to reach the voice from the vent, but there was no reply. Talking to the voice through the vent had not only benefited him by possibly providing a way to escape from the facility, but kept his sanity.

He picked up his dad's note from the cot and re-read it. In typical fashion, his dad was a man of few words.

> Son,
>
> Keep your chin up. Embrace your new beginning.
>
> See you when you are better.
>
> Dad

Barely enough words for any redaction, Ian thought. Ian put it aside and picked up his mother's note, easily identifiable by her swishy lettering and the bold smiley face next to his name on the envelope. Her extended message implored him to return to God and encouraged him to use his time in the program for quiet introspection. Two sentences near the end were redacted. The thick black marker that concealed these words didn't bother Ian. In the context of his mother's note, he had a good idea of what they were. They probably mentioned a timeframe for seeing him again or a desire to visit him, both of which Dagny would say risked generating unwanted anxiety. He folded the note without reinserting it into the envelope and stacked it on his dad's.

He picked up Kate's note. When he opened it, his shoulders sagged. The redactions still infuriated him. For two months, he had desperately wanted to know how she was and anything about her life. Dagny had no right to hide any of Kate's words from him, but given the abuse Ian had seen Dagny dole out, the torture of redaction wasn't a surprise. He raised the note, trying to see through the black marker, but the light in his room wasn't bright enough. He tucked it back into the envelope and slid it into his back pocket.

• • •

Ian spent most of the following day locked in his room. The door opened only once for Garland to shove a food tray into the room with his foot. Without more visits from Dagny and Garland, there was no opportunity to test adjustments to the door closer.

He'd lost track of time, making it difficult to estimate how long he had been in solitary confinement. The next time Garland visited, Ian asked about briefly getting out of the room for some fresh air. Garland only said, "Dagny's decision." As he quickly closed the door, Ian carefully watched it. The door took approximately 3 to 4 seconds to close from an open position. He went to the door and pulled out the plastic piece hidden there. He used it to adjust the closer slightly. He knew the door would close noticeably slower if he added too much tension. He also made a note of the latch's sound. It had a firm spring that created a double click, one when the latch hit the strike plate and a second click when the latch sprung, locking it into place. This distinct sound was consistent among all the doors Ian heard many times throughout the day. He wished he could test-flick the latch. Recreating this sound on his first try would require some luck.

A couple of hours later, Ian heard a welcomed sound. The rhythmic tapping from the vent sent him rushing to it. He kneeled and answered, saying, "I'm here."

"Did you find the map?"

"What's going on? Where have you been?"

"It's been too risky to talk. You have had a lot of activity in your room. If I hear any sounds, I don't say shit," the voice answered. "Did you find the map?"

"Yes."

"Awesome! What about anything else?"

Ian considered whether to tell the voice about the plastic door-closer tool. To some degree, Ian felt indebted to whomever the voice was. On the other hand, earlier, the voice made a good point that knowledge was a commodity that patients could use to gain favor with Dagny.

"Still looking, but I think I might be getting closer."

"God, do I wish I were in your room."

"Listen, if I get out, I'll make sure this place pays for every person they've victimized."

Ian's door flew open. Dagny briskly walked in and stood over Ian before he could climb to his feet. She dragged the bullwhip on the floor behind her.

"Who are you talking to?"

The door slowly closed, latching behind her.

"Myself, again."

Dagny cracked the whip and then pointed to the corner of the room opposite the cot. "Over there. Now."

Ian scrambled to comply. "I'm the only one here. Who would I be talking to?"

"Quiet!"

Dagny squatted to one knee and flicked the vent with her fingernail. "Yoo-hoo… Who's there?"

Prickles of terror rushed up Ian's back. He held his breath, hoping the voice wouldn't answer. The vent remained quiet.

Dagny put her mouth closer to the vent. "I heard you. I suspected this for a long time." She whistled. It echoed in the vent.

Ian said, "I'm telling you, I wasn't talking to…"

"Quiet!" Dagny snapped.

"I'm sorry!" A faint voice came through the vent.

Dagny grinned over her shoulder at Ian. Those menacing little teeth. "Aren't you sneaky—and incredibly dishonest?" She returned her mouth to the vent and said, "A confession will lessen your punishment. Identify yourself."

"I'm so sorry, Ms. Conger. It's Annabel. Please, have mercy."

"My mercy has run dry with you," Dagny said, climbing to her feet.

"No! Please! I'm sorry!"

"You have a steep price to pay."

"Ms. Conger, I beg you, please! I promise it won't happen again."

"An addict's favorite line," Dagny said. She pointed the whip handle at Ian and said, "After Annabel, it will be your turn." She walked to the door, holding her gaze on Ian.

"I didn't know who that was!" Ian said. An honest statement.

"Now we do, and that's all that matters." Dagny backed out of the room and firmly pulled the door closed.

Ian went to the vent and listened. He held his breath, straining to hear. He detected a verbal exchange, too faint to understand, but he recognized Annabel's begging tone before the muffled sound of a slamming door muted it.

For nearly two hours, Ian wondered what consequences Annabel faced for communicating with him. Catching them gave Dagny another opportunity to satisfy her sadistic urges.

He heard footsteps approaching and heard someone whimpering in the hallway. The key went into his door before it opened. Dagny and Garland each held the arm of Annabel, the young woman with the piercings.

Dagny said, "I thought it was important for you to see a before and after of her face. Take a good look at the before. I doubt you'll recognize the after when we bring her back."

Ian pressed his hands down on the cot. He considered making his run out the door right now. They would no doubt let go of Annabel to chase him. The rear door was certainly locked, and even if it wasn't, he'd forfeit Riddick's critical head start. Running in a panic now would only make things worse for himself. He had to wait for a better time.

Annabel panted. Sweat covered her face, and her short hair had been pulled from the ponytail. Some of it stuck to her forehead. She looked at Ian and said, "I'm so sorry."

Garland pressed something into her back, and she shrieked. Her knees buckled.

She looked up at Ian and said, "I believe in you. Please save me!"

"Enough," Dagny yelled. She and Garland dragged Annabel away from the door.

Ian forced his attention from Annabel's cries to the door as it slowly closed. When the latch clicked, Ian rushed to listen. He heard them open the rear door. The alarm briefly sounded until Dagny hollered at Garland to turn it off.

Ian stood stunned, wondering what they would do to Annabel and then him. After confessing their secret communication through the vent, he wondered if Dagny had used torture to get Annabel to share more details of their conversation. If she genuinely wanted Ian to save her, ruining the secret was the stupidest thing she could have done.

Ian heard movement outside the room's blocked window.

"No, please! Don't!" He heard Annabel beg.

A gunshot blast right outside the window was so loud he felt it in his chest.

Annabel's cries went silent.

Ian backed away from the window, the blood draining from his face. He backed to the door until he bumped it. He pulled from his pocket the plastic tool that Riddick had left. With trembling fingers, he reached up to the door closer and felt for the groove to adjust the tension. When the tool slipped into the slot, he turned it, tightening it as much as possible without breaking the plastic piece.

With no way to test it, he could only wait for the next time Dagny or Garland entered.

A few minutes later, the door opened. Dagny stepped in and said, "We expect uncompromising obedience. Normally, Annabel's offense would be forgivable, but it was a particularly egregious offense and wasn't her first. Makes sense?"

"Yes, Ms. Conger." Ian's voice cracked.

"As for you," Dagny continued, "I don't think it will come as any surprise that you have earned an additional demerit that will need cancellation. Consider yourself lucky because we have a new patient arriving tomorrow morning. The timing is right, so I am postponing your cancellation procedure until morning so that you will serve as a lesson for our new patient during intake."

"Thank you, Ms. Conger."

"Very good." Dagny stepped back into the hall. Ian felt a surge of adrenaline when he saw the door was closing much slower than before, and Dagny had walked away. He rushed to the door, catching it before it latched. Dagny's footsteps grew fainter at the end of the hallway. He held the latch with his thumb. When the door came to within an inch of closing, he snapped the latch against the strike plate and held his breath.

Dagny's footsteps continued without so much as slowing. Ian heard her open the door to the lobby, and he heard the door close.

After waiting another 30 seconds, he slowly opened the door and peered out into the hallway. It was dim and empty. To his left was the back door exit. He knew Garland had disabled the alarm after mistakenly setting it off while rushing Annabel outside for her execution, but there was no way to tell if he had reactivated it.

Given the horrors slated for his demerit cancellation tomorrow morning, taking a chance that the alarm was still disabled was a risk worth taking.

He looked back at his cot and saw the copy of *Our Beloved*. He pulled the door open as far as it would go, then ran to the cot and grabbed the book, returning to catch the door just before it closed. He used the book to prop the door open. After rechecking the hallway, he ran to the back door and turned the knob. It was open!

Ian ran back to his door, picked up *Our Beloved*, and flipped through the back of it, searching for the map page while trying to keep his hands from trembling. When he found the map, he pressed the book against his leg and tore out the map page. He tossed the book back across the floor, and it spun to a stop beside the cot.

"God help me," Ian said under his breath as he quietly stepped into the hallway, still holding the door. He knew that when he released the door, it would click. He worried Dagny might hear it wherever she was in the facility.

He let the door close. The moment it clicked, he raced to the back door. He gently turned the knob and pushed the door open... The cool, fresh air hit him in the face, and there was silence. Beautiful silence. The alarm was still disabled.

He stepped outside, easing the door to close it quietly. He looked toward the shed, having forgotten about the dogs. His hunting experience with his dad and brother kicked in. He checked the wind direction. There was a slight crosswind. Angling to his right would keep dogs upwind, allowing him to at least make it to the woods at the edge of the property.

Ian sprinted across the open space, crossing the unpaved driveway. He knew the twigs and gravel crunching under his feet might trigger the dogs, but at this point, his sole focus was getting distance between him and the facility of nightmares. As he neared the trees, he put all his effort into maintaining his full sprint. He crashed through the bushes that lined the woods and continued running without looking back, dodging trees and hurtling fallen limbs. Branches slapped him, briars scraped his legs, and thistles clung to his scrubs.

He ran for nearly five minutes before he briefly stopped, completely winded. If only he had taken Kate up on her constant urging for him to exercise with her, he'd be in better shape.

Behind him, he heard something that made him forget he was winded. The dogs were barking.

Twelve

POWERED BY THE vivid image in Ian's mind of the dogs ripping him limb from limb, Ian took off again, putting everything he had into every stride. The rubber-soled water shoes were light and easy to run in, but provided little arch support, so he felt like he was running barefoot. The rugged terrain and the thick accumulation of fallen debris from the trees hampered his speed.

He remembered from Riddick's map that taking a straight path through the wooded area behind the facility should eventually bring him to a river. There was no time to pull the map from his pocket to confirm it.

As he came to a ridge top, he saw it descend into a ravine flanked by an opening. He gained speed. The barking dogs hadn't grown louder, but their volume seemed steady. He ran into a thicket at the edge of the ravine and was thrilled to see water and hear it trickling over the rocks.

If he stopped, the dogs would have him in sight in minutes. He'd be forced to climb a tree if they got too close. He imagined Dagny grinning up at him while he clung to a limb. She'd love that. When he considered what she'd do if she caught him, he decided it would be better to let the dogs have him on the ground rather than to suffer Dagny's punishment.

Ian was no survivalist, but he had learned enough from hunting with his dad and brother to understand throwing a scent. He splashed into the water and turned, running upstream as fast as possible. The water splashed as he high-stepped. The rubber-soled shoes provided an excellent grip on the rounded stones on the creek bed. If his captors wanted to limit their victims' ability to escape, they should probably force future patients to wear boots, he thought.

He jogged for another quarter of a mile, sometimes slipping on the smooth, moss-covered stones protruding from the water before he stopped to listen. He leaned onto his knees, his chest heaving and his lungs burning as the water rushed around his ankles. The dog barks had grown quieter, but he didn't want to fool himself into feeling too safe. He pulled out the map for a quick review. It showed that he should come to a bridge if he continued east on this creek.

He alternated between walking and jogging for three or four miles, he estimated, relieved to hear the dogs' barks fading behind him. With any luck, he had successfully thrown them off his path. The creek widened, and the water level rose above his knees, forcing him to move to shore, where he continued running along its muddy bank. After a couple of miles, he saw something ahead that excited him. A weather-beaten orange bridge spanned the river ahead and matched Riddick's description. Ian trudged toward it, feeling the effects of his lack of exercise.

He wondered if the bridge could have traffic. If it linked to any road accessible by Garland's motorcycle, Ian expected to see or hear it at any moment. He didn't underestimate how vigorously Dagny and her people would search for him. He'd be a great example to the other patients.

As Ian neared the bridge, he discovered it was a railroad bridge, and its orange tone was because of large patches of rust that had spread, nearly covering its sides.

Knowing that he was on the correct path excited him. He hurried to it and climbed down the embankment to a place tucked underneath it. The mid-afternoon sun was stretching the shadows of the bridge and the surrounding trees. If the rest of the journey followed the accuracy of Riddick's map, he should be able to reach the settlement before dark if the map was anywhere close to scale.

He picked some briars from his pants and dumped wet sand from his soaked shoes. He brushed off his backside and felt Kate's note in his back pocket. He pulled it out and skimmed through the unredacted parts of the message. Then, on a hunch, he held it up to the sky. When the sun's bright light hit the paper, the writing Dagny had attempted to blot out with black marker became faintly legible. He went to the paragraph that began with:

When you get back, I want you to…

He tilted the paper against the sun, adjusting it until he could make out the next words:

…pick me up and spin me like you used to.

Ian's heart skipped a beat, and he lowered the note, grinning at it. Kate's request made him forget his exhaustion. For a moment, his anxiety fell away. He reread the message. It felt almost as good as the first time. It was just what he needed to refuel his determination to get back to her as soon as possible.

He pulled out his map again. Although it would've made his travel easier, he couldn't follow the railroad tracks because they took him in a direction that didn't come close to the outpost. According to Riddick's map, he was approximately a third of the way to the outpost. From the bridge, a dotted line on the map jutted upward at a northeast angle for what Ian estimated to be about five miles before coming to a dirt road, clearly noted on Riddick's map. Going to another place where Garland and his henchmen would have easier, quicker access to him via a motorcycle wasn't comfortable. Still, the ability to travel faster on it was worth the risk, as he'd soon run out of sunlight.

He trudged ahead on his trek through the woods. After traveling for another hour, he felt despair. He came to something that could hardly be called a road. It was like two parallel dirt trails with faint vehicle wheel tracks dulled by recent rain. A thick ribbon of grass grew in the center, and trees on opposite sides of the road encroached on the shoulders so closely that their branches occasionally entangled overhead.

Ian followed the road for miles, and his legs and feet ached as his exhaustion grew. The scratches that decorated his legs on his initial sprint from Biding Wellness Center now stung. He wandered a short distance from the road and found a spring. He drank deeply and splashed water on his face and neck. He sat and took off a shoe. Blisters were forming on the soles of his feet.

The temperature noticeably dropped as late afternoon gave way to evening. A new panic set in. At this rate, returning the way he had come wasn't an option, not only because he'd be captured by Dagny but also because he probably didn't have the stamina to make it. He questioned whether he had followed the map correctly. Or what if the outpost shown on the map didn't exist, and that's why Riddick never returned? He tried to dismiss the concern. He estimated he must have traveled at least 10 to 12 miles by now. He knew he was committed to reaching the outpost at this point.

After a brief rest, he returned to the road, moving as fast as possible while limping to ease the pressure on his blistered foot.

He made it only another mile or so before the excruciating pain caused him to stop again. He looked ahead as far as he could see, but the trees and a slight curve obscured a view more than a few hundred meters ahead.

A sound jolted him. It was so faint he had to hold his breath to hear it. The unmistakable, enthusiastic wailing of dogs and their barks were growing louder. He dropped to his knees. There was no way he could climb a tree. He couldn't outrun the dogs. And now he heard the shouts of men punctuating the excited barking.

On pure adrenaline, Ian hobbled from the road into the thick trees. He began going up the gentle slope to the top of another ridge. Each step burned.

The barking grew louder.

No stream or running water was in sight, so masking his scent a second time wasn't an option. He gritted his teeth and fought to reach the top of the small ridge. When he crested it and looked down the other side, he saw them in the distance. Three men in hunting garb walked shoulder to shoulder, unrushed and deliberately, toward Ian. He didn't see any dogs, but heard the barking fading behind the men. Ian wondered if more hunters were handling the dogs out of sight.

As the men approached, Ian noticed they were dressed in matching gear. They wore camouflage parkas, slacks, green and black knit caps, and matching camouflage knee-high rubber boots. The men wore beards of varying lengths, and each carried a backpack. They said nothing to one another as they marched directly toward Ian. Any sound of the dogs was gone, replaced by the crunch of underbrush under the men's feet.

For a moment, Ian considered trying to hide, but he knew it would be futile. He had no choice but to put himself at the mercy of these men. They came close enough for Ian to make out more details. Ian was relieved that he didn't recognize any of them as staff from Biding Wellness Center.

When they closed in to within about twenty meters, Ian climbed to his knees and rose to bring his entire torso into view. He lifted his arm and waved.

One of them raised his hand in a peace sign. The gesture gave Ian hope that a favorable encounter was possible. He called out to them, saying, "I know it's obvious, but I'm lost and in awful shape here. Can you help me?"

Two of the men exchanged glances. The third smiled and said, "Of course."

"Thank God," Ian said, making a prayer sign to exude as much visual gratitude as he could for them.

"What's your name?" one of them asked. He was the tallest, and his hunting outfit did little to conceal his muscular build.

"Ian—Ian Shaw."

"I'm Jebediah," he said as the men stopped beside him. "And this is Rhett." He pointed to a man with a reddish beard and a clean-shaved head. "And that's Jangy." Ian saw something on Jangy that shot a spike of fear up his spine. Blood caked with dirt clung to his boots, fading to lighter splatter as it went up to his belt. His parka's sleeves were also smeared and splattered, as were his hands, except for a clean spot on the back of one hand where the blood had been transferred to his forehead.

"So, it looks like you had a successful hunt this afternoon," Ian said.

Jangy looked down at himself. "I guess you could say that," he said. The others chuckled. Jangy bent down, scooped up some dirt, and rubbed his hands together to remove the blood from them.

"So, what are you hunting?" Ian asked.

Jebediah spit and said, "A little bit of this, a little bit of that. Mostly whatever we can flush out."

The answer didn't remove Ian's concern about the blood.

"What are you doing out here, Ian?" Rhett asked.

"It's sort of a long story," Ian said, still trying to pry his gaze from Jangy's bloodiness.

"We'd love to hear it," Rhett said, as he un-shouldered his backpack and pulled a water canteen from it. He uncapped it and held it out to Ian. "Drink. If you die, you'll ruin our heroic rescue."

"Thank you," Ian said. He took a few deep swallows but cut his thirsty gulps short, not wanting to disrespect Rhett's generosity by draining the canteen. He handed it back and wiped his mouth.

Rhett slid the canteen back into his backpack. "Now, tell us how you got here."

"I'm an escapee," Ian said.

"Whoa! Prison?" Jebediah asked.

"No, no!" Ian said. "Not that. You guys ever hear about Biding Wellness Center?"

The men looked at one another. Rhett and Jangy shook their heads. Jebediah rubbed his beard while he looked up. "Doesn't sound familiar. What is it?"

"It's an awful place," Ian said. "It fronts as a rehab facility, but it's run by some horrific people who are using it for something mysterious and terrible that's still unclear to me. But I can tell you they are sadistic. I saw them torture people who had been sent there as patients."

"Sounds terrible," Jebediah said. He took off his boot and shook some pebbles out. "How can they get away with that?"

"They have so far, but they won't for long. The minute I get back to town, you can bet they'll be shut down and prosecuted."

Jebediah pulled a small bag of trail mix from his coat pocket and handed it to Ian.

"Thank you," Ian said, accepting it. He tossed some in his mouth, which might have been the most delicious nuts he had ever tasted.

"How did you end up there?" Jebediah asked.

"My parents presumed I had an alcohol problem," Ian said, chewing. "They arranged for me to go there. They convinced me to try it—coerced me, actually. I escaped a few hours ago before I was slated to be tortured."

Rhett and Jangy cussed under their breath.

Jebediah said, "Sounds like a place nobody would want to end up. Where is it?"

"It's out on the main road. I don't know how many miles I've walked, or I could be more specific," Ian said, pointing his best guess as to the direction he had come from.

"Well, we are glad you made it out," Rhett said.

Jangy added, "Sounds like you got real lucky, but here's a question… Where the hell were you trying to go?"

"One of the other patients broke out before I did and left a map to some sort of outpost in this direction. He claimed it had buildings with telephones and that it would be easier to reach than hiking all the way to town."

Jebediah said, "I've got news for you. The only buildings out here are the small structures of our little encampment just up ahead. You said this person broke out ahead of you?"

"That's right. It would've been over a week ago."

Jangy said, "We know every inch of these parts and have never seen what you're describing."

Ian said, "You haven't happened to see anyone else wandering out here sometime in the last couple of weeks, have you?"

"Oh, we see people all the time," Rhett said.

"You do?" Ian's face lit up.

"Yes, every day or two, we'll be huntin', and some poor fool will step right out from behind a tree and start talking to us."

The men exploded with laughter. Jebediah and Jangy fist-bumped while Rhett's laughter sent him into a coughing spell.

"Hell, no, we don't see anyone out here," Jebediah said. "We were shocked as hell to find you."

Ian wasn't amused. The painful joke sadly confirmed for Ian that Riddick had never made it to the outpost and had likely died somewhere out here.

Their laughter, the blood on Jangy's clothing, and the darkening sky made Ian want to abbreviate his time with these guys—as grateful as he was to be rescued. "Can I use one of your phones?"

Jangy said, "We don't have phones. We're escapees, too!"

"I don't understand," Ian said nervously.

"We're escapees from civilization. If you're looking to call somebody, you are shit out of luck."

"Then how do you guys make calls if you have an emergency or something?" Ian pointed to himself.

"We never call out," Jebediah said. "We make it a point to be self-sufficient."

"Then do you guys have an ATV or another vehicle? I'm hoping for some help back to town. I'll gladly pay for your trouble and gas."

"You won't be paying us for anything."

"I don't mind paying—you do not know how grateful I'd be for the help."

"I think we do!" Jebediah said, laughing. The others joined in, and their laughter grew—apparently from a joke Ian wasn't in on. There was something creepy about the heartiness of their laughter from Ian's simple statements.

When they settled down, Jebediah said, "We're gonna help you, but we don't have phones, and we don't have vehicles. Out here, our only transportation is Ford feet and Chevy shoes."

Jangy scooped up some more dirt and massaged it into his pants at his calves to remove some of the drying blood. He said, "I hate to break it to you, but you're not going home tonight."

"Pardon?"

"Sun's almost down. It'll be dark in no time. You're lucky we caught you while there was enough light."

Ian didn't like that he used the word caught.

"You damn near made it over that hill," Jebediah said, pointing in the direction Ian had been headed. "If you had gone a couple of stone throws beyond that, you would have stumbled right into our encampment."

Ian said, "Honestly, I don't know if I could have even made it that far. I might have suffered out here all night if you guys hadn't shown up."

"Nah!" Jebediah said. "The bears would've made it really quick."

Ian had to swallow hard, considering that scenario. He looked at them and said, "Another reason to be grateful to you guys."

"Think you might be strong enough to take a few more steps?" Jebediah pointed ahead.

"I suppose I could. Do you mind if I rest just a few more minutes?"

The men looked at one another, confirming. "Not a problem."

While Ian rested, the men didn't move. They stood over him, examining him. His uneasiness grew. He tried to change their focus by asking, "You never did tell me exactly what you were hunting?"

Jebediah plucked a straw of grass and began picking his teeth with it. "Oh, this and that. There's all kinds of prey out here."

Ian noticed that if they had any guns, they weren't visible. "What are you hunting with—just out of curiosity?"

"You mean our weapons?" Jebediah said.

"Yes."

Jebediah spit the grass out and said, "We hunt a little differently around here. Show him, Jangy."

Jangy unzipped his parka and opened it. A 12-inch blade hung from a knife holster.

Rhett unzipped and opened his parka, revealing a steel club the length of his forearm with sharpened spikes protruding from a spiked ball at the end.

Ian swallowed.

"You seem a little scared," Jebediah said.

"What were you hunting that you could get close enough to use those weapons?" Ian laughed nervously.

The men just watched him, smiling. Jebediah said, "We believe that using guns is cheating. Prey that dies by a man's bare hand is prey that lost a fairer fight. A hands-on kill achieved using brainpower is always more satisfying than a cheap kill using firepower."

Ian quietly stared at the ground.

"We best get going," Jebediah said. "You'll have plenty of time to rest." Jangy and Rhett zipped their coats and adjusted their backpacks.

The feeling of being in danger had become familiar to Ian these past days. In fact, he had felt numb to it and wondered if he was depleted of adrenaline. But blood-soaked hunters who apparently killed some still-unidentified prey with clubs and knives and who wanted to take him deeper into the wilderness to a camp he knew nothing about barely spiked his anxiety because of his exhausted helplessness.

"Need us to carry you, sir?" Rhett asked.

Jebediah flashed him an angry look.

Although Ian's feet were blistered and he was obviously exhausted, having these guys take hold of him wasn't comfortable. "If it's really just over that ridge, I think I can make it," Ian said. He climbed to his feet, gritting his teeth through the pain, and they began walking to the ridge.

They walked single file, Jebediah ahead of Ian, Jangy, and Rhett followed behind him. The trip to the ridge didn't take long, just as Jebediah had promised. Along the way, the men surprised him by offering encouragement, saying things like, "Almost there… You're walking strong… Just a bit further." When they reached the top of the ridge, Ian looked down, trying to spot their camp. At first, he saw nothing, and then his eyes focused on some structures almost entirely obscured by trees and foliage.

"There we go," Jebediah said. "It's all downhill from here. You could practically ride your ass down this slope if you didn't want to use your feet anymore."

"I can make it," Ian said. As they got closer, the outline of five barracks-like rectangular structures became more apparent. Three of them were in parallel, and two of them were offset perpendicularly. Their pattern matched precisely what Riddick had drawn on the map.

Thirteen

IAN'S FEET BURNED like fire. Combined with his exhaustion, he had to concentrate on each step to prevent his knees from buckling.

They reached the edge of the camp. Jebediah, Rhett, and Jangy spontaneously broke into song with no apparent trigger. The song was part musical and part chant containing lyrics about the joy of reaching home and something about being wiser for their journey and their hunt being prosperous. The oddity of the spontaneous song didn't bother Ian, as it was minor compared to the overall strangeness and the scariness of everything he had experienced these last days.

As they came to the door of the first building, Ian noticed the camp appeared to be abandoned, and the disrepair of the entire outpost became more apparent. Bushes and tall weeds enveloped the buildings. Some exterior walls were covered with a blanket of ivy over curled, weather-worn pale green paint. Trees buttressed most of the buildings, providing shade and plenty of concealment. Some branches scraped against the roofs. Ian wondered why they hadn't been pruned.

A narrow pathway, only apparent from slightly trampled debris, connected the first two buildings. They approached the entrance of the closest one. The men stopped singing.

Ian looked around and said, "Seems peaceful." It was the only statement he could make that sounded somewhat complimentary.

"We enjoy the seclusion," Jebediah said. He climbed two small steps to a shallow porch, opened the door, and motioned for Ian to enter.

Ian looked back. Rhett and Jangy pointed to the open door leading to the darkness. It made no sense to step into a dark building with these guys until he remembered they would be no more isolated inside a closed room than outdoors in this godforsaken wilderness. These men were in a position to do anything they wanted to him. Resisting was useless.

Ian winced, climbing the two porch steps, and stepped inside. The men followed him. Jebediah reached up and, after pawing in the darkness above his head a few times, pulled a thin chain for a single light bulb that illuminated a cramped room—a vestibule—only slightly larger than a walk-in closet. Each of the three other walls had a door. An overstuffed easy chair sat against the wall to Ian's right.

"How good does that chair look to you?" Jebediah asked.

"Like a long-lost friend," Ian said, laughing with relief that there were no apparent elements of torture in the room.

The men laughed, too.

"We're gonna go change," Jebediah said, resting his hand on the inside doorknob just to the left of the vestibule's entrance. "We'll leave the front door open for some fresh air. You rest awhile. We'll get you some bandages for your feet."

"Thank you." Ian gingerly positioned himself in front of the chair and fell back into it. Relief spread across his face when the weight came off his feet. "Any chance I could get a little more water?" he asked. "And if it isn't too much trouble, maybe a wet rag for my face?"

"You will be well taken care of," Jebediah said. He unlocked the door to the left of the entrance with a key and pushed it open to another dark space. Rhett and Jangy followed him in. Before closing the door, Jebediah said, "You wait here for a spell. We're gonna get you washed up right there in that chair." He closed the door.

Ian was alone. His emotional teetering between relief and terror with these guys added to his exhaustion. They gave every sign that they'd be helpful to him—so far, but he wondered what Jebediah meant by getting him washed up right here? Although injured and exhausted, Ian could fully wash himself. The implications of *we're gonna get you washed up* didn't sit well.

Ian looked outside the open front door to the leafy trees that had gone still as dusk darkened. He tried listening for any sound from the door behind which the men had disappeared, but heard nothing.

As his total helplessness sank in, the door suddenly opened, startling him. A woman entered carrying a tray. She wore shiny black work boots and a purple slip dress. The straps over her shoulders exposed beautiful skin, and her hair was pulled into a ponytail that fell to the middle of her back. She smiled and said, "Hi there, Ian!" like he was an old friend.

Ian raised his hand in a weak wave, unable to hide his surprise.

She thumbed over her shoulder at the door and said, "The guys filled me in about you."

Ian gave a slight nod, still examining her from head to foot.

She brought the tray and said, "Now, what's a more urgent treat: something to eat or fixing those feet?"

Ian thought momentarily, then said, "My feet are doing better now that I'm off them, so something to drink and a bite to eat would be great if that's okay."

"Fabulous! Let's serve a dish that's just as you wish!" She balanced the tray with one hand while she pulled down its support legs on either side. She set it on the chair positioned perfectly above his lap. Ice cubes clinked against a large glass of water, and condensation droplets slid down the sides. Ian stared at the tray, frowning.

"Is something wrong?" The woman asked as she took a step back.

"No, it's just—I didn't expect anything like this." Ian's tray held two plates, each with a polished silver cover. Silver utensils on cloth napkins were placed beside the plates.

"We are good to our guests."

"I see that," Ian said. "What's your name?"

"I'm Amity," she said with another smile, revealing perfect teeth.

"Hi, Amity. I'm bad with names, but I'll try to remember."

She tapped her head with her finger and said, "Think of Calamity without the Cal. But unlike calamity, Amity means pal."

Ian squinted at her, letting the words sink in.

Amity grinned. "Now you'll never forget it, right? My pleasure to meet you, Ian. Let's get you some sustenance."

She lifted the plate covers for him. Ian's mouth dropped open.

The larger plate contained roasted beef short ribs with celery root and sautéed stemmed shiitake mushrooms drizzled with a red wine sauce. The smaller plate had a crisp tossed green salad and a steamy, warm slice of sourdough bread.

Ian blurted an involuntary laugh, unable to believe what he saw. "What is this?" He gawked at the meal.

Concern spread across Amity's face. "I'm so sorry. Are you a vegetarian?"

"No, not that." Ian leaned forward and fanned the aroma to his nose. "This is extraordinary and smells absolutely delectable. The presentation is amazing."

Amity clutched her chest. "Whew!" She spooned some more of the sauce over the ribs. "I hope you enjoy it."

Ian couldn't stop grinning.

She took the cloth napkin, snapped it open, and draped it over his leg. "Have a taste," she said.

Ian took his fork and gently separated a piece of short rib that fell from the bone. He dabbed it in the sauce and then put it in his mouth. He sat back and closed his eyes, chewing only twice before drawing a deep breath through his nose. He covered his mouth with the napkin and said, "Oh my God. Unbelievable."

"You approve?"

Ian nodded emphatically. "I have to be honest. This isn't the camp food I'd expect."

"What did you expect?"

"I don't know—canned beans in a metal bowl, maybe a charred piece of corn on the cob, or even more trail mix would have been fine."

"We have all those ingredients if you'd prefer them."

"No! This is wonderful." Ian laughed. "Thank you."

Amity did a little dance with her hands raised and said, "Then we conclude that you'll love all our food."

"Hey, that was good! So, you like to make rhymes?"

"Yeah, I'm a rhymester. They've always come easily to me since I was young. I'm known for it out here. The guys tease me by coming up with phrases that only almost rhyme, just to grate on my nerves."

Ian laughed and took another bite of the short rib. He shook his head in amazement. He pointed his fork at the plate and said, "Did you cook this?"

"No, we're lucky enough to have a couple of former professional chefs here. They take excellent care of our tummies."

"Obviously. It's delicious. You better be careful how much you spoil me. I won't want to leave!"

"Oh, I think you will," Amity said, wagging her finger.

The statement startled Ian. The excitement about the food dissolved from his face. "I'm just kidding," he said. "I'll be on my way as soon as possible."

"No rush," Amity said. "We'll get you fixed up and back on your feet to running in no time. Meanwhile, enjoy our hospitality. One thing you'll learn about us is that we're rough and rugged outside. But inside, we strongly prefer luxury."

"Now that's a philosophy I can get behind!" Ian took a large bite of the salad and said, "Mmmm. What type of dressing is this?"

"It's a shallot, white-cranberry wine vinaigrette with a touch of sesame."

"I've never had anything like this," Ian said, covering his full mouth. After chewing, he added, "I used to have a restaurant, so I have a special appreciation for this type of culinary excellence."

"I'll be sure not to tell our chefs," Amity said. She leaned forward and whispered, "They're very competitive."

"They shouldn't feel any pressure. I was always proud of my dishes, but I didn't put out cuisine like this." Ian pointed his fork at the plate.

She went to the door. "Enjoy it. I'll be right back. Don't go running off."

Ian raised his feet. "I can almost promise you I won't be running anywhere. Even if I could, there's no way I'd run from a meal like this. Take your time!"

Amity said, "Good, just finish your meal and let your feet heal," as she exited.

He guzzled the cold water and then marveled again at the delectable meal. Having such exquisite cuisine in such a remote location was a strange juxtaposition. He wondered if the horrible food at Biding Wellness Center made this food seem more delicious than it actually was. He then wondered how they could have brought him the prepared food so quickly. He hadn't been sitting in the chair for two minutes before Amity arrived with the tray. Unless this was already on their menu for the evening, the thick cuts of short ribs would've required hours to become this tender. Even a pressure cooker would have required an hour to achieve this tenderness.

Amity returned about ten minutes later, pushing the door open with her foot before stepping into the room. She carried a bucket in one hand and, in the other, a basket full of bottled products and other supplies.

"Now that you've had some food to eat, it's time to let me work on your feet. Would you allow me to give them some relief?"

A slow smile spread across Ian's face. "I don't know how to explain the feeling I have right now, but it would be something like being snatched from hell and then dropped into heaven."

Amity laughed. She set the bucket and supplies beside his chair. "I'll take that as a yes!"

Ian was better positioned to see the items in the basket, including sponges, emery boards, brushes, lotions, ointments, soap bars, rolls of gauze, and other tools he couldn't identify. The water in the bucket exuded the scent of lavender. "You just happened to have these supplies for me?"

"Wouldn't that be something?" Amity winked at him while putting on some thin, transparent gloves. "Actually, since we have no vehicles, we don't spare any expense for foot care, since we depend on our feet for all transportation."

"Of course," Ian said, taking a big bite of salad.

"May I touch your feet?" she asked, pointing.

"Uh, I have to warn you, I'm disgusting and probably smelly. Maybe I should clean them first."

"Whatever condition your feet are in, I promise you I've seen much worse. If your feet are half as cute as you are, I probably won't smell them at all."

Ian stopped chewing and blushed.

"So, may I take off your shoes?"

"Sure," Ian said. He raised a foot. She gently slid his heel out before gently removing the whole shoe with skillful care to avoid rubbing his skin. "Was that okay?" she asked.

Ian nodded, taking a big bite of the warm sourdough bread.

Amity took off the other shoe and set them both aside. "May I wash your feet? I promise to be gentle."

"Okay," Ian said skeptically. The raw blisters on his sole and the worn skin on the sides of his feet were fully exposed. Unless the liquid in the bucket contained an anesthetic, he fully expected contact to sting like crazy.

She took his ankle, guided his foot over the bucket, and gently lowered it.

Ian gritted his teeth and closed his eyes, bracing for the searing sting. He felt soothing warmth envelop his foot. He opened his eyes. His foot was fully submerged. Ian's whole body relaxed. "Unbelievable," he said. "That feels fantastic."

"See?" Instead of wiping his foot in the water, she gently rocked his ankle back and forth, swishing his foot for over a minute to clean it with only the friction of the water. Then she draped a fluffy white towel over her knee, raised Ian's dripping foot from the water, and gently rested it on the towel. "Tell me if you feel pain, and I will stop." She lightly wrapped his foot with the towel, then slowly pressed the towel around his foot.

Ian smiled. He was amazed that the contact didn't hurt. "What's in that water? It feels amazing."

"A little bit of this and a little bit of that. Your feet will feel so good, you'll wonder why you sat."

"Cute. Secret concoction?"

"You might say that." She unwrapped his foot, pulled a squeeze bottle from the basket, and shook it. "May I apply some salve?"

"Of course," Ian said. "What is it?"

Amity squeezed a dab of yellowish gel onto her glove and rubbed her hands together. "It's something that will help your feet heal quicker." She gently drew her hands along the sides of Ian's foot and slowly massaged the salve into his skin, easing to feather-light pressure on his blisters. At one point, she stopped and closed her eyes for a moment. Despite the gloves, he felt the warmth of her hands on his feet. The soothing feeling spread up to his calf. She took a spool of gauze and wrapped his entire foot. She attached a thin, cream-colored adhesive sole to the bottom of the gauze for walking traction. She did the same with his other foot. When finished, she stood and said, "If you don't mind my asking, how much do you weigh—normally?"

"Normal–normal or normal lately?" Ian wiped his mouth on the napkin.

"What does that mean?" she asked, removing the gloves.

"My life has been rough lately, and it's affected my appetite. Some people are emotional eaters. I'm the opposite, so I've lost a lot."

"I take it from your appetite tonight that you're feeling much better." She pointed at his nearly clean plate. She stepped back and finger-framed him. "I'm gonna say you need to put about 21 pounds back on."

Ian chuckled. "Eating like this would make that easier." He sopped up the last of the sauce with the bread. "Anyway, my weight…" He wadded up his napkin and quietly looked down for a moment as memories of everything that led to the end of his relationship with Kate rushed back. He looked up at the single bulb in the ceiling, thinking while chewing.

"I'm sorry. I didn't mean to pry," Amity said.

"No, it's fine. Let's see… By the time I went to that hellhole, I had probably dropped over 10 pounds. The last time I weighed myself was at the gym about six months ago. I came in at 189 pounds."

"Why do you ask?"

"I might be able to wrangle up some clothing that fits you. What's your waist size?"

"33, last time I checked," Ian said.

She pointed to his feet. "And I'm guessing you wear a size 10."

"That's right—or 10 ½, depending on the make."

"Fantastic. I'll check with the guys. One of them should be a close match."

"I wouldn't want to take anyone else's clothes. I don't mind putting these clothes back on since I won't be here long."

"You really want to keep wearing the clothes the people at that horrible place forced you to wear?"

The urge to free himself from the symbolism of Biding Wellness Center's power over him suddenly grew stronger than his aversion to imposing on someone offering to share a set of clothing with him. "You make a good point," he said. Her comment about the extreme hike from Biding Wellness Center reminded him of Riddick's sacrifice and that Riddick had missed out on all of this pampering. A wave of sadness swept over Ian.

"Why the long face?" Amity said. "You're a survivor! That shouldn't make you sad or mad. You should be glad!"

"I am glad. It's just that there was another guy who escaped before me," Ian said. "He left directions to this camp, but because you haven't mentioned him. He must not have made it here."

Amity frowned. "Someone told you about our encampment?"

"Not specifically. It was a rough sketch." Ian pulled the crinkled map from his back pocket and handed it to her.

She stood and opened it, turning for more light. After examining it, she said, "The scale is way off, and our building arrangement isn't as precise as it could be." Her expression had gone cold. She folded it again and handed it back to Ian.

Ian remembered what Jebediah and the other men said about escaping from civilization. He realized that showing any proof that people on the outside knew of them wouldn't go over well. "Yeah, he could have been drawing directions to a completely different location. I guess I was lucky to be found by Jebediah and the guys." He placed the fork on his plate, that now had only the short rib bones and a few crumbs from the bread.

"Would you like more?" Amity asked.

Ian held up his hands. "I'm stuffed."

"Any chance I could convince you to try at least a bite of some dessert?" she asked.

Ian said, "You can't be serious!"

Amity placed her hand over her heart and said, "I promise you I wouldn't lie, cross my heart and hope to die."

Ian laughed. "I can't imagine how you would top off that meal. Since you have me so curious, I suppose I could go for something small. What do you have?"

Amity grinned at him. "It's a delectable surprise! Stay put."

Amity took off her gloves and exited through the door.

While she was gone, Ian examined her work on his foot. The gauze wrapping was pristine, woven around his foot in a perfect lattice pattern, not too loose or tight. The salve under it still felt warm, occasionally tingling. He set the food tray on the floor beside the chair and put some pressure on his foot. He was surprised to feel only the faintest hint of residual pain. He planted his feet side-by-side and pushed himself up onto them. There was a brief sting from the heel blisters, but it quickly vanished. Whatever treatment Amity had used on him had worked wonders to nearly eliminate the pain in a matter of minutes.

Amity returned, carrying a new tray.

Ian said, "You *have* to tell me what is in this potion you put on my feet."

"Do they feel better?" She said.

"They feel amazing." He raised his feet and wiggled his toes.

Amity said, "If I did your feet right, you'll heal overnight."

"How's that possible?"

"As I mentioned, we've had to master podiatry to survive out here." She set the tray down over Ian's lap. A tall, frothy glass of milk sat beside another silver plate cover. She lifted the plate cover, exposing a thick slice of chocolate cake infused with fresh raspberries and dusted with powdered sugar. A large dollop of vanilla ice cream slowly slid closer to the cake as its underside melted on the warm plate.

"You've got to be kidding me!" Ian said, gazing at Amity incredulously. "You shouldn't even be able to call this camping," he said.

"Please, taste it." Amity stepped back and clasped her hands under her chin, waiting for his verdict.

Ian took a bite and covered his chocolate-covered teeth as he laughed.

"Oh my God, this is so moist and rich. I can't believe it."

"I promise you can believe it, and there's plenty more where that came from if you can find room for it. Do you mind if I wait here with you while you finish?"

"Not at all, but I doubt I can finish this entire piece," Ian said. He forked another bite into his mouth.

"I won't force you." She went to the middle door that hadn't been opened yet and leaned her shoulder against it to face Ian. She crossed her boots and folded her hands.

"So, where are all the others?" Ian asked.

"Others?"

"The other campers." Ian took a drink of milk.

"Most are sleeping, getting ready for the dawn of night," she said.

"The dawn of night. I've never heard that term."

Amity said, "We follow an inverse time schedule. We sleep during the day, and at night, we play. Sunset is our morning."

"So, you got up early to help me?" Ian said, looking through the open door. Only the faintest glow was still visible through the trees.

Amity said, "Actually, I had trouble sleeping today and woke up early, so your timing was good."

"How many of you are out here?"

"That's a tough question. We regularly get newcomers. Sometimes, they stay for only a day, sometimes a month."

"After tasting your food," Ian pointed to the last bite of cake, "I don't know how you could stay only one day." Ian ate a last bite and chased it with a swig of milk. "I didn't think I'd finish it, but I couldn't resist. It was delicious. Thank you!"

"You're welcome." Amity came and consolidated his used plates and trays. She placed them all on the floor beside the mysterious door. Then she went to the center door and rested her hand on the knob. "As luck would have it, we have a spare room after one of our guests departed yesterday. Can you handle a few final steps for me?"

"Thanks to your magic salve, I believe I can." He pushed himself onto his feet and took several steps toward her. "A little sore with my full weight, but bearable."

Amity opened the door, reached in, and turned on a light. She grinned and said, "That's genuine progress. Take it slow. In no time, you'll run like a doe,"

Ian came to stand beside her. She pushed the door wider, motioning for him to enter it.

Ian stepped into a spacious, opulent room with hardwood floors. Centered on the far wall was an ornate wrought iron queen-sized bed flanked by designer bedside chests. A polished, matching credenza on an adjacent wall was positioned beside wall-mounted cabinets and a refrigerator. Full-length draperies were tied back to reveal a large picture window to his left. An open door inside the room led to a sizeable restroom, ornately tiled and sparkling clean.

"You people aren't allowed to call this camping," Ian said, grinning.

Amity laughed and said, "We don't."

Ian went to the window and cupped his brow to look outside. Although it was dark, he could see that the view was partially obstructed by bushes, but beyond the trees, he could make out the rough shapes of the other identical barracks-type structures separated by a wide easement.

A small table and two chairs were in the corner and held some water bottles and candy bars. Ian picked up a water bottle.

"Help yourself to the water and snacks. We'll tally them up for your bill when you leave."

Ian looked over his shoulder at her. She held her serious expression for a moment, then burst into laughter.

"You got me," Ian said, wiping his forehead.

"When we find lost travelers, our treats are free. We're good to our guests. You'll soon agree."

Ian pivoted, taking in all the amenities. He saw another door to the left of the bed. It had a keyed deadbolt. "Where does that go?" Ian asked.

"That's just some additional storage," Amity said. She pointed to the bathroom. "There are plenty of towels, a full supply of toiletries for you, and plenty of ice in the fridge."

"I can't imagine needing more. By the way, how does a person find out about this place?"

"A person doesn't," Amity replied, smiling.

"Are you all friends?"

"Yes. Close friends."

"So, how can I become a close friend?" Ian asked, laughing.

When Amity didn't appear to share his amusement, Ian stifled his laughter. He would love an opportunity to bring Kate here. She loved being out in nature and often jogged in the woods. He imagined her enjoying and raving about all the comforts of this place.

Amity leaned on a nearby wall. "The only visitors who see our encampment are the poor souls who've become lost and need our help. We do our best to show them our utmost kindness and hospitality. But to join our group, we are extremely private."

"So, my stumbling into your camp was my lucky accident, and I won't be allowed back."

"Correct."

"But what if I were to get lost annually?" Ian said, laughing.

Once again, Amity showed no amusement at his comment. She said, "We need to get you off those feet so they can rest."

"Actually, I'd like to wash up first." He took a few gingerly steps to the bed and tested the mattress for firmness.

Amity said, "You can strip out of those filthy clothes. I'll go check on getting you some new ones to wear. There's a robe hanging behind the bathroom door for you."

"Thank you," Ian said.

"My pleasure. Try not to get your bandages wet," Amity said as she exited the room.

Ian stepped into the bathroom. "Of course," he said out loud, once again amazed. Every fixture and surface was polished and pristine. A stack of towels lay fanned beside the sink. A faint and pleasant lemony fragrance filled the air. He closed the door and pulled the fluffy bathrobe from its hook while marveling at the five-star accommodations.

Ian felt the stress relief of total privacy without being incarcerated for the first time in days. While washing his hands, he almost didn't recognize himself in the mirror. Dirt smudged his face, some of it caked to a beard that was longer than he'd ever seen it. His weight loss from heartbreak before the intervention had been exacerbated by his stay at Biding Wellness Center. He must have burned thousands of calories during this journey through the wilderness to get here. He leaned closer to the mirror and turned his head to each side, examining a few scratches before he washed and cleaned his face with warm, soapy water. He watched the grime swirl down the drain with each squeeze of the washrag.

He put on the robe and carried his soiled Biding Wellness Center scrubs out to the room, where he was startled to see Amity. She sat on the bed, leaning back with her legs crossed. When she saw Ian, she feigned surprise and said, "I'm sorry, sir, but I was waiting for Ian. Like him, you're very lean, you can't be him, you're much too clean!"

Ian laughed. "I hadn't seen a mirror since my ordeal began. I really feel like a completely different man."

"It shows." Amity stood and picked up a glass of red wine that rested on the bedside table. "Please, taste," she said, handing him the glass.

As he took it, Ian said, "Unbelievable." After taking a sip, he drew air through his teeth.

Amity studied him. "Good?"

"Fantastic. What is it?"

"It's a 2014 Don Melchor Cabernet Sauvignon." She went and patted her hand on the bed. "I think it's time for you to get some rest. You must be exhausted."

Ian sighed. "I can't argue with that." He drank more wine and imagined Dagny watching him, imagining her fury over this delicious, intentional relapse. He wished she could see him now. He sat on the bed, smirking.

Amity took his wineglass.

He swung his legs up and leaned back, and his head sank into the overstuffed pillow. It exuded the scent of freshly laundered linen.

Amity set the wineglass on the bedside table.

It took only moments for Ian to become drowsy. His adventure-filled day of escape made sleep come easily. And with the good fortune to land in a place where he was pampered like a king, he dozed off with a smile on his face.

Fourteen

IN THE MORNING, Ian stirred and pulled his head from under the pillow. He grimaced from a throbbing headache and raised onto one elbow, looking around the room. It took him a few moments to get his bearings, refreshing his memory of where he was.

The drapes had been drawn, leaving only a narrow opening through which the sun's rays illuminated a line across the floor.

He looked down beside the bed and was surprised to see Amity curled up on the floor, wearing a white robe identical to the one he had donned in the bathroom the evening before. She wore a peaceful expression, a hint of a smile, with her eyes closed.

Ian flung back the comforter, discovering he was naked.

Amity stirred.

Ian pulled the comforter back over him.

Amity sat up, rubbing her eyes. She climbed to her feet, yawned, and stretched. "Good morning. It looks like you got a solid night's sleep."

"Right…" Ian said, distracted as he looked around the room, trying to remember removing his clothes. "Is that my robe?" he asked.

Amity looked down at herself. "Oops!" She wiggled her shoulders out from under the robe and let it drop. She smoothly caught it with one hand and held it out to Ian. She wore nothing underneath.

Ian tried to suppress his surprise as he took it, quickly changing his focus to the robe.

Amity turned and strolled to a cabinet on the other side of the room. She pulled out a purple dress on a hanger. It was the one she had been wearing yesterday—or an identical copy.

"You seem quite comfortable with me," Ian said, laughing nervously.

She removed the dress from the hanger and held it at her side. "Should I be afraid?"

"No, of course not. It's just—"

"Then my instincts keep their perfect record." She slipped the dress on with no bra, no panties.

"Did I miss something?" Ian asked, cocking his head.

"Such as?" She went to a chair at the corner table, sat, and began putting on her black boots.

Ian swung his legs out, keeping himself covered with the bedsheets. "Uh, I don't remember going to bed naked," Ian said.

"Of course you don't. You were immersed in some of the deepest exhaustion-sleep I've ever seen." She grinned at him. "What are you worried about?"

"I'm more puzzled than worried. It feels like I started a movie during the closing credits."

She laughed. "The full-length movie wasn't bad—most satisfying flick you've had."

The cute rhyme didn't console Ian. "Amity, listen, this is a little awkward, but I need to ask you directly. Did something happen last night... between us?"

"It depends on what you mean by the word 'happen.'" She crossed the room to him and leaned onto her knees. She put her face close to his. "I came in to check on you. You fell asleep in the robe. It had you sweating something awful, so I put on my gloves, slipped you out of it, and tucked you in." She stood. "If you're feeling self-conscious, you can relax. As phenomenal as that beautiful body of yours is, I was respectful."

"I didn't wake up through all that?"

Amity shrugged. "Seems I have a special touch. But you were so flaccid, and your breathing became so shallow that I took your blood pressure. By the way, you have the cutest snore. It's so hushed and peaceful. I could sleep with you forever."

Ian ignored the flirt. He rubbed his temples, trying to ease his headache and reconcile her explanation with any memory he could pull from the night before.

Amity watched his struggle and said, "I think it's fair to say you're officially worried."

"Sorry, I just..." Ian said, closing his eyes to enhance his recollection. "I remember lying on the bed and suddenly feeling more tired than I can ever remember. I can't recall anything after that."

Amity said, "Listen, you were severely dehydrated when you arrived at the encampment. I didn't want to alarm you, but I noticed that your mouth was dry, your eyelids were not supple, and I could feel the dehydration in your muscle tone while massaging your feet. I gave you a huge, high-fat meal, chased by some heavy carbs for dessert. Your body had no time to metabolize these nutrients before I offered you some rather powerful vino. I probably should have held off on that. I'm sorry."

"No need to apologize. It's just that wine has never hit me that way."

"We'll be more careful," she promised. "I stayed the night to keep an eye on you."

"Were you able to find a change of clothes for me?"

"They're waiting in the bathroom. If you'd like a shower, you can remove the bandages on your feet." She went to the door. "I'll be back with some breakfast."

"Thanks." Ian still looked puzzled as Amity left the room. When the door closed, he got up and went into the bathroom. He was amazed by how much better his feet felt. Walking was easier with almost no pain. He sat on the toilet and carefully unwrapped the gauze from his feet. The blisters had darkened like they had been healing for more than a few hours. The more prominent blisters remained only slightly sensitive to the touch, and the rest of the skin on his feet was soft and smooth. He wondered if he could hike out of the camp later today.

He turned on the shower and let the spray hit his hand. While he waited for the water to warm, the weirdness of his and Amity's nudity nagged at him. Physically, she was gorgeous. Her fit body reminded Ian of Kate, although Amity was taller with darker hair. Amity's attractiveness was more than the sum of her photogenic face, beautiful skin, and shapely figure. Something about her walk and posture exuded confidence and a commanding presence. As attractive as Amity was, Ian missed Kate. He longed to be back at home with her, to pick her up and spin her around, fulfilling the fantasy hidden in her redacted note.

He stepped into the spacious shower. The water didn't sting on his feet like it did on the many scratches and scrapes on his legs and arms. He noticed some pain coming from his wrist. He examined it and found a small red mark on the underside that looked at first glance like it might be a spider bite.

The shower felt glorious. He dried off and put on the clothes Amity had provided. The outfit included a neatly folded white cotton button shirt, blue jeans, socks, and underwear. He first held the shirt and jeans out, checking their length in the mirror. He tried them on. They couldn't have fit better.

After a last check in the mirror, he exited the bedroom and found Amity waiting on the bed. She smiled and said, "Fit, okay?"

Ian looked down at his outfit and said, "Perfectly. Where did you get these clothes?"

"I have a good eye for sizing up bodies. Your physique is a virtual clone of Sever."

Ian looked confused.

"Sever is one of our hunters—but you're 10 times cuter."

"Thank you," Ian said, blushing.

"I hope you are ready to eat. We scraped together a treat." She got up and led him to the corner table beside the window. The drapes were tied open, and the morning sun streamed in. A tall glass of orange juice sat beside a French press and a couple of covered plates on the table.

"I didn't consider how great that shower might feel to you, so I hope your food is not cold," Amity said. She pulled the cloth napkin from under the silverware and snapped it open.

"The shower felt wonderful. You're gonna tire of me asking about the stuff you put on my feet. They aren't fully healed, but I didn't expect to walk comfortably for at least a few days."

"I'll tell you what," Amity said, pulling his chair out for him. "If you let me re-wrap them while you're eating, I'll give you one of the salve's ingredients."

"I'll take that deal," Ian said.

"Great," she said. She turned the chair slightly so Ian could eat while she worked.

"Good," Amity said. She removed the silver plate covers. "This morning for breakfast, we have a stack of buttermilk pancakes, fluffy scrambled eggs, thick-cut bacon, a bowl of mixed berries, and a flaky croissant striped with a chocolate & honey drizzle."

Ian shook his head. "Does everyone at camp eat like this?"

Amity laughed. "We do enjoy our food, but to be perfectly honest, we don't all eat like this every day."

"Thank you. I feel special."

"You *are* special!" Amity said.

"I won't need that," Ian said, sliding a French press carafe aside.

"No coffee?"

"It's a weird thing about me. I don't like coffee. I don't even like the way it smells."

"I'm so sorry," Amity said. She picked up the French press from the tray and carried it away, setting it on the floor beside the door. She got some gauze and tape from her bag. As she returned, she said, "I was hoping you were the type to enjoy an exquisite brew. This one is special. One of our members recently visited Brazil and secured some Fazenda Santa Ines beans for us. They are out of this world."

Ian said, "I'm sorry if I've wasted something valuable."

"Don't worry," she said. "There's no way a drop of this coffee will go to waste with hungry hunters who will be thrilled to savor it. Now, let me see how those feet are doing." She kneeled in front of him. She leaned back and patted her hand on her thigh.

Ian put his foot there. He began eating while she carefully examined it from all angles, gently touching it in a few places. Then, she repeated the same examination with the other foot. "Your overnight progress was quick. A tad more rest is the trick," she said.

"Great. The pain has almost gone away, so I'd like to begin my hike today."

Amity laughed. "Nice rhyme. You're so silly."

"Actually, I'm not kidding," Ian said.

"I'm sure you'd love to rush back to so-called civilization, but let's not get ahead of ourselves." She began gently wrapping his feet. "Some of our hunters come back after a 20-mile trek. We bandage them up, and the next day, they decide to rip the bandage off because there's a new hunt they think they can't miss. We always warn them, but they sometimes fail to heed the warnings. Invariably, they never make it more than a few miles before the agony requires them to be carried back. This setback can triple their healing time, so you won't be going anywhere today, you adrenaline junkie." She caressed the top of one of his bandaged feet and said, "How does that feel?"

"Very comfortable."

"Fantastic." She got up and returned her tape and gauze to her bag.

Ian said, "Listen, Amity, I appreciate your concern for me and your fair warning about over-exerting myself, but isn't there any way a couple of the men could assist me back to town? I have family waiting, and I'm sure they are concerned."

"Our men are strong, but do you expect them to carry you the thirty miles back?" Amity giggled at the idea.

"It's 30 miles?"

"Yes, as the crow flies."

Ian knew he had probably hiked further than ever before, but didn't fathom it was 30 miles.

Amity squatted beside him. "Are you really eager to get back? I thought it was your family that committed you to that sadistic treatment center."

"True, but I'm sure they didn't know what was happening there. They will be as surprised as the authorities when I report these sadistic criminals."

"It was that bad, huh?" Amity said, grimacing.

"Worse than I've described. Another reason for my urgency is that I left other victims behind. The longer I take to get help, the more they suffer. I can cope with the pain if it means shortening the suffering of other innocent victims."

A slow smile spread across Amity's face as she looked into Ian's eyes. "That's so beautiful. You are willing to sacrifice your well-being for others?"

"Absolutely. Wouldn't you?"

"I like to think so, but you seem so sure of it." She tilted her head as she looked up into his eyes. "I can't tell you how attractive that is." She closed her eyes and drew a long breath through her nose, as if savoring some fine fragrance. When her eyes opened, she sighed and said, "I'm trying to help you, but I'm getting a feeling that you are the one who is heroic."

Ian smirked at her over-the-top gushing. He continued eating his delicious breakfast while Amity made his bed. The pain from his headache was diminishing. After Amity had discouraged him from attempting to leave today, he worked out a new plan for tomorrow.

Amity noticed him sitting perfectly still, looking out the window, and said, "Is everything okay?" she asked.

"It's so quiet," Ian replied. "I can't get over it. Where is everybody? I have yet to see anyone outside."

Amity tucked one pillow back into its case and then fluffed it up. "Don't forget our inverted schedule. She pointed to a clock on the wall that showed 8:50 a.m. It's bedtime for most of us."

"So, I must have gotten lucky that Jebediah, Rhett, and Jangy found me during the day."

"Correct. They found you at your dusk, which was their dawn."

"What's their game of choice?" Ian asked.

"Didn't Jeb tell you?"

"His answer was vague. On the way here, I saw plenty of deer, pheasant, and rabbits."

Amity said, "I can tell you the guys like this area because of the rich diversity of prey. We've hunted everything you just listed. Most of all, we simply love being in this paradise."

Ian forked a final bite of pancakes and smeared it around in the last bit of syrup. Amity's reference to paradise made Ian eager to see more of the outdoors. It would be great to sit outside and listen to the birds on an unrushed stroll without feeling the panic of being hunted. He wiped his mouth on the napkin and said, "You might not believe this, but I'm dying to walk outside."

"You're right. That surprises me," Amity said. "I wouldn't advise it."

"I suspected you might be worried about my healing. I'll be careful, and I won't go far. Some fresh air will do me good." He stood from the chair.

"Ian, I'd strongly advise you to rest a little longer. The men are sleeping and quite sensitive to sounds outside. Also, I want to ask that you not wander outside during the day."

Ian looked at her suspiciously. "You don't want me to go outside?"

Amity said, "Part of our commitment to keeping this encampment undisturbed is to make sure no visible man-made changes are visible from the sky."

"I don't understand," Ian said.

"Satellites," she said. "The rough landscaping you saw outside is by design."

Ian laughed, and then his mouth hung open. "Are you being serious?

Don't tell me you're here illegally."

"Of course not. This property is on state land. The structures are part of an outpost formerly used by the forest service. They've been abandoned for years. We've since respectfully used the property for our encampment. In fact, we've made substantial improvements within the structures at no cost to the taxpayers."

"So you're secretly squatting and concerned about eviction if you are discovered?"

"If I'm perfectly honest, yes."

"Wow, that explains a lot."

"Thank you for understanding. I need you to stay indoors for the time being. More than anything, I want you to heal so you're fit to run."

Ian said, "And I thought my mom was protective."

Amity laughed and came to him. "I know we haven't known each other long, but you are a wonderful man. Even though I may never see you again after you leave, I still want what's best for you, including a healthy journey *after* we completely replenish your reserves."

She stepped close enough to kiss Ian and looked up into his eyes. "All I ask is that you rest today. I promise it will make all the difference."

Ian said, "The bandages feel good. I guess a little more recuperation won't kill me."

Amity smiled. "Of course, it won't. Thank you!"

He went to the bed and sat.

While Amity cleared the table, stacking the dishes on the tray, she said, "After dark is a better time to explore outside, and I can have some hunters show you around then." As she crossed the room to leave, Ian got up from the bed and said, "Let me get the door for you."

Before Ian could reach her, Amity said, "No! Please rest!" She sidestepped to block the door.

"Okay," Ian said, a bit startled by her insistence.

Amity balanced the tray with one hand while she opened the door after fidgeting with the knob.

"Wait a minute," Ian said. "You promised to give me an ingredient." He pointed to his feet.

"Oh, right." She looked up and tapped her chin. "Here's one: toothache plant."

Ian frowned.

"Haven't heard of it?" she asked.

"Never."

"It's not common. The official name is *spilanthes acmella*. It's an antibacterial and antifungal herb. The nickname came from the mild numbing effect it brings while it disinfects."

"Amazing. Any chance you could tell me one more ingredient?"

She wagged her finger at him. "I promised you only one. You got it, so now we're done." She closed the door.

Ian went back to the window. He couldn't wait to get outside and considered sneaking out against Amity's wishes, especially since his feet felt great.

He used the bathroom and then flopped onto the bed, staring at the door to the small foyer where he had enjoyed his first meal, and Amity had bandaged his feet. The room felt a little stuffy. He wanted some fresh air, so he propped the door open for a while. He couldn't see how that would compromise the privacy these people wanted from Big Brother watching from the satellites.

He went to the door and turned the knob. The metal bulb of the knob spun loosely around the lock cylinder. He turned the knob in the opposite direction just as loosely. He tried pulling the door open while he turned it, but it wouldn't catch. He pulled the door harder, trying to force it open, but it was a heavy fire door, and the latch was solid.

He couldn't remember seeing Amity use a key to enter or exit the room. He stepped back from the door, staring at it, then searched a small nearby cabinet, hoping to find a key. He pounded on the door. "Hello! Amity? Is anybody out there?"

No answer.

Ian suddenly felt claustrophobic and became more determined to get some fresh air. He went to the window and pushed the draperies back to see the window's edge. He searched for a latch, but there was none. "You've got to be kidding me," he said, scanning the top and sides of the window frame. The thick glass panes were sealed entirely, with no way to open them.

He went into the bathroom and examined the small window over the toilet. This window, too, was sealed with no latch or handle to open it. He leaned against the sink, rubbing his chin.

The broken doorknob could be a coincidence. But the locked windows lessened that likelihood. Being unable to leave the room created a rather severe fire hazard. If trapped, Ian would have to break the window to escape. Although the idea was far-fetched, he wondered if the locked door and windows were by design. Considering the hospitality they had been showering on him to speed his recovery, it made no sense that Amity and the guys would keep him trapped in a room that had no emergency exit. Still, his concern about that possibility grew.

From its outward appearance, the camp showed every sign of having been abandoned. The absolute privacy of its location made it ideal for any activity these people wished to engage in, with virtually zero risk of discovery.

Even the slightest possibility of being in danger with these people got Ian's heart pounding. He needed some answers. He knew Amity would return soon with lunch. If something sinister was going on, he might have an advantage by concealing his knowledge of it. Rather than confront her directly, he decided to play it safe to see what he could observe first. He'd watch her when she returned to see how she opened the door and how closely she guarded it. Her visits so far had been alone, and he could easily overpower her to get out if necessary. The problem was that if he overpowered her and made it outside, escaping all the way back to town was daunting. In his condition, the other hunters' help was necessary to find his way out and critical to helping him if he physically couldn't make it.

He laughed at his own paranoia. The possibility that these were bad people made no sense in the context of their kindness. He felt a twinge of shame for assuming the worst in them. He imagined having a good laugh with Amity about his inadvertent imprisonment.

He stretched out on the bed for a couple of hours, getting up only to check the window and to use the bathroom. His visits to the window revealed nothing but the same trees, bushes, and other dilapidated barracks. Eventually, he heard something outside the door. He sat up on the bed and scooted back against the headboard. He crossed his legs and tried to put on a casual expression.

Amity pushed the door open with her elbow while carrying another tray. "Hello, traveler," she said.

"Hello, Dr. Amity," he replied. They laughed. Ian noticed she carried no keys in her hand. He quickly checked the door's outside knob. It was a different color.

"Lunchtime!" Amity said. I hope you're hungry. She carried the tray to the corner table.

Ian swung his feet off the bed.

"Sounds good. What gourmet grub have you brought this time?"

Amity removed the plates from the tray, positioning them and the utensils on the table. "I hope you'll enjoy it. And you'll be happy to see that I haven't tortured you with the sight or smell of coffee."

Ian watched the door slowly close, latching on its own. He wished he could run to it and prop it open. He got up and went to stand beside her.

Amity pulled the table's chair out for him and said, "It's time to have a treat. Please come take a seat. Your lunch today, displayed on a tray, includes a special meat."

Ian sat, too distracted to be impressed by her rhyme.

Amity snapped open a napkin and draped it over his leg. "To start, we have a crisp, chilled green salad with frisée, roasted beets, hard-boiled eggs, sunflower seeds, and a balsamic vinaigrette." She lifted the larger plate's cover. "For your lunch entrée, we have a grilled swordfish with a homemade hunter's Romesco sauce over wild rice. I'm keeping your lunch's dessert light today." She tapped her finger on a covered bowl. "Under this, we have a simple wine-poached pear with a dollop of crème fraiche."

Ian looked at the delectable offerings and said, "Simply amazing." While Ian began eating lunch, Amity made the bed for him, smoothing every wrinkle from the comforter.

He was tempted to just ask her about the door. Enough time had passed after she brought lunch to avoid appearing panicked about it. But what if his far-fetched hunch was correct? He decided to get more info by asking some unrelated questions first.

Ian said, "So, do you guys have a better map for me so I can get back to town?"

Amity stood and put her hand on her hip. "Why would I give you a map when I don't want you to leave?"

"Excuse me?" The answer sent prickles down his back.

"You haven't figured out that you're my prisoner?"

Ian stared at her. He felt his mouth going dry.

Amity fell onto the bed, clutching her stomach, laughing.

"What's funny?" Ian said.

She rolled to her other side and, after catching her breath, said, "I wish you could have seen your face. You'd think I was from outer space!"

"Hilarious," Ian said, not sharing Amity's enjoyment at the joke.

"You actually believed me?" she said.

"I admit you had me going for a minute. That was a little creepy."

"I'm sorry," she said, still giggling as she got up from the bed and smoothed the top again. "That one gets them every time."

"What do you mean by 'them?'"

"Pardon?"

"You said 'gets them every time' like it's a regular joke."

Amity paused. "No, by 'them,' I meant my patients. I haven't told you I used to work as a nurse's assistant. If the situation was right, I would joke that they were my prisoners. Some men thought I was cute, so they would say they were happy to be my prisoner. It was all just silliness, pure and simple."

"About the map," Ian said, returning the conversation to his question.

"No, I don't have a map for you. The guys have every tree and trail memorized. Carrying a map is too risky. It would reveal our location if it were to be lost and then discovered by outside hunters—or anyone."

"Amity, I have to tell you that for people who don't want visitors, you're incredibly hospitable and beyond generous with your care and food."

She squinted at him and said, "You sound suspicious."

"I admit I'm having a little difficulty understanding it. Considering your extreme measures to maintain privacy, I'm surprised to have been treated so well."

"We have an ulterior motive," she said.

"Oh?" Ian swallowed and folded his hands under the table, squeezing them.

Amity stood from the bed and strolled toward Ian, stopping to lean against the wall. "You arrived exhausted and injured. We don't have a vehicle to transport you back to so-called civilization. The sooner you are well enough to return on foot, the sooner we regain our privacy. The more rest you get, the better your nutrition, and the quicker we can get your feet healed, the sooner you can be on your way."

"When you put it that way, I feel more like an unwelcome interloper."

"Don't feel bad. Besides valuing our privacy, we believe we have an obligation to help others. We're good people."

"That's great to know!" Ian said, visibly relieved.

Amity looked over her shoulder at the door and then back at Ian. "It's broken."

"What's broken?" Ian asked.

"The doorknob. You've looked at it six times since I returned to your room."

"Oh, the door… Yes, I was wondering about that."

Amity stepped closer. She crossed her arms. "Are you afraid?"

"What would I have to be afraid of?" Ian answered her question with a question he hoped she couldn't answer.

Amity slowly nodded while studying Ian's face. He felt like she was looking straight into his brain.

She broke her stare and glanced back toward the doorknob. "We didn't build this place," she said. "We improved it a great deal, but renovations are ongoing." She went to the door. "Some old hardware, like this old doorknob," she pressed her fingers against it and spun it, "remains in place. Eventually, we'll get it fixed."

"How do you open it?"

She swatted her hand toward him. "With a key, silly!"

Ian said, "Any chance I could borrow the key, or we leave the door open? Being locked in makes me uneasy—you know, with the fire hazard of it and all."

"You're right. I hadn't thought of that. I'm so sorry! You poor thing. If you had said something to me earlier, I could've prevented the stress you must be feeling. Of course, I will leave it open for you."

"God, that is such a relief," Ian sighed. He covered his face and laughed through his hands. "I didn't know what was going on with that!"

"I don't blame you," Amity said. "But all's well that ends well."

Amity clasped her hands in a prayer sign, closed her eyes, and bowed before looking up to the ceiling and saying, "Thank you." She came back to Ian. "Come to think of it, I'm surprised you discovered the doorknob so soon. Truthfully, when I saw the condition of your feet when you first arrived, I expected you to remain in bed with no urge to walk on them for at least another day. If I hadn't done such a good job healing you, we wouldn't have had the small doorknob scare."

"Interesting," Ian said. "My feet do feel great. I understand you don't want me walking around outside during the day, but could I just stand on the porch for some fresh air?" He pointed to the door.

Amity said, "I don't see why not." She thought for a moment and said, "Hold on." She went to the door. This time, Ian saw her pull a key from her dress pocket. She deftly slid it into the lock cylinder and opened the door with barely a sound. "I'll be back in a moment."

"Wait, the door!" Ian said as it closed.

He heard Amity's footsteps fade away. After a couple of minutes, Ian heard them re-approaching. He heard Amity briefly speak to someone outside.

Amity reentered, carrying some black work boots like hers. "Guess what?" she said.

Ian said, "You scared me again. Can you leave that door open?"

"Oh, sorry. Guess what?" Amity repeated.

"What?" Ian played along, expecting a rhyme.

"Not only can you get some fresh air, but I'm also taking you on a walk." She dropped the boots and a pair of thick socks on the floor beside Ian's feet.

"I heard you talking. Is there someone out there?" Ian asked.

"There are many of us out here. I just had a quick word with another member." She kneeled and said, "May I help you get into these boots?"

"I think I can handle that myself," he said. "So, you refer to the others here as members?"

"Did I say members? I meant campers."

"Is your group of campers a type of club?"

"Tell me how they feel," Amity said, ignoring the question. She gently patted the boot Ian had just put on.

"Perfect fit."

"Fantastic, let's go." She led him into the vestibule and pushed open the front door to the outside. Fresh air rushed in. Ian breathed deeply and said, "Ahhh, that's what I've been waiting for." He stepped outside and made a turn toward one of the other buildings.

"No, not that way," Amity whispered.

"Why are you whispering?" Ian said.

"Shh!" She leaned close to his ear and whispered, "Our men sleep with their windows open. We can't wake them. Follow me. I have something special to show you." She led him down a narrow path flanked by heavy vegetation and tree limbs, creating a virtual canopy over them. They walked about thirty meters from their building to a rectangular gazebo with canvas flaps rolled up on each side. The roof consisted of chopped tree branches, and weeds were stacked atop a grid of wooden poles.

A shiny silver material lined the perimeter of the roof. Ian had noticed the same material around the edge of the other structures' roofs. It was almost impossible to see from a distance, but the odd feature became conspicuous when standing close to it.

They climbed several steps to the gazebo's platform. Four wooden chairs faced toward the camp. Amity sat and said, "Let's wait here for a spell." She patted her hand on the seat beside hers.

"My feet feel okay. I could actually handle going a little further before we rest," Ian said.

Amity checked her watch and said, "No, this is far enough for now."

Ian decided not to argue. He sat and took in the beauty of the surroundings. The gazebo was positioned at the end of the easement that dissected the group of buildings.

Ian leaned back. "So, where are you from, Amity?"

"Tennessee—originally. The Memphis area."

"How in the world did you end up out here?"

"It's a long story." She folded her hands in her lap.

"The way you're forcing me to rest to recover, I have plenty of time to listen."

Amity laughed and said, "First, why don't you tell me more about you?"

"Fine, I'll lead by example. I'm an open book." Ian opened his arms, inviting her questions.

"What motivates you?" she said.

Ian smiled. The question came so quickly. It was as though she had prepared for it. "My motivation… Let's see," he interlocked his fingers behind his head. "Lately, my primary motivation has been to survive."

Amity nodded slowly. "I love that answer."

"Why?"

"Because the people I admire most have overcome extreme hardship and survive against the odds."

"Right before I arrived at your camp, I never felt closer to losing my survival battle. The nurturing and hospitality you've shown me have erased that worry. I can't thank you enough."

"You don't need to thank us. We'll have you on your way in no time."

Ian shifted in his seat to face her. "Speaking of that, if it's not too much trouble, can you find out from Jebediah or one of the others when they could help me get back to town?"

"Certainly I can. I'm sorry we haven't pinned down a specific time for you, but I think the guys will be flexible. I'll be sure to update them on your speedy progress, and we'll get a trip onto the calendar."

"Thank you," Ian said, visibly relaxed by the answer. "I told you about my motivation. Now, maybe you can answer the same question for me."

Their conversation was interrupted when they noticed someone exit the front door of the building where Ian's room was.

The man looked both ways and spotted them in the gazebo. Amity raised her hand. The man headed their way.

As he got closer, Ian soon recognized that it was Jebediah. He had cleaned up, and his beard was washed and combed. He wore a denim jacket, a purple plaid shirt, blue jeans, and cowboy boots. His hair was still wet and combed straight back.

"How goes it?" He said as he climbed the steps to join them. Ian noticed his necklace. It looked like a miniature silver machete with a loop threaded to a silver chain. He reached down and plucked a straw of grass before pinching it between his teeth.

"Ian felt a little stir crazy," Amity said. "We're just enjoying a few minutes of outdoor air."

Jebediah's boots clopped onto the gazebo's wooden floor. Instead of taking a seat, he stood off to one side, leaning against a beam. He crossed his arms and, smiling down at Ian, said, "Something wrong with the air in your suite?"

"Suite," Ian said, laughing. When Amity and Jebediah didn't join him, Ian cleared his throat and said, "No, not at all. The air is wonderful in there. I just wanted to be outside for a bit."

"Is this okay?" Amity asked, looking up at Jebediah.

"It's fine, as long as you're careful," he replied, chewing the grass as he turned his back to them, scanning the property.

"Careful?" Ian said.

"About being seen, remember?" Amity said.

"Oh, right."

Jebediah spat the grass out and said, "So, Amity tells me you'd like a tour of our encampment." He looked at Amity for confirmation.

She suddenly looked concerned.

"Is that true?" Jebediah asked Ian.

"My feet are feeling better. I'm willing to see anything you are willing to show me."

"Sounds like a polite enough request to me," Jebediah said, stepping down from the gazebo to the path.

"Are you sure, Jeb?" Amity said.

"It's fine," he said, waving off her concern before he motioned for them to follow him.

Amity and Ian walked in line behind Jebediah back toward Ian's room. When they got to the porch, Ian continued walking toward the center of the easement.

"Whoa!" Jebediah said. "We're going back in here, partner." He pointed inside.

Amity hurried ahead of them and opened the door for Ian.

Ian came back, looking confused. "Sorry, I thought you were going to show me around."

"Patience, young man. Follow me."

In the small entry room, Jebediah opened the mystery door behind which he had seen Rhett, Jangy, and Amity had disappeared when Ian first arrived. The space behind it was dark.

Jebediah stepped in.

Amity held out her hand, motioning for Ian to follow.

When he stepped through the door, he saw they stood on a short landing at the top of a staircase. The ambient light from the entry room wasn't strong enough to reveal what the darkness concealed at the bottom of the stairs. Ian's concerns about ulterior motives rushed back. There was no comfortable reason to descend steps into pitch darkness with these people. Ian felt he had every reason to panic.

Fifteen

IAN'S TREPIDATION TOOK a stronger hold on him as he looked into the darkness. He stalled and said, "I didn't know this door led to a basement," Ian said, remaining at the top of the landing.

"So far, you're saying all the right things," Jebediah said, having descended halfway down the staircase. "Come on down."

Amity coaxed Ian from behind, saying, "Try to keep up."

"Any chance you could turn on a light? My eyesight isn't the best."

"There are no lights, but you'll find that you can see well enough when you reach the bottom."

Ian slowly descended the stairs. His heart thumped as his wide eyes tried to adjust to the darkness. He heard Amity's boots behind him. Jebediah had disappeared ahead of them. They didn't enter a basement at the bottom of the stairs but a narrow, dimly lit, dirt-floor tunnel, its walls shored up with wood beams. The shoulder-height ceiling required them to hunch over as they walked. Jebediah was correct that Ian could see a few feet ahead, but not much further.

After about twenty paces, Jebediah stopped, pointed to a door in the tunnel wall, and said, "Open it."

"Excuse me," Amity said, easing past Ian. She produced some keys and unlocked a wooden door's deadbolt.

Jebediah pulled the door open and reached inside, feeling around in the darkness. After hearing a click, a bulb mounted just inside the door illuminated a storage room. "You can look in here," Jebediah said.

Ian leaned in. Wall shelves were stocked with paper towels, plastic bags, and stacks of clothing. On another wall were more of the tall, closed cabinets like the one in his room.

"All of our basic supplies are in this room," Jebediah said. "You'll see more of this room later."

Ian leaned back out.

Amity locked the door.

"If you don't mind my asking, why do you need to lock this door?"

"Some items in this room are prized among our hunters. We don't have a problem with theft, and I don't believe any of us would steal, but the keys make sure of it."

They continued along the tunnel. About forty more paces and they came to the foot of another staircase. Jebediah led them up the stairs, and when all three had reached the top landing, Jebediah rested his hand on the doorknob and said, "This is our recreation center." He opened the door to a wide-open floor-plan. One side of it was set up as an auditorium, with approximately fifty chairs positioned for an audience to face a small stage. The center of the room had a pool table, several recliners, and some card tables with stacks of games. At the far end, two doors were marked as men's and women's restrooms and two more doors were unmarked. All the windows in the recreation center had rolled shades pulled down. The sunlight that slipped through the cracks along the windows' edges created enough ambient light to see some detail in the room.

Ian stepped further into the room, looking around. "How many people are out here?" he asked.

"It varies," Jebediah said. "Sometimes five, sometimes 100 or more."

"So, you get 100 people out here with no transportation?"

"The arduous journey keeps our members self-selecting."

"Members?" Ian asked, looking at Amity.

Jebediah noticed this and said, "Campers. I meant campers. Our interests are so similar we might as well be members of something together."

Ian saw wall plugs. "How do you get electricity?"

"We have a solar array outside."

"I didn't even see them," Ian said.

"Excellent," Jebediah said. "Then we've constructed them properly."

"Aren't you worried they would be discovered—from the sky?"

"The actual solar cells are camouflaged to blend in with the terrain. They are impossible to see from the sky. Let's continue."

They walked through the recreation center to a door on the opposite end. Jebediah opened it to another staircase that descended with the same type of stairs to the same type of tunnel, continuing another thirty strides to another set of ascending stairs.

At the top, they entered another large room. It has several long rows of tables and a buffet-style serving counter on one end. The faint smell of food lingered from a recent meal.

"This is where we dine," Jebediah said. "We call it the Sustenance Center."

"Is the chef here? Because I don't mind admitting that I'm a little star-struck. I'd be honored to meet him or her."

Jebediah glanced at Amity.

She shrugged.

Jebediah said, "Maybe some other time. Everyone is asleep." He looked at his watch. "We need to wrap this up."

They passed through the dining area and another door, following the same sequence of descending steps, the tunnel, and ascending steps. When they reached the top of this landing, Jebediah turned back and whispered,

"Don't speak and walk softly in this next area. The men are sleeping and need their rest."

Ian nodded in agreement before Jebediah held the doorknob firm to turn it quietly. He leaned inside, looked around, and stepped in, motioning for Ian and Amity to follow.

Once again, the dim room was lit only by slivers of light that seeped around the drawn window shades. Neat rows of bunk beds reminded Ian of the large rooms he had seen on TV that served as sleeping areas in some prisons. Every bunk was occupied by a sleeping man. As Jebediah, Ian, and Amity crept between the bunks toward the opposite side of the room, a couple of the men stirred. One of them sat up and looked at them, and rolled over.

They exited the sleeping quarters, and Jebediah quietly closed the door behind them.

"Are there any other women here?" Ian whispered as they descended the stairs.

Amity said, "More than one woman would be a crowd. That's why I'm the only one allowed."

"Seriously?" Ian replied, stopping to look back at her.

"She got you," Jebediah said.

Amity covered her mouth and laughed.

Jebediah said, "I'm about to answer your question." He pointed forward.

They followed the tunnel, and at the top of the next staircase, Jebediah turned back and said, "Same rule here. Please don't talk while we're in there."

He quietly opened the door, and they went in. There were fewer bunks than in the men's quarters, and the bunks were lined against the walls, creating a wide-open space in the center. Against the back wall was a large ornate king-sized bed pedestaled waist-high. Its taut, pristine bedspread was perfectly made, ornamented with pillows. Polished bedside tables on either side of it held decorative glass lamps.

As they crossed the room, one woman stirred and sat up. She covered her mouth. Then, the other women woke up one by one and sat up to see the visitors.

Amity pointed at an empty lower bunk near the door toward which they were walking and then pointed to herself, indicating where she slept.

"Back to sleep, precious ladies," Jebediah said.

As they exited, Ian heard a faint giggle from one woman. After closing the door behind them, Jebediah said, "It looks like you have some fans."

"They know about me?"

Amity said, "Word travels faster than lightning here. Especially when it involves a cute lost traveler."

At the bottom of the stairs, they took the tunnel for a longer distance this time. Jebediah stopped at another door and said, "Open it."

Amity eased past them with her keys and unlocked the door's deadbolt.

Jebediah stepped in and turned on the lights. He held the door open for Ian to enter and motioned for Amity to follow.

Ian assumed they had entered another storeroom until he realized they were standing in the first storeroom of the tour, having entered it from the opposite side. From this side, he saw many more supplies hidden behind a partition. Neat rows of metal hooks held a variety of weapons, including knives, spears, and spiked clubs. More hooks held coiled ropes and several rows of unusual goggles on the adjacent wall. A wall cabinet had a grid of open compartments, each containing a pair of leather gloves and black boots like those Amity wore. A large lidded red barrel was labeled *Bleach*. Above it, shelves extended to the ceiling, full of rags, scrub brushes, and other cleaning supplies.

Amity closed them in and locked the door's double-key deadbolt when they were all in the room.

Ian looked up and saw wiring zigzagged in a pattern covering the entire ceiling. Small, red boxes were spaced approximately every meter on the wire.

"What is that?" Ian said, pointing up at them.

Jebediah said, "Did Amity explain our desire for privacy to you?"

Ian nodded.

Jebediah strolled across the room, tapping his lips, seeming to contemplate the best response to Ian's question. He leaned against a countertop and said, "This property will probably be reclaimed by the government at some point, and we'll have to leave. We're prepared to do that. We call it our Exodus. Without advance notice, we can't possibly evacuate with all our belongings. And we cannot allow our belongings to be pillaged. So, this room has some incendiary devices we can trigger remotely. The locked doors ensure time for ignition to succeed and flames to take hold."

"I understand," Ian said. He was equally intrigued and terrified by the scenario. At least something about their privacy was making sense. These people seemed to be odd types of doomsdayers. Ian decided not to ask the new questions that further fanned his desire to leave. His attention went to several rows of goggles hanging on the wall.

Jebediah saw what he was looking at and said, "Night is our day. Those use infrared technology to enhance our vision."

"Interesting," Ian said. As he continued looking around the room, he noticed no firearms.

"So, now you've told me how you hunt at close range. Obviously, you hunt only after dark, but you still haven't told me what you hunt."

"I know," Jebediah said.

"Is it a secret?" Ian asked.

"Not everyone would agree with our hunts," Jebediah said.

The answer gave Ian no comfort. "Animal rights activists?" he said.

"No, nothing like that." Jebediah's persistent vagueness triggered more alarm in Ian. The camp, its secrecy, and the engineered self-destruction gave it a cultish, militant feel. The layout of the camp, the secret underground passages, the male-female segregation, and primitive weapons all boosted Ian's urgency to get away from them and get home.

"I'll tell you what," Ian said. "Thank you for showing me around. I'm grateful you've been so open with me, but I think I'd like to lie down."

"Suit yourself," Jebediah said. "Maybe you'll join us on a hunt on our way back to town. You can see us in action for yourself. First-time hunters always get a rush from it."

Amity looked at him, surprised.

Ian said, "That would probably be a great time…"

Jebediah laughed.

Amity turned away, shaking her head.

Ian ignored that he missed the joke. "…but I would like to return home as soon as possible."

Jebediah grinned. "No doubt you would, but we've got to heal your paws before you can run on a hunt. How are they feeling?"

"So far, so good," Ian said. He gently marched in place several times and gave a thumbs-up sign.

Jebediah led them out the door on the opposite side Amity had first opened at the beginning of the tour.

Amity unlocked the deadbolt, then closed and locked it after they had exited the tunnel.

"It's past my bedtime," Jebediah said. "Godspeed for your healing. If things go well, the guys and I will plan a trip to town. Whenever that happens, we'll make sure you're with us."

"Fantastic! Thank you—and thank you for the tour," Ian said.

"My pleasure."

"See you, Jeb," Amity said.

She led Ian up the staircase to the vestibule outside Ian's room. Amity picked up a large bag and slung it over her shoulder. Ian hadn't noticed the bag on the way out. He saw her subtly insert a key into the doorknob to open the door.

They entered the room.

"Can I hold that key while I'm here?" He pointed to her hand.

"How would I enter your room?"

"If you knock, I can let you in."

Amity laughed. "That would work, in theory. But this is a master key." She raised it for him to see. "For security reasons, I couldn't leave it with you. I'll tell you what, though. Tonight, after dark, I'll leave the door wide open for you, and you can explore outside to your heart's content." Amity dropped her bag on the floor beside the corner table. "Do you mind if I hang out with you for a bit?" she asked.

Ian felt tired, and although he preferred quiet privacy, he didn't want to be rude. "Sure, but I must warn you I might fall asleep."

"I'd love that," Amity said, grinning.

"You would?"

"Allowing yourself to fall asleep under the care of someone you barely know shows a willingness to express vulnerability. It's beautiful, really."

He sat on the bed, staring at her as she smiled. Her emoting over his vulnerability only fanned his anxiety.

Amity went to her bag beside the table and said, "I'm so excited! I'm beginning a new puzzle. I'll work on it while you rest." She pulled out a box and took it to the table.

"I might've guessed you are into puzzles," Ian said.

"Why?"

"Being a rhymester, you enjoy matching words. I could assume you also enjoy matching puzzle pieces."

"What a perfect read of my personality," Amity said, dumping the puzzle pieces onto the table. She began flipping pieces so they were all right-side up.

"What's the puzzle of?" Ian asked.

Amity read the box. "It's called A New Dawn. I love the symbolism of a fresh, new start."

"Nice," Ian said. He hoped her work on the puzzle would give him some quiet time. While resting, he reviewed what he had seen on the tour. He had noted that while traveling through the consecutive tunnels, they had made only right turns, following a circuit that had taken them full circle back to the second door of the storage room. He marveled at the ingenious labyrinth these people used to move from building to building, concealing any visible sign of their presence from the outside.

"So, what do you think of our encampment?" Amity asked, rearranging the puzzle pieces.

"Your modifications are amazing. Thank you for showing me. I noticed that, so far, everyone I've seen is thin. Is that a rule?"

"Thinness isn't a requirement, but if you reach our encampment on foot, you're probably thin. Some of our members were heavier when they arrived. Now we're all lean, like you." She looked up and smiled.

"I also noticed that there aren't any children."

Amity laughed. "Who would force a child to hike all the way out here? That would be cruel and unusual!" She shook her head, amused by the question.

"I guess that's understandable," Ian said.

"And what if a child needs more medical care than we could provide? Tell me, would you force a child to come out here?"

"When you put it like that, I understand."

"We wouldn't do that," Amity said, briefly widening her eyes at the idea's absurdity.

Ian rested with his eyes closed, but didn't sleep. Amity worked on her puzzle for nearly two hours, occasionally saying, "Aha," when she found a matching piece. Ian's desire for some alone time grew. He wished there was a comfortable way to ask Amity to leave without offending her.

"How's it going on the puzzle?" he finally said.

"Fantastic. I'm over halfway finished."

"How many pieces is it?"

"1,500."

"Wow, you work fast."

"Some things come easy for me."

"Listen, I appreciate your attention and willingness to keep me company, but I feel like I'm pulling you from other, more important things."

"Nothing is more important for me now than to take care of you." She winked at him.

As impressive as her care was, Amity's doting and almost constant presence felt stickier by the hour. "Shouldn't you be asleep this time of your day?" he said.

"I have insomnia, and I'd actually like to cure myself of it. If I can synchronize my sleep cycle to yours, it'll be easier to help you."

Ian's social claustrophobia surged. He said, "I don't plan to be here long enough for that. You can take off. I promise not to run away."

"That's what they all say," Amity said, chuckling.

The statement sent chills again. Ian sat up. "They all?"

"Guys—guys always say they won't run away, but if that were true, I would have one today."

"That's difficult to believe," Ian said. "You're an attractive woman, witty and smart. I'd think any man would be lucky to be with you."

"You really think so?" Amity said, standing from her puzzle to look at him.

"To be fair, I don't know you well. That's just my first impression," Ian said, tempering his praise.

Amity looked at the puzzle again and said, "I think I'm a catch, too. But guys always freak out and run—eventually. You'd be perfect for me."

"I wouldn't be so sure," Ian said, his mind racing for a way to control the conversation's trajectory. "Besides, as great as you are, my girlfriend would probably have something to say about that."

"You never mentioned a girlfriend."

"I wasn't trying to be secretive. It simply never came up."

"How long have you been together?" Amity's tone was flat.

"Just under five years. We recently split up, but now we are getting back together again."

"How did she do that?"

"Pardon?"

"How did she get you back after you broke up? What did she do?" Amity studied his face.

"Honestly, she took me back with only minimal begging!"

Amity stared for a few moments, processing something. And she returned to the puzzle. "I'd hang my mom from the nearest tree to have a guy who'd beg for me."

"What the hell? You can't be serious!" Ian said.

Amity didn't respond, using both thumbs to insert a puzzle piece into place.

Ian got up. "I think I'll take a shower."

"Do you want some help?"

"Pardon?"

"Your bandages… Do you want help to remove them?"

"Oh, right. I can take them off."

"Enjoy your shower," Amity said. "If there's anything you want from me, I'm all yours."

Ian closed himself in the bathroom. Amity's attention had risen to the level of smothering. He unwrapped his feet and slipped into the warm shower stream. He took his time, staying in the bathroom longer than usual, extending his temporary privacy for as long as possible. He dried off and put on a fresh bathrobe that he found behind the door.

When he reentered the bedroom, Amity was gone. He went to the door and spun the loose doorknob. "Dammit," he said. Amity had taken her bag, too.

He went to the table and looked down at the puzzle. His mouth fell open when he saw what Amity had done. Most of the pieces had been used but were pressed into places where they didn't fit. Amity had forced most of the bent jigsaw loops into sockets that didn't match, creating gaps between the mismatched pieces. Almost all the pieces were black. He looked at the puzzle box's top Amity had propped on the table's edge. The image was primarily black. A thin line representing dawn breaking ran horizontally through the middle. But Amity had randomly placed pieces containing the light, creating a speckled, incoherent image that did not match the box.

He heard footsteps outside the door and hurried to stand beside the bed.

The door opened, and Amity elbowed in, carrying a dinner tray. She saw Ian and said, "Darn it. I was hoping to get back before you were finished showering."

"That's okay," Ian said, still reeling from the puzzle. "Your timing is fine. I just got out. By the way, please don't forget to leave the door open if you leave."

"As I said, I hoped to return before you returned from the bathroom. Did you have somewhere you needed to go?"

"No, I just—"

"Good, then." She took the tray to the bed and set it down. It contained a couple of beverages, silverware, and the usual covered plates. She went to the table, carefully slid her roughly attached puzzle pieces smoothly onto the inverted box top, and placed it on the floor. She brought the dinner tray from the bed to the table and said, "Come and have a seat. It's time for you to eat. I'm sure you'll like this treat."

Ian went to the table and sat.

Amity said, "Hungry?"

Ian's anxiety had knotted his stomach, affecting his appetite. "I might enjoy a few bites."

"Great." Amity lifted the lid from a small plate. "For starters, you'll enjoy a steel-head trout roe with a bowl of creamy wild leek soup." She removed the lid from the large plate. "Your entrée tonight is roasted dry-aged duck breast with foie gras sausage and decadent confit duck legs paired with grapes. And for dessert, we have a 3-layer carrot cake with a special maple cream-cheese frosting. Bon appétit!" She snapped open the napkin and draped it over his leg.

After Ian took a moment to take in the gorgeous dishes, he picked up his fork. Each meal was so spectacular that expressing his amazement was becoming redundant.

Amity moved to the bed and sat, folding her hands on her knees. "Do you have any questions for me while you eat?"

Ian held up a finger for her to wait while he chewed the first bite of the duck. The only question he needed an answer for was when he could get the hell out of this encampment. He decided to test her. After he swallowed, he said, "Not so much a question as an announcement."

"Oh? What is your announcement?"

"I hope you'll take it as a compliment that you've healed me so quickly. If my feet improve tonight as much as last night, I plan to leave tomorrow on my own."

"Aww, what a tragic plan," Amity said. She crossed her legs and leaned back on the bed.

"Tragic?"

"Oh, without a doubt," she said. "I like your pride. I'm on your side, but running now is suicide."

Ian said, "I know you advised against going on my own, but I figure I made it ninety-nine percent of the way here on my own. After having benefited from your amazing restoration, I think I should be able to return to the main road without inconveniencing Jebediah or the other men by requiring their help. If I'm completely spent, I can wait for a passing car if I need more help."

"Sounds like you've tried to think this through as well as you can," she said sympathetically.

"Yes, and as great as you've been, I really need to get back."

Amity got up and strolled to the door, tapping her finger against her lip. She rested her hand on the doorknob, looking at Ian with a steely gaze that disturbed him.

She strolled to him and kneeled. "Give me your feet," she said, sitting back on her haunches.

"Why?"

"Put them here." She patted the front of her thighs.

Ian swiveled in his chair and raised his feet to her.

She examined their tops and sides, gently drawing her fingers across the skin. "Do you feel any pain when you walk on them?"

"At this point, I feel soreness only if I step hard. The recovery has truly been incredible."

"14 miles—tops."

"I beg your pardon?"

"If you try to hike out of here alone, your feet will feel fantastic for the first five to six miles. Your feet will ache from mile seven to mile ten as the blister and tissue injuries quickly revert to your condition when you first arrived at our encampment. If you even make it to mile twelve, you will regret having embarked on a solo journey because you will certainly need help. If you can muster enough willpower to push on, your thirteenth mile will probably take two or more hours because you'll need more frequent rest for shorter distances. At that point, you'll be equidistant between the main road and our encampment, no longer able to walk. You'll wait for darkness when our nocturnal friends will end your misery in a way you'll beg God to make quicker."

Ian stared at her for a few moments after she finished the horrifying monologue. "Wow, you paint an uncomfortable scenario."

Amity stood and said, "Ian, I know you miss your family and woman. But you will rob them of any future with you if you embark on a suicidal trek without our aid."

If Ian wondered how adamant Amity would be about escorting him from the camp, it was now clear. "I suppose I could stick with the original plan and leave with the guys the day after tomorrow."

"Actually, there's been a change," she said. "Their trip has been postponed by four days."

"What? That's not what Jebediah said!"

"Calm down," she said. "While you showered, he stopped by and updated me. It's a relatively brief delay. Besides, is it so awful being with me?"

"Amity, that's not the point. You are amazing, and I—"

"Thank you!" she interjected. "I hoped you would say that!"

"I'm trying to tell you I'd prefer Jebediah kept his word."

Amity said, "Let me talk to Jebediah tomorrow for any alternatives. But you'll owe me if I succeed for you, right?"

"Of course—wait, owe you what?"

She laughed. "I don't want you to worry," she said. "Even if you can't get out of here when you want to, we have plenty of provisions for you. Think of how strong and ready you'll be for the journey by then!" She beamed. "Meanwhile, I hope staying with me won't be torture. I think it's safe to admit that we've grown attached to one another." She held up crossed fingers.

Normally, Ian would have blushed, but anxiety had locked a stern expression on his face.

"I'll let you finish your dinner," Amity said.

Ian tasted the soup. The flavor was rich, creamy, and delicious. As much as he'd like to enjoy the entire meal, the tension in his stomach brought on a hint of nausea. He took a sip of water, and after taking a couple of deep breaths, he moved the massive slice of carrot cake, centering it in front of him. "This is one of my favorites, but I won't be able to finish it."

"That's okay," Amity said. She stepped closer and clasped her fingers under her chin, waiting for him to taste it.

Ian cut a small bite. After chewing several times, he covered his mouth and said, "Another home run."

She clapped and jumped up and down, her boots thudding on the floor. "Why not have another piece? I promise you won't grow obese."

Ian made a timeout sign with his hands while pretending to chew more than was really in his mouth. The cake was delicious. He finished three or four bites of it before pushing the plate away. "I wouldn't have thought I could eat another bite, but that was irresistible."

"It seems like you didn't eat as much," Amity said, taking his tray away. She set it on the floor beside the door.

Ian walked to the bed and stretched out on it.

Amity got her puzzle box and went back to the table. She slid her wacky puzzle concoction back onto the table.

Ian almost immediately felt drowsy. He looked at the clock, and it was only 6:40 p.m. Something about this place made him fall asleep faster and sleep deeper than he ever had. Tonight's drowsiness felt different from the sudden sleepiness that swept over him after getting into bed the previous night. Tonight, he felt some slight dizziness. He looked over at Amity and saw her smiling down at her puzzle. His eyes slowly closed as his consciousness drained away.

Sixteen

IAN FELT HIMSELF returning to wakefulness before his eyes opened. He had experienced the strangest dream in which he was a kid again, and someone had been knocking on the front door of his parents' home. He remembered standing in his foyer, listening to a voice ask him to come outside and play. He thought he recognized it as one of his childhood friends, but then became confused when the voice was a grown female. He tried to reply, but the words wouldn't come out.

A heavy thud opened his eyes, and he realized the sound originating from outside his room had been incorporated into his dream. Someone pounded on the door and said, "Let me in. Come on, you can do it." The voice squeezed through as though the speaker's lips were pressed to the door's crack.

Ian sat up. "Who's there?"

The woman said, "Ah, I knew you were there. Come to the door. I need you to let me in."

The voice wasn't Amity's. Ian cringed from another throbbing headache. He looked toward the voice but couldn't see the door because the room was completely dark except for the illuminated clock on his bedside stand. 3:10 a.m. He reached for the lamp's base and then felt his way up to the switch. He turned it on and got out of bed. After a few steps toward the door, he felt dizzy and reached to the bed to steady himself. The headache stabbed harder. He sat on the bed.

"Open up!" the woman said. She tapped again rapidly.

Ian stood and immediately felt lightheaded. The room spun. He dropped to one knee and then sat on the floor.

"Are you coming to the door?" the woman asked. "I need you to unlock it for me."

Ian crawled the rest of the way to the door. He turned the knob. As expected, it spun loosely, not affecting the latch. "I can't open it. I don't have a key."

"I need you to find something you can pry with and help me break the door open. Do it right away." She was desperate.

Ian reached up and spun the knob again. "It's broken. I have no tools. There is nothing to pry it with."

"Are you turning it?"

"Yes." Ian closed his eyes to wait for a fresh wave of dizziness to pass.

"Who are you?" Ian asked.

"Let me in. I'll tell you everything. They're planning to kill you."

"How do you know that?"

"I can protect you. I know how to keep you safe. You can trust me."

"Where's Amity?"

"She's the one I'm protecting you from. I'm giving you a chance to live. You have to help me break this door open." She slammed something heavy against it.

Ian's fogginess didn't lessen his sense of danger. Something wasn't right. "Listen, I can't help you open the door. If you're trying to save me, why don't you just tell me what I need to know?"

"Because you need me to protect you. Without my help, you will die a horrible death."

Ian reached up and rattled the knob without pulling it.

In a throaty scream, the woman said, "Open this fucking door!"

Ian scooted away from it.

She pounded and kicked the door and then swung something solid that cracked it. Ian wondered if she had switched to an ax or a sledgehammer. The pounding continued. Ian felt each impact vibrate through the floor. Whoever this person was, she tried to destroy the door to get to him.

"Go get Amity," Ian yelled. "She can let you in."

The woman stopped her pounding to laugh. Between panting, she said, "You're a helpless little sheep begging the shepherd to go fetch the wolf. Unbelievable."

Ian heard something wedging into the door crack, followed by squeaking as wood popped and splintered. He looked around for anything he might use as a weapon. The only loose object in the room was the lamp on the bedside table, which was too small.

He ran into the bathroom, searching for anything that he could use to defend himself. He raised his foot and kicked the side of the towel holder, breaking it off the wall. The dowel crashed onto the counter beside the sink. It was a solid piece of wood about an inch thick and the length of his forearm. He returned to the bedroom and waited beside the door, ready to swing his makeshift club.

The pounding had stopped. Ian leaned close to the door, listening. There was only silence on the other side. He leaned closer to it, expecting a final blow to crack the door open, if not knock it from its hinges, but his visitor seemed to have left.

He waited five more minutes beside the door before taking the towel rack dowel to the bed. As his adrenaline rush subsided, his headache flooded back. He felt utterly helpless behind his severely damaged door.

He took the only measure possible to conceal and protect himself. He turned off the light, lay on the floor, and scooted under the bed, still grasping the dowel at his side. The space underneath the bed was too tight to roll to his side, so he remained on his stomach. As uncomfortable as it was, this was his safest option—for the time being. His hand slowly relaxed on the dowel, and he fell asleep.

· · ·

Ian woke up to footsteps outside his room toward the vestibule. It took a few moments for him to orient himself, remembering that he was tucked under the bed and why.

A key slid into the knob, and the door opened. Heavy footsteps clopped into the room, scuffing to a stop inches from his head. They looked like Amity's black boots, but he needed to be sure. "No! Ian … Ian!"

The voice sounded like Amity's.

She ran into the bathroom and frantically called him more. "Ian… please don't tell me you're gone!" She ran back into the bedroom.

Ian knew she would eventually find him, but her reaction to his disappearance was fascinating. He kept quiet.

Amity ran out into the vestibule, then immediately returned and went to the window, where Ian could see her from his position. She turned back and put her hands on her hips, scanning the room. She looked down and spotted him.

Ian stretched his arms, pretending to be waking up.

"Oh, my God!" she rushed to the bed and kneeled. "Are you okay?"

"Someone tried to get in last night. It was a woman. She sounded crazy."

"I know. I'm sorry. I'm so glad you are okay."

"What was that about?"

"I can explain. First, come out so we can talk."

Ian wiggled out from under the bed and got up. It was almost 11 o'clock in the morning. Ian couldn't remember sleeping that late since he was in high school. After the incident with the voice behind the door, he must have fallen into another deep sleep. "I need to use the bathroom," he said, leaving her.

After using the toilet, he looked in the mirror while washing his hands. He wondered if he was only imagining his cheeks filling in with the weight gain Amity had set as her goal. If true, his progress was impressive after only three days of rest and well-fed recovery.

He felt a twinge of pain on the side of his calf. He rubbed his hand against it and felt a point of tenderness. He shifted to see it with more light. Barely visible was a mark that looked like a single puncture wound surrounded by some faint redness the size of a dime. A white strand of string adhered to his skin about a centimeter away. The tiny puncture was almost unnoticeable unless he pressed against it, feeling its sensitivity. He checked his wrist to find the mark he had discovered previously. Though the marks were similar, his wrist had almost fully healed. He hadn't noticed any bed bugs or spiders in his room during his entire stay.

He recalled how deep his sleep had been these last nights and how he had remembered nothing upon waking—not even dreaming or tossing and turning. In fact, he hadn't slept so hard since he was in high school. He wondered if Amity had done something. Had she injected him while he slept? That would be difficult to do without waking him unless he had been sedated. He remembered the food. Given the wide variety of dishes and beverages he had enjoyed, she could have laced almost anything to achieve that.

His urge was to confront her about it, but he was almost sure that wouldn't go well. If she had been secretly doing something to him, then revealing his knowledge could trigger her. She had already tried to restrict him to this room. He was virtually, if not literally, captive. Thirty miles of rugged wilderness gave Amity and the hunters more control over him than Dagny had with the heavy locks and doors of Biding Wellness Center. Once again, his total vulnerability to these people made him feel sick. He needed to understand whatever was happening. Either he was a prisoner or free, and it was time for him to find out.

When he came out of the bathroom, Amity sat on the bed. "Everything okay?" she asked.

"I'm fine," Ian said. He went to the open door and saw deep gouges in the wood around the entry knob and splinters scattered on the floor below it. A large crack ran up the center of the door.

"I should have been here for you. I'm sorry," Amity said. "I had planned to only take a nap, but when I woke up, it was late morning—your morning, anyway."

"Who was she?" Ian asked.

"Her name is Angelica. She's been acting strangely. I'll deal with her for you. Obviously, she's not someone we want at our encampment. Tell me everything that happened and exactly what she said to you."

Ian recounted how Angelica's tapping on the door had awakened him and how her pleas for Ian to let her in had escalated to shouts and pounding that had damaged the door. He omitted the woman's dire warnings about Amity.

She quietly listened, wearing a concerned expression. When Ian finished, she said, "I'm so sorry you had to go through that."

"Which leads me to say…"

"Don't say it." Amity closed her eyes.

"I'm leaving. Today. Immediately."

Amity slouched. "I told you not to say that."

"I need to be on my way. I realize it's risky, and I'm willing to take that risk. Thank you for everything you've done to help me."

"What can I do to change your mind and stay one more day?" she asked.

"I really need to go."

"Then please let me at least give you a running chance."

"I don't understand."

Amity said, "Before each hunt, we prepare our men. We have developed a prep routine that increases their stamina and endurance by at least one-third. This procedure and a small backpack containing some energy bars, electrolytes, and bear repellent spray can boost your odds of surviving the journey even if your feet quit on you."

Ian looked at her skeptically. "How long does it take?"

"Maybe a half-hour." She stood and came closer to him. "I don't want you to die. Will you accept my help—pretty please?"

"I appreciate the offer, but I'd rather leave immediately."

Amity's expression clouded, flashing anger before quickly dissolving. Ian knew that provoking her would only make it more difficult. He sensed the need to appease her, even if only temporarily. "Listen, I can give you my number, and maybe when you come to town, we can get together."

Amity looked at him sympathetically. "I hate to disappoint you, but it's been years since I've seen town."

"Seriously?"

She raised her hand. "I swear on your life!" she said, laughing.

"My life? That was funny," Ian said.

"Getting together in the future would be nice, but if you want to make me feel better right now, you'll accept my help so you can avoid a suicidal journey. Come with me."

Ian decided that the cost of a few minutes for her prep was a fair price to keep her calm, as long as her prep didn't require injecting him or eating anything on the spot.

She led him from the bedroom into the vestibule, where she used a key to unlock the door to the staircase. They descended and took the tunnel to the next set of stairs. At the top of the next landing, Amity opened the door. They entered the large recreation room. She led him past the rows of chairs to the back of the room. One door next to the restroom was slightly ajar.

She opened the door wider, revealing a rectangular room, narrow and deep, the size of a small closet. A gritty, dark vinyl covered the floor from edge to edge. A faded wear-stripe stretched up the middle.

Centered on the far wall was a shoulder-high slat of tinted glass. Hanging from the center of the ceiling, an oxygen mask and a tangle of wired electrodes dangled.

"What is this?" Ian asked, leaning in.

"This is where we quickly check our hunters' vitals to determine their fitness for our longer hunts."

Ian said, "Don't your hunters already have a good sense of their capabilities?"

"You'd think so, but we cannot afford to have a hunter stranded because of exhaustion. It isn't reasonable to ask the other hunters to deplete their reserves to carry a hunter who miscalculated his own ability. Therefore, we perform these simple tests and insist on the supplements. It's designed to be brief, leaving you plenty of reserves."

"Are the supplements given orally or by injection?"

"Which would you prefer?"

Ian didn't trust her. He no longer trusted anything. At this point, he just wanted to get out of this place. "I won't be needing any of that. I'm good to go as is. You've rejuvenated me plenty."

"Okay, but at least let us check your vitals," Amity said. "You might find this to be fun and informative."

"I'd rather not."

"Why won't you do this simple thing for me?" Amity snapped.

Ian kept calm, not reacting to Amity's flash of anger.

She pressed her fingers to her temples and took a deep breath before calmly saying, "You'll be on your way so fast once this simple test is passed. I'm begging you, please, I'll get on my knees. The test is a breeze." She pressed her cheek against the door's edge playfully.

Ian hesitated, then said, "Okay. Just the readings, no supplements."

"I promise!" Amity clapped. "It'll be over in a jiffy. We measure your heart rate, respiration, and distance to calculate your stamina level. We use our proprietary software to tell you how your biological age compares to your calendar age. What's the worst thing that could happen?" She led him into the room, slipped on some gloves, and connected electrodes to Ian's chest, forehead, and wrists.

A chime came from Amity's pocket. She pulled out a phone. "Hello…"

The shock of seeing Amity using a mobile phone spread an

incredulous look on Ian's face. If these people had phones, he could've borrowed one to arrange a rescue. And even if they were unwilling to allow rescue from their camp, he would've gladly hiked to an easily reachable rendezvous point these people felt was a safe enough distance away to maintain their privacy.

Amity plugged one ear. "...That might be possible... I understand, but can it wait?" She pulled the phone from her ear and whispered to Ian. "I have to run a quick errand. I'll be right back. The analysis will start automatically." She resumed her phone call and backed out the door, saying, "Yes, I will check, but I'm helping Ian and want to pick up some survival supplies for him." She stepped out of the room.

A motor hummed, and Ian began sliding toward the door. He looked down and discovered the entire floor was an enormous conveyor belt for a treadmill. Ian almost stumbled. There was no place to step off. The floor carried him at a walking pace toward the door that closed with a heavy clunk when Amity slammed it.

When he was close enough to reach the knob, he walked backward while trying to turn it. It was locked. The tread sped up slightly. He pounded on the door. "Amity! Wait! Keep the door open!" he shouted.

There was no answer.

He turned to face forward and jogged to reach the center of the floor. Amity had promised that the test would be brief. There were no handrails, which seemed odd, if not dangerous. The floor had sped him to a brisk pace. He put his hands on his hips while he walked, waiting for the testing to finish. He waved at the tinted rectangle in front of him.

The treadmill sped up again, forcing him to speed-walk, and then it increased again, taking him into a slow jog. "Hey, that's fast enough," he shouted, hoping some out-of-sight operator could hear and adjust the speed. The floor didn't slow down. Ian pounded the wall with the butt of his hand. "That's fast enough. Stop it! " The floor's speed increased, bringing Ian to a full jog. He waved his arms above his head at the tinted window, shouting, "Stop it! This isn't funny." He pounded the wall again, screaming, "Stop! Is anyone there? Stop this thing!" He was feeling winded.

After jogging for nearly five minutes, Ian had broken a sweat and worked to catch his breath. He jogged to the room's center, now understanding the faded strip that ran up the center of the floor.

He was furious that Amity had abandoned him for so long and soon realized he had been trapped in the perfect sabotage. He needed every ounce of energy for his hike back to town. He put everything he had into running to reach the front of the treadmill so he could pound on the tinted window, but each time he came close to it, the floor sped up, keeping him centered in its middle no matter how fast he ran. When he stopped running, it only slowed to a brisk walking pace. "The joke is over. You're pissing me off!" he shouted at the window. He drew his hand across his neck, motioning for anyone who could see him from behind the tint to turn off the moving floor. "I need to stop!" he yelled. The floor continued sliding under his feet with no response to his pleas.

Thirty minutes into his run, Ian's shirt was soaked. Twice, he rode the tread to the door, where he bumped the back wall and fell, but the tread had not stopped. It rolled him against the wall, causing abrasions on his arms before he could scramble to his feet again. An hour into his run, he felt his stamina depleting as his remaining energy waned. "You've got to stop. Please," he panted. His voice had grown hoarse from shouting.

He tripped and fell a third time. The floor did not stop. It carried him back, where it slammed him into the door. Ian yelled in pain as the moving tread flipped him over and over, like knotted blankets in a dryer. It slowed enough for Ian to get up and resume jogging. He cussed at the window and fell again.

The moving floor finally stopped. Ian collapsed. He felt a burning on his back and arms where the floor's tread had scraped his skin.

Moments later, the door opened, and Ian's feet slid out onto the rec room carpet.

Amity stood over him. She pressed her hand over her mouth, looking stunned. "Oh, my God! What happened?"

Ian lay on his side, still working to catch his breath. He didn't look up at her. His sweat-soaked head rested on his arm, the rest of his body completely limp.

"Ian, answer me. Are you okay?"

"No!"

"I'm so sorry. I should never have left you. They didn't stop the treadmill for you?"

Ian tried to lift his head to look at her, then let it fall back down.

"Can I help you up?" Amity said, reaching out to him.

"No, get away from me," Ian said.

"I'm so sorry about this," Amity said, stepping back. "It's never happened before, and you can trust I'll sort this out."

Ian ignored her. He closed his eyes, teeth clenched.

"Ian, I beg you to forgive me," Amity said, kneeling beside him. "I know this is bad, and you're probably mad, but soon you'll be glad. You know I will take care of you."

Ian divided his words between deep breaths, saying, "I … want … to … leave."

"And you will leave. Soon."

Ian struggled to get himself to a sitting position. His back burned.

"Let me help you." Amity reached out to him again.

Ian waved off her hand. "You've been enough help." He climbed to his feet, feeling the wobbliness in his legs from the punishment they had just taken. He pinched the front of his soaked shirt and fanned himself.

Amity held up her finger for him to wait. "On my errand, I grabbed a refreshment pack you can wear on your back." She went to a nearby table and returned with a black vest with two pockets centered on its back, each containing full water bottles. The vest had green fluorescent tape along its shoulders, down its sides, and around the waist. "This vest is light, easy to slip on and off, and will give you some extra hydration on your trip."

"Are you kidding me?" Ian said.

"What?" Amity replied, looking confused.

"You honestly expect me to hike back to town after you forced me to run a marathon?"

"Actually, yes, I do, because you were insistent. You seemed adamant about leaving today."

"You've done your best to ruin that, right?" Ian said, staggering toward the staircase door.

Amity ran ahead of him and opened it for him. She followed him down the stairs and said, "While you are resting, I'll get your lunch ready. Do you have any special requests?"

"Yes, I'd like an ATV with a full gas tank with a side of a shotgun?"

"Listen, Ian, I'm sorry about the treadmill malfunction. I can't undo it, but you already know how fast we can help you recover."

Ian turned to her and held out his hand. "Can I use your phone?"

"I told you I don't have a phone." Amity seemed almost offended.

"I saw you use it before you locked me in that marathon room!" Ian shouted.

Amity stepped close to him. She looked up. Her eyes bored into him, seething. "Don't you dare holler at me!"

Ian glared back at her, unflinching.

Amity stepped back, and her shoulders visibly relaxed. "They aren't phones. They're radios." She motioned for him to follow her. They headed along the tunnel, returning to Ian's room. She unlocked the door and pushed it open for Ian to enter.

While she watched, Ian eased onto his bed and used his fingertips to gingerly remove his shirt so it wouldn't brush against his injuries.

"May I see?" she asked.

Ian shrugged, feeling completely deflated and too tired to fight her.

Amity examined his back without touching it. "I have a salve that will fix these scrapes. May I bring it to you with some lunch?"

Ian shrugged. "Sure." Under normal circumstances, he would have expected his appetite not to return so soon after a vigorous workout. But he felt hungrier than ever. He'd need all the calories he could get if he was to have a chance of getting out of here on his own—whenever that happened.

Amity headed out of the room, pausing in the doorway. She crossed her arms. "Are you still planning to leave today?"

Ian gave a disgusted laugh. "It looks like you got your wish."

Amity seemed hurt momentarily, then said, "I can apologize again for what happened if it will help."

"I'll deal with it," Ian said.

"I'll get your lunch. I hope you'll love it." Amity said. She exited and closed the door again, failing to leave it open for him.

Ian wasn't surprised. He laid back gently on the pillow. He welcomed the quiet time alone, but it also allowed his paranoid speculation to rush back. He knew Amity probably wouldn't drug him until dinner. Whatever they were doing to him, it happened during the night.

When Amity returned, she carried a tray and placed it on the bed beside him. She removed the plate cover. "I kept this meal light for you. We have a citrus-marinated rotisserie chicken strip salad on crisp shredded spring mix heaped high and topped with grilled chili-lime corn, crumbled goat cheese, toasted almonds, and garnished with avocado slices." She removed the smaller plate cover. "For dessert, you'll enjoy crème brûlée rimmed with alternating raspberries and blueberries and a light Manuka honey drizzle."

Ian examined the salad. Thankfully, the dressing was in a small ramekin on the side. He ate the salad dry. The tray also included a glass beaker of lemonade and an empty glass cup. There was no way Ian would so much as sip it.

He tasted the salad. As with all the food he had enjoyed, the flavor was spectacular.

Amity said, "It's been a rough day so far. I think I'll give you some privacy. When you finish, I'll return with a soothing salve for your injuries. Can I get you anything else?"

"No, this is delicious." Ian pointed at the salad with his fork.

"I'll be back soon—this time, I promise."

He waited a couple of minutes after Amity left before he eased out of the bed. He carried the food tray into the bathroom, pouring the lemonade from the beaker into the sink. He scooped the salad dressing into the sink and rinsed it down the drain. The crème brûlée was too thick to rinse the sink, so he scooped half of it into the toilet and flushed it before returning to bed. He finished the rest of the dry salad and then set the tray on the bedside table.

Although he was in better shape than he was when he first arrived at this place, the toll his unexpected exercise had taken on him was apparent. He fell asleep. When he woke up, he looked at the bedside table. His lunch tray was gone.

"Good evening, sleepyhead," Amity said. She sat in the corner chair, watching him.

Ian sat up and covered a yawn. "How long was I asleep?"

"About four hours? And you sure needed it."

"I drew a bath for you. I'll heat the water again," Amity said, walking past him. She disappeared into the bathroom.

Ian heard the tub faucet flowing. He wondered if he had been sedated despite his caution with the food. But he had no headache or dizziness.

Amity appeared in the bathroom doorway, holding a bathrobe. She tossed it onto the foot of the bed. "I'll give you some privacy. I put some healing salve in the water. It might sting initially, but you can expect your back to heal as quickly as your feet."

"Thank you," Ian said.

After she left, Ian took the robe to the bathroom and slowly waded into the large tub. The discomfort was minimal when the water reached the scrapes on his back, and the warmth soothed him.

Seventeen

FOR TWO HOURS, Ian lay on his bed, staring at the ceiling, having exhausted every escape scenario he could imagine.

He heard footsteps approaching his door. Amity knocked and pushed through before he could answer. She carried a dinner tray.

"I hope you're hungry," she said.

"Actually, not so much," Ian said.

"Well, there's a first," Amity said. She took the tray to the table.

Ian got up and went to her. "Thanks, but my appetite is shot."

Amity gave him a quizzical look.

"Don't get me wrong," Ian said, "I'm sure whatever you've prepared is, once again, Michelin Star worthy. But I couldn't hold down much right now."

"Hmm," Amity said, studying him.

"You need your strength. You should eat something even if you don't finish it all." She lifted a plate cover and said, "For dinner this evening, we have an appetizer of fries coated in Parmesan cheese and drizzled with white truffle oil. For an entrée, we have citrus and honey-crusted lamb with mint gremolata in a wine and shallot jus. If you want to skip ahead to dessert, we've prepared a special ricotta crepe with vanilla bourbon strawberries." She pulled the chair out for him.

Ian reluctantly sat. "How do you keep such a varied inventory fresh?" Ian said, shaking his head. "I know some of this food couldn't have been frozen."

Amity laughed.

"I'm serious. How do you do this?" Ian pointed at the tray.

"Camping doesn't have to automatically mean roughing it. Is it wrong for us to appreciate great cuisine?"

"Not at all. I'm just curious how you get such a wide variety of fresh ingredients that I know don't grow outside your door."

"I wish I could tell you more, but I can't give away a trade secret. You'll be leaving soon, so meanwhile, why not just enjoy it?"

Ian picked up the fork and stabbed a fry. He bit a small piece of it and smacked his lips. "Delicious," he said. He pressed the fork to the plate to pull the remaining piece of the fry off.

Amity said, "Nutrition is a vital part of your recovery."

"I know food is important, but rest is what I need most now."

"I'm trying to keep you alive."

"Alive?" Ian frowned.

Amity paused. "What I meant was that I want you to have the nourishment you need so that you have the strength to complete your journey."

Ian could see Amity's anxiety rising each time he resisted the food. He picked up the partially eaten fry and popped it into his mouth. Then he cut into a piece of the lamb. It fell from the bone, and the sauce smelled heavenly. He took a small bite and said, "Maybe I can force myself to enjoy a few bites."

Amity grinned. "Good! Any amount will help. I need to step out for just a few minutes."

Ian cut a larger piece of lamb and raised it with a smile when Amity looked at him before exiting through the door.

As soon as the door closed, he grabbed the tray and hurried into the bathroom. At every other meal, he had gorged himself, only to wake up after having experienced odd sleeping patterns, headaches, and puncture wounds on his body. Strangely, after such a strenuous workout, he had little desire for this food, which surprised him.

He scraped two-thirds of the lamb entrée into the toilet and flushed it, then used the napkin to clean the edge of the plate. He cut the crepes in half, disposing of them the same way. He returned to the bed and smeared some of the wine shallot jus along the corner of his mouth.

About fifteen minutes later, with no footsteps to warn him, the door opened. Amity stepped in.

His shoulders jumped.

"I'm sorry," she said.

"For what?"

"I must have scared you. Your face looks so concerned. I told you I'd be right back."

Amity approached him and placed her bag on the floor beside the bed. "I see you found at least some of your appetite," she said, examining his plate. "Finished?"

"Yes." Ian rubbed his stomach and then stretched. "Delicious as usual, but I couldn't finish it all."

"That's okay," Amity said. She took away his dinner tray, placing it on the floor beside the door, her voice suddenly infused with new enthusiasm. "If we got some food into you, you'll surely get stronger, too."

Ian's attention went to Amity's bag on the floor beside him. She carried it with her everywhere. He wondered what was in it. He wanted to find a way to get a look inside it.

Amity said, "I'll be back with a special nightcap we have for you tonight before it's time to sleep."

"No need for a nightcap," Ian said.

"It's no bother. It'll be yummy."

"I'll be fine. I think I could use some privacy right now—no offense."

"It's a delicious warm drink. I think you should try it."

Ian lost the grip on his patience. "What do I have to say to get you to understand?" He felt the blood rushing to his face.

Amity slowly walked toward him. "What did you just say to me?" Her face had traces of the anger Ian had seen her flash at him in the tunnel.

He softened his tone slightly. "Why don't you just tell me what's really happening here?"

Amity's face lost none of its tension. "If you have a question, why not simply ask it?"

"When Jebediah and the guys found me, I only needed some rest, a simple meal or two, and some direction. By now, I would've been on my way back to town alone without infringing on you or anyone else here. But the level of care you've given me is beyond anything I can understand. I can't imagine the cost of the food you've given me. Why are you treating me like a king despite your hatred of visitors?"

"You were injured and probably would have died out there." Amity pointed to the window. "You needed us. We stepped up and helped. We're trying to do the right thing."

Ian said, "And then there are your off-the-chart privacy concerns with the rules about not walking outside during the day because I might wake someone up or some satellite might see your camp. You can't help me get to town for days, so I'm stuck in this fire-trap of a room because the doorknob is broken and hasn't been fixed even though one day of your food budget would buy an entirely new door."

Amity sat in the chair opposite him. She folded her hands on the table. "Anything else?"

"I'm sorry, I just…" he put his head back and sighed. Something caught his eye that he hadn't noticed before. He pointed up. "What's that?"

Between each ceiling beam, the same zigzagging wires connected to the incendiary boxes he had seen in the supply room crisscrossed from one edge of the room to the other. They were difficult to see, having been painted to blend in.

"Jebediah explained that to you, remember?"

"You said you didn't want anyone finding your possessions in the storage room."

"You must have misunderstood. Our possessions are dispersed throughout the entire encampment. The bed, furniture, and completely remodeled bathroom with all the fixtures you've enjoyed are our property. We aren't leaving them to anyone. Does that make you uncomfortable?"

"If I'm honest, it terrifies me," Ian said.

"I don't want you to be worried, so let me put your mind at ease," she said. "We will do everything necessary to protect the property until that becomes impossible. The ignition devices cannot be accidentally triggered. You have no reason to be concerned."

Ian shifted in his chair. "Why not see if your group can use the property instead of preparing for some sort of confrontation?"

"Oh, we're nonconfrontational. We won't engage them in a battle. If the government returns to reclaim this property from us, we will destroy our belongings, abandon it, and they'll never find us. You can be sure of that. We call it our Blessed Exodus."

"Interesting. But why destroy it?"

"The structures on this property were virtually uninhabitable when we found them. We restored each and installed the very best amenities at our own expense. What right would the government have to profit from our upgrades? Does that seem fair to you?"

"Honestly, yes, because you don't own it."

Amity poked her tongue into her cheek, then said, "I'm sorry you feel that way."

"I don't understand why you need to destroy the property."

"If it comes to that, and we purge the property in our Blessed Exodus, we'll leave them in a better financial position. An insurance claim will pay them much more than the structures were worth before our upgrades."

"Listen," Ian said, "You want your privacy, and I want to leave. I wish I knew why we can't both get what we want."

She stood, went to the door, and rested her hand on the knob. "Be very careful what you wish for, Ian. We're good at granting wishes here. If I were you, I would accept every teensy weensy bit of help I offer. I'd take my advice instead of rolling the dice." She picked up her bag and stepped into the vestibule. Before closing the door, she said, "I'll be back with your nightcap."

Before the door latched, Ian said, "Wait!"

Amity leaned back in.

"You said you'd leave the door open."

Amity briefly looked at Ian's legs while chewing her cheek. "Okay. This time." She went into the bathroom and returned with a roll of toilet paper. She set it on the floor as a door jamb.

"Thank you," Ian said. "I can't tell you how much that helps me psychologically."

"Get you anything else?" she said with no warmth.

"No, thank you."

Amity disappeared into the vestibule.

. . .

Ian spent the next hour resting. The soreness from his unexpected workout earlier that day was settling in. His legs felt stiffer. Looking out the window, he wondered if he could step outside for some fresh air. It was dusk, and there was little chance of being seen from the sky. He'd be quiet so as not to wake any of the hunters. He went to the door and opened it. He stepped into the vestibule and gently brought the door back to rest against the toilet paper roll so he wouldn't get locked out. When he stepped to the door that led outside, he found it locked. The door to the top of the staircase was locked, too, as well as the other mysterious door to a room he had never seen. What good was propping his bedroom door open if you were still trapped in the building? "Dammit, Amity," he said, going back into the room. He waited another two hours until Amity returned a few minutes after 8:00 p.m. carrying a tray. It contained the nightcap she had promised. "Did you miss me?" she asked.

"I was still trapped. Every door is locked." he pointed to the front room.

"Were we trying to leave?" Amity said, taking the tray to the corner table.

"You've removed my ability to leave. I'm imprisoned here."

"That's not true." Amity walked, her boots clopping hard to the door. She stepped out into the vestibule. Ian heard keys jingling. When she returned, she kicked the toilet paper roll across the room, unraveling it in a long tail. She pushed the door open as far as it would go, blocking it with her foot. "Would you like to leave? You can leave right now. No one will stop you."

Ian tried to control his surprise. "I didn't mean to upset you," he said.

"Why would you think I'm upset?" Amity said, laughing. "There it is. The great outdoors." She held her arm up to the open door. "Do you see any iron bars? High fences topped with razor wire? Towered guards with sniper rifles? Have we put handcuffs or ankle cuffs on you? Have your meals consisted of disgusting prison grub? Are you sure you don't want to break out of this torture chamber to escape from complete freedom directly into the comfy, cozy deathtrap of the wilderness?"

"Yes, I'm sure," Ian said, swallowing.

Amity put her hand on her hip and moved her foot from the door, allowing it to close. The latch clicked into place. She came closer to him. "You're not a prisoner. You're a guest. You shouldn't doubt how you've been blessed."

"I understand," Ian said, realizing that claiming to feel imprisoned was clearly a trigger for her.

After a contemplative stare at Ian, she said, "Let's get you that nightcap." She motioned for Ian to follow her to the table. "You resisted this nightcap, but I think it's critical if you are serious about making the journey tomorrow. It will relax you. We need to make sure you get plenty of sleep tonight."

The statement fanned Ian's paranoia. The nightcap might as well be a syringe of sedative.

"I've brought a delicious open & shut brandy cocktail alongside a few slices of Asiago cheese, coppa cold cuts, and pretzels."

Ian sat at the table, examining the elements on the tray.

"I have a request," he said.

"Sure, anything."

"Could I get a tall glass for some water?"

Amity said, "You have some bottled water in the refrigerator."

"Yes, but there's something about drinking it out of a nice clean glass. Is there any way you could go get me one?"

Amity's expression clouded with suspicion. "Of course," she said.

It was a long shot, but Ian hoped she might run out to get a glass and that such a quick errand wouldn't require her to take her bag.

Instead, Amity went to the cabinet. She opened it and clicked her tongue several times as she looked inside. To his disappointment, she pulled a tall glass he had forgotten about and held it up for him to see. "This okay?" Her suspicious expression remained unchanged, and Ian detected a slight smirk.

"Yes, that will work fine."

"We aim to please." She pulled a bottle of water from the refrigerator and brought both to him. While filling the glass, she said, "Is there anything else I can get for you?"

"No, everything's great."

"I know it is." She went to the door. "Angelica hasn't left the encampment yet. We're monitoring her, but she's sneaky. I want to close the door to prevent her from becoming a nuisance to you—just in case she tries to pay another visit."

Although Ian wasn't thrilled about having the door closed again, he decided not to make an issue out of it since he had already triggered Amity only a few minutes ago. Besides, he wasn't in any condition to leave tonight, anyway.

"Get some rest, won't you?" she said.

Ian raised the brandy, miming a toast to her. "Thank you, I will." The moment Amity left the room, he examined the cheese and meat. He considered taking a small bite of cheese, wondering if he might detect bitterness if it had been laced. He was hungry but not ravenous like on his first day. He bit a pretzel, crunching it while he carried the drink into the bathroom. There was no way in hell he would take even a sip. He rinsed his lips from the fake toast he had shown Amity. He poured it into the sink, stopping when only about a tablespoon was left. He held the glass up to the light and swirled the remaining brandy. He saw a faint powder orbiting in it. He put his finger in the glass and pressed it to the bottom. He rubbed his fingers together, sensing an unmistakable grainy residue. He poured the rest down the drain and washed his hands. He took the glass back out and placed it on his bedside table. He laid down, hoping his anxiety would ease enough without alcohol for his first normal night of sleep. He wondered if he would experience the roller coaster drop into unconsciousness he'd been experiencing.

He turned off the lights. He did not know what time Amity came into his room each night, but he remembered the possibility that he might wake up to find her sleeping on the floor beside him.

He eventually dozed off into a restless sleep. Footsteps in the vestibule woke him up. He checked the clock. 11:15 p.m. He worried it might be Angelica, but heard a key slide into the knob. The door opened. Ian closed his eyes, relaxed his face, and parted his lips to feign sleeping. Footsteps quietly approached his bed. Although his eyes were closed, he sensed someone standing over him. He cracked open his eye closest to the pillow. The open doorway created enough ambient light to see a woman's waist. He closed his eye.

"Can you hear me?" she whispered. It was Amity.

Ian didn't answer, working to remain perfectly still. He sensed her moving closer to him. She leaned down and put her face next to his head. She blew a puff of air into his ear.

Ian used brute force to resist even the slightest twitch.

"Good, good," she whispered as she picked up his glass and set it on the tray. She balanced the tray while opening the door with a key and exited.

Ian exhaled, but the door opened again after only a few moments. He subtly adjusted his head to bring the door into view.

He saw Amity lean down and place something on the floor to prop it open. She then backed into the room, pulling an IV stand behind her. When the wheels rolled over the bump of the door threshold, a dangling bag of solution swayed back and forth. Below it, a transparent tube looped on a hook.

Ian's fears of having been intravenously sedated were confirmed. His heart thumped.

Amity wheeled the stand to a place beside the bed and unraveled the

IV tube. He saw her pinch the base of the needle connected to the tube. When she pulled his sheet back, Ian released a deep sigh and stirred, turning to his back.

Amity sidestepped to move the IV stand behind her, blocking Ian's view of it.

She waited for almost a minute, quietly observing him. Ian knew better than to fully wake up. He worried that his ignorance of the sedation brought the comforts he enjoyed. If Amity's covert plan for him was exposed, his experience might no longer need to be cloaked in fine dining and fancy accommodations. He needed to maintain their hospitality and dodge the sedation until tomorrow, when he could make a run for freedom.

Ian kept still, eyes closed.

Amity bent down and put her face close to his. He felt warm breath from her nostrils while she studied him for any twitch. She gently took hold of his wrist.

Ian stirred, rolling to his side.

She reached behind her, lifted the IV stand from the floor, and slowly crept out of the room, carrying it. She closed the door behind her.

After lying in bed wide awake for a half-hour, authentic sleepiness finally seemed to win over anxiety. Ian dozed off before a strange sound rushed him back to full wakefulness. It sounded like a bird's chirp. He sat up on his elbows. A faint light seeped under the vestibule door. He wondered if Amity was preparing for another attempt to drug him or to take her place on the floor beside his bed.

He heard the chirp again, and it seemed to come from outside. He heard it again. The chirp was followed by a drumming sound that vibrated the floor, lasting about 10 seconds. He sat up.

When he heard the chirp and drumming a third time, it was followed by some faint cheers.

Ian got up and went to the window. He pulled open the drapes about the width of his head to peer out. Whatever was happening outside was being done in pitch darkness. He saw motion as he stared toward the other structures. In the distance, a group of thin, glowing green lines undulated as they came nearer. Ian squinted, trying to determine what it was, but he couldn't. As the green lines moved closer, he saw they were attached to men—a group of about twenty. They walked back to a place about ten meters from Ian's window. Ian could now see that the green lines were fluorescent stripes on each man's uniform. Although he could only make out their silhouettes accented by the fluorescent markers on their clothing, he saw they had formed a huddle. A light flashed from its center, and a flame illuminated the bearded men. They listened to the one who held the torch. Most of them carried knives—long machetes. Others had cleavers, and a few held clubs like the bloody one he had seen under Jangy's coat. The men eventually shouted one word in unison that Ian couldn't understand. They all clapped once in unison. The man with the torch put a whistle to his lips before snuffing the torch's flame. The green stripes glowed brighter in the darkness, having been recharged by the torch's light. The men lined up.

Ian heard the chirp. The men took off running in a direction away from Ian's room. Their feet created the drumming that quickly faded as the men traveled to the far end of the easement that separated the buildings. The shouting and cheers in the distance repeated.

Ian tried to make sense of what they were doing. There was no way he could ask Amity, since there was no doubt he wasn't supposed to be awake for this.

He returned to the bed and laid on his back, listening to the men engaged in some bizarre late-night ritual for over an hour before silence returned.

Ian drifted into restless dozing, startling awake many times for the next few hours. He was awake when he heard his doorknob jiggle. It was still dark outside. He glanced at the clock before closing his eyes to feign sleep. It was 5:34 a.m. After the door latch clicked, footsteps approached his bed.

Ian cracked one eye open when he felt a puff of air. Amity had flung out a comforter, spreading it on the floor beside his bed. She laid down and curled up, wrapping the comforter around herself.

Within a couple of hours, he knew she would present him with a gourmet breakfast tray.

He wondered if she would again throw open the building's doors and invite him to make a run for it. If she did, he'd do it.

• • •

When dawn broke, the opening in the drapes slowly brightened. Ian pretended to stir to wakefulness.

"Good morning, sunshine!" Amity said, sitting up.

Ian stretched his arms high above his head. "Good morning," he said, sounding as groggy as possible.

Amity climbed to her feet. She went to the window, then stopped, staring at it.

"What's wrong?" Ian asked.

"I could've sworn I closed those drapes."

After viewing the late-night hunter show, Ian felt the prickle of fear, having forgotten to close the drapes.

Fortunately, Amity seemed to brush it off. She opened the drapes all the way, filling the room with light. She came close to him, closely studying his face. "You look so tired. How did you sleep?"

Ian pretended to yawn. "My sleep every night here has been wonderful."

"Hmm," Amity said.

Someone knocked on the door. Amity went to it.

Ian noticed that she'd left her bag on the table.

When she opened the door. Someone handed her a tray. "Thank you," she said, closing the door. She returned to Ian, lowered the tray's foot stands, and set it in front of him on the bed. "Breakfast in bed is served." She took off the plate covers. "This morning, we have a Denver omelet with juicy vine-ripened sliced tomatoes with a side of New Zealand venison sausage. If you still have room after, you can enjoy some sticky maple crescent buns still steamy-warm from the oven."

"What's the drink?" Ian asked, pointing to the tall glass of juice on the tray.

"It's a special apricot nectar ale. I'm sure you'll love it."

"You're probably right," Ian said. Once again, there was no way he would sip or eat anything that could hinder his ability to make the hike today. "I need to use the bathroom," he moved the tray, setting it aside on the bed. He went to the bathroom doorway and stopped. "I have another request that might surprise you."

"Anything!" Amity said, stacking the plate covers.

"I'd like some coffee from that French press you brought before."

Amity's brow furrowed. "Are you serious?"

"Absolutely. You've already commented that I look a little tired. Being practical is more important than my taste preference. What better way than some hot java to give me the boost I need today?"

Amity thought for a moment and then shrugged. "As you wish. I'll be right back with it."

Ian went into the bathroom, leaving the door open a crack. He peered through it and saw Amity heading to the bedroom door.

"Cream and sugar?" she hollered over her shoulder.

"Please," Ian said. He watched her exit. When the bedroom door clicked, excitement flooded him when he saw her bag still on the table. He ran across the room. When he slipped his hand into the bag to search it, he heard Amity's footsteps in the vestibule. He pulled his hand out as he heard her keys jingling. There was no time for him to run back to the bathroom before she entered. Catching him standing beside her open bag would be beyond suspicious. With nowhere to run, Ian took his only option to conceal himself. He slipped behind the full-length drapes, pressing himself against the window. He sucked in to make himself as thin as possible.

Amity entered and hurried to the table, saying, "...don't know how I'm supposed to go anywhere without my keys." She approached and stood within an arms-length of him.

Ian held his breath.

She picked up her bag, slipping it over her shoulder. "This might take a few minutes," she hollered toward the bathroom.

When Ian didn't respond, she said, "Did you hear me?" She went to the bathroom door and put her ear to it. "Ian, are you okay?" She pushed the bathroom door open wider and looked in.

Ian felt his pulse throbbing in his neck. He remembered her freaking out when she couldn't find him while he hid under the bed. The curtains were a crappy hiding place, and it would take only a casual glance to see his toes jutting out from under them.

Amity stepped into the bathroom. "Where are you?" He heard the shower door slide open.

"I'm out here," he said, reaching back to stop the drapes from swaying.

Amity came out of the bathroom, looking confused. "But you..." she thumbed over her shoulder. "How did you get there?" She pointed at him.

"What do you mean?" Ian said. "I'm right here."

"Wait a minute," Amity said, looking back into the bathroom and then at Ian several times.

"I'm right here," Ian said, seizing on her confusion to make her believe she had simply overlooked him.

"No, no," she said, waving him off. "I know for a fact that when I left, you were standing in that bathroom. I stepped out and instantly realized that I had forgotten my bag. I turned around and opened the door only ten seconds later, and suddenly, you are standing beside the window?" She pointed to Ian's feet.

"I don't know what to tell you," Ian said, shrugging. "I came over here to tie the drapes open. I love the light." He turned and used the tassel to wrap and tie back the drapes.

"Oh, my God!" Amity covered her open mouth with both hands.

"What's wrong?" Ian looked concerned.

Amity shook her head, still clasping her mouth. Her eyes were wide.

"What's the problem?" Ian said, walking toward her.

Amity stepped back and dropped her hands from her mouth. "You're him, aren't you?"

"Who?"

"You don't have to pretend with me," she said. "I know it's you. You were in the bathroom. I left the room and immediately returned to find you standing over there." She pointed to where Ian had stood beside the window. "You couldn't possibly have physically moved that quickly."

"I'm sorry, Amity, I don't understand."

"You performed a material displacement from the bathroom to the opposite side of the room, didn't you?"

It was Ian's time to be dumbfounded. He stared at her, thinking of the best way to respond.

"And you allowed me to detect your displacement." A tear slid from her eye, and she wiped it. "I had such a strong feeling you were much more than a lost traveler. Thank you for giving me the gift of certainty."

Ian tried to mask the fear he was feeling from whatever bizarre epiphany Amity was experiencing. The safest route was to play along. "Amity, I want you to tell me more."

"You're testing me, aren't you?" she said, grinning.

Ian's mind raced, trying to make sense of the realization about him Amity had experienced. Whatever she had confirmed in her mind, it seemed helpful. He decided not to ruin her new perception. He crossed his arms and raised his head higher. "Actually, no, this isn't a test. I want you to know I appreciate how good you've been to me."

Amity let her bag slip from her shoulder and fall to the floor. She dropped to her knees and crawled to Ian.

Ian hid his surprise and resisted his urge to step back.

Amity kissed each of his feet and said, "It has been my pleasure to serve you."

Ian watched her in utter disbelief.

Amity crawled back to her bag and pawed through it. She pulled out a book and raised it for him to see.

Ian released an audible gasp when she held up a book for him to see. It showed a man climbing a rugged hill, his eyes looking upward with gleeful anticipation of something. The title: *Our Beloved.*

Eighteen

AFTER CONVINCING AMITY to get up from her knees, Ian held the book, pretending, for the time being, it was the first time he had ever seen it.

"I know you can't tell me directly that I'm correct, but I have never felt stronger about any of you than I do right now."

"Any of us?"

"I knew the others were all imposters."

"Thank you," Ian said, keeping his response generic.

"I have a request for you," Amity said. "I hope you'll forgive me if I'm being too forward." She dug out a pen from her bag and held it out for him.

Ian took it.

"I know you aren't the author, but you're the star. Is there any chance I could convince you to sign it?" she asked. She chewed her fingernail, seeming afraid that he might say no.

He opened the book's cover. "After you've been so good to me? Of course," he said, keeping her delusion intact. "How shall I sign it?"

"Please write, 'For Amity Mae, together we'll stay, your love and great care I can never repay.' Can you write that?"

Ian pressed the pen against the paper of the title page and paused.

Amity clasped her fingers under her chin and wiggled her legs, willing him to hurry with the coveted autograph.

Ian scribbled the words Amity had requested and returned the book to her.

She opened it to confirm what he had written. "But you didn't sign it," she said, handing the book and pen back to him.

Ian was unsure of which identity Amity expected him to use. He took a chance. He scribbled a messy *O. B.*

When Amity took the book back from him, she looked at the signature, then pressed the open book around her face, drawing a deep breath as if trying to inhale the ink of his signature. New tears welled up in her eyes. "I've never felt so overwhelmed by the truth."

Ian watched, amazed. He knew things could be worse. Whatever revelation Amity had experienced during his attempt to snoop through her purse couldn't have played out better. He hoped to extend its benefit. Her glassy eyes looked at him, combining with her broad, toothy smile to create a gaze of adoration reserved for a deity.

She slipped the book back into her bag.

Ian noticed her hand trembling. "Now it's my turn for a request," he said.

"Anything! Anything in the world!" Amity managed to further broaden her grin.

"I'd like to hold your copy of *Our Beloved* for a while."

Amity frowned, and then her face lit up. "To bless it?" Amity asked.

"Precisely," Ian said.

"Thank you, my beloved!" She pulled the book out and gave it to him.

"I need some time alone with it," Ian added.

"Absolutely," Amity said. "I understand. I will not interrupt you until it's time to bring your lunch—oh my God, I forgot your coffee! I'm so sorry!"

Ian raised his hand to stop her. "Skip the coffee. Sending you out for it has served its purpose."

"Thank you for your leniency, my beloved," she said. "I'll give you the privacy you've requested to bless your book."

"Thank you."

As Amity left the room, she said, "Be warned that Angelica is still planning to kill you." She pulled the door closed.

"Wait! What?" Ian called out to her.

Amity opened the door again.

Ian said, "What did you say?"

"Angelica. She wants to dispense with you. She's sure you're an imposter."

"Right," Ian said, trying to avoid appearing naïve despite being totally confused.

"Which reminds me…" Amity said, coming back in. "I've gone above and beyond in my preparation to protect you. The best defense is avoiding the need for defense. Come with me." She motioned for him to join her beside the bed. She moved the food tray, kneeled, and flipped back the bedspread. She tore a long seam of Velcro along the entire length of the box spring mattress, revealing an open compartment. "I'm so grateful that you're thin. You should hide in there if you hear anyone other than me trying to get into your room while you're alone. I'm the only one who knows about it. I want you to try it."

Ian kneeled and raised one leg into the compartment before sliding the rest of his body inside. It was cramped, but the length and width of the mattress gave sufficient air for at least a few minutes.

"Close yourself in," Amity said. "You need to know how to do this on your own."

Ian reached out and pulled the end of the side flap, connecting it and sealing himself inside.

Amity flipped the bedspread down.

Ian saw the edges of the seam go dark.

"See?" Amity said. "The bitch would need a dog to find you."

"I'd like to get out," Ian said, his voice muffled.

Amity opened the flap.

He slid out and said, "I could have used that compartment when she first tried to enter my room."

Amity said, "To be honest, I wasn't certain of your identity back then."

"I'm glad it's now clear," Ian said, desperately hoping it would remain clear. "Thank you for looking out for me. Now, can you fill me in on why Angelica wants me dead?"

Amity looked at him suspiciously, then said, "Ah, you're testing my knowledge."

Ian smiled and winked.

She said, "Any rescue nurturer who accurately recognizes an imposter and submits a written ballot before dispensing with him is rewarded for their insight. They also improve the chances of the person they nurture for a successful Blessed Egress. You're lucky she failed to enter your room on her first try." Amity smiled and backed away from him, almost bowing, on her way to the door. She opened it and said, "I want you to know that I'm going out to make my declaration of faith immediately."

Ian didn't even try to make sense of the statement. "That is good," he said.

"There's one more thing," she said, slowly shaking her head as more tears flowed.

"Yes, what is it?" Ian said.

She held up her finger for him to wait. When she regained her composure, she said, "I love you so much, my beloved." She closed the door.

• • •

Ian knew the book in his hand linked Biding Wellness Center to Egress Encampment, but he didn't know how. He only knew the answer must be hidden in the pages of the *Our Beloved* book. During his captivity at Biding Wellness Center, the book's boring content gained appeal only after the voice in the vent told him it contained Riddick's map. Amity's revelation of Ian's participation in the storyline gave the story a new relevance.

He got himself comfortable on the bed, and for the next four hours, he read *Our Beloved* in earnest for the first time. He virtually devoured every word of every page. As the story unfolded, he realized that the first two-thirds featured a protagonist whose experience was nearly identical to everything that had happened to him since his intervention. And if those first two-thirds of the book were accurate, then the prophecy of the last third was absolutely horrifying.

Our Beloved chronicled the journey of a troubled young man who was rescued from a life of sin by devout Saden believers and forced into rehabilitation against his will. The young man soon discovers that he is one of the many people the Sadens have acquired, purportedly for addiction treatment. The protagonist is transported to a secret place where he's held captive while his handlers test his ability to cope with horrible conditions. He is held in isolation and regularly threatened with punishment. He is forced to watch others being punished. He is given small amounts of unpalatable food. After several days of suffering, a special messenger from God provides insight, bringing hope through a secret map and the tools he needs to escape. The protagonist uses the special map to embark on a journey. When the time is right, he escapes, beginning a grueling trek deep into the wilderness. Eventually, when he is nearly depleted of all physical strength, he reaches a place called Egress Encampment. The Sadens that live there assign him a female nourisher who revitalizes him with the finest foods and plush accommodations while he rejuvenates his resources. After a few days, he is forced to take part in a ceremony. At its conclusion, he is set free to run back to civilization. After a brief delay, the Saden hunters from the camp pursue him on foot at nighttime. He spends an entire night on the run with the Sadens in pursuit. While fleeing, he suffers injuries, close calls, and several near-death experiences.

If the Saden hunters can catch him before he reaches civilization, their success proves he is an imposter. They then mercilessly slaughter him with the brutality reserved for a person who has betrayed all Sadens.

If the beloved reaches the road that marks the threshold of civilization, it symbolically represents the conclusion of his Blessed Egress. A group of well-rested Saden hunters wait there for him. Instead of killing him, they carry him back to Egress Encampment, where he is celebrated for having proven himself to be the genuine beloved. He is given all the accolades of a victorious king, including continued indulgence in the best food and constant doting. He becomes a representative for the Sadens, taking the message to the world where he preaches it, restoring their reputation, and converting many thousands of new followers to Sadenism.

. . .

Ian finished the book a few minutes after noon and put it on the bedside table. The last events of the story had his pulse racing as though he had just sprinted a hundred meters. The accuracy with which these Sadens had masterfully enticed and coerced him to follow each of the protagonist's steps in the book was stunning. His arrival at Egress Encampment was positioned precisely two-thirds of the way into the story. If the final chapters proved to as accurate as the earlier ones, he was about to endure a horrific nightmare with no way to avoid it.

His shoulders jumped when a knock at the door startled him. The door opened, and Amity leaned in. "My beloved, I have some lunch. Are you ready to munch?"

Ian waved her in, trying to appear normal. "I've been expecting you," he said.

Amity blushed. "Really?" She pushed the door open with her elbow and entered with a tray.

Ian pointed to the corner table.

Amity carried the tray there. As she crossed the room, she sneaked a couple of glances at him like a fan passing by her idol.

Ian got up from the bed and picked up *Our Beloved*. He tucked it under his arm and went to the table where Amity busied herself, arranging the plates and silverware.

Amity forced herself to pause her grinning and said, "For lunch, we have grilled sea bass in a sake miso butter sauce beside sautéed baby carrots and—"

"Hold on," Ian said, raising his hand.

Amity's smile dissolved. She looked closer at Ian. "You're sweating. Is everything okay?"

"No, it's not." Ian picked up the food tray and set it on the floor. "We need to talk," he said.

Panic filled Amity's face. "Is something not acceptable, my beloved?"

Ian took the book from under his arm and tossed it onto the table.

"No, the food is fine, Amity." He motioned for her to sit in the chair on the opposite side.

She complied, still looking worried.

Ian sat and tapped his finger on the book cover. "You think I am this person? Our beloved?"

"No," Amity said.

Ian frowned.

"I don't think you are our beloved," she said. "I *know* it!" She folded her hands on the table and grinned. "If I didn't believe it with all my heart, you'd already be dead."

"How's that?" Ian asked.

Amity used two fingers to pull a capped syringe from her cleavage. She held it up for him to see. "Because I would have murdered you in that chair before you set foot in this room." She pointed the syringe over her shoulder toward the vestibule.

Ian swallowed. "By injection?"

"It's called T-61. It's a cocktail of embutramine and mebezonium that paralyzes respiration and causes circulatory collapse in a few seconds. In other words, it stops your heart and the muscles that make your lungs work. It's typically used by veterinarians, but we use it for imposters. They're less than human, so it's completely appropriate."

Ian looked back and forth between the syringe needle and Amity's face.

"You look so scared," Amity said, sliding the syringe back between her breasts. "You can relax. It would have been painless. In fact, Jebediah trapped a buck and gave us a demonstration out in the easement. It was so peaceful. The buck shook its head several times, then its legs simply buckled. The only sign that it was dying came from its eyes—they grew huge for about two minutes before slowly shrinking back to normal size as they faded away. We knew it was gone because Jebediah used tongs to press a lump of red-hot coal to its ass. It didn't move."

Ian had to consciously close his mouth. "Why not just shoot it?" he asked.

"We don't believe in using guns. We believe in only using the direct kinetic energy of muscular effort to kill imposters. We forbid bullets, hanging, and electrocution because these bring death by using energy other than the muscular force God gives us. Stabbing with a knife, impaling with a spear, or crushing a skull with a club are all blessed methods of dispensing with imposters. Our hunters occasionally fight one another for the coveted opportunity to use their hands to snuff an imposter's unworthy life. The intimacy of strangulation is our ultimate and most sacred method. Even so, our hunters are extremely competitive and prefer to flaunt their skill with handheld weapons during a Blessed Egress."

Ian sat back in his chair. He felt a wave of nausea coming on.

"I've never seen you so pale, my beloved," Amity said. "Trust me, my syringe will never touch you."

Ian slowly nodded. "What you're telling me... It's just a lot to take in."

"I don't expect you to know everything. We don't believe that our beloved is omniscient. That would be unfair. Only God is omniscient. According to prophecy, part of our job is to teach you the truth. Because of your special calling, any knowledge you gain from us will be multiplied as you are granted a special blessing of knowledge. Soon, you will know more about us and our purpose than we do, which is why you will be our leader." She wagged her finger at him. "I had a hunch about you, but I should have been certain you were our beloved much sooner. You are more cooperative than an imposter—not to mention cuter."

Ian ignored her flattery. "You've actually injected people with that?" He pointed to where she had tucked the syringe.

"I've had the pleasure of dispensing with only two imposters that way. The T-61 keeps the job clean. Before a pharmacist joined Egress Encampment, we had to kill imposters the old-fashioned way." Not taking her eyes off Ian, she stood, reached behind her, and drew a 9-inch knife from some hidden sheath concealed in the back of her dress.

"Whoa," Ian said, sitting back to give her more space.

"Don't worry," Amity said. "If it's true you haven't lied, this blade will never slit you wide." She raised the knife, putting the tip inches from her nose. The room's reflection danced on the dark, serrated blade. She seemed lost in a momentary trance, then said, "What was I saying? Oh, I remember. We used to rely on the knife. The contour sheets on your bed are waterproof to make cleanup easier. The syringe gives us a bloodless way to dispense with imposters. I feel comfortable revealing these things to you because you revealed yourself by allowing me to see your material displacement." She flipped the knife in the air, catching it perfectly by the handle, then twisted her torso, smoothly sliding the blade back into a hidden sheath in the back of her dress that Ian had never seen. "You have nothing to fear," she said.

Ian knew this was a lie. He had everything to fear, but it was time for extreme care with every word he said to Amity. According to the book, imposters were always killed the moment they said or did something that confirmed they couldn't possibly be the beloved. Those who survived until their Blessed Egress ceremony were set free to be hunted and killed by a throng of physically fit hunters who knew every inch of this wilderness. Ian knew it was virtually impossible for any man to elude them for thirty miles successfully. "I'm not afraid," Ian said. "If I were an imposter, you or someone would have tried to kill me by now, right?"

"Absolutely. Except that we don't try to kill imposters, we do kill them. Each sacrifice has been exhilarating because we knew it brought us closer to your arrival, our true beloved."

"How many imposters have there been?" Ian's mouth had gone dry.

Amity looked up and began counting on her fingers before she shrugged and said, "Many."

"I'm pleased you recognized and listened to your feelings about me," Ian said.

"It's more than a feeling. I'm absolutely certain of this truth. I know what you did—you showed me a miracle. I know for a fact that you displaced from the bathroom to the opposite side of the suite, and I know you allowed me to see it. It was such a special gift. I can't thank you enough."

Ian felt light-headed as he stared down at the copy of *Our Beloved.*. "You're welcome," he said in barely a whisper.

"I will ensure you are fully prepared for your Blessed Egress," Amity said.

"I trust you," Ian replied.

Amity's face filled with affection. "Aww, that makes me happy. I also want you to know I have submitted my declaration of faith."

Ian didn't remember this term being mentioned in the book. "And tell me how you did that," he asked, carefully wording the question like a quiz rather than an inquiry.

"My declaration of faith means I've given official written notice of my faith that you are our beloved. If our hunters successfully kill you during your Blessed Egress, my declaration will result in my punishment. If I'm right, I will attain a new status among our members, and it will come with enormous privileges."

"What would your punishment be?"

"Death."

"My God," Ian said, covering his mouth.

"Yes, God is good!" Amity said, grinning.

After Ian took a moment, he said, "So then, what privileges would you get?"

"I'm afraid we must save that as a surprise." She leaned slightly to see his eyes. "You still look so worried."

"Tell me your camp's connection to Biding Wellness Center?"

"I expected that one." Amity sat back. "Biding Wellness Center is our blessed gateway from your world to ours. You were selected as a beloved candidate to pass through it."

"Who selected me?" Ian said, raising his voice. "I need to know how this happened!"

"Stay calm. All of your questions will be answered. According to prophecy, our beloved is a man of the world who is afflicted with addiction. But his addiction to sinful substances and behaviors can be cured, transforming him into something absolutely magnificent, like a caterpillar to a butterfly. The hardship you experienced at Biding Wellness

Center inspired and compelled you, without our force, to embark on your blessed journey to our encampment to finalize your transformation. Subconsciously, you knew it was your destiny."

Ian put his head down on the table and sighed. He sat up and let his hands drop to his lap. "Listen, I have a request, but I don't want to anger you."

"Okay, my beloved, I won't get mad. If you're honest, I'll be glad."

"I don't want to be a bother to any of you fine people. I don't want to influence or change any of your beliefs. I don't want to intrude on your privacy. I want to give you your privacy as soon as possible because I respect you."

"Thank you for all that," Amity said. "What's your request?"

Ian said, "I no longer want to burden you with my care. And I don't want to risk the physical harm our hunters might experience while chasing me in blessed devotion to our faith. Catching me will be futile, because you and I know I'm your beloved. Therefore, I am canceling the Blessed Egress ceremony. I will journey alone to close my affairs in town before returning to resume my duties here. I need you to arrange for me to leave without being hunted."

Amity smiled at him and drummed her fingers on the table. "Is that what you truly want?"

"Yes."

"Of course I can allow you to leave."

"Thank you," Ian said, clasping his hands in gratitude.

"But I'm afraid that hunting you is our duty. Your method of arrival proves that God selected you for us. He inspired you to sacrifice almost all your physical resources to reach us. The physical and emotional toll you willingly paid to arrive at Egress Encampment is awe-inspiring. Failing to fulfill the final part of the prophecy would cheat you and us."

"See, that's the thing," Ian said, adjusting himself in the chair. "I wasn't inspired to go on a mission. As wonderful as your encampment is, arriving here wasn't my goal. I was simply trying to survive."

"You are so modest, my beloved. Your innocence and how you downplay your importance perfectly fit our prophetic description of you." She went to her bag and pulled out a crumpled piece of paper. She brought it back and flattened it on the table. It was Riddick's map. She tapped her finger on it. "From Biding Wellness Center, you could have run in any direction, but Egress Encampment was the destination you clearly chose and made every effort to reach. Prophecy told us you'd arrive under your own power and of your own will. You've fulfilled that to a tee. We've spent tremendous effort and many resources to get you here. Why would we squander that expense? It would be like a farmer spending weeks to fatten a calf, only to throw its pen open for it to go free. Absurd!" She waved her hand, dismissing the idea.

Ian cleared his throat and said, "Listen, I am your beloved, right?"

Amity grinned. "Oh, that sounds so wonderful! Yes, you are!"

"Okay, if I am your beloved, then I am giving you a direct order. I'm directing you to release me. I want to officially forbid anyone in this camp to follow me. You are to suspend all hunting activities for a minimum of three days. I am your beloved, and I'm commanding it."

Amity held back as long as she could before bursting into laughter. She bent over, clutching her stomach. After she caught her breath, she said, "You are hysterical! Wouldn't my premature obedience be nice? I refer to you as my beloved, because that's what I believe. But you have no authority over us until after your Blessed Egress!" She pushed *Our Beloved* closer to him. "On the other hand, if you want to place your hand on this book and solemnly swear that you are not our beloved, I can dispense with you now. I'd make it quicker and much less painful than any hunters will." She reached back for the sheathed knife.

"No! No!" Ian said, eyes wide.

"Aren't you adorable?" Amity said. "I knew you wouldn't do it because our beloved would never do such a thing. But letting you go without a hunt introduces too much risk. A hunt is an important validation of your identity. As Sadens, we've been mistreated by the press. Allowing someone not our beloved to return to civilization alive risks reigniting old questions about our practices. Soon, new inquiries, investigations, and unwanted attention from an even more aggressive press would occur. Your idea doesn't work. Unfortunately, if you are revealed to be an imposter, it will be easy for us to replace you with a new addict in this world that's so saturated with sin. You're lucky I observed your material displacement from the bathroom. Otherwise, I'd already be mopping blood from around your pathetic carcass."

Ian's heart pounded so hard he thought Amity might see his pulse in his neck. He felt nausea rushing back. He hurried into the bathroom and splashed water on his face. Amity stood in the doorway when he came out, her boot propping open the door. The vestibule's outside door was also open.

"Want to run away?" she said.

"No," Ian said, giving the answer he knew she wanted.

"Good," she said. She moved her foot to let the door close. She scuffed her heels as she strolled back to stand beside him.

Ian considered jumping her. There was a good chance he could physically overpower her. She wasn't large, but her knife handling intimidated him. If he could restrain her and tie her up, he could make her his hostage to escape the encampment. He didn't know where she ranked in the Saden hierarchy, but using her for a freedom ransom might work if she was important enough.

Amity said, "I'd be shocked if you even considered attacking me."

"I beg your pardon?" Ian said. She seemed to have read his mind, but that was impossible. "I wouldn't attack you. Why would you say that?"

"When you came out of the bathroom, your eyes scanned me from head to toe. Then you did it a second time as I approached you." She leaned closer. "The calculating eyes are unmistakable."

"No, I'm not planning to attack you," Ian said, ridiculing the idea with a small laugh.

She sat on the bed. "Ian, no one will stop you from running, but I hope you avoid that mistake for your sake," she said. "Fleeing before your Blessed Egress ceremony is the unmistakable sign of an imposter. You will be caught and slaughtered probably before you complete enough strides to be winded."

"I understand," Ian said, still feeling lightheaded.

"I wish you didn't look so sad and afraid," Amity said.

He took a seat beside her. "If you're wrong, I'm a dead man walking."

Amity jumped up and faced him. "I'm not wrong! May I have permission to touch your skin?"

"Why are you asking me that?"

"Touching our beloved without his permission is strictly forbidden and severely punished. If someone in our encampment touches you, you can be sure they think you are an imposter. To be safe, most of us err on the side of caution and avoid touching imposters." She came closer. "But I'm ready. I'm sure. Let me touch you… please. Just a little hug."

Ian looked shell-shocked. He backed away from her.

She stepped forward.

He backed away more, bumping into the wall.

She came within reach and looked into his eyes. "I really need your permission. Please let me," she said, opening her arms.

"You've already touched me."

"No, I haven't."

"You treated my feet with your hands."

"I wore gloves. I asked for your permission. You granted it. None of us, not even the Biding Wellness Center staff, have ever lifted a finger to you."

Amity's claim seemed utterly impossible. Ian thought back to when the nightmare had begun, from when he got into Dagny's car at his parents' house to when the seatbelt had restrained him. He remembered punching her, yet she had not retaliated physically. He could still hear the crack of

Garland's bullwhip but had never been whipped by it. He remembered when Jebediah, Kyle, and Jamie found him and how they didn't offer to carry him despite his condition. Instead, they gave him water and encouraged him to take the final few steps to the encampment. Then he remembered his escape attempt on Garland's motorcycle and said, "You broke your own rules. You told me you don't believe in guns. Two of your men aimed shotguns at me, forcing me to get into a car."

"They did not force you into the car. You willingly complied. If you had disobeyed and attempted to walk past them, they would have stepped aside. The true beloved should not require physical force to accept his mission. The gunmen knew this. Your compliance with all the commands you've been given proved to us you were a suitable candidate."

The maddening realization that he could have avoided all of this by simply walking away only added to Ian's emotional distress.

"Now that you understand why I've kept my distance, may I hug you for the first time?" Amity said. "Knowing who you are while not being able to touch you is driving me mad."

Ian had become so paranoid he worried that denying her might indicate he was an imposter. He gave a slight nod.

Amity grabbed him and hugged him tightly. She nuzzled her nose into his neck and inhaled deeply, rubbing her hands up and down his back and squeezing him as if trying to melt into his body. "You feel so warm. You smell so good. It is heaven to touch you."

Ian didn't participate in the hug, but that didn't affect Amity's enthusiasm as she squeezed his arms to his sides.

"Thank you, my beloved," she said as she released him. "I can feel the vitality exuding from you, and I'm more certain than ever." She looked up into his face and pulled his hands around her. "I want you to make love to me."

Yet again, disbelief filled Ian's face. He pushed her away to arm's length and said, "I need some alone time to think—please." He pointed to the door.

"First, listen," Amity said, putting her finger to his lips. "I know the idea might seem odd, but I can explain. If I already carry our beloved's seed when he concludes the Blessed Egress, I will be rewarded for my foresight. Impregnating me is your ultimate blessing. If it is later shown that I'm carrying an imposter's seed, I'll be killed and buried with your carcass. If you had doubts about my commitment to you before, my desire to make love to you should give you certainty."

Ian looked into her wide eyes, which now projected an unmistakable instability. He had no idea what bizarre revelation would come from her lips next. The potential for her affection to change to rage instantly was clear if he denied her. He paused to construct the gentlest no he could muster and said, "Amity, I am so flattered by that offer, and that might happen, but I think a better time for that will come soon."

He was relieved that only the slightest disappointment registered on her face.

"Okay, when?" she asked.

"Why don't I tell you when I'm ready?" Ian replied. "For now, I need time alone for introspection and preparation. I'm sure you understand."

"Of course. Anything my beloved wants." She looked at the tray on the floor beside the table. "Your lunch is cold. Can I replace it for you?"

"That isn't necessary. I don't have an appetite." Ian said.

Nineteen

IAN PACED BETWEEN the bathroom doorway and the windows after Amity exited. His whole body felt sweaty. Everything happening to him was making sense in a way that was yet more horrifying. He sat at the table and spent the next hours brainstorming with the disturbing new information Amity had given him. He racked his brain for any way to change his fate, but none of his devised schemes seemed workable. There were no vehicles to steal. There were no horses. He couldn't even get his hands on a gun because these people didn't use them. The remote location was perfect for the Sadens' sick ritual and anything else they wanted to do to him. He wasn't in peak physical shape and wasn't fully recovered from the incident on the treadmill. The threat of death along the thirty-mile distance to the main road was more effective at detaining him than steel bars and handcuffs. Even if he recuperated for an entire week, eating the fantastic food, the odds of eluding and then escaping these physically fit hunters in a foot chase were solidly stacked against him.

He got up, and on his way to the bed, he heard a new sound. A muffled voice was coming from behind one of his walls. He strolled the room's perimeter, listening to each wall. He soon discovered that the conversation came from behind the door in his room that Amity had told him was only a storage closet. It had been completely silent during his entire stay, so he had completely forgotten about it. He pressed his ear to the crack. One voice was female, the other male. It certainly wasn't a closet. It was a room at least large enough for two people. He heard the woman laugh at one point. He spent a few minutes trying to understand their conversation, but couldn't make out their words.

A knock at his door jerked him from his eavesdropping. He stepped away from the door as Amity came in, holding a tray.

"Since our gabbing made your lunch go cold, I found dinner if you've found your appetite. Hungry, my beloved?"

"Is this my last meal?"

"No, silly. Your Blessed Egress isn't for a couple more days. Don't be so dramatic." She carried the tray to the table and set it down. "I know you'll escape—you'll see." She motioned for him to come and eat.

As he went to her, he said, "So, I didn't know this building had another room," he said.

Amity didn't respond, preoccupied with removing the plate covers and arranging Ian's silverware.

"I heard voices in the storage room," Ian said, pointing to the door.

Amity held up her finger while looking at the dinner setting and said, "Tonight we have wild-game venison bourguignon, fingerling garlic mashed potatoes with burgundy wine gravy, and a delicious butter lettuce, watercress, and chrysanthemum salad with 25-year-aged balsamic vinaigrette on the side. For a beverage, we have a delicious hibiscus strawberry rhubarb iced tea. For dessert, you'll enjoy a beignet-topped tiramisu with chocolate ganache."

"That sounds delicious, but you didn't answer me. Who did I hear in the room next to mine?"

Amity came to him. She nibbled her lip briefly, then said, "That would be a recent visitor who I believe to be an imposter."

"You've captured someone else?"

"We didn't capture anyone. He journeyed to our encampment from Biding Wellness Center of his own free will, just like you did."

Ian felt sorry for the person, but the prospect of having someone to commiserate with was a relief. If he could communicate with the person, maybe they could devise a plan.

"His room isn't as secure as yours, so, honestly, I think he's going to make a run. He's a little pudgy. He won't make it far. Our hunters will quickly fetch and slaughter him, just like so many others." Amity rolled her eyes and made an on-and-on motion with her hand. "Normally, dispensing with an imposter was something to celebrate, but after you revealed yourself to me, it seems like a waste of time."

The voices from behind the wall resumed. Amity tilted her head, now able to hear them, too. When the woman finished speaking, Amity said, "That's Angelica. Your late-night wannabe visitor."

"You told me she wouldn't be at the camp long."

"And I meant it, but she's been assigned to be the new imposter's nourisher, like I have been yours."

"It's funny," Amity said, "after tending to him for only fifteen minutes, Angelica is certain that the new piece of trash next door is our beloved." She rolled her eyes again.

"The same way you are certain about me," Ian said.

"Except that I'm right. You gave me a visible advantage. There can only be one of you, so I know your new neighbor won't be materially displacing for Angelica, ever."

Ian's anxiety finally yielded to his hunger, and Amity convinced him to eat. She stayed with him. Someone knocked at the door. Amity went and opened it. Another woman stepped in. She was shorter than Amity, attractive, and had darker hair. She wore a purple dress identical to Amity's, which visually added to the cult-like feel these people exuded.

"I need some snow," she said to Amity.

"Storage, in the bookcase," Amity replied.

"I also need—"

"Shh!" Amity said. She shooed the woman out with her hand.

The woman looked at Ian, scanning his details with disdain. Before she closed the door, Ian noticed a loaded IV stand parked in the vestibule behind her.

When the woman left, Ian said, "Angelica?"

"Yep, that's her," Amity said, returning to the table. She snapped open a napkin and draped it over Ian's leg.

The IV stand had been visible to both of them, making it fair to ask about it without revealing that he had already figured out more than he should have. He seized the opportunity.

"What was the IV stand for?" he said.

"What IV stand?" she said.

"The one I saw right outside the door," Ian said.

"Her visitor has a medical condition that requires it."

"Do I have that same condition?" Ian watched her carefully.

Amity's expression tensed, then slowly relaxed and smiled. "Anything we do is designed to be helpful, not harmful."

"I know I've been drugged," Ian said.

"You have nothing to worry about."

"I'll skip the part about you having no right to medicate me without my permission because my permission isn't needed for anything that happens to me here, right?"

The corners of Amity's mouth went down. She nodded.

"So, what did you give me?" Ian asked.

Amity didn't answer.

"What was it?" Ian repeated louder.

Amity sat in the chair opposite him. She folded her hands in her lap and said, "We have worked so hard to put everything you need in place to help you succeed at your Blessed Egress. The intravenous solutions are part of a regimen that rapidly heals you from your arduous journey. We have refined it many times, making it more effective than ever."

"Why won't you tell me what is in the IV?" he said.

"The solution includes a pre-hydration formula. It includes magnesium, potassium, zinc, thiamine, folate, vitamins B6, B12, and several other ingredients. We follow that infusion with a mild sedative to enhance your rest."

"You sedated me before giving me the IV. After eating your food, I've never been knocked out so fast."

"To be completely honest with you, yes, we do season your meals with several ingredients that, together, are completely flavorless and help you rest."

"Is that what you call it—seasoning?"

"It's perfectly safe. Your sedation is controlled, and I closely monitor you. The only other part of your infusion I can share with you is Somatropin, which enhances your appetite a wee bit."

"Your food is extraordinary. Why would you need to enhance my appetite?"

"An efficient, carefully calculated minimum calorie intake is vital to ensure that we see your best effort in your Blessed Egress."

Ian had slouched in his chair.

Amity smiled and slapped her hands onto her lap. "We have a special dessert for you." She got up and went to the door. "I need to bring it on a separate tray. I'll be right back."

Ian picked at his meal with his fork. His few bites were delicious, as usual, but he lacked the ravenous appetite he now knew to have been at least partially drug-induced.

Within a few minutes, he heard something that made him stop chewing and put down his fork. The sound was faint at first but grew, giving him more excitement than he had felt for days. It was the unmistakable beating of an approaching helicopter.

He jumped up from the table and scanned the portion of the sky visible through the window, but saw nothing. In all his time at Egress Encampment, he hadn't heard any vehicle's sound, and there was no telling when another helicopter might pass over. It was his last chance to communicate with someone from the world of the sane.

He ran to the door and looked into the vestibule. The door to the outside was closed and locked as usual. Despite the Sadens' warning to respect their privacy and not to bring any visual attention to their encampment, he kicked the door, slammed his weight into it, and somehow broke the latch. He ran out into the easement between the buildings. The setting sun stretched the shadows from the trees and buildings, and he hoped there was enough light for the helicopter pilot to see his movement below. If he could get the pilot's attention, he might elude his captors long enough for the helicopter to land for his rescue.

The helicopter neared and was on a trajectory that would take it almost directly overhead. He jumped up and down, waving his hands and screaming, "Help! Down here! Please Help!" He quickly scanned his surroundings. Amity and the hunters were nowhere in sight. He continued jumping and shouting. The helicopter came so close that Ian read the number on its belly. The cockpit windshield faced forward. Ian realized the angle would make it difficult for the pilot to spot him directly below. He screamed louder and ran as fast as he could, still waving his arms, but the helicopter passed overhead without slowing or turning. Ian shouted, "No, down here!"

He heard footsteps behind him. He looked back and saw three shirtless hunters in shorts sprinting in his direction. The one in the middle swung something beside him like a lasso. The second carried some type of package, clutching it like a football. The third had a long pole that he carried like a spear.

The helicopter faded away.

"No!" Ian said as he turned and raced toward the woods.

The hunters quickly overtook him, even though Ian pushed for all the speed his legs could give.

The hunters' feet barely made any sound. They didn't shout or command him to stop. Something struck the back of his legs. He glanced down briefly and saw a rope tether connected by two balls orbiting his legs tighter and tighter until they were locked. He fell forward, spreading his arms to break his fall.

The hunter with the package flung it out and over him. A net spread, doming in the air before settling on Ian while he frantically tried to free his legs from the tether. Each of the men took hold of the ends of the net. They ran a choreographed maneuver, two running clockwise while the third running counterclockwise, ducking and moving their arms to avoid entangling each other. The net quickly tightened around Ian's body. He tried to grab the netting material to pull it off, but the openings were large enough that his hands slipped through the holes on his first attempts, further entangling him. In less than ten seconds, the men had fully restrained and secured Ian in a cocoon of netting.

One hunter retrieved a long wooden pole that he had tossed to the ground. While the other men held the net's loops open, he threaded the pole through before lifting Ian from the ground.

Ian yelled, "No! Get this off me! I am your beloved! You will pay for this." His struggle only tightened the net.

The men lifted the wooden pole to rest on their shoulders and carried Ian back toward the building. He dangled, swaying back and forth in rhythm with their strides. He felt wrapped like a helpless fly in a spider's silk.

The beating of the helicopter's rotors grew stronger. It had turned around and was returning in the direction it had come.

When the helicopter crested the trees and came into view, the hunters stopped and stood perfectly still.

Ian screamed, "Down here! Help me!" But all he could do was shout and wiggle his hands and feet.

The men stood like statues until the helicopter passed over again and disappeared from view. They then finished their trek to Ian's building, carrying him into the vestibule. The third man produced keys and opened Ian's bedroom door. They took him inside and set him down on the center of the floor between the bed and the corner table.

"It's hard for me to breathe. Please…" Ian said.

The men tugged several parts of the net, slightly loosening it and avoiding touching Ian. Without a word, they filed out of the room.

"Can you please loosen it?" Ian called out.

The door slammed, latching.

A few minutes later, Amity barged into his room. "Why did you do that?" she asked. She looked angrier than Ian had ever seen her.

He twisted and raised his head to look at her from inside the netting.

She came toward him. Her boots scuffed to a stop near his face.

"I'm just trying to live," Ian said. Resting his head again.

Amity said, "And you will live when you survive the Blessed Egress." She paused and added, " I should thank you."

Ian strained to lift his head again. "For?"

"Prophecy tells us to be prepared for our beloved to attempt an escape before his Blessed Egress ceremony. It's his way of testing our vigilance and preparation for the event. But deep down, our beloved wants us to catch him before he reaches the encampment boundary. He wants us to ensure a successful Blessed Egress."

"Well, you passed your test," Ian scoffed.

Amity grinned. "I knew you would stop before reaching our property line, and for that, you are lucky."

"I feel anything but lucky," Ian said, glaring at her.

"If you had taken one step off our encampment boundary before your Blessed Egress, it would have been an unmistakable sign that you are an imposter. The hunters who fetched you would have killed you on the spot—probably after arguing over which of them would have the pleasure."

Ian was becoming callous to Amity's shocking revelations.

"Now that you're thrilled to have passed the test, can you get me out of this net?"

"Of course, my beloved." She reached back and pulled her long knife from its sheath. She took hold of the net and pulled it from his chest and stomach. She slid the blade underneath it. Ian held his breath while she sliced through the net loops all the way past his stomach to his groin. She then cut the tether that bound his legs.

Ian breathed deeply and wiggled out of the sliced netting.

She stepped back while Ian brushed himself off. "Your guys overtook and wrapped me from at least twenty meters in less than thirty seconds.

And do you seriously expect me to outrun more of them for thirty miles?"

Amity poked her tongue into her cheek and slowly nodded. "Are you testing my faith?"

"No, I really want you to answer that."

"At the ceremony, you will have everything you need for a successful Blessed Egress if you are truly our beloved. I expect you to materially displace if necessary. By the way, you've damaged yourself." She pointed.

Ian raised his forearm. Some blood trickled toward his elbow from a cut he had suffered in his struggle.

"It's not much. I'll wash it," Ian said.

Amity said, "I'll get you a bandage. Meanwhile, the time for your Blessed Egress is fast approaching. You will take part, no matter your physical condition. I advise you to reverse your sleep cycle for an added advantage."

"Because…?"

"Because Blessed Egresses are always held after dark. You need all the rest you can get right beforehand."

Ian lay in bed, fully dressed, as he continued to rack his brain for ways to save his life. So far, the only idea with an ounce of promise was to flee midday while the sun was at its brightest. With any luck, any element of surprise would combine with the Sadens' concerns about being spotted from the sky to create an advantage, even if small. A fresh idea came to him.

Amity made one more visit to Ian's room to bring the bandage she promised for his arm and to offer more food for the calories she insisted he'd need. Ian had no appetite. Despite her protests, he rejected a tray of marinated rib-eye steak with herb garlic butter, grilled baby asparagus, and strawberry shortcake topped with a dollop of freshly whipped cream.

"I have a concern I need to share with you," Ian said.

"Oh?"

"Yes, I think it's time for us to leave. I think you called it the Exodus."

"Why would you say that?"

"Initially, I wasn't going to say anything, but I've decided that not sharing any information with you would be selfish. Today, when the helicopter passed over, I made eye contact with the pilot."

"So what?" Amity said.

"The pilot signaled me. He gestured to me with his finger as if to say, 'I'll be back.' I think you should carry out that Exodus you mentioned."

"So, you think we should make our Blessed Exodus immediately?"

"Absolutely. If you want to save any of your possessions without having to burn them, we all need to leave now."

Amity slowly said, "Are you sure you want that?"

"*You* should want that. I'm giving you this information for your own sake. You've been good to me, and I don't want you to lose everything you've built. If I'm correct, and you do nothing, you can expect this camp to be swarmed before morning."

Amity tried to resist laughing. "Thanks for the warning."

"You think I'm joking? Listen, we all need to leave on the Blessed Exodus right away. If we do, we can cover a good distance before dark."

Amity couldn't hold it anymore and clutched her stomach, laughing.

"I don't see what's funny," Ian said.

Amity caught her breath and said, "The Blessed Exodus doesn't involve fleeing into the woods, silly! We leave directly from our rooms."

"I don't understand."

"We leave this earth through fire. Only Dagny's partner, Garland, can call for the Blessed Exodus. If someone breaches Egress Encampment to take it from us, Garland initiates the Blessed Exodus. He will order all the beloved's Sadens to our rooms, where we'll secure the doors. Then we are to flush our keys down the toilet. The always-locked doorknob in every room that makes you so uneasy seals our commitment. It ensures that the fire cleanses and transports us from this place. If you are still here, you'll have the privilege of participating in our Exodus, and you'll take the journey with us. Ready to go?"

Ian shook his head.

"That was a clever attempt," Amity said, laughing. She went to the door and opened it with a key. "I really can't blame you for trying. You have yet to realize and truly feel your new identity as our beloved. That will happen soon enough. That you're a horrible liar only makes you more adorable."

Twenty

WHEN THE SUN went down, he turned on the bedside lamp, filling the room with a soft yellow light. The stress and many adrenaline surges were taking a toll. Although he fought to stay awake, he soon drifted off.

Just after midnight, a new, growing sound woke him up. He sat up in bed, listening to an approaching vehicle. He turned off the bedside light to conceal himself and went to the window, parting the drapes just enough to peek through. He saw a large group of people—more people than he had imagined being at the encampment. Each person held an illuminated stick, so that, combined, they created enough ambient light to make out some of their features. Most of them were the athletic, bearded men Ian recognized as hunters. They wore shoes resembling moccasins, dark shorts, and no shirt. He counted about 30 of them. Each man had a canteen slung over his shoulder. Their bodies were ornamented like warriors, their arms and faces brightly painted with hieroglyphics. Their beards were dusted white. They wore back necklaces with several tufts of hair tied vertically down their backs. They stood near a raised wooden platform connected by a narrow staircase of about five steps.

Off to the side, a small group of women stood together, their hands comfortably folded in front of them as they supervised the men.

A van backed its way between the buildings toward them. The men and women lined up while holding their light sticks at a 45-degree angle, creating a pathway for it to follow. They guided the van to a large table. The light sticks illuminated the van's brown exterior. Twigs and branches protruded from the door cracks and fenders after passing through the narrow vegetation-encroached roadway Ian remembered.

It came to a stop. In unison, the men and women cheered. The driver got out and walked around the front of the van to the side closest to Ian's window. He couldn't see who it was because the men quickly swarmed the driver, blocking his view. Eventually, he realized they were taking turns hugging the person. When the last man had given his hug, the driver stepped from the crowd, moving to stand beside a lit table. The driver was Dagny Conger. She raised her hand. Everyone went silent and turned to face her. She pointed to a hunter. He opened up the rear doors of the van. She pointed to two others, and they began unloading crates from the van, placing them on the table. She pointed to other men and women who joined to help carry the crates through an open door into the structure Ian assumed was the Sustenance Center.

Ian's shoulders jerked when a voice startled him from behind. "I thought that scene might excite you."

He spun to see a silhouette in the open door.

"It's me, my beloved," Amity said.

"You startled me," Ian said, clutching his chest.

"I'm sorry," she said. She came and set her bag on the table before joining Ian at the window. "I'm glad you turned off the lights before looking."

"Don't they know I'm here?"

"They do, but it's almost 10:00 p.m. At this time of night, they expect me to have sedated you. I'm the only one who knows you are awake. The imposter next door is sound asleep and will hear nothing." She put her face in the opening of the drapes.

While she looked out, Ian noticed a blinking light inside Amity's bag. He reached back and quietly widened the bag's opening a bit. Although it was too dark to see clearly, he was reasonably sure it was the phone he had seen her use just outside the treadmill room.

Amity said, "Usually, the only visitors allowed to remain awake at this hour are those in final preparation for their Blessed Egresses."

"That's interesting," Ian said. He slipped his hand into her bag. He felt the phone and pulled it out.

"Did you see him?" she said, pulling her face from the window.

"No, who?" Ian said, slipping the phone into his back pocket.

"Look again," Amity said. "He's about to climb the steps."

Ian put his face to the window. "I don't see him yet," Ian said,

She opened the drapes enough to put her face beside his. "Look right there." Amity touched her finger to the window.

"The only person I see is the awful, cruel woman from Biding Wellness Center."

"That would be Ms. Conger. Before you judge her so harshly, don't forget that she was merely playing a role. If it weren't for her, we wouldn't have met!"

"Of course," Ian said sarcastically.

"Ms. Conger is delivering provisions. You can thank her for the fresh supply of delicacies you've enjoyed. The men are taking the crates inside for refrigeration and storage. She's also here to observe the launch of tonight's Blessed Egress. Everyone is so excited when she shows up. Can you see the lowlife imposter now?"

About half the men had moved to one side to wait with the women. The other half of the men moved away from the van and surrounded the platform. They strapped goggles to their heads, giving their eyes a futuristic alien appearance that contrasted with their primitive body painting and sparse garb.

A shirtless, muscular black man stood atop the platform. He was gagged. His hands and ankles were bound around a pole behind him. His green shorts glowed.

"Who is he?" Ian asked.

"My opinion? An imposter." Amity flicked her fingers toward the window dismissively. "His name is Riddick."

Hearing the name come from Amity's lips took Ian's breath away. He had to pause before he could speak. "How long has he been here?"

"Almost a week longer than you have."

Ian pulled his face from the window and stepped back. "He's the one who drew the map I followed."

"No, he isn't. Dagny drew your map. She uses the name of one addict as the map's author for the next addict. There's nothing more inspirational for visitors to Biding Wellness Center. It works every time."

Ian clenched his teeth.

"Come see," she said, motioning for him to look out the window again.

Ian complied. He didn't want to see what they were about to do to this man, yet he was still desperate to learn anything possible about their ceremony in case it could be used as an advantage. "Why are his shorts glowing?"

"He's wearing Blessed Egress garb. The luminescent material is most visible during the first thirty minutes of the hunt. Most imposters are slaughtered naked after they quickly realize the luminescence of the shorts is a liability. Such a limitation won't affect you because of your ability to displace."

Ian wanted to tell her he couldn't displace. He wanted to convince her, but he knew if he did, she'd immediately kill him.

He still felt the phone in his pocket.

"The ceremony is about to happen," Amity said. "It'll be quick. I'm required to join them. You can watch, but don't let them see you, or we'll both have colossal problems."

• • •

After Amity closed the door, the room went completely dark again. Ian felt his way to the bathroom and shut himself where he could use the light. He pulled Amity's phone from his pocket. He finally had his best chance for rescue if he could get any kind of signal for any length of time. He tried to keep his hands from trembling as he pressed a button to turn on the screen. It showed the dimmed image of a padlock. He swiped it. To his relief, the phone unlocked without a code or pattern. Instead of finding a screen of icons, it looked like an app was already open. A dark rectangle covered the top third of the screen. The bottom two-thirds of the screen slowly subdivided into smaller and smaller squares. One by one, a face appeared in each square. They were all lit with a yellowish light, most bearded men.

He tried to close the app, but nothing he tapped on the screen closed it. He heard faint shouts outside. He turned off the bathroom light and carefully returned to the window to look. The men surrounding the platform had each held a phone at arm's length, staring at their screens. Someone was running from them toward his building. He soon recognized it as Amity.

She stomped into the vestibule. As she fumbled with the key, trying to get it into his knob, she shouted, "Shut it off!" Ian quickly placed the phone face down on the table an instant before Amity burst through his door.

"Give it to me! Now!" she said, running to him. She snatched the phone and held it, arm outstretched, the screen illuminating her face. "It was a misplacement. I apologize," she said into the phone. The shouting outside stopped. She turned off the screen and scowled at him. "You are testing me like none of the others did." She left and closed the door. He heard her check the knob to make sure it was locked.

He went to the window and saw Amity run to rejoin the group of hunters. She pointed back toward Ian's room while speaking to them. After a brief animated conversation, during which Amity gestured emphatically, the hunters tucked their phones back into their waistbands.

Ian realized he had underestimated the technical savvy of these people. Aside from their use of solar power, he was surprised that they had incorporated the mobile connectivity of a modern civilization they claimed to despise.

As he watched the ceremony continue, the hunters moved away from the platform and formed a single line. Dagny moved to one end of the line and stepped between the men and the platform that held Riddick. She read from a book, her voice too faint for Ian to hear. Several times during the following minutes, the men raised their hands in unison in response to something Dagny had said. When she closed her book, all the men pulled canteens strapped over their shoulders. On Dagny's signal, they all tipped the canteens back, drinking at once. They guzzled deeply, some spilling water from the sides of their mouths. Then, they threw their canteens into a pile nearby. Dagny raised her hand. All the hunters slid their goggles from their foreheads down over their eyes. Ian suddenly remembered asking about these goggles when Jebediah and Amity gave him a supply room tour. They were night vision goggles and clearly not on Riddick's head. The ridiculous advantage of night vision for physically fit hunters familiar with the terrain was so disproportionate that Ian wondered if it was even worth it for the Saden's victims to run at all.

Each hunter dropped to one knee, assuming a starting block position like Olympic sprinters.

Dagny checked her watch while raising the other hand above her head. She nodded to one woman, who stood off to the side. The woman, dressed in a purple dress identical to Amity's, climbed the steps to the platform. She pulled out a large knife from under the dress when she reached the top.

Ian's stomach clamped down, and he forced himself to watch.

As the woman approached Riddick, he bucked his head and appeared to be begging through his gag. The woman walked behind him and raised the knife. She slid the knife slowly between Riddick's bound feet, slicing his ankle bindings free. She did the same to free his wrists.

Riddick lunged forward, leaping from the platform, clearing all five steps. When he hit the ground, he sprinted toward the woods. His glowing shorts bobbed up and down as his strides took him away until he vanished into the darkness.

The hunters stayed on the line, frozen in place, their goggle-strapped faces looking forward.

Dagny's hand remained raised high above her head, still looking at her watch. After waiting for what seemed like two minutes, Dagny dropped her hand. All the hunters shouted in unison and ran, racing in the direction that Riddick had disappeared. All the light sticks the men had been holding remained on the ground. Because they carried no lights and didn't wear Riddick's illuminated shorts, the hunters disappeared from Ian's view much sooner than Riddick had. The women and a few hunters who weren't taking part filed into one of the other buildings, leaving the easement abandoned with only the scattered light sticks whose illumination was already fading.

Ian closed the drapes. He knew Riddick was fleeing for his life, trying to escape an eager, vicious pack of master hand-to-hand assassins who held every advantage.

Overwhelmed with pity for Riddick and fear for himself, a new thought came to Ian. With most hunters off chasing Riddick, now was probably the best opportunity he would ever get to flee. But he had no way to get out of the room. He went to the door. The knob spun as usual. He put his mouth to the door crack and called for Amity. If he could get her to return, attacking her would have better odds with so many hunters away from the property. He pounded and kicked the door, shouting, "Amity! Please come back. I need you!"

He ran to the window and flung open the drapes. The easement between buildings was still abandoned. He couldn't wait anymore. The hunt for Riddick could be over in a matter of minutes.

Ian pulled the wooden table away from the window to the middle of the room. He picked up a chair, stepped back, and threw it as hard as possible at the window. It bounced off. Ian wondered if the loud sound it made would bring Amity. He picked up the chair, moved closer to the window, and swung it, landing a solid blow to the glass. Again, it bounced off the window, almost throwing him off balance. He tossed the chair aside and went to the table. He tipped it to its side and lifted it by its center post. He turned it and charged, gaining as much speed as possible in three strides, and slammed the table's base into the window. The window didn't break. Ian fell back onto the floor, the table toppling topside down beside him.

He looked out the window, panting. He couldn't believe no one had heard him yet. He scrambled to his feet, picked up the table, and carried it further from the window near the bed. He adjusted his grip and ran as fast as he could toward the window, raising it high enough to slam its corner into the glass with as much force as he could muster. The glass didn't break, but the tabletop split into two pieces. The center post detached from the feet. The table lay in three pieces on the floor. Ian sat among the broken pieces, fully expecting Amity to rush in at any moment to investigate the crashing sounds he was sure should have been audible from any of the other buildings. There was only silence, and no one came to investigate.

Ian picked up the table's center post and detached it by unscrewing it from the base, giving himself a solid post to use as a battering ram. He went to the edge of the window, and instead of trying to break the glass, he began swinging the post at the window's framing. If he could do enough damage around the edges, perhaps he could push out the entire window with its housing or break through the wall to freedom. He felt encouraged when the window's casing began to splinter and separate. He kept swinging blow after blow with the post, slowly working until he had broken a hole in the sheetrock. He dropped the post and used his hands to peel away the damaged wall and window framing. He pulled out a large piece of fiberglass insulation. His heart sank. Behind it, a narrowly spaced row of vertical steel bars was embedded in the wall. They were spaced too narrowly for his head to fit through them. Ian crumpled to his knees. He looked at the dusting of sheetrock powder that covered his hands. He was no longer trapped only by distance. He was physically imprisoned by steel.

Ian sat on the bed and waited. He couldn't believe no one heard him pummeling the window with the table and chair. At this point, he wouldn't be surprised if Amity showed up with her knife to tell him that the destruction of his room was a sure sign that he was an imposter and that the Blessed Egress ceremony would no longer be needed.

After waiting thirty minutes, he heard something, but it wasn't the footsteps he expected to be rushing to his room. Outside, voices chanted, slowly growing louder in a marching cadence. He went to the window and saw the doorway to the women's quarters open. Several women exited carrying recharged light sticks. Dagny followed them.

On the opposite side of the easement, the doorway to the men's quarters opened. The men who had not taken part in the hunt streamed out, also carrying light sticks.

They all formed an open lane that led to the van. Dagny went to it and opened the rear doors.

The chanting voices soon came into view. It was the hunters, marching single file. The two in front rested poles on their shoulders, which hung a body bound to the pole by wrists and ankles. The image reminded Ian of how he, his dad, and his brother sometimes transported a freshly killed buck through the woods back to camp. As the men marched into the light, Ian saw Riddick's limp body sway back and forth with the synchronized strides of the hunters who carried him. Ian gasped when he saw that Riddick's head was missing. Ian knew this scene foreshadowed his own fate after his Blessed Egress. Riddick had looked fit and strong—much stronger than himself. If anyone had a chance to escape based on strength, it was Riddick.

The men came to the rear of the van and then set the headless corpse on the ground. After disconnecting it from the pole, they lifted the limp body and heaved it into the back of the van. They closed the doors. Dagny took her time, shaking hands and hugging each of the hunters who had participated. Then, before moving back to the van, she donned her pair of night-vision goggles and climbed into the driver's seat. The van's engine came to life, and it slowly drove out of the easement, headlights off, only the brake lights briefly illuminating twice as she approached the boundary to the encampment.

As Ian listened to the van's engine grow faint in the distance, he wished he could have somehow escaped his room to wait nearby in the woods. Jumping onto the back of the van would have been an ideal way to be transported out of this nightmare.

• • •

A key sliding into his doorknob sent a shiver up Ian's back. He sat up straight. Two men wearing jeans, flannel shirts, and work boots entered the room. The first one backed in, holding one end of a new table identical to the table Ian had broken. They carried it to the corner, kicking the broken table pieces out of their way.

Ian expected them to question, comment, or reprimand him for destroying the first table, but they said nothing like Ian wasn't present. One man retrieved a broom from the vestibule and returned to sweep up the wood shavings and sheetrock dust Ian had created. Then they gathered the broken table pieces and headed for the door.

"What do I owe you for the damage?" Ian said sarcastically.

The men ignored him, pulling the door closed and jiggling the knob to ensure the latch had clicked.

Ian laid back on the bed in the darkness, feeling despondent. Minutes later, he heard a gentle knocking from the door that held the Sadens' other prisoner, whom Amity claimed was an imposter. At first, the knock was soft, but then grew louder. From behind the door, someone whispered, "Hello... Are you there?"

Ian got up to investigate. He put his mouth close to the crack. "Who are you?"

"I'm Travis. Listen, could you open this door?"

"No, I can't."

"Can't or won't?"

"I can't. When did you get here?"

"Why?"

"Just tell me."

"Got here yesterday. A couple of hunters brought me in. A woman has been helping me, but I have no way of reaching her. She told me to stay off my feet, but I'm feeling better today, and I can't get the door to my room open. Can you come over and open it or get someone to help?"

A terrifying thought struck Ian. Why wouldn't Travis, another mysterious voice belonging to someone he had never seen, be any different from the voice in the vent?

"I can't help you," Ian replied.

"Why?"

"You're a prisoner."

Travis laughed. "No, seriously..."

"I wish I was joking," Ian said. "Did you come here from Biding Wellness Center?"

Travis didn't respond.

"Hello?"

"Yes, I did."

"Travis, listen carefully. You've been tricked. You didn't arrive here by accident. You were lured here."

"I don't believe you," Travis said. "Who are you, anyway?"

"My name is Ian Shaw."

"Oh, my God!"

"You know who I am?"

"Of course I do. Hang on…"

Ian heard movement, and then a wrinkled piece of paper slid through the crack under the door.

Ian immediately recognized a map similar to Riddick's, but it wasn't identical. It was drawn in green ink, and the proportions were slightly different. It provided a rough relationship between Biding Wellness Center and Egress Encampment with the familiar landmarks—the bridge, the stream, and the narrow winding road.

Travis said, "I was told that you drew this map and had escaped before me."

"Told by whom?"

"A person who spoke through a vent. They said that you were familiar with every inch of these woods. You worked for the Bureau of Land Management. I know all about you."

"Travis, I didn't draw the map. Dagny did. She got you to use the map by making you desperate to escape Biding Wellness Center. These people are Sadens. I'm trapped here, just like you are. We've both fallen victim to a cult, and we're both on death row."

Travis said, "I don't know how they treated you, but my food and the attention I'm getting have been fantastic. It's a strange way to treat someone you're about to kill."

"I don't need you to believe me, although it could help our chances of survival if we worked together. Did you see what happened outside about an hour ago?"

"No, I heard some cheering. My window faces the other direction. What happened?"

"Let me first tell you what leads up to it so you'll understand." Ian described the process for Travis. He told him of the fine food and sedated rest to speed recovery. He told them about the Blessed Egress and the impossible odds of escaping against skilled hunters. He explained the handheld weapons and the scalps worn as trophies. He told him of Riddick's slaughter and beheading in the celebration that followed.

Ian paused when he heard Travis heave.

"You okay?" he asked.

Travis cleared his throat. "What do we do?" His voice trembled.

"I have an idea. When the women bring us our breakfasts, it will probably be at about the same time tomorrow morning. They showed me where they keep their supplies underground. I think if we can overpower them, we can use their keys to the supply room for weapons and any other provisions we need to escape successfully."

"Sounds risky," Travis said. "Are you sure we can't wait for a better opportunity?"

"I wish I had that luxury, but my Blessed Egress is tomorrow," Ian said. "If we can get our hands on some of their weapons and both run simultaneously, they'll have to hunt both of us, doubling our odds of success."

Travis sighed. "Look, I want to escape as much as you do, but your plan puts me at a disadvantage. Don't forget that I got here less than a day ago. I'm still recovering. I'm in no shape to outrun anyone at the moment. You've had time to rest and are probably in better shape. That's a tremendous advantage."

"Are you insane? You want to scrap the plan because you think I have some advantage over you when we will both be equally dead if we don't act quickly?"

Travis didn't respond.

"Are you there?" Ian asked.

In a hushed voice, Travis said. "Someone's coming."

"Okay," Ian said. He heard footsteps, followed by muffled voices that quickly went silent. Travis had been surprisingly reluctant to escape, especially after hearing Ian's information about their impending executions. Travis's willingness to wait for a better option was unbelievable for someone who would be murdered within hours. Also, Travis had not spoken ill of the Sadens in any way. He showed no resentment. His responses to the horrors Ian described were muted and lacked emotion. His heaving could have been faked.

Ian's hunch that Travis was a Saden grew. Travis had to be a Saden spy planted next door to convince Ian to cooperate with their agenda a little longer.

Ian flopped down on the bed and buried his face in the pillow. He screamed as regret flooded him. He couldn't even trust himself. Travis might have successfully tricked him into revealing the details of his only escape plan. He ran to Travis's door and pounded, shouting, "Where are you? Come back! I know what you're doing."

There was no answer.

After about an hour, Ian sat at the table when he heard footsteps in the vestibule. A key slid into the door. It opened. Two new men, also wearing jeans and flannel shirts, entered. One of them had a work belt on and still wore face paint from Riddick's ritual murder.

Ian stood, wondering if they were here to take him now to a rescheduled Blessed Egress ceremony. "What's going on?" he asked.

The men ignored him. One of them checked to make sure Ian's door had latched, then went to the door that connected Travis's room. The other man slid a key into the lock, and they opened Travis's room. Ian stood and moved, trying to see into the room.

The face paint man raised his hand and said, "No," giving Ian a warning look.

Ian backed away, returning to his chair. He sat and watched them remove the door's deadbolt and install the new one. After testing it by locking and unlocking it several times, the men exited.

A few minutes later, Amity entered the room with her bag slung over her shoulder.

"I was wondering when you'd show up," Ian said.

She went to the window and leaned against the wall beside the hole Ian had created. She looked at him and crossed her boots. "If you wanted to run away, you could have waited for me to return. I would've thrown the doors wide open for you, saving you the need to destroy our property."

"If I live, maybe I'll write you a check," Ian sneered. "Who's next door?"

"I told you already. He's an imposter."

Ian slowly nodded with an unconvinced smirk.

"You've been talking?"

"You knew we would," Ian said. "He's a horrible actor, by the way."

"Why would you say that?" Amity seemed confused.

"He's not an imposter, and he's not your beloved. He's one of you. I know it."

"Ah," Amity said. "Let me fill you in." She walked across the room, her hands folded behind her back, and said, "He's not one of us. I hate Angelica only a little more than she hates me. Earlier today, our members enjoyed a celebratory meal in the Sustenance Center in honor of your Blessed Egress. Angelica bragged to the other women about how quickly you'd die and started spouting off about how her new imposter was our beloved. She irritated me. So, I told her that instead of blabbing her mouth, she should clean up Travis's remains. You should've seen her face—she looked like someone had drowned her puppy. Then I said, 'Your fake beloved is missing his head. Go to his room. He's already dead.'"

"You... killed him?" Ian asked.

Amity walked back toward the window. "No, but she sure thought I did. I've dispensed with more imposters before their Blessed Egresses than any other nurturer, and they all know it. Your conversation probably ended abruptly because Angelica ran back to check on him. When she saw he was

fine, she called Dagny at Biding Wellness Center and got permission to
change the locks to his room."

"I knew your phones could make calls," Ian said.

"They aren't mobile phones. They're walkie-talkies."

Lonnie scoffed. "There's no way you could call someone that far away
on a walkie-talkie."

"If these were common walkie-talkies, you'd be correct, but these are
modified GMRS radios with a range of thirty-five miles. Anyway, Dagny
approved her request, and the guys changed the lock." Amity went to the
shiny new deadbolt and drew her finger around it, then said, "It's so
funny."

"What?"

"It's funny they think a new lock will stop me from slicing and dicing
Travis." She pulled an insulated metal flask from her bag and held it to Ian.
"I brought you a vitamin drink designed to provide a nice nutrient boost
for your Blessed Egress tomorrow."

When Ian didn't take it, she shook it and said, "Here…"

"I'd rather not be drugged."

Amity looked offended. "What makes you think—"

"Don't lie to me!" Ian said.

"The beverage is for your own good," she said. "It won't hurt you. It
will restore your appetite, and then it will help you rest. Not drinking this
severely limits your chance of success. You need to trust me on this."

"No, I don't." Ian crossed his arms.

"Fine. Have it your way." She watched him with an icy stare.

"I just want to decide what goes into my body. I'm not trying to anger
you."

"I'm not angry. Let me explain something to you, Ian. My certainty
about your identity was strong. But if I'm candid with you, your refusal to
accept advice has brought me back to the cusp of doubt about you."

Ian sensed the extreme danger that came with any loss of Amity's
confidence in his identity as our beloved. "That's okay," he said. "Doubt
is acceptable as long as the wrong conclusion doesn't win."

Amity thought about it for a moment, and then a slow smile spread
across her face. She held out her hand and wiggled her fingers for him to
take it.

Ian forced himself not to hesitate and interlocked his fingers with
hers.

Amity pulled him close and said, "Thank you for tolerating my doubt.
I don't know how you can allow my faith to wane only to swoop in at the
very last second and provide perfect encouragement that restores it like
you did."

"You're welcome," Ian said, covering his relief.

"I like how you haven't fought me on your identity," she said. "The only time imposters say they're our beloved is when my knife is pressed to their throats. At that point, the claim is so pathetically dishonest and desperate that it becomes a pleasure to watch their last lie gurgle through their severed neck. I can't tell you how grateful I am that you've chosen to accept your identity and prove it tomorrow."

"Of course."

She squeezed his hand tighter and dragged him to the bed. "Sit."

Ian complied.

She gently pushed him onto his back. She hiked her dress, revealing she had nothing on underneath, and climbed onto him. "Make love to me," she said. She raised up onto her knees, reached down between her thighs, and tugged at his belt buckle.

"Wait," Ian said, taking her wrist.

"What's wrong?"

"It's not time yet. You told me I need all of my physical strength. As much as I'd like to have you now, I cannot afford to be distracted before my Blessed Egress."

Amity tilted her head back, looking at the ceiling while she grinned. Looking back down at him, she wagged her finger in his face and said, "You know you're making me crazy, don't you?"

As Ian gently guided her off him, he said, "Crazy could be fun—when the time is right. Right now, I need to rest."

Twenty-one

AFTER AMITY RELUCTANTLY left Ian's room, a dark thought came to mind, instantly making Ian feel shame for thinking it. What if he not only overpowered Amity, but killed her? If it happened quickly, there would be no time for her to signal anyone. Given his dire circumstances and the ticking clock, the disturbing idea grew on him. With no trust in Travis, Ian knew he was on his own.

His biggest problem was that he had no weapon. The flimsy towel rack dowel was no match for her knife. He looked around the room, searching for some object he could use to club or cut her. The bed's frame was wrought iron, and all its parts were welded and bolted together too securely to disassemble without tools. The bathroom towel rack was too flimsy. He could break the table again, but its center stand and legs were held together with steel brackets. Combined, they were too heavy to swing quickly enough. She'd certainly have her knife out before he could make contact.

In the best scenario, he could take her to the floor and wrestle her knife away. He had no martial arts or other hand-to-hand combat training, but wondered if his intense adrenaline surge and desperate fight to save his own life might be enough to get the job done quickly.

He sat on the floor beside the door to wait for her. He wondered if she would make another visit before breakfast. If she entered his room carrying a tray, he could tackle her at the waist if her hands were already occupied. He yawned and felt the mental fog of sleep deprivation. His eyelids felt dry and scratchy.

He got only a few restless naps in the following hours before the sunlight squeezed between the drapes at about 5:30 a.m. Amity had not come in to check on him during the night. He supposed that his refusal of any sedation gave her no reason.

About an hour later, Ian left his post by the door to use the bathroom. When he came out, he went to the fridge to get a water bottle and heard a knock at the door. Amity opened the door before he could answer.

Ian cursed himself for leaving his post at the worst time, missing his opportunity. Something was different about her. She wore her familiar purple dress, but this one was different. The lacy and low-cut, sheer fabric was more like lingerie. The bottom edge barely covered the top of her thighs. Her boots were gone, too.

The other noticeable change was that she carried no food tray. "Today's the big day," she said, beaming at him. "The time is near for your premiere! Let's celebrate your special date." She stepped closer and pivoted with her arms out for him to see.

Ian saw the nine-inch knife sheathed behind her at her beltline, now more difficult for her to conceal through the wispy dress. "You look different," Ian said. The door latch clicked shut behind her, and he instantly realized he hadn't seen where she had put the key. He held out his hand to her.

She took it.

Ian raised her hand as if wanting a better look at her, but wanted to see if she held a key. The key wasn't in either of her hands. She must have tucked it somewhere immediately after entering the room, but her new dress had distracted him long enough to miss it. He let go of her hand.

With a mischievous grin, she tilted her head and said, "Does my new attire spark your desire?"

"You look lovely."

"Lovely?" Amity said, looking disappointed.

"I mean, great, actually," he said.

"Thank you." Her smile returned. She took both of his hands.

"No breakfast this morning?" Ian asked. If he could get her to leave and return, he'd have another opportunity to see where she put the key.

"Not yet. Since this is the day your true identity will be revealed, I wonder if I can convince you to enjoy me before breakfast—to celebrate my faith in you."

Ian released her hands.

She pulled his arms around her waist and slid one of his hands down. "That's better."

Ian immediately thought of Kate. He tried to think of a way to stave off Amity without triggering her anger. Having sex with Amity would physically deplete him and make his death more certain than it already was. "Your offer is so tempting," he said, "but I'm focused on proving that you have correctly identified me. I must reserve every ounce of my energy for the Blessed Egress, right?"

Amity's smile faded slightly before returning. She pulled him toward the bed, guiding him to sit. She cupped his cheek and said, "I can limit your exertion. I know how. It's the stress that drains your resources. You look so tightly wound. Let me release it. Trust me." She put her hands on his shoulders and raised her leg, wrapping it around his waist.

Ian gently pushed her away.

"Please don't be offended," he said. "You have to understand that given what I am about to go through, I'm not in the frame of mind for anything but preparation for my journey. And what about my breakfast? I'll need nourishment for energy, right?"

"Are you hungry?"

"Yes, I'm starving," Ian lied, desperately hoping she'd need to leave to get his food so he could watch her next entrance to see where the key went.

"That's perfect!" Amity said. "I want you to channel your hunger into desire. Today, you will not eat food prepared by man. Today, the food that will pass through your lips is the love that flows from my body. You'll drink it for strength and nourishment from above."

Ian gawked at her.

"Now, stop denying me and give me a small taste of what we will have." She tugged at his belt. "I want you in me. I want to be your first."

"Wait, I have to tell you…" He cut himself off. If Amity wanted to be the first woman to experience him, it was too late for that, but he was reluctant to share anything more at this point for fear it might instantly prove that he was an imposter. He carefully worded his response. "You want my virginity?"

Amity laughed. "No, silly. I want to be the first of our nurturers—our women—to carry your seed."

Ian's mouth opened, but no sound came out.

She giggled. "The other women are already talking." She reached down and tried to open his zipper flap. "They've never seen me so certain of any previous imposters, and my declaration that you are our beloved shocked them. They're tired of me going on and on about you, but they're starting to see you the way I do, one by one. They can't wait for their turns with you."

"Turns with me?"

"Of course! How else will we get babies? According to prophecy, our numbers will be rebuilt from the seed of our beloved. Your offspring will multiply, spreading our word, and eventually, we'll become our own nation. The other nurturers can't wait to become lovers, but I've made it crystal clear to every one of them they must get in line!" She closed her eyes, imagining it for a moment, then took Ian's arms and said, "If you won't give me your seed now, please promise me I'll be first when you return triumphantly as our beloved."

Ian searched for a thread of sanity on her face.

Amity's smile faded a bit. "Can't you promise me?"

"I promise," Ian replied in a whisper.

"You look so confused."

"The weight of my future responsibilities is overwhelming."

Amity seemed to approve of that answer. "No need to worry. Tonight will be your only night of difficulty. After your victory, you will return here to sleep in the bed of our beloved at the center of our nurturers' quarters.

As our leaders, you and Ms. Conger will direct us with your wisdom. I can't wait until you let me love you in every way."

Amity's over-the-top sincerity was almost comical. It was also impossible to imagine Dagny sharing control of these people with him. No wonder the so-called Blessed Egress was impossible to achieve.

"Amity, for now, I want to have some privacy with some food for breakfast. Please get me some food."

Amity stepped back, and her face lit up. "You see? It's beginning!"

"What?"

"Your tone with me has changed. You've never directed me like you did by instructing me to bring you food."

"Maybe my role is starting to suit me."

"I wish I could obey you, but I can't in this case. Your every wish will be my command after you are proven to be our beloved. Until then, I must follow the rules, and they state that the hours before your Blessed Egress will be spent in quiet introspection while fasting."

"Then why are we talking?" Ian snapped.

"I understand why you might be mad. Obey the rules, and you'll be glad."

"Enough with the rhyming."

"I'm sorry I've offended you."

"I want privacy. Didn't you just say quiet introspection?"

Amity went to the door.

Ian followed her, watching the knife under the back of her dress, riding the movement of her hips. When she opened the door, it would be his best chance to overpower her.

She stopped and turned to him. "You should know by now that you can't go with me."

Just get your key out! Ian thought. "I was just escorting you to the door."

"You've never done that."

"I was inspired to do it. I'm experiencing urges that are new to me. Maybe it's my transformation already beginning. I can't explain the changes I'm feeling."

Amity smirked at him, then backed away from the door. She reached into her pocket on her dress, feeling around for something.

"I'd like you to wait over there." She pointed to the corner table.

"Why? Do you think I have any chance of escape at this point?"

She reached behind her and, with a sharper tone, said, "Go over there."

Ian knew she was going for the knife. He raised his hands but did not move away from her. His proximity to her was perfect if she would only turn her back and open the goddamn door.

He heard footsteps, then a key slid into the doorknob from outside. The door opened, and Jebediah leaned in. He was winded. "Everything okay here?" he said.

"Thanks, Jeb," Amity said, keeping her gaze on Ian.

Jebediah stepped in, holding a machete at his side.

Amity said, "Everything is happening as it should, right?" She raised her eyebrows at Ian, prodding him for a reply.

Ian nodded and stepped back. Amity exited. Jebediah backed out and closed the door, giving it a firm tug to secure the latch.

• • •

Ian remained locked in the room until almost noon without breakfast. Withholding food from him only made him more confident that Dagny wanted him dead and that this whole Blessed Egress charade was nothing more than a lynching.

He stood from the bed when he heard a faint knock at Travis's door, followed by "Psst."

He went to the door and said, "What?"

"Thank God you're there," Travis blurted.

"What do you want?"

"You sound pissed off."

Ian said, "You're one of them. Go fuck yourself."

"That's not true! They took me to another room. I don't know why. Then, for no reason, they brought me back here a few minutes ago."

"What's it like to be a Saden? What's it like to be crazy?"

Travis said, "I don't know why you insist I'm one of them."

"Curse the beloved," Ian said.

"What?" Travis let out a surprised chuckle.

"Curse the person the Sadens claim is the beloved. Say you hate him and hope he will never be discovered."

"That's a ridiculous—"

"Then you're on your own." Ian turned and walked away.

"No! Come back!" Travis said, pounding on the door. "I'll say whatever you want. I promise I'm not a traitor. Tell me how you plan to escape."

Travis gave up and went silent after pounding on the door and begging for another twenty minutes.

Ian heard footsteps before he heard a key slide into his door. Amity, still wearing the purple lingerie, entered carrying a food tray.

Ian jumped up from the bed. "You told me I couldn't eat today."

"There's been a schedule change. We've postponed your Blessed Egress to tomorrow."

Ian looked at her incredulously.

"I'll explain after you eat." She carried the tray to the table. "Still hungry?"

"Yes," Ian said, knowing how critical nourishment would be for any plan. She pulled the chair out for him.

"Good." She removed the plate covers. "For lunch this beautiful day, you'll start with a chilled Caesar salad with a delectable dressing made with Pujado Solano white anchovy fillets and the finest imported Greek olive oil, topped with exquisite aged Parmigiano-Reggiano shavings. For an entrée, we have a delicious al dente linguine with trumpet mushrooms and scallops. And, for dessert, we've created a scrumptious, rustic chocolate raspberry tart with a homemade pastry crust. Bon appétit, enjoy this great treat."

Ian took a fork and picked through the salad, examining the ingredients. "No drugs?"

"I promise. Cross my heart and hope to die, stick a needle in my eye," Amity said, snapping open a napkin.

Ian began eating. If Amity had laced the food with a sedative, he wouldn't have enough time to see the effect of a small sample bite. The food's flavor was extraordinary, as usual, but he couldn't risk enjoying it— even a little.

Amity went to the bathroom door and leaned in, looking around to check on his supplies.

After finishing a bite of salad, Ian said, "Tell me why there's been a postponement."

Amity came back to him. "I'll explain, but I think it would be better for you to finish eating first."

Ian stopped chewing and put his fork down. "Just tell me."

Amity took a seat opposite him. "I had another altercation with Angelica. She started spouting off about Travis again. It almost came to blows. Jebediah had to intervene. Eventually, we came to an agreement that we believe will settle our squabble."

"That doesn't tell me why."

"As part of the agreement, our men need some time to clear brush from around the gazebo to accommodate chairs for our members to watch a special ceremony. If the hunters capture you during your Blessed Egress, they will not kill you as they normally would."

Ian felt a rush of relief that Amity had arranged clemency for him. The nightmare could be coming to an end. "Thank you," he said.

"You're welcome. The men bring you back to the encampment alive so that Angelica can dispense with you on the gazebo however she wishes. I'll be required to watch. She wants this ceremony recorded, claiming that the method of execution she has planned for you will be, in her words, 'legendary.'"

Ian felt the blood draining from face.

"But the hunters will never catch you, right, my beloved?"

Ian couldn't reply.

"Anyway," Amity continued, "if the unthinkable happens and Angelica gets her way with you, then I'll be given the same opportunity when it's time for Travis's Blessed Egress. If the hunters capture him, they'll safely return him to the gazebo where I'll be waiting. In whatever way Angelica chooses to dispense with you, I promise to double Travis's suffering—trust me." She looked up at the ceiling and grinned. "A thousand ants that sting his skin won't pay the price for his great sin. He will not die with bludgeon blows. I'll block his mouth and clamp his nose. He'll squirm for air, his eyes bugged wide, then through his groin, my blade will slide." Amity's grin faded, and she blinked as if coming out of a trance. She looked at Ian. "You look pale. You're not afraid, are you?"

Ian covered his face, still unable to speak.

"I could understand some fear if you weren't truly our beloved. But I *know* you are, so that means Angelica made a sucker's deal. You will return from your Blessed Egress to rule this encampment, and I will be at your side forever. After I finish with Travis, I hope you'll consider a creative punishment for Angelica for her attempts on your life. We'll finally give her what she deserves. I cannot wait to see her face."

• • •

Ian's unfinished food remained on the tray for an hour after Amity left him. His appetite had vanished entirely, and he could only swallow a few bites. Another delay in his Blessed Egress ceremony execution didn't feel like a reprieve. Having to suffer longer only intensified his occasional waves of nausea. He had thrown a towel over the food and placed the tray on the bathroom floor, closing the door to avoid smelling it.

The boredom-filled isolation seemed to slow time. He was tired of contemplating the innumerable and ridiculous disadvantages he faced compared to the hunters.

Wandering around the bedroom, he heard a voice from Travis's door. "Ian, are you there?"

He ignored it.

"I want to work with you." Travis knocked on the door. "Come talk.

We can work something out that's good for both of us."

Still, Ian didn't reply.

"I have a game-changer for you. You've got to believe me."

Travis's begging irritated Ian more. For over 10 minutes, he ignored Travis before he finally went to the door and said, "What?"

"Thank God you're there," Travis replied, laughing with relief. "You'll be glad you answered me. I have something for you."

"More bullshit?"

"I understand why you suspect me, but maybe this will win your confidence." A metal key slid under the door.

Ian picked it up and examined it.

"I wanted to make sure you were there before I slid it to you. I can't imagine what they would do to you if they discovered either of us with it."

"What does it unlock?"

"I don't know. I lifted it from Angelica."

"How?"

"Before she left after bringing my lunch, she went into my restroom to check supplies. I pulled the key from her bag that she left on my bed."

Ian squeezed the key into his fist. "It's a trap. None of these people would make a mistake like that."

"It's not a trap," Travis insisted. "I snagged it in less than two seconds. She didn't know I took it."

Ian tried to open Travis's door with the key, but it didn't fit. "It's useless without knowing what it opens," he said.

"Look, I'm doing everything I can to show that I'm not one of them. I'm behind a double-keyed deadbolt. All I can tell you is that the key doesn't unlock my door, but it might open yours. Handing it over to you is all I can do to convince you I'm not one of them."

"Thank you. I'll try it," Ian said.

Travis said, "I'm wishing you luck. If you can get me out of this room, we'll have a better chance of making a run for freedom together."

"Absolutely," Ian said, infusing as much feeling as possible.

After ending his conversation with Travis, Ian wondered how soon Angelica would discover the missing key and return to squeeze Travis for it. He took the key to the bedroom door and slid it into the knob. It turned, and the door opened. He felt a rush of excitement. For the first time since his arrival, Ian could leave his room alone, and he was ready to take it, no matter what.

He ran to the credenza and grabbed a sock. He rushed back to the door, where he used his precious key to open it. He stepped into the vestibule and propped the door open, using the sock as a door jamb to enable quick reentry. Then, with two strides, he rushed to the door that led outside—to his freedom. It was locked. No matter how he tried to insert the key, it wouldn't fit. The vestibule contained only the oversized chair. There was nothing with which to pry the door open. He would certainly wake the hunters if he tried to kick the door open. If that happened, he'd have less of a head start to escape than Riddick had.

His insides knotted with an overwhelming sense of despondency. He turned to the staircase door, tried the key, and was surprised that it slipped easily into the keyhole. He turned it, and the key worked. Excitement flooded him, but before he opened the door, he stopped when he realized an unsettling new possibility.

He wondered if the Sadens were using Travis to set him up with this key in some ultimate test of an imposter. Ian imagined using the key to open a door behind which Amity and other Sadens waited. He could also imagine Amity revealing some obscure belief that any person who attempts to use a forbidden key of deception is an imposter and must be killed.

On the other hand, he had nothing to lose. In a matter of hours, the Sadens would hunt and kill him. Failing to try the key only guaranteed their success.

With the sun still high in the afternoon sky, the Sadens should be asleep, except for Amity and Angelica, who were up and about several times during the daylight hours to tend to their respective victims. Ian estimated Amity had left him about two hours ago. It was possible she wouldn't return until his dinnertime, between 5:00 and 6:00 p.m.

He opened the door and saw the empty staircase landing. No one waited there for him. So far, so good. He descended the stairs, sidestepping on his toes to keep quiet. Without a flashlight, he was soon enveloped in pitch darkness. As he neared the last steps to the tunnel floor, he paused, holding his breath to listen for any approaching Saden. Just before he reached the dirt floor, the bottom step squeaked. Ian grimaced.

As he felt along the tunnel wall, he eventually felt the supply room door he remembered from his tour. He used his fingertips to search it until he found the deadbolt. He raised the key to the knob, but before inserting it, he paused. This had been too easy. Either he was about to be the victim of a setup, or Travis had hit the ultimate jackpot for a couple of imposters.

He tried the key. His heart sank when it wouldn't fit. He buried his face in his arm against the wall and whispered, "Dammit." He tried the key again, this time flipping it upside down. He felt a rush of euphoria when the key slid into the cylinder and turned, unlocking the door. He felt a drop of sweat slide down his back. He took a deep breath and pushed the door open. He stepped inside and closed the door before feeling the wall beside it for the light switch. He turned it on, expecting an audience of killers.

The light illuminated the storage room with no one in it. Ian froze for a minute, still not quite believing his good fortune. The supplies and weapons he remembered were still stacked neatly on countertops and shelves. The smell of leather and cleaning solution hung in the air.

He saw the open cabinet containing a grid of compartments filled with boots and gloves. On another wall, he saw the knives, ropes, clubs, and spears neatly hung in rows. Below them were additional machetes, their handles protruding from a wooden crate like a bouquet. Next to them was an industrial-sized sink. A slow drip of water dropped from its spigot every three to four seconds. On the next wall were rows of the canteens he remembered seeing slung over the shoulders of the hunters at the Blessed Egress ceremony. He recalled how Dagny had given a command, and all the hunters drank simultaneously. Ian went to them and picked one up. He took off the cab and tilted it. A few residual drops of water dripped out.

He went to the opposite side of the supply room and discovered something that seemed out of place. It was a small bookcase on the floor against the wall. Something about it didn't fit the hunting weapons, clothing, and other practical utilities the Sadens kept here. He remembered the recreation room had a large bookcase filled with Saden reading material. This small one seemed out of place in the supply room. As Ian stared at it, he remembered the exchange between Angelica and Amity in the vestibule while Ian's bedroom door was open. Angelica had said, "I need some snow." And Amity had replied, "Storage, behind the bookcase." Ian only remembered it because the exchange was so bizarre, and he wondered what snow was.

Ian tried to look behind, but it was too close to the wall. He wanted to pull it away, but it seemed anchored to the floor.

He pulled out a book. It was fake. The spline looked authentic, with a title and a leather binding, but the body of the book was a plastic case. Ian pulled out the next book. It was also fake. The book on the far right side looked a little different. It was taller and thicker. When Ian tried to remove it, it slid out only a couple of inches. The top of the bookcase clicked. He pulled the book harder, and the entire bookcase swung open, the left side hinged. It concealed a mini-refrigerator like the one in Ian's room. He opened it and found an assortment of IV bottles on the top shelf, and syringes lined up in a row on the second shelf. On the bottom, two large glass jars sat side-by-side. One was two-thirds full of blue pills. The other contained a bluish powder. The pill jar had a label that read:

Dormicum Midazolam 15Mg. Pre-medication 20 to 40 minutes prior to anesthesia.

The last word was all Ian needed to see to understand that he had discovered their tool of choice for sedation. He marveled at the number of pills—there had to be a thousand or more.

He stepped back from the bookcase and noticed a stainless steel contraption with a hand crank bolted to the edge of the countertop. Traces of blue powder were on a metal plate attached to it. Ian leaned closer for a better look. A metal tag on its base read:

Pill Pulverizer

Ian stepped back and bumped into a shelf. He was about to close the refrigerator and the bookcase when he heard a faint scratching sound. He cocked his head, listening. A shadow near the floor on the opposite side of the room streaked along the wall before turning. It darted, seeming to come directly at him.

Ian jumped backward, colliding with the shelf. Several canteens toppled to the floor as he rushed to the door. He looked back to see a huge rat dart behind the base of the countertop in the corner.

Ian clutched his chest while the adrenaline subsided. He was sure the canteen crash had been loud enough to reach the tunnel. If the crashing canteens had reached the Sadens, Amity, or worse, Angelica would appear at the door for him any moment now.

He grabbed a machete and a club from the wall and went to the door where he stood, his back pressed against the wall. He was prepared to fight for his life, attacking anyone who came through that door. He waited with the club in one hand and the machete in the other, listening. After a couple of minutes, the room in the hallway outside remained quiet.

He set the club on the counter but kept the machete. He picked up the fallen canteens and arranged them on the shelf again. That's when an idea struck him. It was a long shot, but given his dire circumstances, the long shot was his only shot.

Twenty-two

TEN MINUTES AFTER his secret excursion to the supply room, Ian returned to his room. He closed the door quietly and tossed the key onto the bed. He went to the window, where he carefully tucked a machete behind the outside edge of the drapes. He rested it against the wall, carefully positioning it within the end folds of the drapes that never moved. He opened and closed them several times to ensure their motion didn't cause the knife to fall. He stepped back, examining it to verify that it was concealed well enough to be inconspicuous. Ian figured he had at least a ten-inch length advantage over Amity's knife if he was wielding a machete. He sat at the table and sighed. Not only did he have a key to open his door, he finally had a viable weapon to defend himself with.

Travis called to Ian from behind Travis's door. "Pssst. Where did you go?"

Ian didn't respond.

"Talk to me. I know you left. I heard you leave."

Ian got up and went to Travis's door. "The key doesn't open the door to the outside. I have no way to get you out."

"So, what were you doing out of your room for so long?" Travis said.

"I was trying to get the key to work on another door. No luck."

"I guess we are screwed, then," Travis said.

"Looks like it."

"Then give me the key back."

"Why?"

"It did you no good. Slide it back under the door to me."

"I'd rather hold it."

"It was mine. I gave it to you as a show of trust. You tried it, and it didn't work. Give it back."

Ian didn't respond.

"Goddammit, give me the key now!" Travis yelled.

"Lower your voice and calm down," Ian said. "You gave me the key because it was useless to you. I'm holding it."

"Isn't that ironic? You accuse me of being a traitor and then steal my key."

Ian left the door and sat at the table.

Travis said, "I told Angelica that we talked."

"What did you say?" Ian immediately returned to Travis's door.

"She asked me if you had attempted to convince me to flee."

"And?"

"I covered for you."

Ian couldn't shake his skepticism. "I suppose I should thank you."

"You're right. You should. Angelica told me that if either of us moves before the Blessed Egress, we're dead."

"There you go again. If you are a victim, why would you try to convince me to embrace their draconian ceremony again?"

"I'm trying to convince you to be logical. Angelica told me more about the head start we get. They are all yearning to find their beloved, so it's illogical for them to make it impossible for someone to escape. They watch our building from the outside. If we run for it, we forfeit any head start, and a team of hunters will finish us quickly."

"Curse our beloved."

"What?"

"Curse our beloved. I asked you to do that before, and you didn't. Do it if you want to prove you're not one of them."

"I'll curse anyone you want me to."

"Then do it! Say, 'I curse our beloved.'"

"I curse the beloved."

Ian listened closely. "No, say, *our* beloved."

"Our beloved."

"Say the whole thing!"

"This place has made you crazy," Travis said.

Ian went to use the bathroom and closed the door. When he came out a few minutes later, Travis no longer called to him.

Ian stretched out on the bed. His new plan had tempered his fear of his Blessed Egress. He could leverage the Sadens' ritual against them with a little luck.

• • •

Amity came to his room with dinner. She pushed the door open with her foot, holding a tray. "Ready for a little bite, some yummy grub this special night?"

Ian didn't answer, only staring at her.

She carried the food to the corner table. She lifted the plate covers and said, "Today we have chicken saffron paella with a side of duchess potatoes, perfectly crispy on the outside and creamy on the inside. For dessert, we have apricot tartlets with a scoop of fresh-churned French vanilla ice cream."

Ian came to the table and stood as close to the edge of the drapes as possible, trying to hide his nervousness. If he could get Amity to walk away, turning her back for just a few moments, he could grab the machete and strike her from behind while she was on her way to the door.

He looked over the food and then said, "Sedatives?"

"Could you use some?" Amity asked, holding out his napkin for him. "No."

"No worries, then. We've kept the delicacies virgin for you." She tried to walk around him, but Ian sidestepped closer to the machete, bumping into her.

"Oh, sorry," she said. She eased around him and pulled out the chair, motioning for him to sit.

"I hope you won't be offended, but I'd prefer to eat alone tonight."

"Of course, my beloved," she said. "I wasn't planning to stay. We have an important planning meeting to prepare for your Blessed Egress."

"Wonderful," Ian said.

She walked away.

Ian stood from his chair and was about to reach for the machete when Amity stopped and turned back to him.

"Did I forget to give you something?"

"No, uh, everything's fine," Ian said.

She looked at him suspiciously as she continued to the door. She was out of reach.

Ian felt the urge to just go for it. He could grab the machete and rush her, but she was already at least seven or eight running strides away. He remembered the lightning speed with which she had unsheathed her knife. Then he remembered how she had flipped it in the air and perfectly caught it by the handle.

Amity stopped at the door and said, "I've never seen that expression on your face. What's on your mind?"

"I'm anxious. I think that's understandable at this point."

"Of course. I didn't mean to offend you, my beloved. If it's any consolation, the truth will soon set you free. It's so exciting!" She slid a key into the doorknob, grinning at him. "I'll be back for your tray in a bit," she said, exiting.

He wadded his napkin and threw it to the floor. He ate some of the food, but once again, his knotted stomach ended any appetite.

After dinner, Ian lay down on the bed. With his Blessed Egress fast approaching, he expected another rough night of sleeplessness. Without a meal laced with a sedative, he expected to be both sleep-deprived and tired by morning.

A few minutes after 9:00 p.m., he heard footsteps approaching his room door. There was no reason for Amity to come back unless she had news for him.

Someone pressed against the door, rattling the knob a few times before it went silent. If it was Amity, she would have used the key to enter. Then something metal clicked against the outer deadbolt and scraped against the wood.

Ian thought of calling out to whomever it was but waited. The scraping against the wood grew louder.

The chopping and prying intensified. The person slammed into the door, creating a thin crack down the center.

He rolled off the bed and quickly opened the hidden compartment in the mattress. As he slid inside on his stomach, the door took another blow that Ian felt through his knees on the floor.

Once tucked inside, he pulled the bed linen down and sealed the flap to the compartment. The door cracked open after a final hard blow, and someone stumbled into the room.

Ian heard footsteps that sounded like boots. They moved to the center of the room and stopped. Then they approached the bed, scuffing to a stop inches from him. He felt the bed shift slightly when the person pressed their hands down on it several times. He held his breath, cursing himself for not grabbing the machete, but there wasn't enough time.

The footsteps moved to the corner table. The intruder yanked the drapes back, then sucked their teeth in a shame-on-you sound. After another pause, the footsteps crossed the room to the bathroom. The door opened hard enough to slam against the wall. The footsteps scuffed on the tile floor before returning to the bedroom. After a moment of silence, the person exited into the vestibule. Ian heard the footsteps fade as they descended the stairs.

He waited a few minutes before pushing the flap open to see out. The room was empty, but the bedroom door was wide open. Spikes of splintered wood protruded from the latch housing.

Ian didn't dare get out yet. If he heard someone climbing the steps, he wasn't sure he could get back into the compartment quickly enough to hide. Whoever had been in his room would no doubt report to the rest of the Sadens that he was missing. For a moment, Ian's heart jumped at the thought of the hunters rushing from camp into the woods, searching for him. But that wouldn't happen before the Sadens swarmed his room. Amity was the only one who knew where he was hiding. He knew she wouldn't give up the secret, so he expected to hear hunters' feet trampling to his room, scouring it inside and out. Instead of feet stomping, he heard a single set of footsteps running up the stairs.

The person ran into the room, stopped by the bed, flipped back the bedspread, and yanked the flap open. Light poured in. Amity squatted beside the bed, looking in at him. "Thank God you're okay," she said.

"I'm not okay," Ian said.

She patted the floor. "Come out." She moved back to give him room. Ian climbed out and said, "Was it Angelica?"

"Yes, the bitch," Amity said. "You're lucky to be alive. She'll be furious that I tricked her by hiding you. I can't wait to rub it in her face." Amity pulled the covers down over the side of the bed and smoothed them.

Amity's expression had a concern he hadn't seen before. He wondered if she had already been told he had been hiding a machete.

"There's something I need to discuss with you," she said, stepping closer to Ian. The strange way she looked at him sent a chill through him.

"Something made Angelica more certain than ever that you are an imposter."

"What's new?" Ian said.

Amity appeared to struggle to get her next words out. She took a deep breath and said, "At our meeting, Angelica announced you stole a key."

Ian needed a moment for the implications of having been ratted out by Travis to sink in. His hatred for Travis spiked. "That's absurd," Ian said, forcing a small laugh to enhance the ridiculousness of the idea.

Amity watched him carefully, then said, "Angelica shared this news during our weekly meeting about an hour ago. If true, I'm sure you can understand how unfortunate this would be for you."

"Well, it isn't unfortunate because it didn't happen!"

"Anyway, Angelica immediately excused herself to use the restroom. I should have known where she was going. When I realized she had likely gone to your room, I chased after her but couldn't get here before she broke your door. I apologize for the scare." Amity kept her eyes locked onto his, her inquisitive expression unchanged. "Did you steal a key, Ian?"

"And how could I possibly get a key from Angelica?"

Amity poked her tongue into her cheek, nodding. "That's an interesting way to answer my yes-or-no question."

"I don't have a key!" he said. His last memory of the key was when he tossed it onto the bed. His heart pounded harder as he stepped back from her and shifted his position to see the bed. The bedspread pattern was a complex pattern of interlocking gray rectangles zigzagging like a latticework, making the key challenging to see without effort. Still, Ian spotted it because he remembered where he had placed it. His mouth went dry. Ian pulled his front pockets inside out to keep Amity's focus on him. "You're welcome to search the room if you want to waste your time."

Amity nodded with the corners of her mouth turned down, considering his offer.

"I want to believe you."

"You can."

"At the same time that Travis claimed you boasted to him about having a key, he also said you told him about the launch of a Blessed Egress ceremony you observed through your window. He described things he couldn't have possibly seen from his room. Is this true?"

The rage Ian suddenly felt toward Travis almost matched the terror of Amity believing Travis or, worse, spotting the key. "He's a liar!"

Amity smiled sympathetically. "Travis also told us you would deny it. He certainly didn't lie to us about that, did he?"

"I don't know what you expect me to say. How am I supposed to prove something that never happened?"

Amity walked toward the window with her hands folded behind her.

Ian felt the chill when he saw her approaching the drapes where he'd left the machete.

"Travis insisted to Angelica that you attempted to lure him into some far-fetched escape plan before your respective Blessed Egresses. Is this true?"

Ian turned and walked away, saying, "I can guarantee you I won't try to escape with Travis."

"Look at me," Amity said, coming back to him. She reached behind her and pulled out her long knife. She raised it and said, "Let me share something about Sadens that should be obvious to you by now. We have a saying: The moment we catch a lie is the moment the liar must die."

Ian swallowed and said, "Travis can't be trusted."

"But his accusation against you is grave, wouldn't you agree?"

"What else can I tell you?" Ian raised his shoulders. "He's not telling the truth." It was time to kill Amity. He had to get the machete now. He had to position himself close enough to her to take a swing. He went to the table, bent down, and began reorganizing the plates and silverware on the food tray.

Amity strolled toward him but didn't come within striking distance.

"Are you hungry? Shall I get you some fresh food?"

Ian reached out and pushed the drapes aside. The machete was gone. He pulled the drapes apart wider, hoping he had miscalculated its location. His heart dropped to his stomach as panic gripped him.

"What are you doing?" Amity said, stepping closer.

"Nothing, I just thought the spoon might've fallen off."

"It's right there." Amity pointed to the spoon on the tray.

"Oh, right."

"You're acting weird. Why did you look behind the drapes?"

"I told you, I thought the spoon—"

"You never clean up the tray. You know I always take care of such tasks for you."

"I guess it's just nervous energy. The Egress and everything."

Amity raised the knife and examined its tip, close enough for Ian to grab her wrist. Before he could lunge for it, she moved the knife behind her and stepped closer. He knew the knife handle was still firmly in her grasp. If he made any move, she'd have the knife through him in an instant.

"I really, really want to believe you," Amity said. "But do you know what would be worse than your dishonesty?"

Ian swallowed.

She lowered the knife to her side and tapped the side of the blade on her leg. "It would be worse if that bitch turns out to be right about you. Her gloating will make my life unbearable."

Ian nodded, his eyes locked onto her knife-hand.

She stepped out of his reach and pointed the knife at him. "On the other hand, if I were to dispense with you here and now, I would rob her of a privilege she desperately wants."

Ian raised his hands. "Hold on. Be careful." He had to come up with something—anything to prevent his immediate execution. "In a moment of anger, would you sacrifice everything I want to do for you?"

"For me?" Amity seemed surprised at the statement, then took on a look of shame. Her fingers loosened on the knife handle. She looked down. "I—I'm sorry. You're right."

"I've already forgiven you."

"Thank you, my beloved," she said, her eyes welling up.

"I think it's time to solidify your commitment to me now." He went past her to the bed and climbed onto it. As he crawled toward the pillow, he placed his palm over the key and squeezed it into his fist.

"You mean... Are you serious?" Amity looked at him, her face filled with disbelief. "Right now?"

Ian nodded while grinning.

Amity dropped the knife to the floor and clapped both hands over her mouth.

Ian slid his fist under the pillow and let go of the key. He used his fingertips to push it further toward the headboard. "It's time for me to reveal something to you," he said.

Amity nodded vigorously, mouth still covered. Tears slid down her face.

"I resisted making love to you to test your patience. I wanted to see if it would cause you to doubt my identity. Because you have expressed that you still believe I am your beloved despite the temptation of an imposter," Ian pointed to Travis's room, "I couldn't be more pleased with you, and I'll remember your unshakable faith after my Blessed Egress."

Amity's fingers trembled as she pulled one hand from her mouth to wipe her tears.

Ian sat up and held out his hand. "Come to me. I believe you are ready to receive my seed."

Amity ran and leaped into his arms, not bothering to take off her boots. She hugged him tightly. They fell back onto the bed. As they kissed, her tears smeared onto his face. He had never cheated on Kate. He felt shame for what he was about to do. So many times during his captivity, he had longed to be back in Kate's arms. But he knew that if Kate knew his predicament, she'd tell him to do whatever was necessary to save his life. The bigger problem was that it would be practically impossible to achieve an erection with the terror he felt. Would the true beloved have such a limitation? He wondered if Amity would freak out and claim that impotence was a sure sign that he was an imposter.

She tore open the front of her dress, popping the buttons as she grinned down at him.

He briefly turned his head and saw the knife on the floor. He could dispense with her if he could get to it before she did. The idea of murdering someone seemed utterly foreign to him, but desperation strengthened his resolve.

She pulled his shirt off, threw it aside, and then reached down between her legs, trying to unfasten his pants. After several failed attempts, she put her lips to his ear and said, "Get them off!"

"I hate to interrupt the moment, but I need to get up for a minute."

"Why?"

Ian pointed to the bathroom.

"Don't be self-conscious," she said.

Amity leaned onto her arms, putting her face close to his, and smiled.

"What's wrong?" he said.

She touched her finger to his lips and said, "Do you know what the most beautiful thing I've ever experienced in my entire life is?"

Ian said, "Of course I know, but I want to hear you say it."

Amity giggled. "The most beautiful thing I've ever experienced in my life is my absolute certainty of who you are. I will remember this moment forever."

"As will I," Ian said. "You are the only woman in our encampment worthy of my trust. I've been waiting to confess that truth to you."

After looking deeply into his eyes, she clasped his face and said, "You can't imagine how much I love you!" She kissed his forehead. "Don't move. I need to make our situation perfect!"

She pulled the dress back up onto her shoulders and climbed off him. She ran to the knife and grabbed it from the floor.

Ian sat up, swung his feet off the bed, and said, "What are you doing?"

Amity raised the blade high and said, "I hereby offer my ultimate demonstration of faith." She turned and ran toward Travis's door. She leaped, landing a blow with her boot. Ian felt the impact through the bed. The door cracked but didn't open. The sudden ferocity with which Amity had charged the door shocked him.

From behind the door, Travis yelled, "My God! What's going on?"

Ian said, "Amity, what are you doing?"

She pointed the knife at him. "I'm doing something for us." She slid the blade into the crack beside the latch and tried to pry it open. The door made a cracking sound but did not open. Amity stepped back and charged again. Her whole body went airborne this time, and she slammed her shoulder into the door. The latch broke, and the door flew open. She fell to the floor inside.

Ian heard Travis shout, "What are you doing?"

Ian could only see her legs from his position, but she quickly scrambled to her feet and disappeared from view.

Amity's frantic and maniacal breach of Travis's room stunned and terrified Ian. He sat, incredulous, staring into the open doorway.

He heard Amity's boots run as Travis screamed, "No! Please! … Angelica, help me!"

Ian got up and approached the door. Before he reached it, he heard a loud thud. Travis screamed, "No, no, no!"

Ian leaned to see inside and got his first glimpse of Travis, who lay on his back, his arms wrapped over his head to protect it. Amity had mounted him and repeatedly swung her arm, impaling his chest with the knife.

"Amity, no!" Ian shouted.

Travis made a couple of desperate swipes at her wrist, but Amity deftly dodged each, obviously practiced with the weapon.

Travis's resistance weakened, and his struggle slowly subsided. His arms went limp. A thick pool of blood spread from under him.

Amity finished him with a slice across his neck. His last plea gurgled.

She slowly turned to look up at Ian, her face freckled with blood. Her chest heaved as her smile grew. "How about that?" she said.

Ian couldn't speak.

Amity leaned forward, bringing her face close to Travis's, and screamed, "You lied! You lied! And now you've died!"

She climbed to her feet, wiped her bloody hands on her dress, and approached Ian.

He backed out of the doorway to make room for her to pass by.

She stopped beside him. "You never answered me."

"I beg your pardon?" Ian said, feigning calmness while his heart pounded.

"How about that?" She pointed the bloody knife blade over her shoulder at Travis's corpse.

Ian swallowed hard. His tongue was dry. He forced the words, "Again, you've shown your commitment to me, and I'm pleased."

Amity dropped the knife and grabbed him, hugging him tightly, smearing blood on him. "Now everything is perfect. Don't you agree?"

They heard footsteps running up the stairs to the vestibule.

They turned to look. Before Amity could let go of Ian, Jebediah, and Rhett rushed into the room.

"What are you doing here?" Amity said.

Jebediah raised a machete, pointing it at Ian. "You stay put." He pointed it at Amity. "Drop it."

The knife thudded on the floor.

The men approached Amity.

She bolted, trying to run between them.

They grabbed her arms. She fought them, shouting, "Let me go! I have not retracted my declaration of faith!"

When she refused to walk, they dragged her toward the door.

"You'll ruin everything!" she screamed. She got an arm free and swung it at Rhett. Jebediah dropped the machete to the floor to get her arm restrained.

Ian saw the machete, hoping Jebediah would forget it.

Amity twisted and kicked at them, but they overpowered her, dragging her to the door. Before they exited, she yelled, "Let me have him! Give me ten minutes. I'm not finished!"

They pulled Amity into the vestibule. Jebediah stepped back in and picked up the machete. He held it up and said, "Wouldn't want to forget that!"

Amity's voice faded as they dragged her down the staircase. She yelled, "Please don't! Not yet! He's the One!"

The door to the staircase slammed shut, muting her.

Ian thought the men had taken Amity downstairs, but Jebediah reappeared in the doorway a moment later. He looked at Ian, then slowly looked at the broken door that had separated Travis's room. "I need you to step back and have a seat," Jebediah said, pointing the machete at the table beside the window.

Ian backed away from him with his hands up. "Okay, take it easy." He reached behind him, found the chair, and sat.

Jebediah tossed the machete onto Ian's bed and then strolled to Travis's door, examining the damage around the latch.

From where Ian sat, the machete on the bed was about the same distance from him as Jebediah was. Jebediah was muscular and fit. But if Ian could get a solid grip on the machete and get a good swing, he could do some fatal damage. He was already doomed to die during the Blessed Egress. It was time to use some fucking initiative to at least have the satisfaction of inflicting some damage on one of these maniacs before he died. He adjusted himself in the chair.

Jebediah stepped into Travis's doorframe and, after looking at Travis's body, he turned back to Ian. "That Amity is a firecracker. Never know what might set her off."

"I understand that," Ian said, working not to look at the knife.

"She thinks you are our beloved."

"I know."

"I don't agree with her."

Ian adjusted himself in the chair, leaning slightly forward, preparing for his move.

Jebediah leaned against the doorframe and crossed his arms. "Your ceremony is only hours away."

"I know," Ian said, glaring.

"Why the angry face, then? The way Amity talks, I'm surprised you have any trepidation about fulfilling your destiny. I've never seen her so convinced that an imposter is our beloved. She better be right—for her sake." He motioned toward the window with his chin. "Look."

Ian stood and backed to the window, being sure to keep Jebediah in his peripheral vision. He pulled back the drapes. For the first time during daylight hours, he saw a group of hunters outside in broad daylight. They were perfectly spaced at an arm's length from one another, arcing around the building. They wore cargo shorts and were shirtless. Their torsos and faces were painted with the primitive designs of war paint. Their beards were dusted with a white powder. Each had a club in one hand and a long, thin knife in the other. They stood motionless, their feet slightly apart and their arms pulled slightly away from their bodies.

Jebediah said, "At least half of them can beat a five-minute mile. They can't wait to play some tag with you."

Ian let the drapes fall closed and then sprinted for the bed.

"Hey, stop!" Jebediah yelled, taking off after Ian.

Ian reached the bed first and grabbed the machete handle, hearing Jebediah right behind him. Ian pivoted and swung the knife as hard as he could, landing the blade's edge squarely on Jebediah's neck. The blade bent, wrapping around Jebediah's neck before it bounced away.

Jebediah fell to the floor, clutching his stomach as he laughed.

Ian tossed the rubber knife to the floor and ran to the door. As usual, the knob cover spun. Ian put his foot on the wall and tried to force the door open.

Jebediah got up and tackled Ian to the floor. Ian fought back, but Jebediah was too strong and quickly overpowered him. He flipped Ian to his stomach, pulling his arms behind him. Then he pulled some zip ties from his back pocket and secured Ian's wrists. He rolled Ian to face up, then stood and straddled him. He looked down and said, "Our beloved is expected to do almost anything to escape, but any attempt to physically harm one of us is a sure sign of an imposter. Our true beloved's overwhelming desire is to escape, never to harm."

Ian panted, saying, "You're not allowed to touch me."

As Jebediah opened the loops on the zip tie, he said, "That would be true—if I thought you were our beloved. If I'm wrong, I'll be killed after your Blessed Egress." He leered at Ian. "I'm not worried."

"Please… I don't want to be bound. I promise not to run, and I promise not to attack you."

Jebediah laughed. "Your word is your bond, right? The restraints stay. Now that my doubts about you have been confirmed, the next question is whether to tell Amity the truth about you." He looked Ian up and down. "You can't imagine what she'll do to you for deceiving her. But it might be more interesting to give Angelica some private time with you."

Jebediah guided Ian to the bed. He flipped back the bedspread and shoved Ian down onto the bed face. He zip-tied his ankles and connected zip-ties with a chain to a solid metal ring that decorated the wrought iron bed's footboard. Ian could move his feet only a few inches to the left or right.

Jebediah covered him up to his neck with a bedsheet. He turned and chuckled as he retrieved the rubber machete from the floor.

Jebediah hollered a word Ian didn't understand. The door opened, and two hunters entered wearing rubber gloves and vinyl bib aprons. They carried a stretcher between them. Jebediah exited. The men went into Travis's room. After a couple of minutes, they came out carrying Travis's body on the stretcher. Ian noticed blood dripping from the edge of the stretcher on its way to the vestibule. They took the body from the room, returning a couple minutes later to scrub Travis's and Ian's rooms. They said nothing to Ian as he lay there.

After they finished, two other hunters entered, carrying a new door. They wore jeans, tool belts, and short-sleeve shirts. After they leaned the door against the wall beside Travis's demolished door, they stepped back into the vestibule and brought back two large toolboxes. They went to work, replacing Travis's and Ian's doors.

Ian tried calling out to them, but they ignored him, barely glancing his way. In less than an hour, the new doors were in place.

Twenty-three

IAN TRIED TO pull his legs up, but the already tight zip ties dug into his ankles, causing more pain. His wrist bindings were also becoming painful, even though none of his weight rested on them. It was almost dinnertime, but he doubted they were planning a scrumptious meal for him at this point.

He heard a faint set of footsteps climbing the steps to the vestibule. When the door opened, Amity stepped in, closing the door behind her. She had showered and changed into a new purple dress. Her wet hair was pulled back into a ponytail. "Thank God!" she said. She dropped a shoulder bag on the floor and came to the bed. She leaned over and kissed his head. "You should have seen Angelica's face when she saw his blood all over me! It was priceless! They still have her restrained because they don't want us to kill one another. Surprised to see me?"

When Ian realized Jebediah hadn't told Amity of his failed imposter test and that she hadn't come to finish him, he said, "Get these ties off my wrists and ankles." Ian moved his wrists under the sheet.

Amity threw it back and saw his hands bound behind his shirtless back. "Oh, my God! You poor thing! What are they doing to you?"

"Amity, seriously, my ties... cut them. I've lost circulation in my hands," Ian grunted through the pain.

Amity raised her knee and pulled a 4-inch black push-dagger from the side of her boot. She squeezed the handle between her knuckles and reached for his wrists before she paused and said, "Did they say why they restrained you?"

"What do you think?" Ian snapped. "Get them off!"

Amity's face flashed with anger before it relaxed. She held a warning finger and said, "You should know that making me mad is never good and always bad." She moved to the foot of the bed and examined his ankle bindings. "Aside from the physical discomfort, the stress of being restrained this way won't help your Blessed Egress. They should know that. How can you effectively fulfill your Blessed Egress if your ankles are sore?"

"It's what I've been trying to tell you," Ian said, working to control his temper.

"Let's remove your restraints, but first, I need to ensure I won't be making a mistake." She slid the dagger back into her boot and went to her bag by the door.

"A mistake?" Ian yelled. "Cut me loose now!"

"Hold on, my beloved." She pulled a phone from the bag and pressed a button. As she placed it to her ear, waiting for someone to answer, she walked to the window and said, "I'll sort this out right now." She turned her back to him and spoke softly. "Yes, it's me... Why is Ian Shaw bound? ... Uh-huh... I see..." She parted the drapes to peer out the window. "Right... Okay, thanks." She hung up and slowly returned to the bed, nibbling her cheek.

"My hands have gone numb!" Ian shouted.

"Well, I have good and bad news," Amity said. She went back to her bag and dropped the phone into it. "Which do you want first?"

"No more fucking games!" Ian shouted. "Get these ties off my goddamn wrists and feet."

"I've been informed that your Blessed Egress is imminent. That means," she paused to look at the clock, "it'll happen in two or three hours at the latest. This is so exciting!" She clapped and jumped up and down. "No wonder our hunters have surrounded the building. Did you see them?"

Ian glared at her. "Why can't you unbind me until then?"

"When we reach the threshold of your Blessed Egress, hunters begin a vigil to make sure that you remain available for the ceremony. We are required to keep you bound during this threshold, but I have an idea." She ran into the bathroom, returning a few moments later with a few wads of toilet paper. She kneeled beside the bed and folded it several times. "I'll tuck this between your wrists and those horrible plastic cuffs."

While she squeezed the toilet paper between the zip tie and Ian's wrist, Ian squeezed his eyes closed and took a few deep breaths. He needed a big move. He said, "If I can do just one good deed, will you accept my seed?" He opened his eyes.

Amity squinted at him. "That was awful. The rhyme worked, but the cadence was atrocious."

"It was my best attempt to creatively tell you I think we need to finish what we started before Jebediah came."

Amity laughed, then pointed at him. "*Now* you think it's time?"

"I can't think of a better gesture to show my commitment to you than to share in this intimate act while I suffer."

Amity nibbled her cheek, thinking. Her suspicious look didn't feel promising, so he added, "The time is perfect. I want you to have a foretaste of what's coming." Amity smiled and rested her warm hand on his back. She closed her eyes and drew her fingertips down to his stomach. "Your body is magnificent. Enjoying a little unrushed exploration while you are bound arouses me."

"Please cut my wrists free. The pain is awful."

"Shh, shh, shh," she said. "Give me just a minute. I promise you'll forget the pain." She climbed over him and laid down beside him. She wrapped her leg around his waist and began unbuttoning her dress. "I'm going to roll you to your side. I want you to let me do all the work. I don't want to deplete your energies."

Ian tried to raise his head.

"Wait," she said. "Don't strain your neck. Use a pillow." She lifted his head and positioned the pillow under it.

"Thank you," Ian said.

Something seized Amity's attention. She raised up onto her elbow. Her face clouded up.

"What's wrong?" Ian said.

She leaned forward and reached to where the pillow had been. She picked up a key and held it up. "What's this?"

The terror that shot through Ian was so powerful he gasped. "That's a test," he said. "Because we have crossed the threshold, I'm giving you a final test of faith in me."

Amity climbed back over him and got up from the bed. She backed away and said, "You lied to me."

"No, I didn't! If you believe in me, I will reward you a hundred times more than anyone else in the encampment. Amity, please! You have to believe me! I'm your beloved!" He twisted and tried to reach her arm with his bound hands, but couldn't. "Don't make a foolish decision. Don't lose your faith in me."

Her expression grew icier. She stared at him contemptuously before she flung the key over her shoulder. It bounced against the wall and spun to a stop on the floor near the corner.

She went to her bag, ignoring Ian's pleas. She pulled some wound rope from it and slid the dagger from her boot. She started slicing the rope into pieces of varying lengths.

Begging hadn't worked. Ian played the confidence card. "Amity, my triumphant return is inevitable, and I want you to benefit from it, but first, you must believe."

She came to him and put her hand over his throat and squeezed, staring down at him with eyes that had grown dark. "You fooled me for a while with your tricky little smile, but I'm no longer sold on the tales you've told." She lifted the lamp on the bedside table. A ball gag sat under its hollowed base. She lifted the gag and slammed the lamp back onto the table. While she stretched the rubber strap to loosen it, she said, "I'm known to get real freaky with imposters who've been sneaky."

"I'm not an imposter! I'm your beloved. Don't do anything that you'll regret!"

Amity climbed onto the bed and mounted him.

He bucked and twisted, trying to get out from under her, but his struggle only inflicted more pain from his bindings.

She waited for him to finish a round of thrashing before she stretched the gag's elastic band and pressed it down over his head.

"No, please!" Ian said. "I'll be quiet, I swear!"

"It would be simplest for me to end you quick and dirty right here, like I ended that filthy imposter, Travis. But I've decided to keep my agreement and wait to observe whatever creative slaughter Angelica has planned for you." She dragged the gag's ball down over his mouth.

Ian clamped his teeth, pressing his lips together.

Amity said, "Pretend my ball's a treat, something great for you to eat."

Ian's nostrils flared with each breath. He shook his head.

She pressed the ball, twisting it against his lips so hard that Ian thought she might break his teeth. He cracked his mouth. The ball popped in.

With Ian unable to produce more than a sputtering hum, Amity climbed off and picked up a few lengths of the rope. She fastened one to each of his wrists and then to iron rings in the headboard before she sliced the zip tie free. While holding both ends of the rope connected to Ian's wrists, she pulled the rope through the iron rings, stretching Ian's hands until his knuckles bumped the headboard. Amity worked quickly, securing each length of rope to the bed with constrictor knots.

She cut two more lengths of rope and secured each ankle with the rope just above the zip tie, looping the rope through wrought iron rings on either side of the footboard. After she secured each rope to the footboard, she severed the ankle bindings before pulling the rope to spread his legs, tying his feet to the footboard.

Ian yelled through the gag while Amity finished the last constrictor knot. She stepped back and observed her work.

Ian's chest heaved as he looked wide-eyed at her.

She looked him over, nodding after confirming that he was satisfactorily secured. She returned to her bag and retrieved a pair of surgical scissors. She brought them back to Ian and snipped them a few times in front of his face. "You've embarrassed me," she said.

Ian vigorously shook his head and cried out with an unintelligible plea smeared by the gag.

Amity grabbed the cuff of his jeans. She slipped the scissors under them and cut a straight line up to his knee, then continued to cut them open to his waist. She walked around to the other side of the bed and did the same with his other pant leg. She then took hold of the elastic of his underwear and cut a straight line down the front with quick precision. She opened the cut flaps, smoothing them on the bed.

Ian was completely naked. He stared at the ceiling, trying not to freak out about what might happen next.

Amity reached down and took hold of his penis, examining it from several angles. She squeezed it a few times while looking at his face.

He closed his eyes.

She tossed the scissors into her bag and went to the door.

After discovering the key, Amity had morphed from the hyper-attentive nurturer into a detached, emotionless dominatrix engaged in a rote preparation for an awful ceremony.

She returned a few moments later, carrying a brown paper bag. Jebediah and two other hunters came in behind her. They stopped at the foot of his bed.

"Looks like you lost your biggest fan," Jebediah said. He looked at Amity's bindings that had Ian spread-eagle on the bed. He checked Amity's bindings for tightness and then showed his amazement by whistling. He looked at Amity and said, "If he is our beloved, you're in big trouble."

"I'm not worried," Amity said, reaching into the paper bag. She removed a pair of latex gloves and a syringe.

Panic filled Ian's face. He bucked hard against his restraints, thrusting his pelvis and writhing to break free.

She placed the syringe on the bedside table while she wiggled her fingers into the gloves, then snapped each while her cold eyes bore into Ian.

Jebediah came around to the side of the bed. He gently squeezed each of Ian's upper thighs. "Nice muscle tone and strength," he said. "You've done well, Amity." He rubbed his hands together and grinned like a little kid about to open a present he expected. "And nothing gets me more excited than a good hunt."

Ian bucked.

Jebediah said, "Whoa! We love nothing more than feisty game. The boring ones are always lame—Amity taught me that rhyme!" He looked over his shoulder at her.

She rolled her eyes.

Jebediah slid his fingers through Ian's hair and said, "A lock of this gorgeous mane will make a fine trophy for a lucky hunter. It might be long enough to get a small braid out of it."

Amity brought the syringe to Ian's arm. He fought to pull away, yanking on the restraints to dodge her grip a few times. "Help her," Jebediah snapped.

One hunter grabbed Ian's arm and used his weight to steady it on the bed.

Jebediah said, "Your eyes are filled with fear. Not something I'd expect from our beloved. We need to check your glucose, oxygen level, and metabolites to better understand what type of stamina we can expect from you. I'm sure you'll forgive us for this pinprick."

Amity slid the needle in and drew several vials of blood before she and the men left, leaving Ian alone.

He heard the preparations for his Blessed Egress outside. The murmur of conversation and occasional shouts with instructions. The darker it got outside the window, the louder the sounds became. The hum of the returning van's engine approached the encampment, no doubt with Dagny at the wheel. He heard excited voices and some hammer blows near the Egress launch platform.

An hour later, Amity, Jebediah, and the two hunters returned. "Your blood tests are excellent," Jebediah said, grinning. "You are good to go— so to speak!"

Amity seemed unwilling to even look at Ian anymore.

The hunters went to either side of his bed while Amity snapped open a loincloth with strips of luminescent plastic sewn onto it. On either side of the bed, the hunters lifted Ian's pelvis while Amity threaded the cloth between his legs and around his waist, securing it with safety pins like a diaper. They put new shoes on his feet. They were specialized rubber shoes similar to those worn by the hunters. Finally, they removed the gag and bindings before helping him stand up.

When they pulled him toward the door, Ian said, "I have to piss."

They changed directions, dragging him toward the bathroom.

Jebediah said, "Let him go alone. If he runs, I'll get my pretty lock of hair sooner."

The hunters let go of Ian's arms.

Ian entered the bathroom and slammed the door shut. As he relieved himself, he looked over his shoulder at the small window beside the shower. Knowing many hunters were posted outside, prying the window open to escape was impossible. As he looked, a hunter's face startled him when it slid into view through the window.

They took him by the arms again when he came out of the bathroom. A chime sounded. Jebediah held up his finger for them to wait and pulled his phone from his pocket. He plugged one ear and stepped away as he said, "Yes… We're ready." He looked at Ian. "He seems excited and ready to run. We'll be there shortly."

· · ·

They guided Ian from the porch, and around the building toward the wide easement that separated the buildings. Ahead, Ian saw the platform from which Riddick had been taken to launch his Blessed Egress. A group of hunters already surrounded it. They cheered when they saw Ian approaching, clapping their hands and waving weapons over their heads. They wore the same garb Ian had observed them wearing for Riddick's ceremony, including the night vision goggles pushed up onto their foreheads and water canteens draped around their necks.

Ian resisted walking toward the platform, but his handlers pulled him, forcing him to move at their pace. As they neared the platform, the waiting group of hunters parted, creating an open path to the platform's steps.

Ian's legs felt wobbly as he experienced the sensation of imminent doom that men sentenced to hang must feel during their final steps toward the gallows.

He saw Dagny's van parked with its rear doors open and the edge of a tarp hanging out. She came from around the opposite side carrying a book in one hand and a bullhorn in the other. She approached the platform and went to a small podium off to one side, where she turned to face the hunters. She raised one hand.

All the hunters went silent.

She looked over at Ian on the platform and smiled. "Well, here we are!"

Ian used brute strength not to scream at her.

Dagny said, "Can I just tell you again how exquisite that rhubarb cobbler your mama made was? Um-mm-mm." She smacked her lips.

Ian said nothing.

Dagny opened the book on the podium and began reading passages describing the Blessed Egress's preparation and initiation. When she finished, Dagny said, "I know you are all eager to begin. But before we launch this Blessed Egress, I will ask Jebediah to assign our earned advantages. Those he designates may step up to the advantage line and be granted the coveted one-minute head start over the other hunters."

Jebediah stepped out from the group of hunters and turned to face them. One by one, he pointed to ten of the hunters in the group. These men moved to an adjacent square outlined in white powder. A few bumped knuckles and grinned as they looked up at Ian on the platform.

Dagny turned to Ian and said, "And now the time has come for your true identity to be revealed. I speak for everyone here when I say we truly hope and pray that you are our beloved. But if you reveal yourself as an imposter, we still thank you because your sacrifice brings us closer to that glorious day when our beloved reveals himself. As is customary at the Blessed Egress, we will give you a moment to address us." She motioned for him to speak.

Ian stared at her, saying nothing.

"All right, then. Before we begin our countdown, please raise your canteens to provide your bodies with blessed hydration." She raised her hand.

The hunters holstered their clubs and knives, then removed the slung canteens over their shoulders.

"And now, in unison, we drink," Dagny said. She lowered her hand.

Ian's heart pounded. *Please drink, please drink*, he thought.

The hunters brought the canteens to their mouths and tilted them back, guzzling the water. Dagny watched Ian with a smile, rocking back and forth on her feet, rising on her toes a few times.

After the sounds of swallowing stopped, a few hunters coughed as they removed the canteens from around their necks and threw them into a pile beside the platform. They shook their legs and arms to loosen them.

Dagny raised her hands and said, "Hunters, please prepare for the revelation of the Blessed Egress."

Two of the hunters approached the platform and took up positions on either side of it. They raised two flashlights, aiming a narrow beam directly at strips of plastic sewn into Ian's loincloth. They kept the flashlights aimed until the attached strips illuminated intensely green.

Dagny turned to the hunters and loudly said, "Your feet are quick, your eyes are keen, your hearts are strong, and your bodies are lean. Rush into the night and track down the liar. Our passion for truth burns hotter than fire. Keep your eyes peeled and don't spare your sword, dispense with a fraud, and gain a reward." She paused and turned toward the group of women who watched from a short distance away. "I want to thank Amity Mae for that beautiful rhyming pre-hunt affirmation." She turned to Ian and said, "When I drop my hand, off you go. Makes sense? Advantaged hunters will wait for my other hand. Godspeed."

The hunters with the flashlights turned them off. The other hunters clapped when they saw how bright Ian's loincloth glowed.

"Advantaged hunters ready," Dagny said.

The hunters Jebediah had called out for an advantage lowered their infrared goggles onto their eyes. They carefully placed their fingers on a starting line like sprinters. A few stretched their legs out, shaking their feet behind them. Eventually, they all looked up, waiting for Dagny's start.

She grinned at Ian, showing her menacing smile full of little teeth. Her eyes widened a bit as she thrust her right arm downward.

The hunters shouted and began chanting, "Go, go, go…"

Like Riddick, Ian ran to the platform's edge and leaped from it. He sprinted at full speed toward the woods where he had seen Riddick disappear. The hunters' chants behind him slowly faded, leaving only the sound of his breathing and footsteps.

All the ambient light produced by the light sticks near the platform quickly faded, leaving Ian in complete darkness except for a glow from his waist. The night sky was slightly overcast. He could see only a few meters ahead of him. He hurtled a fallen tree trunk and ducked under outstretched branches. He soon saw a bright red laser dot about waist high, connecting a row of tree trunks that marked the perimeter of Egress Encampment. Ian charged through, knowing that breaking the beam would likely confirm to them the precise location of his flight.

The hunters' excited yelling behind him had faded almost entirely away. He tripped on a rock and fell, quickly scrambling to his feet to continue. He zigzagged between trees and noticed that he was on a slight incline. After running for a distance, he estimated to be about the length of a football field, he came to a small clearing. He wondered if the hunters were on their way yet.

He pulled off the loincloth, unwrapping it from between his legs. He threw it down to the ground, illuminating the surrounding ground. He also took off his shoes, kicking them a short distance away, feeling that the challenge of running barefoot was offset by the advantage of not being trackable. It was odd to feel safer while naked.

He remembered that the orientation of the Blessed Egress platform encouraged him to flee directly south, the direction from which he had arrived from the Biding Wellness Center. He had to ruin the Sadens' every expectation if his plan was to succeed.

He continued across the clearing, about 20 meters, then removed the special shoes the Sadens had put on him and committed to the next part of his plan. Instead of continuing his long run toward the main road, he turned and cut back, following a wide arc that took him toward the backside of Egress Encampment. He slowed as he felt winded, carefully checking trees until he found the laser beam perimeter. Off to his left, he saw a depression in the ground. He ran to it and discovered a dry gully with tree roots protruding from its sides. He laid down, slid under some roots, and scraped leaves over himself.

He soon heard the twigs snapping and the pounding of the hunters' feet as they raced through the woods after him. There were no more chants or shouts. He heard twigs snapping and trampling feet of physically fit men competing to kill him.

The footsteps faded in the distance. Ian remained motionless, trying to calculate when they might reach the clearing where he had left his loincloth. He wondered if the hunters would assume he had continued ahead or determine he had doubled back. In the dark stillness, he eventually heard only crickets and the sound of his own breathing.

After waiting for what he estimated to be about fifteen minutes after the footsteps had gone silent, he raised his head and sat up. He climbed to his feet. Leaves and debris fell from his body like he had come to life from a grave. He looked around. His eyes had adjusted somewhat to the darkness. He could see about the distance of a stone's throw.

He began walking as quietly as possible. He returned along the arc he had followed from the opening where he had left his loincloth and shoes. Each time a twig snapped under his foot, he froze, waiting and listening for any nearby motion.

He eventually returned to the edge of the clearing. A few meters away, he saw his loincloth. Its glow had dimmed substantially. He took a couple of steps toward it before a rustling sound to his right froze him in his tracks. He crouched, straining his eyes to detect anything toward the sound. The rustling happened again, followed by a moan. It was a sound of pain. The sound excited him. His heart thumped. He quietly stepped toward it. A figure slowly came into view. It was a person sprawled at the base of the tree. The person did not acknowledge him.

Ian took his time, stepping carefully, pausing after each step. As he closed in, he saw a Saden hunter lying on his side, his back to the tree. The hunter's legs had scraped the nearby dirt smooth like a windshield wiper.

Ian's exhilaration was momentarily tempered when he realized this might be a horrible trick. He picked up a branch and broke it over his knee. The hunter didn't move. Ian moved closer and tossed the branch pieces, hitting the hunter in the leg and torso. The hunter didn't react. "Hey," Ian said in a loud whisper.

No response.

Ian went closer and saw that the hunter was still wearing his infrared goggles. Ian moved to within a stride. Ian swung his foot into the hunter's gut with all his strength. The body jerked, but the hunter was clearly unconscious. Ian pulled the infrared goggles off and put them on. He gasped as he looked around. It was as though someone had flipped a light switch in the forest. Everything became crystal clear. Ian rolled the hunter to his back and struggled to take off the man's shorts for a few minutes before putting them on himself. The hunter had a club in a sling at his hip and a six-inch dagger with a leather handle in his hand. Ian took these items as well. Ian pulled a phone—supposedly only a radio—from the hunter's pocket. A padlock illuminated on the screen. Ian knew better than to unlock it. He couldn't take the chance that the device could be tracked. He dropped it beside the hunter.

With his new visual acuity, he quickly found the clearing, where he saw a scene that terrified and thrilled him. Eight to ten hunters lay near the loincloth and shoes Ian had left there. He had been unable to see the sprawled-out hunters before putting on the night vision goggles.

They weren't moving. He cautiously approached them, now able to see his surroundings for at least fifty meters in every direction. All was still. When he came to the hunters, he stopped and observed them. Their chests didn't seem to move. He kicked several of them. A slight movement of a hunter's arm startled Ian. He raised the club high, ready to bring it down. But the hunter went motionless again. Ian walked around behind the body, crouched, and pressed his fingers against the hunter's neck. He couldn't feel a pulse. Ian checked the other hunters. All had no pulse.

He hurried to remove the shoes from a hunter whose shoe size was close to his and put them on. If tracked, the shoes would identify the hunter's location, not Ian's. He then quickly removed the infrared goggles from every hunter. He gathered the weapons from each hunter, carried them to the top of a ridge a short distance away, and heaved them down into a ravine. He then went back and gathered up the infrared goggles. He ran a safe distance before stopping to stomp on them, breaking each one. He ran southward through the woods toward the main road.

He passed several bodies on the way. He removed the infrared goggles, breaking them with his club or stomping them. He also removed weapons, hurling them as far as possible from the hunters. One hunter had a digital compass with an illuminated LED readout. Ian pocketed it, then turned roughly south. He knew that direction would eventually cross the narrow road Dagny used for van access to Egress Encampment.

He settled in at a comfortable jogging pace and soon came to the narrow road. His goggles allowed him to see the van's fresh tread marks clearly. Along the way, he counted seven more Saden hunters who had collapsed alongside the road or wandered a short distance from it. After running for another 20 minutes, his lungs burned. He slowed to a walk to catch his breath, and as he looked around, his thoughts went to the poor soul en route from Biding Wellness Center. If they met, what a story Ian would have to tell.

As he alternated between jogging and walking, he remembered traveling many miles on the road during his flight from Biding Wellness Center. His physical strength waned. For two more hours, he walked, not seeing or hearing any more Saden hunters. This sign of success exhilarated him, giving him new hope that he might be on the verge of escaping the worst nightmare of his life.

He hiked for another hour, occasionally stopping for water at springs he found off the main road. He felt his energies depleting with each mile. The blisters Amity had so deftly healed were back, forcing him to walk gingerly. He left the road and entered a grove of trees, where he found a safe place to sit and rest. His legs burned, and when he rubbed them, he felt the sting from briar scratches and insect bites.

He ended his brief rest and continued his journey until the eastern sky showed the first signs of dawn. The rising sun brought into view a familiar sight in the distance. The rusty truss bridge he remembered from Riddick's map came into focus. He lifted his infrared goggles and saw the first hints of the bridge's orange patches. The beautiful sign that he was on course excited him and energized him. As he closed in on it, he remembered that Sadens were supposed to be waiting ahead on the road to welcome him. According to Amity, he could presume that they wanted to embrace him as their beloved and crown him as a leader in their horrific cult. Ian wanted nothing to do with this ceremonial victory. These were just additional people he wished to elude.

He gazed up at the bridge as he neared it. Although the rising sun was illuminating the sky more, it was still dark enough to require the goggles to see its features clearly.

To his right and slightly behind him, twigs snapped.

Ian spun to see a Saden hunter burst from the trees. Jebediah sprinted toward him.

Although Ian still had a club and a knife, he knew hand-to-hand combat with Jebediah was a death sentence. Ian fled, mustering every ounce of his waning strength to race toward the bridge. He heard Jebediah gaining on him.

"Keep running, imposter," Jebediah said. "Tired prey makes easier prey."

Ian pushed for all the speed his adrenaline could fuel, but his legs were virtually spent. He glanced over his shoulder and saw Jebediah closing in. When Jebediah got close enough to swing his club, Ian cut hard to the right and ran off the road into the trees.

Jebediah overran Ian's dodge, putting a few more precious strides between them, but quickly made up the lost distance.

Ian tried to hurtle the trunk of a fallen tree but couldn't clear it and tripped, tumbling face-first to the ground.

"Thank you," Jebediah said, slowing to a stop beside Ian while they both panted. "I like how you gave us some privacy."

Ian rolled toward the fallen tree and tried to squeeze under it, desperate for any way to shield himself.

"Nice glasses," Jebediah said, strolling toward him, a knife in one hand and a club in another. "I'm actually glad you stole a pair. I want my smiling face to be your last memory before you fade to black."

Ian said, "Please, I won't cause you any trouble. I won't tell anybody what I've seen."

Jebediah laughed. "All imposters make that promise before we tenderize them with a club. They suddenly become eager to proclaim their extreme respect for our privacy." He walked around the tree trunk and came back to stand over Ian, blocking any chance of Ian's escape. "I'll tell you what… You roll out from under there and lie face down, and I can make it hurt less. But stay tucked away, and I'm liable to break some bones and strip plenty of flesh trying to pry you out. Imposters deserve pain," Jebediah said. "And as an imposter, you enjoyed our hospitality for days. Now it's time to pay up."

Ian was out of options. If this was how he would go out, a painless blow to the back of the head was better than the slow torture of a battle with an opponent who outmatched him.

Jebediah's phone chirped. He put it to his ear. "No, Ms. Conger, I haven't found him yet, but I think I'm close." He slipped the phone into his pocket. "They'll discover what's left of you soon enough. I want to take my time."

Jebediah raised the club and swung it straight down at Ian's head. Ian dodged it, and the club hit the tree trunk, sending chunks of bark flying from it and stinging the side of Ian's face.

Before Jebediah could raise the club again, Ian rolled out and swung his club as hard as possible, landing a clean blow to Jebediah's shin.

Jebediah dropped the club and cried out in pain, clutching his leg. He hopped backward before Ian could swing again and unsheathed his knife. He dove at Ian with the knife, thrusting its blade toward Ian's torso.

Ian rolled just before the knife impaled the ground, lodging in a buried tree root.

"You bastard!" Jebediah shouted. While he wiggled the knife handle, trying to free it, Ian rose onto his knees and swung his club again. He landed a solid blow to Jebediah's back with the spiked end of the club.

Jebediah howled in pain and briefly curled up into the fetal position. Before Ian could deliver another blow, Jebediah worked through his agony to reach for the stuck knife again.

Ian brought the club down directly onto Jebediah's outstretched arm, shattering the bone.

Jebediah rolled in agony. At one point, he rolled face down, screaming into the dirt. He swept his legs, trying to hook Ian with them.

Ian jumped out of reach before charging again. He raised the club high and landed a solid blow to Jebediah's head, smashing his skull. Blood splattered onto Ian's legs and the tree trunk. He swung again and then again, pummeling Jebediah until all the twitching stopped. He dropped to his knees and fell to his side, exhausted and sobbing.

Twenty-four

THE SUN CRESTED, swelling an orange glow above the eastern horizon. Through the trees, Ian watched it grow brighter. He pushed himself up to a sitting position. His muscles had stiffened. He climbed to his feet and plodded from the trees to the road. As he continued to the bridge, he considered that if he hadn't ducked into the woods, Jebediah would have certainly killed him in this wide-open space.

He came to the base of the bridge and climbed up the angled slope underneath it toward the girder. At the top, he climbed over a small railing to step onto the railroad tracks. Based on his memory of his escape from Biding Wellness Center, the bridge had been only four or five miles from Biding Wellness Center. He wondered where the Sadens were waiting for him on the road. The most logical location would be where the dirt road intersected the main road, so continuing on the dirt road was out of the question. If he could accurately backtrack through the woods, he could exit at a different location along the main road and perhaps flag a non-Saden for help.

He resumed his trek. He remembered the stream between Biding Wellness Center and this bridge. He had already been limping, but now the blisters on his feet made each step feel like walking on hot coals. He longed to soak them in the cool water.

He hiked through what he hoped would be the last stretch of his journey. He heard water trickling ahead. He continued climbing over fallen trees, circumnavigating briar patches, and slipping a few times on mossy rocks. The water grew louder, exhilarating him. He slid down an embankment, grimacing when his feet landed ankle-deep in the creek. He collapsed onto his hands and knees and put his face into the water. He splashed his face and shoulders, washing Jebediah's blood off.

The sun had warmed the air. While he rested, he wondered if the Sadens that were waiting for him knew yet that many of the hunters were dead or dying. Nothing in the *Our Beloved* book mentioned a scenario where the beloved succeeded by taking out all the hunters that chased him. He remembered Jebediah's admonition that doing harm to a Saden was a sure sign of an imposter.

He climbed up a final ridge. At the top, he saw a clearing beyond the trees with Biding Wellness Center centered in it. He couldn't believe that the sight of the horrible building actually gave him a warm feeling. It wasn't the building itself that brought relief, but the promise of passersby on the main road in front of it. He kept moving.

As he neared it, he saw no vehicles parked in the back of the building. He changed course to move closer for a better view, hoping the dogs didn't hear or smell him. All the lights in the building were off, and the generator was silent. Biding Wellness Center appeared to be abandoned.

When he came to within fifty meters, he squatted and leaned against a tree. He waited, watching for any activity. From this vantage point, the road was visible beyond the building. Technically, if he set foot on it, he was officially the Sadens' beloved, yet no one was in sight to declare it. Maybe Amity or someone still at Egress Encampment had radioed word of the dead hunters to the Sadens who had been waiting for him out here. If he could be so lucky, his captors might have already returned to Egress Encampment.

He stepped out of the thick woods and walked along the edge of the back lawn toward the road. When he took his final steps and planted both feet on the pavement, the completion of his successful escape made tears well up. He looked along the road in each direction, knowing it could be hours before a car passed by him. He wanted to get as far away from this place as possible, as quickly as possible. He wanted it more than food and rest.

He decided to travel in the same direction he had driven Garland's motorcycle on his first escape attempt from this wretched place. But after taking only a few steps on the hard asphalt, his feet burned more than ever, and his exhausted legs ached. Pain spread to his lower back, and the limp that pain demanded had become a stagger. He looked at the long road ahead and knew he couldn't even reach the first curve.

Since hiking any significant distance was out of the question, his only other option was to summon help somehow. Loitering outside the Biding Wellness Center building was foolish because he knew the Sadens would be back. If he broke in, he could use the phone and hide somewhere in the building until help arrived.

His face contorted as he staggered toward the entrance. His thigh cramped, dropping him to one knee. He clutched it, and after resting and massaging it for a minute, he crawled the remaining distance. He kept his eyes on the front of the building, searching for any movement or other sign that someone was inside. The dark windows revealed nothing. When he reached the front door, he used its handle to pull himself up. He couldn't see through the narrow crack at the door's edge. The entire property, inside and out, was eerily quiet. Even the birds had gone silent. He pulled the front door's handle and was surprised when it opened. He leaned in and listened. Still quiet.

He pushed the door as wide as possible, locking it open, then stepped inside. He crept across the lobby. The ambient light from the open door gave him enough light to navigate to the front counter, where he stopped. He saw the door to the hallway where the rooms were located.

The manager's office was just ahead and to the right. He went to it and slowly pushed it open. He reached in and felt for the light switch. When he located it, he pushed it up, but no light came on. He felt another, larger switch. He leaned in and put his face close to it, straining to make out a small label taped under it:

Power-Main.

He pushed it from the bottom. It snapped upward. A familiar sound he had grown to loathe sputtered in the distance. The generator behind the facility growled to life. He heard several pops and clicks as lights in the lobby, the hallway, and the office blinked on.

He stepped into a room he remembered well. This was where Dagny held her so-called group sessions. Chairs were folded and stacked against the wall. A stack of food trays sat in the corner. He spotted a wired landline telephone on the desk and felt relief. He stumbled, grabbed the handset, and put it to his ear. No dial tone. His heart sank. He frantically pressed numbers on the keypad, but the phone was dead. "Dammit!" He slammed it down.

He noticed the open closet where they had taken his fellow rehab patient, Clarence, for a demerit cancellation. Ian vividly remembered Clarence's cries of agony and pleas for mercy. Maybe he could use one of their instruments of torture as a weapon to protect himself. He went to the doorway and looked in. Long chains still hung from the ceiling by the far wall. A small table held some papers and a microphone on a small tripod. Ian went to it. The page on top read:

Room 151 Vent Script

Engage Our Beloved with a curious sound.
Tapping, whistle, something noticeable.

When the Beloved speaks, be his best friend.
Ingratiate yourself to him.

Tell Our Beloved the previous occupant paved the way to freedom.

Tell Our Beloved of the map to Egress Encampment.

Infuse Our Beloved with the hope that the journey will help others, too.

Warn Our Beloved of the danger of inaction.

Urge Our Beloved to have faith in his ability.

Encourage Our Beloved to believe in the destination.

May God bless our efforts to bring forth Our Beloved.

"You people are insane," Ian said under his breath.

A shelf on the wall behind the door contained swabs, bandages, and a gallon container labeled:

Makeup Stage-Blood, (Dark Venous)

Ian picked up the half-empty container and shook his head.

He noticed an electronic tablet mounted to the wall on the other side of the door. He touched the screen. It came on, showing an already-opened music app. It displayed three audio files, each with the play arrow beside them.

The first file was labeled:

Cries of Repentance

Ian pressed it and flinched when Clarence's screams blared from speakers mounted in a row across the small room's ceiling. They blasted the same contrived screams and begging Ian remembered. He quickly stopped the awful sounds.

The next file was labeled:

Guns

Ian pressed play. The distant, sharp crack of gunshots came from behind the facility.

The third file was labeled:

Dogs

When he pressed play, the howls and excited barking that had tortured him nightly replaced the gunshots behind the building. The dogs barked themselves into their familiar frenzy and included sounds of their paws scratching against a wooden pen.

"Son of a bitch," Ian said.

Without a landline phone as an option to call for help, Ian wondered if there was any chance someone might have left a mobile phone behind. At this point, he'd be thrilled to discover a flare to shoot skyward after dark. Searching the entire facility in his condition daunted him, but he had to survive. He was thirsty and hungry, so maybe he could find food, too.

As he headed out of the office, something caught his attention that filled him with more hope and excitement than he had experienced throughout his ordeal. Two black shotguns he hadn't noticed on his way in were tucked against the wall. He recognized them as the guns aimed at him by the two men who ruined his first escape attempt on Garland's motorcycle. "Thank God," he said. Finally, he could defend himself. He only hoped they were loaded.

As he moved toward the guns, movement in the doorway took his attention. Terror shot through him when Dagny and a hunter stepped into view in the office doorway. Dagny wore the same navy blue military uniform she had worn at the group session. The hunter was in full warrior garb, shirtless, with shorts, black face paint, and markings on his chest and shoulders. He wore gloves and held a machete.

Dagny said, "There you are! I wondered who got the dogs all riled up!"

The massive adrenaline surge of pure survival masked all of Ian's pain as he ran for the guns.

"Wait! No!" Dagny shouted.

Ian grabbed the closest shotgun, raised it, and aimed. His heart sank. The feather-light gun was a highly detailed plastic replica. He let it fall to his side and dropped it to the floor. Knowing he couldn't run or overpower them, he collapsed to his knees and covered his face.

"I made it. You can't harm me," Ian said.

Dagny said, "Of course I wouldn't think of harming you, my beloved. It's my honor to be the first to greet you."

The hunter approached him, dropped to one knee, and said, "Don't be afraid. Your Blessed Egress is complete. You were successful!" He grinned.

Outside, Ian heard the grumbling of an approaching vehicle that moved from the front to the rear of the building.

The hunter held his hand to Ian and said, "It's time to restore you to your full strength. It's my honor to be the first to offer aid in your recovery from the successful Blessed Egress. May I have your permission to touch you?" He held out his gloved hand.

Ian hesitated, then took it, suspicion etched into his face.

The hunter helped him to his feet.

"I don't want to go anywhere with you," Ian said.

"We have an obligation to get you healed," Dagny said. "After you have recovered, we can discuss your options."

"I don't want any of your options. The only option I want is a phone or a vehicle." Ian pulled his arm from the hunter and tried to navigate around him, but almost fell before reaching out to the wall to steady himself.

The hunter grabbed Ian and kept him from falling. "Please let me help you!" He draped Ian's arm around his neck. "You've given your all for us. Now we will give you our all by restoring you." The hunter guided Ian through the door and into the hallway.

Dagny stepped back to give them room, watching with a satisfied grin. They guided him along the hallway he remembered from his imprisonment there days before. They passed by room 151 and continued to the rear door, where they exited to the outside.

Dagny's van sat a short distance away, its side door slid open. As they moved closer, Ian was stunned by what he saw inside.

The van's interior was outfitted with an ornate golden throne, and flower petals were strewn around its base. A large sign hung on the inside wall read:

We Welcome Our Beloved!

A row of 8 x 10 photos featuring the women of Egress Encampment was taped to the wall. The first one was Amity.

A small table draped with a white tablecloth in front of the throne held an oversized tray containing the familiar plate covers that concealed a feast Ian could smell.

The hunter let go of Ian and climbed into the van. He pulled an IV bottle from a medical bag and untangled the tubing.

"Not happening," Ian said.

Dagny said, "My beloved, we need to replenish your electrolytes to boost your recovery."

"I don't want that," Ian said, looking toward the road.

"Nothing in this treatment should concern you," Dagny said. "You've already enjoyed our restorative benefits at Egress Encampment. We need you to be strong because you have much work to do in your new home."

The hunter reached out to Ian with a bottle of water.

Ian took it, cracked the cap, and returned it to the hunter. "You first."

The hunter raised his hands in protest and said, "No, it's for you."

"I insist," Ian said. "You would disobey my first request?"

The hunter looked at Dagny. She closed her eyes and gave him a slight nod.

The hunter sipped the water.

Ian took the water back and threw it over his shoulder.

Dagny said, "My beloved, none of the food or drink is laced. It is purely for nourishment. Your mission is complete. We are here to ensure your well-being."

"I really just want to leave."

"We'll be leaving soon, but we need to wait for sunset," Dagny said.

"Then let me use your phone."

"We don't use phones outside the encampment."

"It wasn't a question. I need a phone," Ian demanded.

Dagny said, "If you refuse to listen to us, we just might have someone who can convince you."

Another hunter Ian hadn't seen peered out from the back of the van. At first, Ian was confused about why Dagny thought this hunter had any influence. He looked somewhat more familiar, but his identity didn't register with Ian.

As the hunter climbed from the van, Kate's face slid into view, beaming at Ian. She exited wearing a purple dress identical to Amity and Angelica's. "I'm so proud of you!" she said.

Ian was speechless. During his absence, he had fantasized a hundred times about reuniting with Kate. He wanted to rush to her, pick her up, and spin her as she requested in her note. He could never have imagined having that reunion with this audience and with Kate wearing garb whose symbolism repulsed him. He couldn't believe she had fallen under Dagny's spell.

"May I hug you?" she said, opening her arms.

Ian gaped at her. His mouth hung open, but he couldn't speak as he tried to process what he saw.

"Please?" Kate stepped closer.

Ian nodded.

She rushed to him, threw her arms around him, and rocked him back and forth. "I'm so proud of you," she said.

"Praise God," Dagny said. She stepped back and dabbed her eyes with a tissue, smiling proudly.

Ian barely returned the hug.

When Kate released her embrace, she held him away from her to inspect him. "You're fuzzy," she said, twiddling her fingertips on his beard.

Ian plowed through his shock to say, "You've got to be kidding me."

The hunters and Dagny laughed. The familiar-looking hunter that came out of the van right before Kate came to stand beside her.

"Oh, I'm sorry," Kate said. "You remember my nephew, Preston, right?" He was dressed in garb, identical to the other hunter.

"You're... a Saden?" Ian said, frowning at Kate.

She nodded and took his hands. "I've been dying to tell you how much they've changed my life for the better. And now we've completely changed your life, too!"

"Wait a minute," Ian said. He shook his head as if trying to wake up from a dream. "You set me up for this?"

"Yes, isn't it wonderful? Preston introduced me to the blessed truth."

She blew a kiss to Preston. He smiled with pride. She turned back to Ian. "Ian—I mean, my beloved—I never wanted to break up with you, but it was the only way we could achieve the mandatory abstinence we needed to cleanse you since you weren't a believer. I promised you we'd look back and realize that it would be the best decision we could have made. It's been over sixty days, so now we're both renewed. You've proven you are our beloved, so we can end our abstinence." She tried to kiss him, but Ian let go of her and stepped back.

"What's wrong?" Kate said.

Ian's feeling of betrayal now outweighed his pity for her. He squinted, trying to make sense of the crazy talk coming from a woman he thought he knew so well. A woman he had wanted to marry.

Kate approached him again and tried to take his hands, but he pulled them away. "The best part of our new life is that we're going to make babies—lots of them."

Dagny cleared her throat.

Kate looked at her.

Dagny made a scissor motion with her fingers.

"Of course," Kate said.

Ian said, "What does that mean?"

Kate looked at him apologetically. "All our men, especially our beloved, must be circumcised. I told them you aren't."

"Is this a fucking joke?" Ian said.

"You'll barely feel it," the hunter beside Dagny replied.

"And we've improved the process," Dagny added. She turned to Ian. "We've got all the tools and numbing cream necessary to get you trimmed quicker than you can say snippity-snip. There's no time like the present."

Kate said, "You'll heal quickly, then we will make love to your heart's content. I can't wait to be the first lover of our beloved!"

"Let's get you ready," Dagny said, pointing into the van.

Ian backed away. "I'm not going anywhere."

The hunter stepped forward and took his arm.

"Please don't fight it," Kate said. "You are required to fulfill your triumphant return to Egress Encampment to conclude the Blessed Egress. Then you will be free to make any decision you wish to."

"I'm not going back," Ian said.

The hunter guided Ian toward the open van door.

Ian let his legs give way. It was the only way he could resist.

"You must take the throne," Dagny shouted. "Take the throne!"

"No!" Ian said.

Preston was about to grab Ian's other arm when a voice from the corner of the building said, "Let him go!" A figure stepped into view and approached the group, aiming a rifle at the hunter who held Ian. He wore camouflage gear and carried a pistol holstered on his hip.

The hunter stopped pulling Ian, but didn't let him go.

Ian climbed to his feet.

"I said get your hands off him," the man said.

Ian felt a flood of elation when he recognized his brother, Tim.

Twenty-five

EVERYONE FROZE AS Tim speed-walked toward them, his rifle steady and aimed.

"I've got you, Bro," Tim said. "Last warning," He approached to within a few meters.

In a smooth motion, the hunter grabbed Ian from behind and pulled a knife, putting it on Ian's neck. "Don't come any closer. Put down your gun," he said.

Tim adjusted his aim to the hunter.

Ian said, "Bro, they won't kill me."

Tim stopped. "I know they won't." He fired. The headshot splattered the hunter's blood onto the side of the van. His body crumpled beside the knife.

Kate shrieked and collapsed to her knees, clasping her hands over her mouth.

Preston dropped to the ground, holding his hands out in surrender.

Dagny raised her hands, too.

Tim moved closer. "Ian, get the van keys!" he shouted.

Ian stepped over the dead hunter and hurried to the driver's side. He reached in and pulled the keys from the ignition.

"Everybody over there," Tim said, pointing with this rifle barrel to a place a short distance away.

As Preston climbed to his feet, he pulled a long knife from behind him and charged Tim.

Tim fired, hitting Preston twice in the torso. Preston fell face down to the ground, moaning. His body jerked a few times before going still.

Kate screamed, "Noooo!" as she crawled toward Preston.

"Stop! You're next," Tim said. He pulled his sidearm and aimed it at her.

"No, don't shoot her," Ian said, moving to stand beside Tim.

Kate froze, staring wide-eyed at Preston. She turned to Tim, clasped her hands, and said, "Tim, please leave us. You have no right to interfere. This has nothing to do with you."

"My brother has everything to do with me," Tim said. He pulled another pistol from his belt and handed it to Ian.

During the exchange, Dagny had subtly moved her phone to her ear. She hollered, "Garland, Initiate the Blessed Exodus! Initiate the Blessed

Exodus!"

Tim raised his pistol and shouted, "Drop the phone!"

Dagny let the phone fall to the ground and smiled as she said, "It's too late. It is all finished."

"Kick the phone over here," Tim said.

Dagny raised her foot and stomped it with her heel. "Now, there's no way to cancel what is about to happen."

"Good. Your horrific game is over," Ian said, raising his pistol to her.

Tim, too, aimed his gun at Dagny and said, "Move away from the van and keep your hands where I can see them."

"Don't worry. They don't have guns," Ian said.

"You can't be sure."

"I *am* sure," Ian said. "They don't believe in them."

Dagny sidestepped to join Kate a few paces away.

Kate said, "I just want to—"

"Shut up," Ian snapped. He wondered how long she had been one of them. Her conversion to Sadenism was a bigger blindside than her breakup with him. Any remaining promise of a future with her evaporated. Her wide-eyed, hollow gaze made it clear that she shared every bit of the insanity Dagny had nurtured in Amity.

"Shouldn't we call the police?" Ian asked.

"Keep covering them," Tim said. He lowered his gun to pull his phone from his pocket. "No signal, not even half a bar out in this godforsaken place. We'll have to call inside the building."

Ian said, "Phones are dead in there. I already checked."

"Then we need to tie them up and drive until we get enough signal to place the call."

"No need to tie them," Ian said. "It'll be easy to lock them up inside, right, Dagny?"

Tim pocketed his phone. "Then let's get them in," he said, motioning with his gun.

Dagny smiled and stepped toward Ian. "Listen, my beloved—"

"No, *you* listen," Ian said, lifting the gun to aim it at her head. "This gun is my beloved. One more step, and you'll experience your own Blessed Exodus. Makes sense?"

As they marched the women to the rear entrance of Biding Wellness Center, Kate said, "I can't believe you're willing to let your brother ruin our future."

Ian ignored her and opened the door. He held them in the hallway and told Tim where to get the keys from the manager's office. When Tim returned, Ian pointed to a door and said, "That one." It was room 151.

Tim pressed the rifle under his arm, found the key, and opened it. He stepped back and nodded to Ian.

"Get in," Ian said to the women.

"You're making a mistake," Kate said, stepping into the room.

Dagny followed, but stopped and pivoted in the doorway. "It's not too late for you to do the right thing, my beloved."

Tim frowned and looked at Ian.

Ian dropped the pistol to the floor and lunged, shoving her.

Dagny tried to catch her balance but fell, crashing onto her back in the middle of the floor.

Ian said, "You've just earned a demerit that will need canceling."

"Why are you doing this?" Kate shouted. "I don't even recognize you anymore!"

As Ian picked up the pistol, he and Tim exchanged an incredulous look.

"Please forgive me, my beloved," Dagny said as she slowly climbed to her feet and moved to stand beside Kate.

Kate clasped her hands as if praying and said, "Babe, please don't ruin everything we have. I'll do absolutely anything you want me to."

Ian took hold of the doorknob. Before he closed it, he said, "I have a request."

"Anything, my beloved," Kate said. Her eyes suddenly gleamed with hope.

"I think it would be best if we didn't see each other or communicate for a while."

"Very funny," Kate said. "If payback will win you back, I'll accept it. How long?"

"The suggested first round is forever." Ian pulled the knob, slamming the door shut.

"Nooo!" Kate screamed. She ran to the door and pounded on it. "You're making a huge mistake!" she cried.

Ian confirmed the door was locked.

The brothers shared their first unguarded moment while Kate continued to beg from behind the door.

"How'd you find me?" Ian asked.

Tim tapped his pistol on door 151. "I told you she was no good. When we couldn't reach you, Mom and Dad got worried. They called Kate. She claimed to be as worried as they were, but insisted they do nothing to look for you. I didn't buy her act. I knew you were her ultimate bait, so I tracked her and her man."

Ian said, "Not that it matters anymore, but the guy's her nephew, not her man," Ian said.

"Is that what she told you?" Tim said, holstering his pistol.

The question clobbered Ian.

Tim said, "Look, I don't need to tell you what I saw, but they aren't related unless she's sicker than I thought. She lied to you, Bro. Let's get out of here." Tim headed toward the lobby.

"My legs are wasted. I'm gonna need a minute," Ian said, limping.

Tim tucked the rifle under his arm, returned, and helped Ian slowly walk toward the front. When they reached the door, Kate's cries had gone silent. They went through the lobby and stepped outside. Ian's new freedom felt wonderful. He turned to Tim and said, "I've never been happier to see you."

They hugged, and then Tim took a moment to look Ian up and down. "You look like hell, Bro."

"I've been there," Ian said, wiping a tear.

"Are you crying?" Tim said, smirking.

"No, my eyes are sweating."

They laughed.

"I hope you don't expect me to call you my beloved," Tim said. "What the hell is that about?"

"It's a long story," Ian said. He looked around the driveway. "Where's your ride?"

"I parked my truck down the road and hiked here so they wouldn't hear me. You wait here. I'll go get it. Looks like you don't need any more walking today."

Tim took off, jogging down the driveway, rifle in hand, to the road.

Ian sat on the curb outside the front door, elated by Tim's dramatic rescue. Within a couple of minutes, Tim's truck turned into the driveway. He pulled to a stop, rolled down his window, and leaned to open the passenger door for Ian. "Get in. Let's go," he said.

"Did you try your phone again?"

"Yes, still no signal. Don't worry about it."

"What you mean, don't worry about it?" Ian said.

Tim smiled.

Ian said, "What's your problem?"

"Leave this situation to me. It's all gonna work out fine."

Ian stared at him momentarily, then said, "You're rushing me out of here so you can come back and finish them off, aren't you?"

Tim said, "Don't be an idiot. You think I'd do something that would get us both in trouble?"

"You can't do this. They'll find the bodies. They'll arrest you."

"That won't happen." He tapped the front of his baseball cap.

Ian recognized the micro-video cam embedded in the hat's brim.

"You should know I never miss recording a hunt," Tim said.

Ian couldn't believe what he was hearing. "You've always hated Kate, and what they put me through was hell, but God damn, Tim, you can't just murder them."

"Do you know what kind of problem you'll create if we turn them over to the police?" Tim asked.

"Yes, smaller problems than going to prison."

Tim said, "Listen. We turned you over to that bitch on her promise that she'd take care of you. She not only let us down, but she tortured you damn near to death. As for Kate, look at how she's talking to you. Her eyes are as bat-shit crazy as her words. She can't be cured from whatever she's got, and you know it."

Ian looked away.

Tim said, "Let's not be stupid here. I was forced to kill to save your life. If it comes to that and I have to defend myself, I can show that your life was in imminent danger. They would have killed you. The footage will prove it."

"We can't do this," Ian said.

Tim raised his hands and let them fall onto his lap, laughing in disbelief. "You're about to make this messy for both of us. If we transport these women anywhere, they'll spin that into a kidnapping charge. They get a good prosecutor, and we're screwed. And do you really want to give that Dagny the chance to do her mind-control shit with a jury? Let this situation be my problem. Leave me to handle it."

A loud crash from inside the building startled them. They looked toward the door. Tim turned off the truck and got out, pulling his pistol. He ran inside.

Ian took his pistol and followed, hobbling as quickly as he could.

He saw Tim grab the keys from the countertop and then run to the hallway door ahead of him. When he opened the door, they heard another crash. When Ian reached the door, he realized it came from the room where Dagny and Kate were locked. Tim stood at the door of room 151, sorting through the keys.

"Just shoot the knob," Ian shouted.

Tim tried another key and said, "This isn't the fucking movies."

Ian reached Tim just as he found the correct key.

Tim turned the knob, pushed the door open, and raised his pistol. "My God, what have you done?" he yelled.

Ian leaned to look in.

In the center of the room, Dagny stood, her dress blood-soaked. More blood smeared her face and speckled the walls, ceiling, and floor. She held a bloody broken table lamp at her side, its smashed base dangled from wires.

By her feet lay Kate's body, face down in a pool of blood. Her arm jutted out behind her at an unnatural angle.

"God, no!" Ian yelled. He hurried to Kate and fell to his knees beside her. He put down his pistol and rolled her onto her back. Her face was smashed beyond recognition.

Dagny stepped back and wiped her mouth with the back of her hand, smearing the blood that framed her smile. "She chose this, Ian. She renounced her faith. She said she wanted to return to how things were with you before her blessed conversion. After months of strenuous teaching, she took it upon herself to reject all the truth she had learned. My only choice was to dispense with her. Makes sense?"

Ian climbed to his feet and charged, launching himself into a full tackle. They crashed to the floor. Dagny landed on her back and covered her face while Ian swung at her, landing several blows before Tim could holster his pistol and pull him off.

"You're full of shit, and you know it," Ian shouted at Dagny as Tim dragged him away. "You tricked all these people. You tricked Kate. This entire scheme—the beloved, the silly rules, the blessed this and blessed that—it's all bullshit, but you'll never admit it, will you?"

Dagny stood, touched her lip, and then smiled at the blood on her fingertips. "Needy people welcome tricks." She looked up at Ian. "A magician's best audience is filled with people willing to believe."

"This is real life, and people want the truth." Ian pulled away from Tim and grabbed the pistol from the floor. He aimed it at Dagny. "Admit that you're a fraud."

"Hold on, Ian," Tim said. "Be careful, here."

"Admit it was a scheme!" Ian yelled.

Dagny's mouth stretched into a broad grin that showed her tiny teeth. "I'll admit that I gave Kate what she wanted. I'll admit that I gave them all what they wanted. Like it or not, truth is learned from those who teach it. Truth becomes true the moment it's believed. Your parents believed that sending you to this facility would improve your life. You believed a simple map I left in this room would free you from this facility. I'm not a fraud. I offer people the truth they desire. They gobble it up. They can't get enough." Dagny stepped toward him.

"That's close enough," Tim said.

Dagny stopped. "You're a smart young man, Ian. Perhaps we could work together to spread the truth to satisfy a new flock that craves it."

"You want me to join you?" Ian said.

"There's no reason this unfortunate situation has to end uncomfortably for either of us."

"Oh, it's gonna end uncomfortably for you. I guarantee it." He adjusted his grip on the pistol.

"If you want to get away with my murder, you could do yourself a favor by turning off the camera that's recorded our entire conversation."

Dagny pointed to the wall behind Ian.

He looked over his shoulder.

Dagny lunged, arms outstretched.

Tim fired, hitting her in the torso.

Ian spun back as Dagny crashed to the floor at his feet.

"You okay?" Tim said, still pointing his gun at Dagny.

Ian nodded, looked down at Dagny, whose body was draped over Kate, and said, "I believe you are finished, and that's the truth." He kneeled and leaned close, looking into her eyes as they glazed over. "Makes sense?"

Tim and Ian left the room and locked the door. Tim helped Ian to the lobby and outside, where they got into the truck.

As they sped away from his nightmare, Ian rolled down the window and enjoyed the cool air as it bathed his face. He knew Dagny would never have stopped. She would have regrouped to recruit and brainwash a new batch of poor souls if given the chance. He had no doubt that Tim's simple trigger-pull had spared so much pain. The small bullet had done the world a huge favor. If their loved ones found out about it, they'd forgive Tim. As awful as it sounds, they'd secretly be grateful.

· · · · · · · · ·

Free Guile Bonus Chapter & Riddick's Map

Visit: gneil.co/guile

Reviews

Thank you for reading *Guile*. Word-of-mouth is crucial for any author to succeed. If you enjoyed this book, please consider leaving a review at Amazon, even if it's only a line or two. It would make all the difference and would be very much appreciated.

To be notified when I release my next books, let's keep in touch:

BookBub:
gneil.co/bookbub

Instagram:
gneil.co/instagram

Facebook:
gneil.co/facebook

Twitter
gneil.co/twitter

Website:
geoffreyneil.com

If you enjoyed *Guile*, you might also enjoy *Human Resources*. Here's a preview:

Human Resources - Preview

One

IF SOMETHING SEEMS too good to be true, enjoy the hell out of it before it ends. That was Nelson Dupar's philosophy.

His perfect life began when the hospital elevator closed him in alone with her. She stood six feet tall and dressed to wither other women. A mile of toned leg stretched between candy-apple high-heels and a black leather miniskirt. She flipped her dark hair, sending a wisp of perfume—or something—to his nose. Whatever it was, Nelson smiled. Standing so close to her was a treat. She made the 28-year-old self-confessed slob wish he owned an iron.

Nelson's daily wardrobe was unimportant while buried in a tiny cubicle at the CPA firm. Today, he wore his standard attire: scuffed gray deck shoes, wrinkled slacks, and an untucked button shirt that failed to conceal his gut.

The woman moved forward to crowd the door and closed her eyes. Nelson leaned slightly to enjoy a deeper whiff of her while he sucked in to tuck his shirt. He then enjoyed an unrushed visual tour of this magnificent being's backside, taking in her smooth curves and generous display of skin and hair that shined where it bent at her shoulder.

She sighed and wrung her hands.

"You okay, ma'am?" Nelson asked.

She shook her head, not looking back. "I'm always nervous in elevators," she replied.

Nelson reached to pat her shoulder but reconsidered. "We'll be fine," he said. "And if anything happens, there's a hospital real close."

She laughed a breath through her nose and bowed her head as if praying. When the elevator bumped and lifted, she teetered and pressed her hand against the wall to steady herself.

Nelson watched, intrigued. *I wonder if she might faint,* he thought. The slim chance of a CPR opportunity excited him despite having no training for it. He reasoned that the honorable thing to do if she collapsed would be to give her a little mouth-to-mouth. He'd seen it a thousand times on TV. Just ease her to her back and tilt her head. Her moist lips would part ever so slightly. He'd gently place his mouth over hers. And, not forgetting the chest compressions, he'd need to unbutton…

The elevator door opened, popping Nelson's fantasy.

"Thank God," the woman said as they stepped out.

"See? We're elevator survivors!" Nelson said.

She laughed and turned to him. "Yes, we are!"

The brightness of the hallway added detail to her features. Her hair, almost black, contrasted with piercing blue eyes over a perfect smile. Nelson wished she had fainted.

"You take care, ma'am," he said, reluctantly turning to leave.

"Wait! What's your name?" she replied, fanning her face.

From the side of his mouth, Nelson whispered, "Clark Kent." She laughed again—a bit longer than he expected.

"Nice to meet you, Clark. I'm Morana."

"Actually, my name is Nelson, and it's even nicer to meet you. Come here often, Morana?"

"Only as a last resort."

"Some 'resort' this is, right?"

She laughed harder. Either Nelson was on a roll, or this woman was just incredibly giddy after conquering the elevator.

They walked toward the hospital exit. Morana sidestepped moving gurneys and oncoming foot traffic, hurrying to stay near him. When Nelson noticed they had taken on the appearance of a couple, his chin lifted, and his stride took on some swagger. As they passed through the crowded lobby, Morana drew intrigued smiles and lustful examination from people. Nelson knew she was out of his league, but for this fleeting moment, he relished being the nerd who baffled the jocks by seducing the hottest cheerleader.

Outside at the patient loading zone, their linked journey ended. Nelson pointed to the far side of the parking lot. "My car's way over in the last row. You take care."

Morana smiled. "Thank you for calming me with your comedy." She extended her hand.

As they shook, Nelson said, "Hey, I'm here all week—be sure to tip the veal and try your waiter!"

Morana bent over in a belly laugh that turned nearby heads.

Flattering, but the line wasn't that funny, Nelson thought. Never had his cheesy jokes impressed any of the women he wanted. He scratched his neck, waiting for her to finish laughing.

She caught her breath and said, "You are absolutely adorable."

"Thanks. You know, I get that all the time," Nelson said, finger-framing his face.

She laughed again and touched his arm, saying, "Oh my God—I want to take you home with me."

Nelson felt blood rush to his head as he realized that her flirtation might have traction. *How is this possible?* He knew that when Morana stepped from the dark elevator, her first glance had swept up the details of his grooming and pegged his socio-economic rung, yet her enthusiasm toward him hadn't dimmed.

"Hold on," she said, digging in her purse. She handed him a business card. "Call me."

Centered on the card was one word: *Morana,* printed above a barely visible gray phone number. No company, no title, and no address.

"Secretive much, Morana?" he asked.

"I can explain some other time. Please call me 'Mo' and call me soon."

"Sure thing," Nelson said. He watched her walk away—graceful, confident, gorgeous. *Not a chance in hell,* he thought.

He was wrong.

• • •

Nelson waited outside a hangar at Nadi Airport in Fiji two months later. He rested against the leather headrest in the chartered helicopter and fanned the front of his shirt for relief from the humidity. The twelve-hour flight from San Francisco had him foggy despite the many naps he had enjoyed fully reclined in first class.

On the floor beside him, dangling her feet outside the helicopter door, sat Mo, or *Cover Girl,* a nickname Nelson's envious buddies back at the office had given Morana after seeing her pick him up from work a few times. She wore a denim mini-skirt and a men's dress shirt with the sleeves rolled up—a neglected gift she had purchased for Nelson weeks ago.

It seemed not even jet lag could dampen Mo's excitement about this impromptu trip until the helicopter's charter company rang her cell phone to say the pilot would be late. She reached back, gently twisted Nelson's wrist to check the time, and then frowned.

"What's your rush?" Nelson asked.

"We have lunch waiting," she said. She poked out her bottom lip and blew the hair from her face. "And I wanted so badly to have you at the resort already."

After seven weeks of dating, Nelson had given up trying to understand Morana's infatuation with him. Whenever they ventured out in public, men and women hit on her. Some of her suitors appeared wealthy, and many were incredibly attractive. She withheld her phone number and dodged all advances with polished finesse. But for some reason, she couldn't get enough of Nelson. When he asked what she saw in him, she would only stroke his chin and say, "You make me crave you."

Nelson didn't know where her money came from—she wouldn't say. But he knew he could never have afforded the lifestyle Mo gave him. She showered him with expensive gifts of artwork, furniture, and concerts. Any material indulgence he mentioned to her in passing seemed to materialize for him within days, sometimes hours. She always paid when they went out, and when they returned to his place, she insisted on massaging him every night before the sex—lots of sex—sex that she joked was all the repayment she needed.

A month ago, he came home to find a new, white Porsche Carrera parked in his apartment's carport, the dealer spec sheet still taped inside the window. After he circled the car twice, grinning, he said, "Mo, there's no way I can accept this—it's far too expensive."

"You are so worth it! Don't hurt my feelings!" she replied, feigning a pout. She tossed him the keys, and when he caught them, she squealed and jumped up and down, clapping. Obliging her by accepting her lavish gifts made her so happy. It was the least he could do. He had it good, real good, too good.

Finally, they saw their pilot jogging toward them from the hangar office. He climbed into the helicopter with a clipboard tucked under his arm and wearing a bright tropical shirt.

"Hi, I'm Captain Kurt. Welcome to my *Skyship Enterprise*," he said. Nelson laughed. Morana rolled her eyes. "I'm sorry for the delay, folks. I can make up the time," Captain Kurt promised. He eased into the cockpit and donned a headset. The helicopter's turbines whined.

Outside, a man in a grease-smeared outfit shut the helicopter's door, muting the whipping rotors. He and Captain Kurt exchanged salutes.

Mo pulled the cockpit's partition closed for privacy in the passenger cabin. She nudged Nelson with her bare foot and said, "I have a new game for later." He grinned and rubbed his hands together. Mo's games for him always included happy endings and two winners.

She pulled a plastic grocery bag from her purse and removed a black leather-studded dog collar attached to a long leash. Nelson wrinkled his nose to raise his thick glasses for a better view. A slow smile of recognition spread across his face. He wagged his finger at her, saying, "I didn't think you were serious!"

They felt the helicopter cabin tilt. They were airborne.

Mo winked at him and said, "Bow-wow-wow." She opened the collar and whistled. "Here boy!"

Nelson laughed and leaned to her. She wrapped the collar around his neck and secured the chrome latch. The lengthy leash bunched on the floor. Nelson picked up the end, swatted his thigh, and said, "I'm such a naughty pup. Teach me to obey—*arff-arff.*"

They laughed. Mo said, "I wish I had my camera."

Nelson pointed to the collar. "Sure, you can hold out 'til later?"

Mo nodded. "Your hotness is burning me up, but yes, later."

They looked out the window as the helicopter ascended, nosing its way over the ocean, headed to a surprise paradise for some relaxation, tropical sex, and stress reduction—at least that's how Mo had billed it.

After a few minutes, the view locked onto a two-toned blue portrait of the sky over the sea, so they turned their attention back to one another. Captain Kurt cracked the partition momentarily to say, "Folks, weather's perfect. We'll be about an hour. Get comfortable."

Nelson's inner ear pinched with the pressure change. He pushed his duffle bag under his seat. Morana lowered an armrest and adjusted her vents for some face-on air conditioning. She carried no luggage, only a purse, having promised Nelson that she'd be naked for most of their trip.

Nelson looked around the supple helicopter cabin and then to Morana. He smiled at his life's unfair bounty. He was accustomed to merely counting the money of people who lived like this.

Morana peeled back the wrapper of a homemade energy bar and broke off a bite-sized piece. Nelson held up his bent wrists and doggie-begged. She giggled and popped it into his mouth. Before he could chew it, she pecked him on the lips.

He palmed her knee, rubbed a few circles, and slid his fingers up her inner thigh toward her skirt's opening. She crossed her legs.

"What?" he said as if she had robbed him of an inexorable right. He cocked his head like a curious puppy and whined, "But later feels *so* far away!"

She laughed and said, "Let's wait until we get there."

Nelson frowned. "So you'll bang me in a cramped 747 lavatory with a line outside the door, but a spacious private helicopter cabin is too risky?"

"I'll make it worth your wait," Mo said. Nelson's frown deepened. It was unlike her to deny him anything—especially sex. "Is the possibility of getting caught what gets you off?" he said. "Let's open the partition. The pilot *might* look back." He slid his fingers up her leg again. She gently pushed his hand away, grabbed the edge of her skirt, and wiggled to pull it lower.

"What happened to you?" he said, leaning in for a kiss.

She turned away. "Nothing happened. Trust me, I'm saving my energy for you… Give me your back." She twirled her finger for him to swivel and then pulled a gel tube from her purse. She slipped her hands under his shirt and rubbed the gel onto his shoulders. She put her mouth close to his ear so he could hear her over the smooth hiss of the engines and whispered, "What's most important right now is to get you as relaxed as possible. I promise I'll give you more excitement than you can handle later."

Mo's massage and the gel's tingly warmth weighted Nelson's eyelids, and after a few minutes, his head fell forward. She massaged deeper. He nodded off. She raised the armrests and laid him down on the entire length of three seats. She moved to the facing seats, inserted earbuds, and watched the sparkling ocean slide beneath them.

Fifty minutes later, Nelson awoke when Captain Kurt opened the partition to announce, "We have a ten-minute ETA, folks." Nelson sat up and checked the window. Still only sky and sea. Morana sat with her purse strap over her shoulder and arms crossed as if ready to step out the door at any moment.

"You look worried," Nelson said as he yawned. "According to Captain Kurt, it's our last chance." He slipped off his seat to his knees, reached down, and tried to spread her legs. She kissed him and gently pushed him back into his seat.

"What's wrong? Ever since we got on this helicopter, I'm smeared with shit to you."

"We're almost there. If you can wait until we get to our room, I'll be the naughty stray that dug up your petunias, and I'll wear the leash this time," Mo said.

"Deal," Nelson said. He fumbled with his collar, turning it, tugging at it, but it would not open. "Would you unlatch this?" he finally asked.

Morana made a feeble attempt and then said, "It's broken. We'll get a paper clip at the lodge. It looks good on you. And that you can't get it off gets me hot."

"You tease," Nelson said. "I want it off. I want to see if it fits you." He continued pinching and pulling on the latch. When it wouldn't budge, Nelson wound and tucked the leash into his shirt to hide it. He couldn't understand Mo's need to delay a quickie. She was always game. Damned mood swings. PMS—it must be.

Outside the window, a slit of land on the horizon stretched and became greener as they neared. Like all the small islands within 500 miles, it was blanketed in lush foliage from beach to beach. The helicopter sank into a narrow clearing amongst trees whose branches leaned away and trembled under the whipping rotors. When the struts touched down, Morana moved to rest her hand on the door handle.

"I guess you're eager to get out," Nelson said. "Can't wait to get to the room, right?" he asked.

Morana smirked. "Baby, I want you so bad I could burst," she said.

A man's dark face appeared in the window. He cupped his hand against the glass to peer in, and Morana signed thumbs up. Captain Kurt opened the cockpit partition and said, "Welcome to Mapetoa Island, folks. Have a good time." Morana shook his hand, transferring a folded hundred. Then she pulled the handle, and the door swung open. A motorized step slid out.

A thin white man in a safari outfit—complete with a brimmed hat, shorts, and black boots—stood outside. Six men, islanders dressed in hats and white uniforms, stood in a half circle at the door. One of them leaned on the handles of an empty wheelchair. The safari man offered his hand to Morana as she stepped down.

"Welcome, Sweetheart," he said.

Nelson wasn't crazy about this man calling Mo "Sweetheart" but chalked it up to island protocol that required extraordinary hospitality for high-value guests.

He felt firm hands take his arms to help him from the helicopter, but he shrugged them off and said, "I'm fine." So the man grabbed Nelson's duffle from under the helicopter seat. Some of Nelson's leash slid out from under his shirt. He tucked it into his belt.

"Mister, would you like a ride to the lodge?" the wheelchair man asked.

"No," Nelson said. He looked at Mo, who had walked with the safari man toward the edge of the clearing. The others followed, so Nelson did too. They came to a narrow dirt path barely wide enough for the wheelchair pushed behind Nelson.

"Mo, Mo!" he yelled, trying to catch up.

He felt a hand on his shoulder. "Please relax, mister. Why not have a ride?" the wheelchair man said.

"I don't want a ride. What am I? Crippled?" He pushed the man's hand off.

Morana turned back and said, "Sweetie, would you just relax?"

"You're practically jogging," Nelson said. "Would you just slow your roll so I can catch up?"

"Sorry. I'm hungry," Mo replied. Safari man chuckled.

They walked single file uphill on a trail through lush gardens lined with palm and balsa trees, some connected by hammocks. Soon, a grand log cabin lodge enclosed by a wide porch and log railings came into view high on a bluff. Huge picture windows faced a break in the foliage to a panoramic ocean view under the cloudless sky. Waves crashed, and sea birds shrieked on the beach below. Nelson heard the distant sound of their helicopter revving up.

He also noticed a glass-enclosed watchtower atop the lodge. A man stood inside holding a rifle with its butt rested on his hip, barrel angled upward.

"What's with the prison guard tower?" Nelson asked.

Mo nudged safari man and said, "This island has been a target for pirates, so the resort goes overboard with guest security. It was one reason I liked them."

Nelson said, "I wish that made me feel more secure." Safari man whispered into a wire connected to an earpiece. The tower gunman dropped out of sight.

They climbed the steps to the lodge entrance. Above the front door hung an ornate carved sign that read, El Sabor de La Vida. Two other uniformed staff washed windows and swept the porch.

Inside, the lodge was laid out with the care and attention to detail of a 5-star resort. A rock fireplace tapered to a thirty-foot chimney dividing two indoor balconies that overlooked the Great Room. An adjacent dining area featured a twenty-foot table made from a solid balsa trunk, polished to a mirror shine. Sofas, a set of massage tables and reading nooks, were interspersed with painted vases filled with tropical flowers cut from the gardens they had passed. A curved wooden staircase led to the upstairs guest rooms. The aroma of seasoned grilled onions and peppers wafted throughout the space. Nelson's stomach growled.

The delicious smell and fancy accommodations would usually have wowed him, but he'd prefer to take the tour later. Mo had him horny with the thought of a quickie. She should have pulled him straight to their room for some overdue sexual "heeling," but she chatted up Mr. Safari. As they moved to the center of the Great Room, Morana laughed, hugged one worker around the neck, and then kissed him. Jealousy flooded Nelson.

"Did you bring kinky-collars for the help, too?" Nelson said, stepping up to her. His voice had a strained pre-tantrum tautness.

Safari man stepped between them. "Hold on, pal."

Nelson shoved him hard. "I'm not your pal, asshole. I'm talking to my woman, and I need a private word with her, or we're back on that helicopter." Morana bit her lip to avoid laughing. The staff slowly encircled them. Some shook their heads as they chuckled and watched.

"There is no more helicopter," Mo said.

"What?"

"We aren't leaving."

"The hell we aren't," Nelson said. He pulled her arm, and before safari man could stop her, Morana planted a foot behind Nelson's ankles, grabbed his throat, and slammed him to the floor on his back. His glasses flew off. His mouth froze open to catch his breath as Morana mounted him, her knee in his chest. She raised her elbow behind her to drive the heel of her hand into his face.

"No!" safari man hollered, "Morana! No damage! No damage— please!" He lunged and pulled her off. Before Nelson could make a move, four workers jumped him. They pressed his arms and legs to the floor.

"Get off me!" Nelson yelled. "I'll sue you and own this island!"

The men raised him to his feet and forced him into the wheelchair. A cloth gag pulled firmly over his mouth absorbed his screams. They tied his ankles, wrists, and arms to the chair using lengths of soft cloth in a tight candy stripe pattern. He felt the leash sliding out of the top of his shirt as a smiling worker pulled it hand over hand and wrapped it around a bollard mounted to a shoulder-high banister. After the brief struggle, Nelson sat strapped to the wheelchair, his collar moored to the banister like a docked boat.

He bucked once, but the collar dug in and choked off a yell. A worker smoothed the top of Nelson's shirt, brushing the wrinkles from his shoulders and chest. He then pulled a spray bottle from his back pocket and misted Nelson's face with water before dabbing it dry with a fluffy white cloth. Another worker combed and smoothed Nelson's hair, checking his work from different angles.

Safari man and Morana strolled away from the scuffle. They sat on the far side of the Great Room by the front window. Morana's voice pierced the ongoing commotion. "Yes, we have a serious problem, Clay, if I don't see the money."

Safari man held up his hands to her. "Mo, calm down. Try again. I just got the wire confirmation a few minutes ago."

Morana tapped on her phone and waited, watching the screen. After a few moments, she said, "It transferred. Finally. That's more like it."

"See? What did I tell you?" the safari man said, beaming.

He and Morana made their way back to the workers surrounding Nelson. Morana continued to the staircase, saying, "I'm going to my room to freshen up. Begin the rub and include two ounces of shuttle fuel. We have less than thirty minutes."

Two workers yelled, "Yes, ma'am!" and then ran, disappearing into a hallway.

Nelson's heart pounded. What was she talking about? He wiggled under his restraints. His mind raced through the sequence of his two-month relationship with Morana. She claimed to have never visited this resort, yet her familiarity with safari man and the cryptic instructions the staff seemed to understand gave Nelson every reason to panic.

A man dressed in white brought Nelson's glasses to him, and after polishing them with a white towel, he placed the glasses back onto Nelson's face. Another man appeared from a hallway with a silver tray holding scissors and four small bowls. He put on latex gloves and nodded to the men surrounding Nelson's wheelchair. One cut the top of Nelson's shirt to expose his shoulders. The man with the tray dipped his fingers into the bowls one at a time and massaged Nelson's lower neck and shoulders until they glistened. The massage was gentle, and the citrus aroma was familiar to Nelson because Morana had often used such scented ointments on him. The liquid from one bowl produced heat that penetrated his skin. It was uncomfortable but not excruciating, so Nelson bit into his gag and took it—desperately trying to understand what was happening.

Nelson examined the tether that anchored his neck to the bannister. Without the use of his hands, it didn't have to be strong to deter a run for the door. Even if he made it outside, eluding these people on this small island was absurd and escape impossible.

A worker approached him with a bottle of beer. He placed his finger to his lips, instructing Nelson to be quiet, and then said, "Mister, drink this beer." He loosened Nelson's gag, and it fell to his neck.

Nelson's upper body relaxed with the sudden ease of breathing through his mouth. "Please tell me what is going on," he said, panting.

Immediately, the gag returned, pulled tighter. The man with the beer shook his head and leaned close to Nelson's face. "When we remove the gag, you will drink all the beer without talking, or I will have Miss Morana feed it to you, and she will make you eat the bottle, too." He pointed up the stairs.

Nelson nodded. The gag fell to his neck again.

He parted his lips and took in healthy swallows of beer. The worker cupped his hand under Nelson's chin for spillage, and his smile grew with each gulp Nelson took. "Eeeexcellent, mister," he said as he put the empty beer bottle into a bag slung over his shoulder.

Nelson had looked forward to massages and beer as part of this getaway, but not like this. The forced massage, beer, and careful restoration of his glasses had become forced doting that fueled his terror. He hoped he was the center of a joke that had gone too far.

They re-gagged him and left. He heard voices from the other side of the bannister. One of them was safari man—Clay—giving some sort of instructions. A jarring electronic melody sounded, and Clay answered his phone. "Fantastic. We're ready," he said.

As one worker left the lodge to go outside, the faint beating of a helicopter seeped through the open door. The sound grew, and soon, the windows rattled lightly as another helicopter landed in the distant clearing.

Morana hurried down the stairs, having changed into a safari outfit that matched Clay's, and her hair was pulled back into a ponytail. Nelson tried to call out to her, but his scream only heated the gag. She rushed outside and out of sight.

The gloved man returned and resumed massaging his shoulders. After a few minutes, two men and two women who looked like tourists entered the lodge with Clay and Morana. They led the guests to Nelson and surrounded him. The older gentleman with a camera around his neck turned to Clay and said, "I must admit, this is new for me. I can hardly wait. If price is any indication, this will be spectacular."

"You'll consider it a bargain, I promise you this," Clay answered.

"Oh my, absolutely exquisite," said the older, silver-haired woman. She let go of the man's hand and pointed to Nelson. "May I?" she asked.

"By all means!" Clay said, hands in his pockets. He rocked from his heels to his toes, wearing a broad, cartoonish smile.

"Wait—hold on," Morana said. She stepped forward, rolling something between her fingers. She raised her hand toward Nelson's head. He winced. Morana twisted a compressed foam earplug deep into each of his ears. The foam expanded, and within moments, Nelson heard only his heartbeat thumping.

The silent mouths of his small audience moved. The older woman donned gloves. She approached him and touched his shoulder, gently squeezing it. Her mouth dropped open, and she turned to the others in amazement. When she turned back, Nelson read the word "fabulous."

Clay directed the guests' attention to the edge of the Great Room, where a man entered from a hall door. He wore a stethoscope draped around his neck and a white lab coat with the name Dr. Lawrence Pradin embroidered on it. With a somber, flat expression, he acknowledged the guests, approached Nelson, and placed the stethoscope on Nelson's chest. He aimed an infrared thermometer at Nelson's temple and read the results aloud. After he poked and prodded Nelson's upper body a few times, he spoke a few words to the guests. Nelson watched the silent clapping. Morana pointed over the banister to a distant part of the lodge, directing everyone to leave.

When the guests had departed, Clay nodded to Morana. From the banister beside Nelson, she opened a shallow drawer the size of a spaghetti box. From it, she pulled out a ten-inch boning knife with the curve and point of an eagle talon. Crisscrossed hairline lacerations along its cutting edge told a story of frequent over-sharpening. Nelson screamed, but the gag dulled it to a hum. He shook his head hard enough to dislodge one earplug, and his glasses again flew off.

Morana dropped the knife to her side, her knuckles whitening around the handle. She watched Nelson—to see his chest heave like it had so many times after his asinine, animal-role-playing sex games she pretended to enjoy in his shitty apartment.

Nelson squeezed his eyes closed and bit into the gag. *How could she do this?* His too-good-to-be-true had become too-horrific-to-be-possible. He expected searing pain in his chest or across his throat but felt a gentle touch on his legs. He opened his eyes. The knife rested on his lap. Its blade reflected a silent spinning ceiling fan above.

Morana pointed, and a worker rotated Nelson's wheelchair while another untied his tether from the banister. They wheeled him out of the Great Room. The temporary reprieve brought Nelson a flash of relief, but now having to carry his own presumed instrument of execution brought a psychological cruelty akin to Roman crucifixion. Nelson strained to understand. If they were going to kill him, they could have easily done so already. They followed a carefully ordered agenda—that much was clear.

They wheeled him across the lodge, where he passed the visitors, who now sat on sofas in a lounge area. Morana joined them. The joyous, celebratory sounds of Mozart's *Symphony No. 40* filled the air. Laughter erupted from the group as Clay held his phone up for each guest to view a photo on its screen. After viewing the photo, the older woman closed her eyes and rocked back and forth to the music with a slight smile. They were festive.

Nelson's two handlers wheeled him down a dark hallway, stopping beside a door with three deadbolts. They flanked his chair and then slipped their fingers under the cloths that bound his arms and legs, checking for tightness. One worker picked up the knife while the other unlocked the door and pushed it open.

Light streamed into the hallway from the room, and the bouncy melody of Mozart's symphony swelled. Nelson saw his fate in unmistakable clarity. His eyes widened in utter horror. He screamed his muffled scream and bucked, swinging his torso in every direction.

The workers did not try to hinder him. They only steadied the wheelchair by stepping between the rear spokes. The one with the knife leaned against the door frame, whistling along with the music. The other pulled a phone from his pocket and scrolled it for new messages.

- Sample End -

More on *Human Resources*, including the audiobook at:
gneil.co/humanresources

Acknowledgments

Special thanks to my beta team:

Mom and Dad—You know what you did.

My wonderful wife for your patience, mastery of language, and gentle use of that loving, slow-blinking facial expression that told me which of my subplot ideas should be abandoned.

Cyndie Chen for sharing your wonderful eye for logic and uncanny sensitivity to word patterns. Nothing escapes you! Your advice is golden.

Dean Gamburd for the firearms counsel and high-powered sense of story logic. Any inaccurate references to firearms or their use in this story will have been the author's fault for not checking with Dean first.

Jackie Rankin for your masterful way of ensuring that each scene's context agrees and your ability to spot logic problems.

Julie "Schmuggums" Harreld for your encouragement, sound medical advice and suggestions, and constant support.

Michelle Martin-Stroup for sharing your extraordinary literary talent with me. I'm constantly amazed by your skill and so grateful for your friendship.

Shanna Gray for your grammar prowess and keen ability to find typos seen by nobody else.

Steven Claborn Your spot-on hunches kept my plot on course and tremendously enhanced my readers' experience.

Wileen Maldonado for your sharp eye for typos, thorough proofreading, and enthusiasm for my stories.

www.ingramcontent.com/pod-product-compliance
Lightning Source LLC
Chambersburg PA
CBHW070312260626
47160CB00003B/817